Simply IRRESISTIBLE

FLATIRON 5
BOOK ONE

DEBORAH COOKE

ISBN-13: 978-1-927477-76-2

Dear Reader;

Many story ideas come out of the blue and many disappear just as quickly. Every once in a while, though, a story just won't go away. **Simply Irresistible** is one of those books. Not only did the story come to me all at once, but the characters stuck with me. I dreamed of them. I heard their dialogue in my thoughts. I thought I didn't have time to write their story, but Amy and Tyler haunted me until I did.

One of the details I enjoyed about this story was Amy's resolve to write a romance and publish it herself. I hadn't written much of this book when I decided it would be awesome to include excerpts from Amy's book. A collaboration was born of this idea: Ella Ardent has written a series of fairy tale romances called *Euphoria*, beginning with **Her Dark Prince**. We've agreed that I would present these as "Amy's" books, and Ella has given permission for me to excerpt **Her Dark Prince** in **Simply Irresistible**. If you like the excerpts, **Her Dark Prince** is available for sale.

The five partners at F5 have moved into my imagination with a vengeance. Kyle's book, **Addicted to Love**, is falling out of my fingertips and I'm loving the story of a bad boy whose resistance to commitment can't withstand the attention of the right woman. Just like Amy, Lauren is a lot more passionate than expected. Kyle and Lauren had one night together before they went their separate ways. When she comes back for more, he can't say no. Look for an excerpt from **Addicted to Love** at the end of this book.

I continue to write medieval romances as Claire Delacroix and have a number scheduled for publication in 2017. *The Champions of St. Euphemia* series will be wrapped up with **The Crusader's Vow**, and **The Rose Legacy series** will launch, too. I'm also writing dragon shifter romances, and you can learn more about my **Dragons of Incendium on the series website**. To keep up with my new releases, book sales and free reads, please visit my website to subscribe to my newsletter, sign up for my new release alert or follow my blog.

Until next time, I hope you have plenty of good books to read.

All my best,

Deborah
Also writing as Claire Delacroix

http://DeborahCooke.com

BOOKS BY DEBORAH COOKE

Paranormal Romances:
The Dragonfire Series
KISS OF FIRE
KISS OF FURY
KISS OF FATE
Harmonia's Kiss
WINTER KISS
WHISPER KISS
DARKFIRE KISS
FLASHFIRE
EMBER'S KISS
THE DRAGON LEGION COLLECTION
SERPENT'S KISS
FIRESTORM FOREVER

Urban Fantasy Romance
The Prometheus Project
FALLEN
GUARDIAN
REBEL
ABYSS

Paranormal Young Adult:
The Dragon Diaries
FLYING BLIND
WINGING IT
BLAZING THE TRAIL

Contemporary Romance:
The Coxwells
THIRD TIME LUCKY
DOUBLE TROUBLE
ONE MORE TIME
ALL OR NOTHING

Flatiron Five
SIMPLY IRRESISTIBLE
ADDICTED TO LOVE (2017)

Writing as Claire Delacroix

Time Travel Romances
ONCE UPON A KISS
THE LAST HIGHLANDER
THE MOONSTONE
LOVE POTION #9

ROMANCE OF THE ROSE
HONEYED LIES
UNICORN BRIDE
THE SORCERESS
ROARKE'S FOLLY
PEARL BEYOND PRICE
THE MAGICIAN'S QUEST
UNICORN VENGEANCE
MY LADY'S CHAMPION
ENCHANTED
MY LADY'S DESIRE

The Bride Quest
THE PRINCESS
THE DAMSEL
THE HEIRESS
THE COUNTESS
THE BEAUTY
THE TEMPTRESS

The Rogues of Ravensmuir
THE ROGUE
THE SCOUNDREL
THE WARRIOR

The Jewels of Kinfairlie
THE BEAUTY BRIDE
THE ROSE RED BRIDE
THE SNOW WHITE BRIDE
The Ballad of Rosamunde

The True Love Brides
THE RENEGADE'S HEART
THE HIGHLANDER'S CURSE
THE FROST MAIDEN'S KISS
THE WARRIOR'S PRIZE

The Champions of St. Euphemia
THE CRUSADER'S BRIDE
THE CRUSADER'S HEART
THE CRUSADER'S KISS
THE CRUSADER'S VOW (2017)
THE CRUSADER'S HANDFAST

Short Stories and Novellas
An Elegy for Melusine
BEGUILED

SIMPLY IRRESISTIBLE

CHAPTER ONE

A ND WILL we be seeing Giselle this weekend?"
Tyler McKay winced, hearing a thousand shades of
nuance and expectation in his mother's question. Mrs. Lowell
appeared in the doorway to his office, her reading glasses in her hand,
and gave him an intent look. He nodded, understanding that his
appointment had arrived, and his secretary pulled the door to his
office so it wasn't quite closed.

Ty spun his chair so that he was looking out the window at
Manhattan in all its spring glory. "I really have to go, Mom. My client
is here."

"But I just wondered, dear. You know that we're finalizing the
table settings."

"It's a potluck buffet," Ty protested and forced his tone to turn
teasing. It was better than letting his mom guess the truth. "You just
want to *know*."

"Of course, I want to know," Colleen McKay huffed. "You're not
getting any younger, Tyler, and I want to see some grandchildren one
of these days."

"You have one."

"I want more."

"Ask the girls."

"A son of a son, Ty. You know it would make your father happy.
And Giselle is just lovely. So glamorous and charming..."

Ty interrupted the list of Giselle's attributes. He'd made a serious
mistake letting her survive in his mother's imagination after their

single date, although it had seemed like a good idea at the time. That's what he got for taking advice from Kyle. "Are you seeing Aunt Maureen any time soon?"

"She's coming on Sunday. Of course! It is a family bridal shower, Tyler. You know, Katelyn is so worried about everyone getting along, but I think it will be just fine. It's been a year since Stephanie's shower, after all. Don't you think your cousin Maxine will have forgotten the toilet paper stuck to her shoe?"

"Not in this lifetime."

"Well, she should."

"She might, if Paige stopped reminding her."

His mother ignored that comment. "These things happen, and there was no cause for making such a scene..."

Mrs. Lowell cleared her throat. Mr. O'Neill could get impatient, and rightly so, given how much capital Ty managed for him. "Gotta go, Mom. I'll talk to you later."

"You certainly will, young man. You might have grown up but that doesn't mean you can evade a question..."

"Bye, Mom." Ty ended the call, telling himself he'd given his mother fair warning. It was only 9:30 in the morning, after all, and this had been her third call of the day. He hesitated only a moment before sending all incoming calls to voice mail.

Then he turned off his cell phone. He might not turn it on anytime soon.

What was he going to do? Giselle was long gone from his life, but if he went alone to any of the events leading up to Katelyn's wedding—never mind the wedding itself—an entire army of well-intentioned female relations would be determined to play matchmaker.

Ty had been there and done that, and he wasn't going to endure it again.

He certainly wasn't going to ask Kyle for advice again.

Ty needed a date. Fast. For self-defense.

What about the Librarian?

What about Mr. O'Neill? Ty straightened his tie and strode to the door of his office, giving his client a welcoming smile. "My mother," he said, then shook his head. "My sister is getting married in a month and everything is a crisis."

Mr. O'Neill chuckled as he rose to his feet, a leather portfolio tucked under his arm. "I thought you were going to say that you were getting married."

Ty shook his head. "Not soon."

"Maybe that's your mother's plan."

"Probably. I'm willing to wait for the right woman, though."

Mr. O'Neill nodded agreement. "That's sound thinking."

"Have you given any thought to our discussion about risk?"

"I have," Mr. O'Neill acknowledged. "Your argument was persuasive but I have a few questions. I watched those stocks you mentioned..."

Ty ushered the older man into his office, then exchanged a glance with Mrs. Lowell who had returned to her desk.

Thirty? She mouthed, guessing how long he wanted to be undisturbed.

Ty wiggled his hand that it might take longer. He'd been suggesting a change of perspective in the management of Mr. O'Neill's portfolio and knew that his client would have a lot of questions. His secretary nodded agreement, then her phone rang. Ty shut the door and gave the older man his undivided attention.

Except for his one thought about the Librarian. Would she do it? Or would she think he was insane? Maybe he *was* nuts. He didn't even know her name.

The worst she could do, Ty figured, was to decline.

He could survive that.

And if she agreed, he wouldn't be at the mercy of his family for the next month.

There he was.

Finally.

Better late than never.

Amy peeked over the top of her book and watched the guy from the wealth management firm on the top floor come into the common area, just the way she did five times a week. Her heart was beating faster, even though that was stupid. She was too old to have a crush on a stranger.

Even one who looked like this. The object of her attention could have stepped out of the pages of one of the books she gobbled up like candy. Tall, athletic, handsome, wearing yet another killer suit that probably cost as much as she earned in a month. Make that two months. No pretension. He was totally at ease and moved with an athletic grace that made her salivate. Confident. Maybe even masterful.

Amy bit her lip. He was almost too good to be true. She watched him surreptitiously, yet again, seeking the inevitable flaw. She didn't find it on this day either.

Perfectly knotted silk tie, French cuffs, Italian shoes. There was no business casual dress code in this guy's world, and Amy liked it.

A lot.

Of course, if he had been like her recent book boyfriends, he'd be emotionally scarred, hiding his wounds from the world. He'd be ruined inside, a wreck of a man who could only be cured by the love of the right woman. She'd be the one to see past his scars and trust him enough to surrender fully to his darkest fantasies. To his needs. He'd give vent to his deepest desires because of that trust, and by the end of the book, he'd be healed.

True love would conquer the obstacles and win the day.

Amy sighed at the perfection of it all. It was a story she never tired of reading. Beauty and the Beast, with a little pain and a lot of pleasure.

In reality, this guy would never notice her, except maybe to excuse himself if she stepped into his path. He'd certainly never talk to her, and maybe it was better that way. She wouldn't have to lose the fantasy, and this one was good enough to defend.

Still, Amy was curious. Even without knowing his name, she'd gleaned a few details. She knew he worked at Fleming Financial, the private banking and investment firm on the top floor of the building, not because she'd stalked him or anything, but because she'd been in the elevator with him once. Fleming Financial had expensive offices, presumably to encourage the sense among their clients that they could be trusted with the management of enormous sums of money.

It seemed to work.

Amy'd nearly had heart failure when she'd realized they'd be the only two in the elevator that day and forgot to push her floor. He'd reached past her to push nine, giving her a delicious whiff of sexy masculinity. Her toes had curled in her shoes. She'd been achingly aware of how rare that scent was in her life and had been ready to just enjoy, but he'd cast her a questioning look. She'd hurried to push five, nearly falling over her own feet, and blushed like a teenager for being an idiot.

That he'd bitten back a smile had only made her feel like more of one. The silence had been painful and the ride eternal, especially since she'd been too mortified to breathe. There'd been a time when she hadn't been a complete moron with other people, or even with gorgeous guys. She could barely remember it.

Maybe his aura of power had unnerved her.

No, it was what he did in her imagination that made her blush.

It was probably a blessing that he'd barely noticed her.

Amy propped her chin on her hand and kept reading about Melissa's misadventures with her new dom. These erotic romances were like crack. Amy couldn't get enough of them. They offered vicarious sexual adventures, ending with the promise of eternal happiness. They were her addiction and she read dozens of them. She wrapped them carefully in book covers, the way she'd done in school with her textbooks, to disguise her reading taste.

That meant she could read anywhere.

She liked print books too much to use her e-reader, even though the keepers had taken over her bookshelves at home. So many of them had a great juicy bit—or twenty. Her dad, the English teacher, had spoken often about censorship and the right to make your own reading choices. The way Amy saw it, buying print books with cash meant that no one could track what she was reading or take her books away.

She'd die if she lost these stories.

Amy's particular weakness was when the master said something tender and hot that it turned his submissive's knees to butter, and her own knees got a bit weak. She liked the trust and capitulation—and the transformation. It was magical how the characters gave each other just what was needed to make them both whole.

Who could resist a happy ending? Not Amy.

The really intriguing thing about Mr. Private Banking was that he read, too. Scottoline, Grisham, Cornwell, Patterson—pretty much always a mystery or suspense story, but she liked that he read women authors as well as men. Was it the violence? The mystery? The knowledge that justice would triumph? Did he see himself as the serial killer or the intrepid hero, ensuring that villains got their due? It was easy to imagine that he was living vicariously too, having an adventure with his choice of fiction. She wanted to ask him why he read what he did. It would have told her a lot about him.

It was also reassuring that at least one other person was as rabid a reader as she was. Observation had revealed that it generally took him two days to read a book. She liked that he didn't cover his up, so she could spy on his tastes. She peeked again to see what today's choice was, but he was in the line at the sandwich bar.

Weird. He usually brought a lunch, just like she did.

Maybe the staff at the mansion had called in sick.

She smiled at that and returned to Melissa's cries of agony and ecstasy. The poor girl was in major trouble this time, having been locked in the dungeon in her master's house. No one knew where she was, and he had her blindfolded and shackled in nothing flat. Of course, she'd been very, very naughty in defying his express command.

And now she was at his mercy. Mmmm. Amy already knew this master didn't have much of that commodity, but Melissa was loving it. Who wouldn't?

Oh, the nipple clamps. Amy bent over the book, fascinated by the description of how they felt. Would he use the riding crop? She tried to savor the sensual build-up, admiring that the author had done a good job, but she turned the pages all too quickly. God, the master was doing that tender-tough thing that just about finished her! Would a man ever talk to her in a gravelly voice? Amy shivered at the prospect and turned the page, desperate to know what would happen next.

"Is this seat taken?" The man's voice was low enough and gravelly enough to start a shiver deep inside Amy.

She looked up to find none other than Mr. Hot standing behind the seat diagonal to hers, sandwich and book in hand. (It was the newest Patterson.) In the common area and food court, the seats were bolted to tables in fours. She had claimed her customary seat by the fountain, where she could see a patch of sky through the atrium overhead. The other three seats were available, as usual.

She was astonished to find him not only addressing her but waiting for her to answer. She pushed up her glasses and cleared her throat. The food court *was* really full. He just needed somewhere to sit. It wasn't personal.

Of course not.

"No. Go ahead." Amy gestured, trying to make it look like a casual invitation. She thought her move looked clumsy or, worse, indifferent.

"That's what I get for being late," he said with an easy smile, then sat down. He had a great voice, just growly enough to make her tingle, even when he said something pedestrian. He could read the telephone book to her and she'd be transfixed. Amy decided to imagine him saying other things later, when she couldn't give herself away. He put down his book, gave the sandwich a skeptical glance, then started to unwrap it. The corner of his mouth tightened in a way that made her want to reach out and touch him.

Gotta flog that mansion staff, spank a few maids, get lunch made on time.

She'd get his lunch packed on time.

Or maybe she wouldn't, just to be naughty and get disciplined.

Amy fought her urge to giggle.

He cracked open his book, conversation over, and Amy returned to the torment of Melissa. Thank God for book covers. *My master has such powerful hands, Melissa thought, stealing a glance, and nearly swooning...*

Amy took a covert look at *his* hands. They were excellent, as men's hands went. Strong, slightly tanned, long-fingered. No rings.

Maybe he was the kind who didn't wear one.

He couldn't be single, could he?

It would be criminal if he was gay.

Her gaze slid over the same sentence seven times but she had no comprehension of what she was reading. His cell phone rang, and Amy gripped her book as if she hadn't noticed.

Of course, she was listening. Any human would have done the same.

"Hi, Mom," he said, his patient tone making Amy smile. "No, Mom, I'm not busy." He sat back to listen, his gaze fixed on the distance, a study in tolerance.

Control. Oh, he had *it*, that was for sure.

Amy could hear his mom's chatter coming through the phone. Even without being able to discern the words, she could tell that his mother was wound up about something.

"I think it will be fine, Mom," he said firmly.

Mom clearly disagreed, her voice rising a little higher.

"I'm sure Katelyn doesn't expect any different, Mom." His tone became soothing. "You've done it three times now and beautifully. The fourth will be easy."

Mom declined to be convinced. Her voice rose another notch, although Amy couldn't make out the words. Who was Katelyn? His wife? His girlfriend? His mom knew her, so she had to be close.

As "Mom" continued, Amy's lunch companion straightened ever so slightly. He'd had this conversation before. Maybe a lot of times.

He was becoming vexed.

What was he going to do about it? His eyes flashed a little and his lips tightened. Amy crossed her ankles tightly.

"I don't want to talk about that, Mom."

Mom clearly did. She was talking faster.

Mr. Yum inhaled sharply and frowned a little.

Amy could have eaten him up with a spoon.

She stared at her book, but had no idea what Melissa was enduring.

And didn't much care.

To her surprise, her companion picked up the cellophane from his sandwich and began to crush it in his hand, making a crinkling noise. Amy peeked to find him holding it close to the phone. "Lots of static all of a sudden, Mom," he said, sounding concerned. "Can you still hear me?"

Amy gasped that he would lie like this to his mother.

Although she could totally understand it. Her aunt was infuriating when she was worried about something and wouldn't abandon the issue.

Maybe she'd steal this trick.

"I can't hear you," he said, holding the phone away from his mouth. Their gazes met for an instant and she saw the wicked twinkle in his eyes. Something quivered deep in Amy's belly at just the implication that they were co-conspirators. "Look, if we get cut off, Mom, I'll call you back tonight."

Green eyes. He had green eyes. Thick dark lashes. A little gold halo around the iris. They looked awesome with his chestnut hair. Amy swallowed and forced herself to look down at her book again. She had a full body blush going on and hoped he didn't notice.

He also had firm lips, the kind that look like sculpture when one corner lifts in laughter. Like his was doing right now. Bite-able, sexy, kissable lips. God, she was a sucker for crooked smiles.

Amy stared at her book, her palms damp.

Even though she wasn't looking, she was aware that he frowned, mostly because he crackled the cellophane louder and simultaneously dropped his voice. "Yes, yes, I *know* why you're worried..."

Then he abruptly ended the call, turned off his cell phone, and dropped it into his pocket. He looked at his sandwich as if he'd rather eat road kill, then picked up his book with a sigh.

Acting like he hadn't just hung up on his mom.

Amy couldn't keep silent. "You did that to your *mom*?"

"An act of desperation," he confided with a grimace. "Don't worry. I'll pay for it later."

"But she's your mom!"

"She's also driving me insane." He looked exasperated, which was both unexpected and cute.

"Some people say it's part of the job description."

His smile was quick and genuine, a flash of perfect teeth that caught Amy by surprise. "There is that," he admitted ruefully. Her heart skipped as he leaned closer. Amy was transfixed to be the focus of his attention, and that was before he dropped his voice to a conspiratorial whisper.

It gave her shivers, that whisper.

"My sister is getting married," he confessed.

"So's my cousin," Amy said. "Stressful times for moms."

He held up four fingers. "My *fourth* sister is getting married."

"Four?"

"All younger than me, one married every spring for the past three years. My mom has been in wedding preparation mode non-stop for more than four years." He sighed, and she sympathized.

"Ouch," Amy said, unable to imagine how she'd endure her own aunt's agitation for any longer than the remaining three weeks until Brittany's wedding.

Let alone Brittany. Her cousin had a serious Bridezilla infection.

"The thing is that it doesn't take a psychic to know what comes after that." He gave Amy a steady look, inviting her to guess.

She did. "You're the last one."

"And the oldest." He shook his head and picked up his book. "I've had a crappy morning, and just don't have any spare patience for unfounded concerns about the weather four Saturdays from now. It'll be what it is, even if the plan is for the ceremony to be in the garden." He flicked her a look. "If it makes you feel better, I'll call her after lunch and apologize, then listen patiently to the whole monolog again."

Amy liked that he told her that. "Perfect son?" she found herself teasing.

"Far from it." That smile made a brief return appearance. "But since there's only one son, she has to make do with my shortcomings."

He started to read, no doubt finding Alex Cross's adventures more intriguing than Amy found Melissa's predicament to be in this particular moment. She was amazed that he'd not only talked to her but she'd been reasonably coherent.

She hadn't talked to a lot of men in recent years, especially sexy ones. Doctors. Care facilitators. All conversations had been without sexual charge.

But she'd talked to *him*, the object of her fantasies, and even made him smile.

It had to be because he seemed nice, nicer than one would expect a billionaire book boyfriend to be. Unscarred. Not tormented beyond getting annoyed with his female relations in the last days before a wedding, which Amy could completely understand.

His interest in her had to be non-existent, so she could continue to employ him in her fantasies. He'd just needed to vent and she'd been convenient. He'd probably forget all about her as soon as he'd had his lunch.

That was a bit of a deflating realization.

The strange thing was that living vicariously through Melissa no longer held Amy's interest. She was intrigued that Mr. Yum had sisters and family tensions, because that made him more real than the men in her books.

Of course, he *was* real.

Even more incredible, she and he had something in common. Weddings on the horizon, and mothers of brides knotted up with concern. But he was reading and the conversation was done, and Amy couldn't think of a clever way to get it started again.

Her mom would have known exactly what to say, which just made Amy miss her even more. Social skills weren't genetic, apparently. Amy would think of the perfect comment in about five hours or maybe in the middle of the night. She smiled a little, thinking of her mom teasing her about that, and felt more alone than ever.

She checked her watch, realized she was due back upstairs, and packed the last bit of her lunch away. Mr. Yum was so engrossed in his book that he didn't even glance up as she did so, which proved all her predictions true.

That might have been the end of it, if Amy hadn't dropped her book.

It slid out of the protective cover when she made a grab for it, as slippery as a fish, then landed face up, right on his expensive and polished shoe.

The cover image left no doubt of the contents.

He looked.

He stared.

Amy was sure she'd die of mortification.

But then he smiled.

Tyler had always known that you couldn't really judge a book by its cover, but he never expected the Librarian to be reading something like the book on his shoe.

He'd never heard of it, or the author, but the handcuffs lined with pink fur dangling from the black stiletto shoe on the cover pretty much said it all. He'd noticed earlier that she was nearly done, so there couldn't be any doubt in her mind what she was reading.

And here he'd imagined that she carefully wrapped her Jane Austen editions to keep them pristine while she read them over and over again.

She gasped when the book fell and then froze when the slipcover came off. All the blood left her face, leaving her pale and horrified, then she blushed redder than he might have believed possible.

Ty was right about the book's content, then. He bit back the urge to laugh at her reaction, but knew that would only mortify her more.

It was cute how flustered she was. She had to be close to thirty, and he didn't think there were that many virgins of that age in Manhattan. He would have expected her sexual appetites to be moderate, even predictable.

Which just proved the old adage of books and covers to be true.

Although he called her the Librarian in his thoughts, Ty had no idea what she did for a living. Chances were pretty good that she wasn't a librarian as there weren't any libraries in the vicinity. Her appearance just fit the stereotype. Those horn-rimmed glasses. That hair wound up tightly. The conservative separates in navy. Always a white blouse and minimal jewelry.

And the loafers. God, the loafers.

Her shoes were a crime against humanity, given the perfection of her legs. He'd noticed her in the first place because of her legs, then become intrigued by how voraciously she read. It had become a habit to check on her presence, to wonder what she was reading, to be reassured in a curious way that she was so constant. Always the same seat. Nearly the same outfit. Every Friday, she bought a coffee, but only on Friday and just one.

She bit her lip when she read. It was impossibly cute.

She crossed her legs repeatedly, presumably when she got to the good bits. He'd surreptitiously watched her legs more than once. Now that he'd seen the book cover, Ty could guess what those good bits might be and her agitation was even more sexy.

In fact, he could imagine her in a pair of shoes just like the ones on the book cover.

Maybe nothing else.

That was an exciting idea, one that he couldn't dismiss as quickly as he should have.

In a way, it was funny. In his desperate need of a date, the Librarian seemed like a good and reliable choice. Safe. Predictable. But she was already anything but predictable.

When she'd first glanced up at him, Ty had been struck by her eyes. They were thickly lashed, like the eyes of a doe, and of a rich golden brown color. He could see that her hair was auburn, even with it tightly pulled back, and noticed that her complexion was creamy. She looked more exotic than he'd expected, and he realized it was because her eyes tipped up at the outer corners.

With a little eyeliner and a different hair style, she'd look like Sophia Loren.

She might not have been entirely comfortable in his presence, but she had warmed up quickly. She'd taken him to task over his treatment of his mom. She'd even given him the ideal reason to present his plan to her. He'd intended to mention it casually, just as she was leaving, in the hope that she might just quickly agree.

Too bad the book had fallen before he could open his mouth.

Ty wasn't used to having his carefully laid plans unravel before his eyes, much less change into something else. That his scheme to get a date for his sister's wedding had done just that, when he would never have expected otherwise, captured his interest and held it tight.

The book was still on his shoe.

She still looked horrified.

This had to be a moment that called for a gentlemanly touch. Ty picked up the book, as if unsurprised, and glanced at the back copy. "Is it good?"

She exhaled in a rush. "Not bad. I've read better and worse."

Not a new genre for her then. Ty offered the book to her, unable to think of a good segue to what he wanted to ask her.

He wished he could put her at ease. She swallowed visibly, thanked him, and just about snatched the book from his hand. She jammed the book into the black purse she always carried, which was massive enough to be considered luggage. The slip cover was then smashed into the bag on top, then she turned to leave. She was so shaken that Ty had to try to make her smile before she left.

"You're not going to tell me that you bought it by mistake?" he asked lightly. "Or that your sister insisted you read it?"

Her gaze met his, then she straightened slightly. "No. I don't have a sister."

"Lucky you," he teased but she didn't smile.

She looked away, then back at him, bristling. "It's currently a very popular genre."

"So I've heard." Ty spoke slowly, drawing out the moment, hoping she felt compelled to linger, if only to be polite.

She flicked a suspicious look at him, the way one of his sisters might have done when thinking he meant to give her a hard time. "From your sisters?"

Ty nodded. It was true. "One of them reads those books, too. I don't understand why, even though she convinced me to see that movie with her."

"You saw the movie?"

"I hated it." He gestured to her seat. "Care to enlighten me?"

"Why would I?" She was as suspicious as Paige on being invited to explain her taste in reading.

"Because women are the last great mystery," he said because he believed it. "Unless it's just about the sex."

The Librarian's eyes flashed and he thought she might give him a piece of her mind. He was more than ready for it. Embarrassment and anger were doing great things for her.

"It's *not* about the sex," she said fiercely, then sat down hard. He wondered whether her indignation would fog up her glasses, then she leaned across the table. She dropped her voice to a murmur that he doubted she knew was sultry. He would have bet that she also didn't know she was giving him a glimpse of her cleavage.

She had Ty's undivided attention.

Now he was the one changing how he sat.

"It's about the healing power of love," she said with fervor. She tapped a fingertip on the table, conviction in her gaze. "It's about someone who is ruined and scarred and tormented finally finding peace and salvation. It's about a woman making a difference to a man because of her love."

Ty thought of that movie. He braced his elbow on the table and his chin on his fist, leaning closer to her. "How is it sexy for a guy messed up enough to be a serial killer to be obsessed with a woman?"

"Because she can heal him."

"You believe that?" Ty shook his head. "A guy like that belongs in jail."

She exhaled. "You don't get it."

"No, I don't. No means no. Unless all that garbage about no meaning yes is true."

She frowned and pushed up her glasses. "It's not." She bit her lip, seeking a way to explain. "It's because she's the focus of his world, to the exclusion of everything else. It's sexy that he can't think of anything or anyone else, that he becomes obsessed."

"There's a justification for every stalker on the planet."

"No!"

"What's the difference?"

"She's complicit. She wants it, that's the difference."

"That's the rationalization of every stalker and rapist," Ty felt compelled to note.

She eyed him. "You really don't get it."

"No, I don't. Why would a woman with any self-respect want a stalker? Why would a woman want a guy to tie her up and 'discipline' her, or keep her as his sex slave? What kind of relationship is that?" Ty flung out a hand, his own protective instinct toward women feeding his exasperation. "Why would anyone *fantasize* about that?"

She exhaled and regarded him, her expression so prim and disapproving that he might have been the one arguing in favor of kinky sex play.

"'We don't see things as they are, we see them as we are,'" she said and Ty blinked.

He didn't recognize it, and that made him feel as if he wasn't keeping up his end of their discussion. "Is that a quote?"

"Anaïs Nin." She shook a finger at him. "You're looking through the lens of your own assumptions, which affects your perceptions and your conclusions."

Ty was struck to silence. She was quoting an erotica author to him. And he had no comeback.

This was easily the most interesting conversation he'd had in years.

The Librarian took another breath and her gaze was steely. "It's not a fantasy, and it's not about the sex," she said flatly. "It's about the connection and the healing. It's about *trust*."

Ty arched a brow. He couldn't help it.

Her disgust with him was clear by how quickly she stood up. "Enjoy your lunch." Before he could continue the argument, she pivoted and marched away.

Chin up

Cheeks still crimson.

And she never looked back.

Ty watched her the whole way to the elevators, just to be sure.

She did have fabulous legs.

Although Ty would welcome the chance to burn those loafers.

He opened his own book, but couldn't follow the thread of the story. His sandwich was even less compelling. He recalled the high heel on the cover of her book. Those heels had to be six inches high. He had to think they'd do awesome things for her already fantastic legs.

It was her eyes that haunted him, though, as well as the way she'd surprised him. It had been a while since a woman had challenged him—at least, a woman who wasn't related to him. He couldn't even remember having a woman set him straight.

It was sexy as hell.

Especially as she was probably right.

Ty drummed his fingers, thinking. So much for his easy solution. He hadn't even learned the Librarian's name. He wasn't daunted, though.

No, he was intrigued.

Well, there was an easy step he could take next.

He would do some research and revive their discussion at lunch the next day.

The truly amazing thing was that Amy hadn't been struck mute in the presence of Mr. Yum. She hadn't spoken in tongues or otherwise been incoherent. She'd even scolded him.

The reason was obvious: it was because he was *nice*. He was the kind of guy who talked to his mom when he was at work. The boy next door, not the billionaire BDSM aficionado with the dark past and more emotional scars than she could count. His fourth sister was getting married. He was helping to keep his mom calm. He'd been pushed too far and had lost it, just a little bit.

There was also, regrettably, no sexual interest on his side. That was why she could talk to him. If he'd been interested in her, she would have been at a complete loss.

Amy would just bet that he was a great older brother. He probably could fix bicycle chains and pitch tents in backyards and build tree forts. He'd always be there for his sisters and would help his dad at the family home with whatever needed doing. He'd be on call at the wedding, picking up elderly relatives and helping them into the church, solving last minute crises, ensuring Uncle Ernie didn't have another drink when he had to drive home—or driving him and Aunt Edna home if Ernie *did* have that drink. He'd be the one everyone counted upon.

Plus he'd look really good in a tux.

His reaction to her choice of reading had been perfectly consistent with that. Thinly disguised horror. No, he would always be the gentleman and the considerate lover. His wife might read naughty books but if she was smart, she'd make sure he never knew. He'd treasure his wife and cherish her, pamper her and never forget her birthday.

He'd probably run from a woman who even owned a pair of handcuffs.

There she went, making up a whole life for him on the basis of a single short conversation. Her dad had teased her about that, once upon a time. Amy was smiling at the memory when she walked back into the office, only to find that chaos had erupted in her absence.

"I'm glad you had a good break," Mrs. Murphy said with her usual impatience. She gestured at the desk. "The internet is down, and I can't access the materials for the case this afternoon...."

"Let me try," Amy said mildly, sat down and got back to work. Mrs. Murphy stood over her, venting her spleen, and Amy wished her boss would go away.

And shut up.

Not necessarily in that order.

At least the afternoon passed quickly, with a hundred crises needing to be resolved. It was Amy who re-established the internet connection, who solved the problem with the printer, who retrieved the survey results "lost" in the computer crash. Before she knew it, it was after five, and she knew she deserved a reward.

She'd finish her book tonight, maybe even on the train on the way home. After the adventures of Melissa ended happily, Amy would be ready for another hot read.

She'd ask Jade to recommend a super spicy one.

CHAPTER TWO

AMY WAS browsing the shelves in what sometimes felt like the last remaining bookstore in midtown.

"Read this one?" Jade demanded on her way past, tossing a book in Amy's general direction.

Amy barely caught the book, turned it around, and nodded. "Yeah. It was good." She put it back on the shelf, ensuring that it was in the right place. She turned the cover to face out because she liked the tattoos on the pecs of the guy on the cover. "I liked it even better than her last one."

"Me, too. This one or that one?" Jade asked, appearing like a jack-in-the-box from the other side of the shelf. She was in the next aisle and offered two books.

"I liked that one better," Amy said, indicating the one on the left. "He was really hot."

"Mmmmmm." Jade rolled her eyes and smiled, then disappeared.

Amy was halfway through the cover copy on a contender, when another book was shoved in front of her.

"Try this one, then," Jade said.

Amy blinked at the cover, which was far more graphic than she would have expected. She stared at the entwined couple, wondering whether they were really doing it for the camera. The title was more than suggestive. Amy thought about putting it back on the shelf but Jade recommended it.

She turned it around to read the back cover copy. Oh. It was dark. She shivered and didn't put it back.

"I would never have picked this one up," Amy said, knowing Jade was listening wherever she was.

"Me, neither," a man said one second before Amy smelled his cologne. Her heart stopped cold, then raced.

Mr. Yum himself. She knew before she looked up.

"Imagine meeting you here," he said mildly, then picked up a copy of the book she'd dropped at lunch.

Amy was astonished. "You're not going to read that."

He had an expression that was becoming familiar. Apparently dead serious but his eyes twinkled. Amy's mouth went dry. "Why not?" he asked, his voice dropping lower.

Amy felt flustered, both by his expression and by her body's reaction to his presence. "You probably won't like it."

"Always a risk with a new author." He cracked a smile. "Want to recommend a better one?"

God, he had a dimple under one corner of his mouth. It was too much.

Amy's face burned. "You're making fun of me."

"No." He was definite. "Absolutely not. Whenever someone tells me that I don't know what I'm talking about, I try to fix it."

"Seriously?"

"Seriously. You made a persuasive argument."

Their gazes clung for a moment and Amy was sure her heart stopped. She couldn't quite take a breath, not when he was looking at her as if she was amazing.

"This one?" he asked again. "Or didn't you enjoy it?"

"I'm not quite done."

"But so far?"

Amy couldn't quite believe that he was serious, but she could play along. "It wasn't as good as her last book," she said casually, and pulled that one from the shelf as if the image was nothing special. A man was blindfolding a woman on the cover, and she was clearly naked, even though her whole body wasn't visible. She had her head tipped back and her mouth open, her pose making her appear to be orgasmic.

If any woman looked that good when she came.

"Okay." His brows rose just a little, then he tucked it under his arm, too. "We can compare our impressions after I've read them both."

Amy laughed. She couldn't stop herself. "Like a book club."

"Just like. But naughtier." He looked amused and she couldn't help smiling back at him. She felt a warm glow from her head to her toes and wanted to just bask in his attention forever.

"I'm guessing you won't be getting a book boyfriend, though." Amy was amazed that she was essentially asking a man she didn't know whether he was gay, but he was so nice that it was easy to be a bit cheeky.

His smile broadened and he chuckled. "Maybe a book girlfriend." He offered his right hand before she could think too much about that. "You left lunch so quickly that there wasn't time for introductions. I'm Tyler McKay."

There wasn't much to do other than slide her hand into his. Of course, his skin was warm and his grip was firm. Those great hands... Were her knees going to give out? "Amy Thornton," she said, and her voice sounded a little more husky than usual.

"I wanted to talk to you about something today..." he began.

"You mean you weren't just looking for a seat?"

To her amazement, he looked a little discomfited. "Not exactly. It was all a diabolical plan to have a chance to talk to you."

Amy laughed again, surprised into it. "You don't look very diabolical to me."

"We all have our dark secrets." His gaze dropped to the book she was holding, as if to imply that her secrets were epic in scope. Maybe they were. His eyes widened slightly at the cover image and she knew he hadn't really looked at it before. At his expression, Amy wished the ground would crack open and swallow her whole.

But then, she wouldn't be talking to Tyler anymore.

He lifted his gaze to hers. "Seriously?"

Amy felt her color rising again in this man's presence. "Jade says it's good."

His lips quirked. "That must be because it *isn't* about the sex."

"Amy! This!" Jade cried, barreling out of the back room with a book clenched in her fist. "Just in. Fresh out of the box. I had an advanced copy. This is the hottest book you will ever read—I promise you. You'll ovulate on the spot when this guy..." A little later than might have been ideal, Jade realized it wasn't just Amy listening to her rave about the book.

She blushed, then smiled, waving the book at Tyler. "Sorry. You're not usually in this aisle, Ty."

She knew him?

Of course. He must buy his books here, too.

Jade's gaze flicked to Amy, then back to Tyler, as if seeking an explanation. Amy wondered what he'd say, but he was the heart and soul of grace.

"Don't apologize. It's good to get enthusiastic about books," he said smoothly, then plucked the book out of her hands. "You'll have to get another copy for Amy." Then he took the one with the graphic cover from Amy's numb fingers. "And one of these, too." He smiled at her and she knew he was going to razz her a bit. "Unless you want to borrow it when I'm done?"

"No, thanks," she managed to say even though her mouth was as dry as the Sahara. "I'll get my own copy."

Ty turned to leave, then paused, dropping his voice to a delicious whisper. "See you tomorrow, Amy."

Both women stared at him as he strolled to the cash, picking up the new Grisham on the way. They watched in silence as he paid, checked his watch, picked up the bag, and left the store. He spared one backward glance at Amy and her heart dutifully skipped a beat.

Talk about ovulating on the spot.

She might have just done so.

Twice.

"You know Ty?" Jade asked.

Amy nodded. "I met him in the food court at work."

"He's one of our best customers." Jade exhaled. "Man candy and such a nice guy." She looked down at the books, then met Amy's gaze again. "You don't really think he's going to read them, do you?"

Amy shook her head. "He's probably going to give the books to one of his sisters."

Jade smiled. "And she will thank him. I tell you, this new book is so smoking awesome. When she opens the box of leather restraints from him in the limo and then strips for him, I just couldn't stop reading until I knew..."

Flatiron Five, also known as F5, the most exclusive fitness club in Manhattan and the company in which Ty was a founding partner, occupied an entire city block. It was the gym frequented by the rich and famous, as well as by the beautiful, and its reputation was such that it had become a tourist destination in itself. People came to F5 to get fit, of course, but they also came to see and be seen, to be part of a beautiful landscape of sculpted bodies. They took classes. They practiced yoga. They lifted weights. They swam laps. They made friends and many of them fell in love. It was amazing to Ty to witness what their little start-up had become after years of hard work and he reveled in it, each and every night when he returned home.

The club was named for the five partners, five buddies inseparable through college, as well as for the district where the club was located and where they had once shared a huge loft apartment. Only twelve years had passed since he, Kyle, Damon, Theo, and Cassie had first started to scribble on a scrap of paper in that loft. Now, their joint venture *owned* this niche.

The old building that filled the block had been purchased when they started out—with financing obtained by Ty—and its space had been renovated in increments as the business grew. Now the ground floor hosted retail shops selling their branded fitness gear and workout clothes, books, and videos. There was a restaurant that catered to every diet—paleo, vegetarian, vegan, raw, and more—and a juice bar, both of which sold F5 merchandise.

The floors at one end of the building had been removed and the structure reinforced to accommodate the highest indoor rock climbing wall on the island. The exterior wall was glass and the climbing wall lit at night. Ty thought of it as an animated ad for the club, like Times Square but better.

Although the ads in Times Square worked pretty well, too. The current one was a shot of Kyle, sprinkled with water as if fresh out of the pool, waxed to perfection and pumped to the max, with the tagline *Get Wet at F5.*

On the second floor was the F5 Club, a stroke of genius on the part of Kyle. He wasn't just the party animal of the partners, but the one who had realized that all those beautiful bodies could be better appreciated in the right lighting, while making the right moves. It had been the project that had demonstrated to Ty just how complementary the partners' skills were. Kyle had had the original vision. Damon had designed the layout, ensuring both privacy and visibility. Ty had found the funding, and Cassie had worked her marketing magic. Theo had the connections to bring in the beautiful people for the launch and get the right media attention. Even now, five years after the hotspot's doors had opened, and that in a city with the attention span of a gnat, it was *the* place to be on Friday and Saturday nights.

The third floor contained the pools, one deep and designated for lap swimming, the other shallower and used for water aerobic classes. The fourth and fifth floors were gyms and workout rooms, big and small, for members to work out and for classes. Floor six had even smaller rooms for private instruction. Floor seven was designated for massage and yoga, and had both serenity and a range of room sizes.

The building's footprint became smaller between the seventh and eighth floors and they had used that to advantage, at Damon's suggestion. They'd added windows on the sloping roof wherever possible and it was a sunny space, with a veritable forest of plants around the perimeter. They'd recently added a trickling fountain to one corner. Floor eight held the showers, saunas, and locker rooms. On the ninth floor, there was offices and storage. Floors ten through fifteen were vacant, but there were permits in the works to convert the upper floors to exclusive condos.

Ty lived in the penthouse apartment on the sixteenth floor and currently was the only resident of the building. Although their building wasn't the tallest in the district, it had provenance, high ceilings, and architectural details. Ty liked both that they owned it and that it had been repurposed with such style. He loved living there, too. There was nothing like going down to swim laps in the middle of the night, having the best fitness club in the city all to himself.

On this particular night, Ty strode along the busy streets, heading for home from his office which was closer to midtown. He couldn't stop thinking about Amy, or his surprise that she was going to read this book. *This* book. He'd peeked inside already and was a bit shocked by the guy's need for power and dominance. This fictional guy was serial killer material, in Ty's view, but he'd give it a chance. He always rose to a challenge and she'd given him one. He'd try to overcome his assumptions.

Either way, they'd have plenty to talk about at lunch.

He was already looking forward to it.

The sidewalks were crowded, probably because the day had been sunny and the air was still balmy. Cafés had put tables and chairs on the sidewalk and the corner store had a brilliant display of fresh flowers. He eyed the people heading into the subway and wondered how many of them had the same reading taste as Amy.

A lot, apparently, given the size of the section in the bookstore.

He wondered how far she took the train and where she lived.

Ty was glad he could walk home. He couldn't have faced the press of people on the train, much less the congestion on the roads leading out of the city. An evening market was setting up in its usual location, and Ty could hear the music from the featured band.

Another time, he would have wandered off, gotten some street food, and listened, but he had reading to do. He crossed the foyer of the F5 building and was going to enter his security code for the private elevator, when he noticed that something was going on at the back of the F5 store. Ty took another look.

The best retail space, the corner window facing the busiest street, was curtained off and stripped down to the walls. The store was closed, and clearly, they were changing out the display for the next day. It was all black and pink, just like the covers of the books he had in his briefcase. Cassie and one of the yoga instructors were helping the retail manager with a new display.

From this angle, it looked like a rack of black leather restraints.

In fact, the mannequin in the display window appeared to be hung from the ceiling by her shackled wrists, her head cast back in ecstasy. She was wearing a pair of black leather thigh high boots with fierce stiletto heels and not much else.

Ty forgot the elevator and went into the store. "What's going on?" The closer he got, the more detail he saw, though he tried to keep his expression calm.

There *was* a rack of black leather restraints, emblazoned with the F5 logo.

And that was the least of it.

"Ta da!" Cassie said, spinning to face him so that her blond ponytail swung out. She looked excited. "Tomorrow's the launch of our new specialty shop. Lucky, lucky, you get a sneak peek."

"Bondage gear?"

"To support our most popular new workshops." Cassie shook a finger in front of him. "We're oversold for the next *three* months. Waiting lists on every single class. I've never seen anything like it. Kyle is *brilliant.*"

Ty wondered whether the world had gone insane when he wasn't looking. "You're kidding me."

"We talked about it during last quarter's meeting."

"I thought you were just exploring the idea."

"It came together perfectly, just the way the best ideas do. And word of mouth booked us up fast. It was like white lightning, Ty. *This* is going to take F5 to the next level. The buffer the better for these kinds of games." Cassie grinned. "And who doesn't like sex?" She poked him in the chest with a fingertip. "We'll practically be printing money and that should even make you happy." She gave him a triumphant smile and returned to the display, leaving Ty with the sense that he'd stepped into a parallel universe.

And the realization that reading these books was now research.

He surveyed the store's merchandise and saw a DVD of the movie he'd watched with Paige. He hadn't liked it then, but had to admit that he *had* been viewing it through his own assumptions.

Ty needed to do better than that to earn Amy's respect. He grabbed the DVD, added it to his tab, ignored Cassie's surprise, and headed home.

He had a lot of studying to do.

Amy felt like she had homework. She'd finished Melissa's story as anticipated, then devoured an entire book, the dark one. It was wickedly naughty and really hot. Outside of her usual boundaries, but exploring that territory in fiction was...potent. She stayed up late to start the new one that Jade had brought out of the back, uncertain which one Ty intended to read first.

She wanted to be ready for their discussion, but Brittany had called around nine and taken too long to reassure. Amy had fallen asleep at three before finishing the second book. That felt like a failure. She slept later than usual, missed the train that was sufficiently empty to ensure she always got a seat, and had to stand all the way from Brooklyn.

No chance to read.

She couldn't even sneak a few minutes of guilty pleasure in the office, given issues with the copier. She was speed-reading in the atrium at lunch, trying to get through the big finish before Ty arrived.

She didn't make it.

She heard his footstep, then saw the dark book being thunked on the table. "Nothing short of the electric chair is going to heal this guy," he said, then sat down and opened his lunch. Brown bagging it today. He gave her an intent look. "That can't be a spoiler. I knew it in the first chapter."

"He has been through a lot," Amy said.

Ty snorted. "Pathetic excuse. Go ahead and finish your book. I'll just check my email and duck my mom's inevitable call."

He looked so weary that Amy couldn't stop her smile. "Up late?"

He slanted a smile her way. "Re-examining my assumptions. Who knew it was so time-consuming?"

Amy was ridiculously pleased. He'd listened to her. There was nothing more seductive than that.

She shut the book. "And do you get it?"

"No, not yet." He looked mystified, then shook a finger at her. "But don't worry. I won't give it up without a fight."

Amy smiled. "Stubborn?"

"Persistent is a better word, I think. It has more of a positive spin."

They smiled at each other across the table and Amy felt warm. "You expect your mom to call again about the wedding?"

"Of course. I can time her."

"The prep isn't that bad. Is it?"

Ty shook his head. "No. We've done it three times to applause and we have our groove. It's the next bit I'm worried about." He actually looked discomfited.

Amy was fascinated. "What next bit? The wedding itself?"

He grimaced. "The part where the truth comes out."

Amy laughed. She couldn't help it. "Did you tell a big fat whopper to your mom?"

Ty eyed her. "Would you stop speaking to me if I did?"

"You don't seem like the type."

"I'm not. It was bad advice from a friend. Now that I've taken it, it just gets worse."

"One lie leads to another."

"Something like that." He gave her a look. "Now that I've admitted it, are you going to stop speaking to me?"

"Not if it was an interesting whopper." Amy would be surprised if he'd actually done something that wasn't nice. "Not if you tell me about it."

He opened his sandwich as if he needed the time to choose his words. It looked kind of sad and not very fresh. Bad, bad staff. Ty considered it without enthusiasm. "That's what I get for leaving it in the fridge for a day," he muttered.

"You bought a sandwich yesterday," Amy reminded him. "Did you forget this one at home?"

She won a very quick look for that, then Ty changed the subject. "So, I told you yesterday that Katelyn's wedding means I'm the only one left unmarried."

"Which is going to make finding you a wife the next agenda item and inevitable development."

She got a very green look for that. "I wish it weren't inevitable."

"No interest in marriage?"

"No interest in being fixed up by well-intentioned meddlers." He studied her for a long moment. "Finding the right partner is important. I'd like to get it right, and that means I intend to do it myself."

Amy liked the sound of that. "Do you have a lot of older female relatives?"

"Hundreds of them, it seems."

"Particularly at weddings."

"And they all know a very nice girl..."

"*Nice*," Amy echoed and unwrapped her sandwich. "That's the kiss of death. When's the wedding?"

"Four weeks."

"My cousin Brittany's is in three. Just for the record, I have way too many aunties, too."

"Well-intentioned meddlers?"

"Every one of them." She shuddered elaborately. "I'm afraid they'll all turn out to know *nice* men by the dozens."

"What's wrong with nice guys?"

"They're predictable. Safe. Boring." Amy wrinkled her nose. "Vanilla."

"I thought vanilla referred to sex."

Amy dropped her gaze and blushed, then found her sandwich fascinating. "So, what whopper did you tell your mom?" she asked, changing the subject.

"It's not pretty."

"Tell me."

"It was an act of self-defense."

Amy smiled. "You're ducking the question."

"Okay, for my grandmother's eightieth birthday party last winter, I invited a woman to go with me, one I'd just met," Ty admitted.

"Harsh. You threw her to the wolves."

"On the contrary. They adored her." He shrugged. "Me, not so much. Well before we even arrived, I knew we had nothing in common. We parted amiably, and that was the last time I ever saw her." He winced and Amy guessed.

She put down her sandwich. "Tell me that you did *not* maintain her as a fictional girlfriend."

27

"Why not?" Ty looked guilty, despite his words. "It's been a great few months because of that tactic. Not one person has set me up. Friday nights have been my own. It's been awesome."

"But you can't bring her to the wedding."

"And I wouldn't want to. If I go alone, though—" Ty made a face that prompted Amy to laugh again. "Talk about being thrown to the wolves." He looked away, then down at his soggy sandwich. "You're kind of in the same situation, aren't you?"

He lifted his gaze to hers and she knew exactly what he was going to suggest.

"You came down here yesterday, looking for a victim," she accused. "That's why you said you wanted to talk to me." She didn't know whether to be insulted or flattered, but she wasn't going to let him have his way easily either way.

"A victim? Excuse me." Ty picked up the book and shook it at her. "This woman is a victim. I'm a nice guy, looking to make a deal."

"A deception," Amy said.

"An exchange," he corrected. "I go to your family wedding, you go to mine. Then we break up."

"It's a lie, another one."

"No, it's not."

"I thought that was what you called a story that wasn't the truth."

That Ty looked so discomfited told Amy that he didn't usually bend the truth. "It's a mutually agreed upon fiction."

"That doesn't sound like something you'd say."

Ty's expression was exasperated. "It's something my friend Kyle would say, who, it must be noted, was the one who gave me the advice that started this whole nightmare."

"It's not going to work," Amy had to point out.

"Why not?"

"If it's just a one-off date, it's no defense. A successful fake date needs depth."

Ty's expression became considering. "Voice of experience?"

"Observer of human nature. Seeds to be planted so that it appears to be a plausible longer relationship." She held his gaze. "Assuming that we're going to be each other's alibis for a whole month."

He took a bite of his sandwich, considering. "You're right."

"If you did this all the time, you'd have known better."

"Point taken. My mom is asking about Giselle coming to the mixed bridal shower this weekend."

28

"See? There has to be consistency for this kind of thing to come off."

"If you're going to be my date for the wedding, you should come to the shower."

"True."

His gaze locked with hers and she couldn't look away from that twinkle. "I probably should ask first, though: how often do you scam *your* family? It's a bit disconcerting that you have the details worked out."

Amy smiled. "Never. But I read a lot of books."

"So?"

"I don't know. Maybe I should think about it."

Ty's expression turned wicked as he considered the book in front of her and she felt her pulse skip. "Is that the secret, then? Do I have become domineering to convince you to agree?"

Amy felt the blood leave her face then rush back again. "Of course not."

"Rats."

"Don't give me that. You're too nice to even consider such a thing."

"Isn't being nice the kiss of death?"

"Pretty much. It might be why this won't get complicated."

"How so?"

"Well, in a book or a movie, the couple making this agreement would fall in love and live happily ever after. But you're not my type, and I'm probably not yours, so we'll be safe."

"Safe." Ty seemed to find that choice of word funny. There was no doubt that he was fighting a smile. "Even though you know just about nothing about me."

"I know where you work. I know you're a lousy liar. Even your mom probably guessed about the cellophane."

"She didn't believe it was really static." He shook his head. "You're absolutely right. My mom will find the holes in our story before you even get a glass of wine. If we're going to do this thing, we should go for dinner on Friday night and prep."

"Prep?"

"You have to study for everything that's important." He nodded, looking decisive. "Research has never failed me."

"So, this dinner would be like cramming for an exam."

"Funny how it doesn't sound inviting when you put it like that."

"Funny." Their gazes locked and held and Amy felt a tingle. "But it would still be a lie."

Ty leaned on the table, his arms folded and his gaze intent. "One that helps both of us. That's got to count for something." His voice dropped to an entreaty. "Come on, Amy. We can have some fun with it."

Before Amy could reply, Ty's cell phone rang. He pulled out the phone and checked the number, then waited for it to ring again before answering it. "Hi, Mom." He listened for a long moment, his mother's voice carrying out of the device. "Even if the weather station says it's going to rain on June 10, they could be wrong. It's weeks away."

He met Amy's gaze and raised his other hand, inviting her answer.

Amy bit her lip, wondered whether she would regret this, then nodded.

Ty grinned, then touched one of the buttons on the keypad. "What's that, Mom? Oh, wait. I have an incoming call, Mom." His voice warmed with enthusiasm. "Oh! It's *Amy.*"

Amy heard his mom repeat her name in a squeak of delight, even as she clapped a hand over her own mouth to keep from laughing out loud.

"Yes, Amy, Mom. Oh, she's incredible." Ty's gaze was fixed on Amy and his tone was so warm that his praise sounded genuine. "I'm meeting her for lunch. I hope she's not caught up at the office. Gotta get this. Later, Mom."

Ty ended the call and met Amy's gaze, his eyes sparkling with triumph as a smile claimed his lips. Damn that dimple.

"You are wicked."

"No, no, I'm *nice.* Remember?"

"You cornered me."

"You didn't have to agree."

"True. Don't make me regret it."

"Never. I might learn to be naughty, just for you."

Amy's heart skipped, then she caught her breath when Ty grinned. He shoved the rest of the sandwich into the bag and threw the whole thing like a basketball, over his head and straight into the trash. Some of the others having lunch applauded, but Ty was watching Amy too intently to notice. "Friday. Dinner. My tab. Just tell me where to pick you up."

"Tell me where to meet you," Amy insisted.

30

"Because I'm a nice guy?"

"Because you just reminded me that I don't know anything about you. You have secrets, too."

"*Everybody* has secrets, Amy." Ty was dismissive. "I'll pick a restaurant." He tapped the book. "Finish up and we'll talk about it tomorrow."

Then he was gone, striding through the atrium like a man who had successfully fulfilled a mission.

Which meant that it *had* been a plan.

She could be insulted, but on the other hand, Ty could only have made the plan because he'd noticed her before.

Amy had butterflies in her stomach, which just showed that it had been too long since she'd had a date, fake or otherwise. She heard her father's voice in her thoughts, repeating his favorite D. H. Lawrence quote: "I want to live my life so that my nights are not full of regrets."

Well, she was following that advice.

Two weddings with Ty as her date. And dinner Friday. And she was going to be in that ghastly dress for one wedding, the fantasy in tangerine with shoes dyed to match. That made her want to twitch.

She should have fought harder against Brittany's choice.

But it was just a fake date. It didn't really matter how she looked or what Ty thought of the dress.

With a sigh, Amy turned back to the fictional Kade and his dark moment.

Even though she was thinking about Ty.

And Friday night.

Cassie felt as if she were a thousand years old.

It was a pretty sad commentary on her life, she thought, that the financial meeting for F5 was looking to be the highlight of her day, week, and month.

Because Ty would be there. The chance to see him put a spring in Cassie's step. It always had, although he'd never even glanced at her. She wondered whether she'd been too subtle in showing her interest over the years. The man had a perfect poker face, but was a complete gentleman. For all she knew, the interest was mutual but he was too polite to make the first move.

It was certainly worth finding out.

His reaction the night before to the new bondage gear hadn't been very encouraging, that was for sure. Cassie had the definite sense that she'd shocked him.

On this day, she'd shock him again with an up-close-and-personal look at the new merchandise. One of the new classes was scheduled right after their weekly meeting. She wore her new black latex catsuit and her highest-heeled pair of black boots. She laced a corset over the catsuit so that her waist was cinched and her breasts pushed upward. With her long blond hair loose, she thought she looked like a hot version of Catwoman.

She felt hot, too.

Maybe it was the bullwhip.

It was such an ideal accessory that every woman should carry one.

Cassie's heels clicked as she strode down the corridor to the meeting and more than one woman gave her a thumbs-up in passing. A couple of the regular guys wolf-whistled after her. Cassie liked how she felt in this outfit, commanding and sexy, too. She knew her smile was more seductive, and that the red lipstick and dark eyeliner worked in a big way. She decided she'd walk the gym floor before her class and maybe muster some more attendance.

She was last to arrive at the scheduled meeting and wasn't surprised to find Kyle and Damon already bickering. They'd done it for so long that it was an ingrained habit, and it had never meant anything anyway. Ty was wearing a navy suit and crisp tie, frowning slightly as he reviewed the financial reports for the previous month. Ignoring Kyle and Damon, just like usual. The phone was on the conference table to link in Theo from London.

"I'm just saying that you could hold up your end a bit better," Kyle complained. He was sprawled in a chair, one foot braced on the conference table as he balanced on the chair's back legs. He looked like the quintessential surfer: blond, tanned, and buff. He was dressed, as usual, in jeans that were snug in all the right places and a tight T-shirt that could have been a second skin. His hair was a hundred shades of gold and tousled, his eyes a sparkling blue, and he looked good enough to eat. Kyle had that perfect blend of confidence and style that made him draw women like bees to honey, and he knew it. He also used it. Cassie had never met anyone with a worse case of commitment disease. Despite his cockiness, there was something playful about Kyle that made him impossible to dislike.

He certainly could make Cassie—and pretty much any woman alive—laugh.

Damon rolled his eyes. A little shorter than Kyle, he spent a lot of time at the gym, too. But Damon had always been the quiet powerhouse. He was intense and brilliant, and a genius with design. He was also a dark horse, the one who could unexpectedly go the distance, and often surprised Kyle when they competed in the gym. "You're the one who came up with the idea of the club," Damon complained. "You're the one who said it had to be monitored by a discerning individual like yourself. So, quit bitching about the job you made for yourself."

"All I'm saying is that you could work a Friday night once in a while," Kyle argued.

"Would the world end if you two stopped arguing like old women?" Cassie asked, pulling out a chair for herself. She stood behind it for a moment, wanting Ty to have the full view. "Maybe we should give it a try, just to see."

"Old women?" Kyle said, apparently insulted.

Damon looked her up and down, then winked.

Ty only flicked her the barest glance of acknowledgment.

So much for the alluring power of latex.

"Maybe elderly sisters," Cassie said and Kyle shuddered.

"I don't think we're that bad," he said, but Cassie was watching Ty.

She saw him blink, then look at her again. She smiled at his astonishment and turned in place, brandishing her whip. "Like it?"

Whatever he was thinking, he hid it well.

And he returned to the financials. "Not your usual look."

"But perfect for the class I'm teaching today. 'Getting Naughty Together 101.'"

"Or knotty," Kyle joked.

That got Ty's attention. "You are serious about the classes, then."

Kyle grinned. "It's not funny how popular they are." He leaned over and pointed to the line item. "There."

Ty frowned. "There are *that* many people, who are already members, who are prepared to pay a premium to attend BDSM classes?"

"Who would have thunk it?" Kyle asked.

"You did," Damon reminded him and Kyle grinned.

"Finger on the pulse of the nation, that's me."

"Maybe women's pulses," Cassie noted.

"Which other ones matter?" Kyle was unrepentant. "I think you all owe me a bonus for this plan. We've got at least one additional session every day of the week, all of them booked out months in advance."

Ty raised a hand in silent demand.

"Three months sold in advance." Cassie plucked a copy of the flyer listing the new classes off the shelf of promotional materials and dropped it into Ty's hand. All three of them watched him read it and Cassie knew she wasn't the only one who felt his surprise.

She'd told him about it.

Sometimes he was a little too much of a straight arrow. Her gaze caught Kyle's and she knew that Kyle was going to pull Ty's chain. She kept her expression neutral and watched.

"Ties that Bind, Spanking Pink, Whip It Good, In the Dark, Pain and Pleasure 101..." Ty frowned. "All under the Safe Erotic Play programming, for adults over 18." He put down the flyer and looked at Cassie. "And people pay for this."

Kyle leaned forward. "You were the one who said we needed new members and new sources of revenue."

Ty nodded in concession. "Well, yeah, our original demographic is getting older, thus less concerned with fitness, drinking less alcohol in the bar..."

"Marriage and babies," Cassie said.

"These classes, though, have kicked things up a notch," Kyle continued. "There's a hum out there that I like a lot. It works for me."

"It's bringing in new members," Damon noted, pointing out the increase between months to Ty. "We're getting a reputation."

"I bet," Ty murmured. He tapped a line item. "What kind of private instruction is this?" He gave Kyle a look that should have been quelling.

Here it went.

Kyle grinned and ran an admiring hand over his own chest. "The very best kind."

"We've always offered it," Cassie said. "Some people like the one-on-one."

"But we didn't offer sex ed classes," Ty noted. "How far does your instruction go?"

"Officially, it's a technique class with a more personal format," Kyle said. "But hey, things happen."

Ty frowned. "You don't..."

"Oh yeah, I do, and very well, too."

Ty was visibly outraged. "But you can't do that. It's not legal."

"Oh, come on," Cassie argued. "It's not any different than Kyle going to Mrs. Markland's condo to help her with her yoga poses and maybe staying a little longer to improve her other moves."

Ty blinked. "You don't."

"Of course, I do." Kyle shrugged. "Sometimes. When the temptation is right."

"You're not a gigolo. You're a bodybuilding instructor."

"Even if he is a man slut," Damon noted.

Kyle wadded up a sheet of paper and threw it at him. "It kind of comes with the territory," he said to Ty. He gestured in the direction of the gym. "Especially *our* territory. All those hot, muscled bodies. All that human perfection, sweating and stretching, and *noticing*. This whole place is built on the power of eye candy. That's our niche. Gorgeous specimens of humanity in every direction. That's why people come to F5. Sex is the natural and inevitable result." He sat back and grinned. "What's not to love about it?"

"No. We're using the sizzle to sell the steak," Ty argued. "Beautiful bodies convince people to join gyms like ours..."

It was Damon who interrupted him. "And what's wrong with a bite of steak once in a while? It happens."

"Right on," Kyle agreed.

Ty put down his pen. "This is a gym, not a brothel!"

"A brothel?" Cassie shook her head. "How Victorian. Are you going to need your smelling salts?"

"It's not a monastery, either," Kyle said, then spoke very slowly. "People have sex, Ty. People have sex with people they meet at the gym. Even at our gym. *Especially* at our gym. I'm sorry to break this to you, but it's true."

Ty rubbed the bridge of his nose. "I *know* that."

"Read about it online?" Kyle taunted, his eyes twinkling.

"My love life isn't under discussion here."

"Maybe the monastery's upstairs," Damon teased.

"There's nothing wrong with having a small dry spell," Ty said.

"I've heard about that," Kyle said. "The Sahara has that problem."

"The Gobi," Damon added and they laughed together.

"Not that dry," Ty said easily. "Just a couple of months."

"A lifetime," Kyle said. "Want help?"

"No. Thanks." Ty frowned. "Now about this so-called private instruction..."

"Take it easy," Kyle said. "The private classes are just that. No sex.

What happens afterward, if anything happens, isn't anyone's business."

"It's not a good idea to muddy the line between professional and personal," Ty insisted.

"I was just seeing what you'd believe." Kyle grinned and Ty shook his head.

"I never know how far you'll go."

"It is part of my charm," Kyle replied easily. "And it's fun to see you get all pissed off." He grinned, unrepentant, and Ty fixed him with a look. "Maybe once it rains, you'll be more philosophical."

"Don't hold your breath."

"Aren't we in better shape than before?" Cassie asked, changing the subject and taking the seat beside Ty.

"I like that we have new members," he acknowledged. "Anything else they have in common?"

"They're joining for the classes," Damon said. "And a lot of them come in couples."

"Really?" Ty said. "That's a new demographic for us."

"The couples' classes book out first and fast," Cassie supplied. "Despite Kyle's bragging. I think there's interest in revitalizing their sexual relationship." She quickly told the guys about two couples who had recently joined.

"Whose idea was it? His or hers?" Ty asked, hitting the nail on the head.

"Hers," Cassie said. "So, we want to target older women in established relationships. The materials will have to be elegant..."

"All our materials are elegant, Cassie," Ty said. "It's what you do, and what distinguishes F5 in the market."

She found herself ridiculously pleased, even though he didn't look at her, and spoke as if it were just a fact. "Spice in the bedroom, or relighting the spark, or rediscovering the passion. Something like that. The idea is that they're finding the passion that's dropped by the wayside in the day-to-day grind of twenty or thirty years, or maybe just with the arrival of kids."

"Advertising uptown, where the established neighborhoods are," Damon contributed.

"Maybe flyers for marriage counselors and therapists," Cassie suggested.

"That's good," Kyle said. "I like it."

"Good starts," Damon said, counting off the elements their action plan on his fingers. "Cost and pricing review, courses for couples. Anything else we can do to diversify our client base?"

"I'll put some flyers at the Museum of Sex, if they'll have them," Cassie said.

"Advertise the BDSM classes in bookstores," Ty suggested. They all turned to look at him in surprise. He shrugged. "Erotic romance is a popular genre," he continued. "You can't predict what kind of women are reading it—the demographic is probably all over the place—but one place you'll find them is in that section of the bookstore, whether bricks-and-mortar or online." He pursed his lips. "Maybe libraries, too. Subway trains."

They stared at him for a full minute before Kyle started to laugh. "That's completely brilliant. Trust you to quietly come up with such a great plan."

"The bookstore near my office has a huge section devoted to it." He looked discomfited, which was interesting.

Ty never looked discomfited.

"How would you know?" Cassie asked, her tone teasing. "Don't you read mysteries?"

He smiled slowly. "Sure, but all the women were in that one aisle. I went over to look."

"The old strategy still works," Kyle said.

Ty grinned.

"*I'm a heterosexual man*," Damon and Kyle sang in unison, fist-bumping each other, then Ty.

"Thank God," Kyle said, wiping his brow with relief. "I was afraid you'd gone celibate on us, Ty."

"Not in this lifetime," Ty said with conviction.

The phone rang then. Damon tapped it to answer and take the call to the speaker.

"I hear laughter," Theo said. "What did I miss?"

"Everything!" Kyle roared. "We're shocking Ty."

"Is that easier than it used to be?"

"You gotta get back on this side of the pond," Damon complained. "What are you *doing* over there?"

"Exploring options, of course," Theo said smoothly.

"This is my kind of guy," Kyle said.

"What happened to being a heterosexual man?" Ty asked, and they laughed again.

"We need some of your mojo back in the club," Kyle said to

Theo. "Come on home. I'll be sure you get an awesome welcome."

Theo chuckled. "All in good time. Come on, let's get to it."

"Financial review," Ty said. "Things are looking good, but we have some actionable items..." He looked as if he were focused on business, but Cassie knew Tyler better than that. She'd bet there was a specific reason he'd gone into that section of the bookstore.

A specific *woman*.

It was only human nature to want to know more.

CHAPTER THREE

S O?" JADE demanded, appearing suddenly on the other side of the shelf in front of Amy. "What did you think?"

"I liked this one," Amy said, stalling for time. She waved the dark erotic romance.

"I knew you would. What about the other one? The new one?"

"Really?" Amy didn't want to disappoint her best advisor.

"Really. Hit me with your honest assessment." Jade leaned over the bookshelves and dropped her voice to a whisper. "Come on. I can take it."

"I didn't think it was hot enough."

"Really?" Jade squeaked. "How could it have been better?"

"Well, what if he'd fulfilled her fantasy instead of exploring his own?" When Jade came around the shelves, Amy lowered her voice and outlined how she thought the book should have ended. To her surprise, the other woman barely took a breath as she described a different plotline, but her hand gripped Amy's arm tighter and tighter.

"Oh. My. God. You're right. That would have been *awesome*," Jade agreed. "It would have been so much better. You're so right."

"Thanks."

"Why don't you write a book?"

"Me?" Amy was startled.

"Sure. All sorts of people are publishing their books digitally and some of them make a lot of money. I think you'd be good at it. You know the market, after all." Jade grinned. "And I want to read the book you just described. Write it!"

39

Amy frowned as Jade continued to enthuse. As much as she liked the idea of making extra money—who didn't?—she was sure that these authors must have experience in doing what they wrote about.

While she, um, didn't.

Wouldn't it show in the writing? They did say that you should write what you know. What Amy knew about erotic exploration based on personal experience would fit in a thimble. She'd just read about a lot of it, and that couldn't be considered the same.

She made her excuses to Jade and actually forgot to buy another book because she was so busy thinking. It was an idea that didn't leave her alone.

Could she write a book?

Could she write a hot, steamy romance that made women like Jade part with their money to read it?

She used to write in high school, and she'd loved her English composition classes. Her dad had let her read whatever she wanted whenever she wanted, including a lot of old-school erotica in his collection. It wasn't an accident that she could quote Anaïs Nin to Ty. She'd planned to take English Lit at college, well, before everything changed.

What if she *could* write a book?

"And the day came when the risk to remain tight in a bud was more painful than the risk it took to blossom."

Thank you, Anaïs Nin.

Amy would try.

Any possibility of losing her nerve died a quick death when Amy arrived home to find the roof leaking.

Again.

Fitzwilliam was complaining mightily about the empty state of his food bowl, even though he twined around her ankles with an enthusiasm at her return that couldn't just be about tuna. She hung up her coat in the bathroom and put her wet loafers on the radiator, then fed him. Then she climbed the stairs with some more buckets and pails, pausing to knock on her tenants' door on the second floor so that Mrs. Petrovsky didn't think the house was being invaded.

"Just me, Mrs. P," she called. "Checking the attic."

She didn't wait for an answer, even though she heard the rustle of Mrs. P. looking through the peephole. Her daughter, Lisa, must not be home yet. Amy and Lisa had gone to high school together. Lisa and her mom had moved into the second-floor apartment Amy created in the house after the death of Amy's dad.

There was one finished room in the attic, at the front of the house, then the back lower part of the attic was unfinished. Amy checked the plastic sheets draped over everything in the finished room, confirming that all her mother's clothes were protected. The leaking, so far, had been in the unfinished part, which was a relief. She walked on the rafters with practiced ease to put buckets and tubs in strategic locations.

One bucket that had already been in place was full, which was a bad sign. That leak was getting worse. Amy switched out the bucket for another one, then lugged the full one down to the kitchen. She opened the back door and dumped it out, then made a note to check that bucket again before she went to bed.

With a sigh, she dug through the contractor's repair estimates that she kept carefully filed in one drawer of the kitchen. The house was due for a lot of maintenance. Nothing much had been done in recent years, what with her parents being sick. Money had been tight and attention had been elsewhere. Now Amy wished she'd been a little more on top of things. It was sobering to go through the estimates and realize just how much it would cost to set everything to rights in her little corner of paradise.

The roofer's estimate made her wince.

And it was two years old.

Amy couldn't move, though. She couldn't ever leave this house. It was too filled with memories and love. It was her sanctuary. But it appeared that she couldn't forgo basic repairs for much longer. Her job wasn't great, but she didn't have the credentials for anything much better.

It wasn't in Amy's nature to sulk about things she couldn't change. She solved things. She had to find a solution to this. Selling the house was out of the question.

Maybe Jade's suggestion had been a timely one.

While she took care of a thousand details, Amy was thinking about the kind of story she'd most like to read.

It should be a story that only she could write.

One that no one else had written yet.

The strange thing was that Amy knew exactly what the story would be. It would be a dark fairy tale, one featuring a scarred prince with dark desires, many secrets and complete authority over his subjects.

He'd pick one to be his sex slave, thinking she'd just be his pet. But in the end, she'd be the one brave enough to challenge him, then win his heart and heal him forever.

And if the prince in question looked like Ty McKay—albeit with a scar—that would be her little secret.

After dinner, Amy took a fresh pad of paper. She made a fresh pot of coffee and found her favorite pen, then sat down at the kitchen table under Fitzwilliam's watchful eye.

Her Dark Prince, she wrote, tapped the pen, then wrote some more.

I first saw the crown prince two days before Midsummer.

We knew he had come to the palace, of course, and that he was the king's nephew and chosen heir. No one had seen him since he had ridden through the castle gates at Midwinter and those who had glimpsed the lone rider on his approach had long been embellishing their brief observations beyond all recognition. He was rumored to be solitary, fierce, and harsh. I could not blame him, not if he had been so disfigured in war as he was whispered to be.

I dreamed of him, even knowing nothing of him. I was curious beyond all. No one came to Euphoria. No one left Euphoria. It was my greatest dream to abandon the monotony of the only life I had ever known. I was prepared to pay any price to see beyond Euphoria's borders, to be more than the sole daughter of a peasant said to be a witch. I created tales about him and spun dreams of a shared future and yearned so fiercely to just see him once that I halfway thought I'd summoned him to me.

Like one of those old tales that I have never believed.

Maybe if I had believed them, I would have attributed his appearance to sorcery instead of coincidence. Or boredom.

It mattered little. I saw him and my life changed.

Ty knew it wouldn't be long before his phone rang again and he was right.

He came up from his evening workout to discover that he'd missed two calls by leaving his cell phone in his apartment. It rang again when he was checking that all the calls had come from the same number.

His mom.

Who was calling again.

He figured he might as well get it over with. "Hi, Mom." He stood at the window and looked down on the traffic in the city streets below. It was raining and the lights were reflected in the puddles. He hoped Amy was safely home, wherever she lived.

"Tyler McKay, I have one question to ask you and one question only."

"Don't be shy, Mom," Ty said. "You know how that confuses me."

His mother exhaled. "Amy."

"Amy?"

"Amy," his mother repeated. "You were meeting her for lunch and I want to know all about her."

"You'll meet her on Sunday."

"I should hope so, but I need to be prepared. Who is she? Where is her family? How serious is your relationship? What does she do for a living? Where did you first meet?" His mom took a deep breath. "Why haven't you mentioned her before? *And what happened to Giselle?*"

Ty grimaced and strolled into the kitchen to get a glass of water. He leaned against the counter and tried to tell his mother as little as possible.

That way she'd have less to use against him.

"It didn't work out with Giselle. I was optimistic, but we broke up."

"When?"

"A while ago," Ty said. "I didn't want to disappoint you. I know you liked her."

"Thank you, dear," his mom said. "But really, if she didn't see your merit, she wasn't worth your time."

Ty smiled. "Thanks, Mom."

"And Amy?"

"She's cute and very sweet. Smart." It was true. Every time Ty talked to Amy, he found more to like and admire. He was going to have another late night, re-examining his assumptions, but it would be worth it to have another conversation with her. Lunch was quickly becoming the highlight of his day.

"How long have you been seeing her?"

Ty chucked Kyle's advice and went with the truth. It was easier. Less complicated. "Not that long, Mom. I wasn't sure whether it was too soon to bring her to a wedding..."

"Don't be ridiculous, Ty. We're so welcoming and friendly. Why, we'll be planning your wedding before Katelyn heads for her honeymoon." His mother laughed, but Ty shook his head.

"That's what I'm afraid of."

"Nonsense. You're always too protective of women, Ty."

"You taught me that, Mom."

"I know, dear, but we're a little tougher than you imagine."

"That doesn't mean she's ready to be engulfed by a huge noisy family like ours."

"I bet she'll love it."

"Provided you don't all terrorize her."

"Ty!"

"Or smother her."

"There you go, being protective again. In this case, dear, I think it's a very good sign."

"Mom..."

"Stop worrying. You bring Amy and we'll make her feel welcome." There was a sound on the line to indicate another call coming in for his mom and Ty realized he'd been saved by the click. "Oh, look, there's the florist. What could possibly be wrong now? I'll see you both on Sunday, Tyler. Two o'clock at Aunt Teresa's."

"I know."

"Well, don't forget. And don't be late."

"I'm never late," Ty protested, but his mom was gone.

The fake date was a go.

For better or for worse.

Amy stayed up half the night, her imagination on fire and her hand racing across the page. Fitzwilliam gave up on her at midnight and went to sleep on her pillow. When the flow of words finally stopped, she looked up digital publishing online and researched the possibilities. It was only when she had been reading for over an hour that she realized she was just as convinced as Ty that preparation was the key to success in any endeavor.

She awakened to Fitzwilliam batting her cheek in a playful demand for breakfast, the alarm clock buzzing, and the realization of one big stumbling block. There was another thing she had to research. She'd thought of it the day before, but in the morning, it seemed an insurmountable barrier. No one had ever tied Amy up and spanked her, and she had a pretty good sense that Ty wouldn't be up for it, even as a joke.

Or a fake seduction.

It wouldn't be hot if he treated it as a joke, anyway.

She did agree with him in a way, though. Doing that with a complete stranger would require that Amy be a lot dumber than she was. She thought about it all the way to work, knowing there had to be a solution. She got off the train at an earlier stop so she could walk past the Museum of Sex and there it was, taped to the window.

A notice that could have been just for her.

Pain and Pleasure 101.

They were teaching BDSM classes at F5—no sex, just sensation. Forty dollars a session, come in yoga clothes and prepare to learn something new.

What could go wrong in a gym full of curious people?

Amy marched to work, thinking furiously.

Did she dare?

Why shouldn't she dare?

When she saw a second similar notice in the window of the bookstore where Jade worked, she pulled out her phone and scanned the QR code before she chickened out. In about fifteen seconds, thanks to Paypal, she was registered for the Saturday afternoon class.

Amy was unable to believe what she'd just done, yet thrilled to bits about the possibilities. Her heart was racing as if she'd run a marathon.

One thing was for sure: she'd never ever tell Ty about it. He'd probably go ballistic.

On the other hand, it might be worth telling him just to see his composure slip.

Something was different. Ty recognized as much immediately.

Amy came into the common area at lunch with a verve that was unusual for her. Her eyes were sparkling and she almost bounced as she walked. Ty dared to hope that it was because she was coming to sit with him, and certainly, his pulse leaped at the sight of her.

She was dressed the same and the loafers were still spoiling the view. It was her attitude that was different.

And that smile. It was radiant.

She was radiant.

The sight of her melted Ty and heated him at the same time.

"Hi!" she said, sitting down in a rush. She dropped her tote bag, the one that apparently never left her sight, on one seat. "Sorry, I'm late." She dug in that bag for her lunch and he wondered if she was like Mary Poppins, carrying around the solution to everything in one enormous bag.

"It's okay. I wasn't going anywhere."

"You're just saying that."

"Nope. True."

She blushed then and looked down at her lunch. The way she blushed was disconcerting. It made her look vulnerable and soft, completely at odds with the bright-eyed woman who fearlessly argued with him. Ty pretended to be fascinated with his ham and cheese sandwich, but it was Amy who intrigued him. He had the book on the table beside him, the one that Jade had gotten from the back for Amy. Had she liked it?

"Something good happen at work?" he asked.

She laughed. "As if."

"You don't like your job?"

"I like that I have a job, such as it is, but the job itself?" Amy shook her head. "No, I don't think much of it."

"Get another?" Ty suggested, not wanting to think about her disappearing from his sight completely. He was acutely aware that he had no way to find her other than meeting in the food court at lunch, and needed to figure out a way to fix that.

Amy pursed her lips, then put down her sandwich without unwrapping it. "The thing is that I have crappy credentials. I only finished high school, so in the job market, I take what I can get. My neighbor helped me get this job. She knows the owner."

Ty was surprised. Amy was so clever and articulate. "You didn't want to go to college?"

"I wanted desperately to go to college, but I only lasted two weeks."

"That's pretty early to chuck it in," he said gently. He knew college wasn't for everyone, but he was surprised that Amy had abandoned it so quickly. "Maybe you should have given it more of a chance."

"Oh, that wasn't it. I loved it. But my mom got sick, and my dad couldn't take care of her, so I came home to help."

"I'm sorry."

"Me, too. Cancer sucks."

Ty nodded silent agreement.

Amy frowned and unwrapped her sandwich with care. "And by the time she died three years later, my dad had been diagnosed with cancer, so I stayed home to help him." She met his gaze, her own so clear and level that Ty knew she wasn't looking for sympathy. "And by the time *he* died, I learned that there was just about no money, so I got a job." She took a bite out of her sandwich and looked philosophical. "I'm lucky to have it, really, even though I'm just a receptionist. It's allowed me to keep the house." She shrugged. "Well, sort of."

Ty didn't know what to say to that. He couldn't imagine being without his parents, even his mother's relentless interference. He hoped Amy had sisters and brothers, but guessed from her manner that she didn't. He didn't want to rub salt in the wound so he didn't ask.

He also couldn't explain how much he wanted to help her.

Well, money was one thing he understood. "Sort of?" he echoed, trying to sound casual. "You have a big mortgage?"

"No. I'm lucky that my parents paid it off." Her smile flashed. "Although I would never have imagined when I was a kid that one day I'd be glad they lived on such a tight budget."

"Taxes and utilities, then?" If the house was anywhere near Manhattan, that could still be a considerable monthly bill.

Amy nodded. "The thing is that it was built in 1899 and needs some work."

An old house. Interesting. Ty was mentally mapping the region around Manhattan for potential locations of Amy's house. "That's understandable. Maintenance wouldn't have been first on anyone's list when your parents were sick."

"Exactly." She smiled quickly and he felt rewarded for understanding, but that smile faded too quickly. "But things need to be done, and no one is going to give me more credit. Not with this job." She met his gaze and smiled sadly. "And we're back to job prospects again."

Ty didn't know what to say for the second time in rapid succession. He wasn't used to that. He realized how accustomed he was to the affluence of his family. Even before he'd built his own investments, he'd always been able to ask his parents for a loan. His life would have been pretty different if that option hadn't been available.

He admired that Amy didn't complain about her situation, but made the best of it. He wished he could fix things for her.

All the same, he sensed that she would be surprised and maybe insulted if he offered to do so. People thought sex was the big taboo topic of conversation, but Ty was pretty sure it was money.

He decided to take a chance.

"Are you sure no one will give you a loan?" he asked gently. He pulled out his phone before she could argue. "I don't want to pry, but I have a buddy from college who works in personal finance." He named a big bank as he flipped through his address book. "He consolidates debt to make the burden more manageable, or to free up capital." He showed her the contact info for Red. "He does free consultations, I know."

Amy put down her sandwich and blinked at him. "Really?"

"A lot of people think they can't borrow what they need. Red says people seldom realize how many assets they have or their worth. You have a house, so maybe there are more possibilities than you realize. He prides himself on finding solutions."

She considered him for a minute. "Free consultations?"

Ty nodded. "Can't hurt to ask."

Amy tapped Red's information into her phone, then smiled at him. "No, it can't." She looked at the number as if she didn't dare to hope. Her expression made everything clench within Ty—then doubled his determination to help her. "Thank you."

"Money is what I do. I hope Red has some suggestions."

"Me, too." As if to prove that she regretted confessing as much as she had, Amy pointed to his book and changed the subject. "Anyway, we were going to talk about that today."

"Right. Have you finished it yet?"

"Of course." Her eyes twinkled. "The big question is whether *you* finished it or not."

Ty shook his head. "I was thinking that castration would be too good for this guy," he admitted, just to make her laugh.

She did and he smiled back. "You're just kidding me."

"I am," he agreed easily. "But you're smiling again."

She blushed as their gazes locked, then suddenly leaned closer, eyes alight. "But it *was* hot. Didn't you think so?"

"Yes," Ty admitted, wishing he didn't have to.

Amy was delighted, though. "And he was redeemed, don't you think?"

Ty wiggled his hand. "Maybe. I wish he'd done something for her, instead of insisting upon his own fantasy to the exclusion of all others..."

"That's exactly what I said to Jade!" Amy declared. She looked around them, then leaned closer again. Her intensity was compelling, and Ty found that he couldn't look away from her. He wanted to reach across the table and take off those glasses, then loosen her hair... "I said to Jade that it would have been so much better if he had thought of her needs instead of just his own..."

Ty listened, as entranced by Amy's enthusiasm as the revision she suggested to the story. He guessed that her version was a lot more naughty than the book had been even though she skimmed over details, blushing. Mostly she talked about story and structure and character arcs. Ty was fascinated.

He wanted to do more than speculate on the ideas she didn't express aloud. He wanted her to tell him all of them, and he wanted to keep talking to her, long after their lunch breaks were over. He should have started a conversation with her ages ago, and regretted all the boring lunches he'd endured alone when she was just a dozen feet away.

Ty was starting to think that dinner was going to be very interesting, when a woman shouted Amy's name.

Amy paled and sat up straight, falling silent as she looked back toward the elevators. Her manner changed right before Ty's eyes, and she was transformed back into the quiet Librarian who had nothing to say to anyone.

He wanted his Amy back.

"I have to go," she almost whispered, hurriedly jamming her things back into her bag.

"Why?" Ty turned around and saw the caller, waving frantically at Amy. Ty had seen her on the elevator before, an older woman with what seemed to be a permanent frown between her brows.

"It's my boss, Mrs. Murphy," Amy said and slid to her feet.

"It's the copier again!" Mrs. Murphy shouted, then furiously summoned Amy again.

Ty reached out to put his hand on Amy's arm. "You get to have lunch," he said, annoyed on her behalf.

"Not when the copier's broken," she said with a smile. "I'll see you tomorrow."

And she was gone, striding across the food court as the other woman visibly harangued her. The pair hurried toward the elevator, Mrs. Murphy gesticulating and Amy walking in silence.

Without a backward glance.

She really did have a shit job.

Ty spent the rest of his lunch wondering what he could do about that.

"Hey, your plan worked!" Kyle offered Ty a high five when he walked into the F5 building on Thursday night. Kyle was in the foyer, apparently just leaving for the day, but stopped when he saw Ty.

"What do you mean?" Ty returned the salute even though he didn't know what it was for. He was still trying to think of how he could help Amy find a better job. They didn't need anyone at Fleming Financial, and he knew she couldn't afford to quit work and go back to school. He wasn't even sure she wanted to do that. A bit late, he realized that he—like the guy in the story—hadn't asked what Amy wanted.

It frustrated him that he couldn't fix that until lunch the next day.

"We got a hit from the bookstore by your office," Kyle said cheerfully.

"How do you know?" Ty's gut clenched.

She hadn't...

"Seriously? Cassie's all about market research. She did these bookmarks advertising the intro course *Pain and Pleasure 101* and put a code on each one to indicate the store where it was placed."

"Of course, she did," Ty acknowledged, amazed as always by the nuts and bolts of Cassie's marketing.

"To the victor go the spoils," Damon said as he joined them. "You should come help teach the class."

"Get lucky. I hear it happens at F5," Kyle said.

"All the time," Damon agreed.

"I'd have to know something about mixing pain and pleasure to do that," Ty said mildly. "I doubt it's about enduring my mom's phone calls. Or wedding plans."

"How hard can it be to learn?" Damon teased.

"Oh, I sense resistance to erotic games," Kyle said. "Don't you think you should try it out, before you decide it's not for you?"

"Just once," Damon cajoled. "You might find out what you're missing."

Tyler spared an exasperated glance at all the gear for sale in the adjacent shop. "It's so complicated."

"He'll always be our vanilla boy," Kyle teased.

"Nothing wrong with that if it's done right," Cassie said in a sultry voice. Ty realized she'd been leaning in the doorway to the shop, listening to their conversation. She'd really gone with the dominatrix look on this day. She wore a pale blue latex dress that left nothing to the imagination and had her long blond hair pulled up into a sleek ponytail. "My demure look," she said, with a curtsey. "You like?"

Tyler knew she wanted him to take a longer and better look, but he just shook his head. "Complicated."

His imagination provided an image of Amy in similar gear, which was considerably more interesting.

"You might like the one who registered from the bookstore ad," Kyle teased. "She looks as uptight as you. Probably will be doing research through Saturday to study up."

"You've seen her?"

"She came in to ask for more information," Cassie said. "And to confirm her registration."

"Double-checking her online registration, like you two were twins separated at birth," Kyle added.

"Checks and balances," Damon said. "Double entry accounting."

"What does she look like?" Ty asked, seeing his opening.

"Kind of cute, in a bookworm kind of way. Glasses."

Ice slid down Ty's back.

No.

"Maybe you'd have chemistry," Damon added. "Great minds thinking alike and all that."

"We should dare him," Kyle whispered.

Cassie came to Tyler's side, showing him the registration in question on her tablet. He ignored the way she put her hand on his arm, never mind the way she almost leaned against him. He could have ignored pretty much anything, once he saw the name on the form.

Amy Thornton.

His Librarian had registered for the Saturday BDSM Intro class.

One of his partners was going to tie her up and spank her, at her own request.

"You look stunned," Kyle said. "Know her?"

"I just can't believe the promotion worked that quickly," Tyler lied. He couldn't wrap his mind around the fact that Amy had really signed up for this.

Fiction was different than real life.

Wasn't it?

And real life was stranger than fiction.

All of his protective urges came to the fore.

Would she tell him about it Friday night?

Should he ask her about it?

If she told him, he'd certainly try to talk her out of it.

Did Amy have a bigger secret than he'd realized? Did she have a secret life, one that was echoed in her reading taste? No. She wouldn't have been taking the introductory course, if that was the case.

Ty wasn't exactly relieved.

He felt a very primal and possessive urge to be the one who touched Amy, one that was completely at odds with his own view of women making their own choices.

But she'd made her choice.

And it would kill him if Kyle touched her.

"Maybe I will join the class," Ty said, trying to sound casual. "Tell me more about what you do."

"So, you can do your research?" Kyle teased, since Ty's fondness for preparation was well known, and a usual target for jokes. "We'll learn some basic knots. We'll try out some blindfolds and gags, just so people can find out how it feels. The whole exercise is planned to build confidence and trust."

"And sales from the gift shop," Cassie added.

Kyle handed him a pamphlet called *Ties That Bind*. "She signed up for the class at one on Saturday. We can go over the material in the morning, if you want to be sure you've got it."

"Good. Thanks." Ty glanced up at a sudden thought. "What do you wear?" He had workout gear, of course, but it wouldn't offer much of a disguise. Amy would recognize him, and that would look like too much of a coincidence.

Like he was stalking her.

On the other hand, maybe she'd like that. He pushed a hand through his hair, feeling that this was all way too convoluted.

"Oh no," Cassie purred. "Not for the teacher. You need to look like a dangerous dom."

"I'm not going to teach..."

"Sure you are," Kyle insisted. "It's more fun. Be my apprentice."

"What if someone from work recognizes me?"

"Be his henchman," Damon said with a laugh. "Go in disguise. That's what I'm going to do. I'll have a secret identity." He lifted his brows.

"No," Ty said, though he was intrigued by the idea.

"I've got just the hood for you," Cassie said. "You can pump up beforehand and we'll give you a big dangerous tattoo."

"I'm *not* getting a tattoo."

"Temporary, my friend, temporary," Cassie said soothingly. "We don't want to mess with perfection."

"But you'd better book in tonight for a wax," Kyle advised.

Ty held up a finger. "Never again."

"You big wuss," Kyle charged. "The girls like us smooth as velvet."

"Says the blond," said Damon. He made a circle with his finger and thumb. "Who has this much body hair to remove."

Kyle looked insulted. "I'll have you know that I have *twice* that much, and it's around my nipples. Very tender place and I'm a fragile flower."

The other partners snorted at that.

"There's nothing wrong with a little body hair," Ty protested. "It's natural."

Kyle did a chimpanzee howl that echoed loudly in the lobby. "We'll call you Conan," he suggested.

"Tarzan," Damon suggested.

"George, George, George of the jungle," Kyle chanted, then did the yell from that cartoon's introduction.

"Ty's perfect just the way he is," Cassie said. "No hair on his back."

"I didn't realize you'd checked," Damon mused.

Ty was well aware that it wasn't an accident how often Cassie met him on his way back to the change rooms from the weight room or the pool. She'd never been so forthright before, though.

He was surprised when she planted her fingertip on his chest and traced the length of his tie. "A perfect dark arrow, pointing down..." She halted at his belt buckle, eyes gleaming, but Ty lifted her hand away.

It was time to have a private talk with Cassie.

"I'll shave tonight," he said. "And I need a review of the course plan on Saturday morning."

"You're on," Kyle said. "You could let Cassie paint your tattoo."

"We've got these temporary ones in the shop," she said. "Trust me. I'll make it good."

"Thanks," Ty said, knowing that might provide the perfect opportunity for that overdue discussion.

Mrs. Murphy couldn't have done a better job of giving Amy the motivation to write. She harassed Amy all day long about the stupid copier—which broke often because it needed to be replaced—and found her a zillion petty jobs to do. If Amy had disliked her job when she met Ty for lunch, by five, she despised it with every fiber of her being.

She charged home, fed Fitzwilliam, and wrote like a fiend. Sleep was a luxury she couldn't afford.

Someone was smiling on her because for the first time in a month, Brittany didn't call about a wedding crisis.

The only upside of Friday was that it was payday. Otherwise, the day was hell from start to finish. Amy only managed to take ten minutes at lunch and she used it to go down and talk to Ty.

He was sitting at what had become their table, and it gave her a huge rush of pleasure that he was obviously waiting for her. He read his Grisham book, but his lunch was unpacked on the table.

"Hi," Amy said, stopping beside him.

He looked up, smiled, then evidently noticed that she didn't have her lunch. His brows drew together in a frown as he stood up. "You don't get lunch at all today?" he asked, his disapproval of that more than clear.

"Eating at my desk as I savor the joys of filing."

"Always a time-sensitive job."

"You'd think it was in our office."

"What about your coffee?"

Amy was startled. "My coffee?"

"You always get one on Fridays," he said with conviction and she was astonished that he'd noticed. He started to stand up. "Let me get you one. How do you like it?"

"Hot, but I don't have time. Thank you, though."

He gave her one of those sizzling looks. "You can take a coffee back to your desk."

"But it won't be hot by the time I can drink it. I love it hot, and one day, when the stars align, I'm going to buy myself one of those single serving coffee makers."

"You can dream bigger than that."

Amy smiled. "It's a good dream."

Ty cleared his throat as if he was going to say something but Amy lifted her hand.

"You're right. My job sucks. I need to find something better. But today, I need to keep her happy so that I get my check. It's a crap job but it's the one I have, and your friend Red won't find me a solution if I don't have a job at all."

"True enough," Ty acknowledged. "And tonight?" he asked as if he expected her to cancel.

Maybe he wanted to cancel. The possibility made Amy's heart skip, and she realized in that moment just how much she was looking forward to even a fake date. "Are you changing your mind?"

"Nope." Ty smiled and at the sight of that dimple, all was right in Amy's world again. "Remember it was my idea. I'm behind it a hundred per cent." He eyed her warily. "Are you backing out?"

"No. We have a deal. I just can't stay for lunch today."

Ty frowned. "We're going to talk about job prospects tonight."

"We're going to talk about family and background tonight," Amy corrected. "And get our meet-cute story straight."

"Meet-cute?" He looked puzzled.

She laughed. "The story of how we met. If this is a romantic comedy, it has to be a cute story."

He got that beleaguered look that made her smile. "I was afraid of that."

"It's good you've seen so many chick flicks. We'll come up with something good."

"Parking lot?" he suggested.

"I don't have a car. Subway platform?"

"They know I seldom take public transit." He arched a brow. "Elevator? We could have talked to each other that day, so it could be true."

He *had* noticed her. Amy felt warm all over. "Oh. Yes. It's better to base things on the truth."

"Absolutely. Less chance of forgetting the details." Ty smiled at her. "Do you usually forget to push your floor?"

"It was a bad day."

"No," Ty countered, his voice dropping low. "It was a good day." His gaze clung to hers as he smiled and Amy felt a little dizzy.

Then she reminded herself that it was all a fake date. "Because it was our meet-cute."

Ty didn't argue. "So, since you don't want me to pick you up, how about we meet here?" he suggested and Amy liked that he found a solution to accommodate her request. "We can walk to a place I like, if an early dinner is fine with you."

"Yes, it is. That way I can take the train home before it gets too late."

Ty looked as if he'd like to argue that plan with her.

Amy tapped her watch. "I've got to go."

He nodded, resolved but unhappy about it. "Six?" He gave her a serious look, one that launched a tingle through Amy.

"Six," she agreed a little breathlessly. "Right here."

Ty smiled slowly, a feast for the eyes that would keep her humming all afternoon. "Deal. I'll make a reservation." He pulled out his phone, then hesitated. "Amy?" he said as she was turning away and her heart leaped at the sound of him saying her name. She looked back to find his expression serious. "Dietary restrictions or preferences?"

"None," Amy said with a smile.

"Steak?"

How long had it been? Amy's mouth was watering already. "Sounds good."

At his nod, she hurried back to the elevator, anticipation bubbling inside her. It was an arrangement, but still.

She was having dinner with Ty. Fake date or not, she would have to have been dead not to feel a thrill about that.

CHAPTER FOUR

I T COULD have been a business dinner.

Ty supposed that in a way, it was.

Funny that he didn't feel as calm about it as he did for business meetings. He wanted everything to be perfect. He wanted the conversation to sparkle. But mostly, he wanted to watch Amy without any distractions.

Since Amy couldn't go home to change, he didn't either. She was wearing the same navy skirt and white blouse as at lunch, along with a plain jacket and the dreaded loafers. Her hair was still up and her glasses were still on, her large bag slung over her shoulder and her raincoat over her arm. She smiled with less radiance than the day before when she strode toward him in the building lobby.

Ty wanted to do injury to Mrs. Murphy.

Instead, he lifted Amy's raincoat from her arm and held it for her. She hesitated, then smiled and turned around.

"Dreading dinner?" he asked.

"No!" she said, glancing over her shoulder. "Why would you think that?"

"You don't seem as happy as before."

"I should be, to be leaving that place for the day," she said with heat. "I'm just a bit tired, that's all. I've been up late a lot this week."

"Me, too. We'll make it an early night," he said, claiming her elbow and guiding her to the door. He felt her start a little, and realized that she wasn't used to a man touching her, even in such socially acceptable ways.

By her own accounting, she'd spent seven or eight years providing palliative care to her parents, then working at a crap job ever since. Ty was pretty sure that Amy Thornton hadn't had a lot of fun since she abandoned college.

He wanted to give her some.

More than some.

They'd start with a good meal.

The restaurant was a favorite of his, a little bistro with an open kitchen and an awesome chef. It was dark and romantic, lit by candles even at this hour, and not anywhere near as busy as it would be by nine. They were given the table he favored, the one tucked out of view that he found more intimate, and their coats were taken away.

Amy ran an admiring hand over the banquette when she sat down. "It's really nice," she said in a small voice that told him a lot. "I thought we'd go somewhere more casual."

"First date for our story," Ty said. "They know I wouldn't take a woman who interested me out for burgers and fries. I need to get back on familiar ground and tell the truth about everything again."

"Everything?" she challenged with a bright glance and he knew where she was going.

"Everything."

"Even the fake date?"

"That might have been the reason I talked to you this week, but I noticed you before," Ty said, wanting her to understand that this wasn't just about convenience. "And now I wish I'd done it sooner. How's that for truth?"

Amy blushed a little. "Why me?"

"Because you read." It was true.

Her eyes sparkled. "But you didn't know what I read."

"No. I assumed you were reading Jane Austen."

Amy laughed. "What if you'd known the truth?"

"Wouldn't have mattered." He shook a finger at her. "If I'd known you were going to tell me off, though, I'd definitely have talked to you sooner. I really enjoy our lunch conversations and that's no lie." Their gazes met for one of those sizzling moments.

Amy smiled at him, clearly pleased, then picked up the menu. He knew the moment she noticed the prices and spoke before she could open her mouth to protest.

"I like this place, and the way I see it, it's been a heck of a week. You've been fixing copiers and I've been run ragged by a couple of clients. I think we both deserve a reward just for surviving it."

She blinked. "You had a bad week?"

"Not bad, exactly, but it was hectic," Ty admitted. "Some of our clients can be demanding, and when more than one of them goes into that mode, it can be a bit frantic."

"And then there's your mom."

"And then there's my mom," Ty agreed. Did she miss her mom? He couldn't imagine otherwise. There was a little bit of sadness in her eyes, and once again, he was determined to make her smile. "Red or white?"

"I like either," she admitted then considered the menu. "But red is better with steak."

Ty nodded agreement, then ordered a bottle of a Cabernet Sauvignon.

Once again, Amy looked like she might argue, but he leaned over the table and dropped his voice to a whisper. "It'll make it easier for us to get to know each other," he said. "And you're not taking the train home." He lifted a finger. "Cab service is part of the deal."

"You're not driving me home."

"I *am* paying the cab fare." He arched a brow. "And I'll make sure you get in the cab, too."

She sat back and regarded him mutinously. "You're bossy."

"I thought you'd like it," he teased and she blushed a little. "Look, it's what I would do for any one of my sisters. You alone on a subway at night?" He shuddered. "I'd be sick with worry."

"I doubt that!"

"Believe it."

Amy heaved a sigh of concession, but her eyes were starting to sparkle. "Normally, I'd say no, but today, thank you." When she looked so pleased and relieved, Ty knew he could get used to spoiling her a little bit.

She was past due.

The wine came and he tasted it, then it was poured. Amy asked the waiter a couple of questions about the options on the menu, then they ordered. Ty liked that she wasn't indecisive and she didn't request a lot of changes. On the one hand, she seemed to be pretty easy-going and to make do with whatever she got. That was an admirable trait. On the other hand, he thought she could have expected a bit more from life, and he wished he could help her to reach a little higher.

He didn't believe for a minute that her current job was the best she could do, but Amy *did* believe it. He was going to find a solution that suited Amy better by the time Katelyn and Jared left for their honeymoon.

Ty had four weeks and a day to make a difference in Amy's life.

He figured it was fair exchange for her going to the wedding with him and saving him from his matchmaking relations. It wasn't possible for her relations to hold a candle to his in that department.

"All right," Amy said, pulling a notepad from her purse. She held up four fingers, mimicking his gesture from their first lunch. "Family summary from Tyler McKay. You have four sisters, three married and one about to be, one a year for three years."

"You have a good memory," he said, a little surprised that she'd remembered all of that.

Amy held his gaze, confident that was true. "It's my gift."

"I think you have more than one," Ty said, then held up a finger before she could argue. "Lauren. Oldest daughter, next after me, probably my favorite sister."

"Are you allowed to have a favorite?" Amy pretended to be horrified and he grinned.

"Only if you don't tell the others."

Amy crossed her heart and Ty chuckled.

"She's thirty, married three years ago to Mark." He tried to hide his dislike of Mark and wondered whether he succeeded. "She's a hairdresser uptown, who unravels everyone's secrets and proposes diplomatic solutions."

Amy started to make notes. "I can see why you like her. That would be a useful talent in a big family."

"Absolutely. Then there's Stephanie, married to Trevor last spring. She's twenty-eight and finishing grad school. He's a lawyer."

"Are they in town, too?"

"No, they're in Boston and will be coming down the week before the wedding to stay with my parents."

"Where?" Amy asked, taking notes.

"Connecticut. My parents moved out there before they started a family and still go to the same church."

She peeked up at him and he really wanted to lift off those glasses. "Episcopalian?"

"Good guess," Ty said and they shared a smile.

"Sister number three?"

"Paige, married two years ago to Derek who has his own

construction company in Brooklyn. She does his books, and they had a son last November. Ethan."

"First grandchild for your parents?"

"Yes, but we're way behind. My mom's sister, Teresa, has nine grandchildren already. One is better than none, but my sisters have to lift their game."

Amy's eyes danced. "But not you?"

Ty winced. "I try to deflect all discussion about the heir to the throne."

"You're going to fail soon."

"You might have to take some of the friendly fire on that. Any defenses?"

She mused and he watched, fascinated, as she tapped her pen and considered the question. "Well, I can't claim that I have too demanding of a job."

"Maybe you're going back to school," Ty dared to suggest.

Amy's eyes lit for a moment, then she shook her head. "I can't lie, even if this is a fake date. I'll think of something else."

"Maybe you just need to not be taking care of anybody for a while," Ty suggested gently.

Her gaze flicked to his. "But then I wouldn't be thinking about getting married, would I?"

"That's not what marriage is about!" Ty protested. "It's about supporting each other and being stronger together. It's not about the woman becoming unpaid staff for the guy."

Amy pointed her pen at him. "That's why I like you," she said and for a moment he forgot that she was talking about their scheme. "Nice guys are more likely to help with the dishes."

"That's not such a bad thing," Ty said, feeling as if he was being slammed.

"No, it's not. It's safe and predictable and a sign of mutual respect." Amy wrinkled her nose. "Every woman's dream."

Ty stifled his annoyance. He'd never thought that being nice was a bad thing before.

On another day, he might see humor in Amy's conclusion that he was safe and predictable, which was what he'd thought about her before that first conversation. On this day, he wanted more from her.

"Sister number four?" she invited.

"Katelyn, the bride-to-be. Jared is an artist, doing pretty well for himself. Big paintings I don't understand. Lots of black." Amy giggled at that. "They live in a loft in Soho and my mother is happy they're making it legal."

"What does Katelyn do?"

"She makes jewelry. I don't understand it either."

"Why not?"

"It's...unexpected."

"I can't wait to see it," Amy said and he knew she was laughing at him. He didn't mind at all. "And the helpful aunties? You've only mentioned one."

"Teresa is my mom's big sister."

"The one with all the grandkids?"

Ty nodded. "And there's Maureen, my mom's baby sister. Her daughter Maxine is unmarried." He sighed. "Someone will mention the toilet paper incident. It was Maxine, last year at Stephanie's wedding. She came back to the dance floor with it trailing from her shoe. My sisters are pretty merciless in teasing her about it."

"Because she's been merciless to them in the past?"

Ty had to think about it. "You know, I guess she was, especially when we were kids. She's the same age as me and kind of lorded it over my sisters."

"That'll do it," Amy said, as if she understood the situation really well.

"Observer of human nature."

"That's me."

Ty had another sip of wine. "My mom is Colleen and has always been a homemaker."

"Five kids would have kept her busy."

"My dad, Jeffrey, is a retired investment banker who pretty much lets Mom steer the course while he works on his golf game. Forty or so years married."

"You don't know?"

"Thirty-seven."

"You can't fool me," Amy said and made a note. "You're detail-oriented and a lousy liar."

Ty was startled that she'd noticed. "Bad traits?"

"Excellent ones."

"Be warned that there will be garden club ladies and church ladies and an entire social network in attendance. My mom was organizing long before the first engagement in the family."

"Big wedding then."

Ty nodded, a little bit weary of it all.

"Not your plan?" Amy asked.

"After four years of this, I think elopements have a certain appeal."

"Family weddings can be fun." Amy shook the pen at him. "And what kind of only son would you be if you disappointed your mom? Not a nice one."

Ty was giving serious consideration to developing some not-nice traits. "One down," he said instead. "Your turn."

The salads came then. His mother would have no quibbles with Amy's elegant table manners. Ty hadn't thought about it until she picked up her knife and fork.

She took a few bites, then had a sip of wine, clearly mustering her words. "My parents, as I told you, are both dead. My aunt Natalie is one of my dad's sisters."

"Which one?" Ty asked, then arched a brow. "Order matters."

Amy grinned. "Second of three. My dad was the big brother."

"Familiar territory, then."

"Aunt Natalie and Uncle Tom live in New Jersey. He's an electrician and she runs their two lighting stores. My grandfather started the business and passed it on to Tom. They have only one daughter, Brittany."

"Who's getting married."

"On June third." Amy winced and looked adorable. "An *enormous* wedding. I can't begin to tell you how much work it's been getting everything organized..."

"Wait a minute," Ty said. "That sounds like you're the one organizing it."

"Well, no, not exactly." Amy shrugged. "But my aunt is working full time and my cousin works at the store, too."

"You work, too."

"But I have a crummy job. Their jobs are demanding..."

Ty put down his fork. "You go ahead and explain to me how you can say Mrs. Murphy isn't demanding."

"It's not the same." Amy leaned closer to explain. "And when they organize things, it's never right. I end up having to fix everything anyhow, so it's easier if I take care of it in the first place."

"It must be a lot easier for them," Ty couldn't help but note. He sounded grumpy and protective and he knew it, but he couldn't bite his tongue. It seemed that her family was taking advantage of her kindness and he didn't like it one bit.

Amy gave him a look that he knew meant trouble. "I'm just helping out. It's what families do for each other."

"Like the way they're helping you keep your house," he observed.

Amy flushed because the point hit home. "It's not the same..."

"No, it's not the same. The house is something that's important to you, but not to them."

"Well, my dad was estranged from his family," she admitted. "My grandparents didn't approve of my mother, but my dad loved her and married her. They didn't speak to him after that."

"They must have helped out when he was sick."

Amy shook her head.

"Come to the funeral?"

She shook her head again. "My aunt phoned about a year ago."

But Amy's dad had passed away a few years ago. Ty bristled. "Because?"

"Well, eventually she mentioned that she and Brittany could use some help with the wedding."

Ty was outraged. "How much time have you spent organizing this wedding?"

"I don't even want to think about it."

"Do it anyway," he commanded.

Amy gave him an impish look. "You're being bossy again."

"It happens when I'm pissed off. I don't like seeing people take advantage of other people." Ty gave her a hard look. "*Nice* people don't do that."

"Well, they're family."

"And it would have been *nice* if they'd remembered that a little sooner."

Amy leaned across the table, her expression earnest. "You can't say anything about this at the wedding. You just can't."

Ty glowered at her. "Depends how they treat you. I just might."

"Ty!"

"How much time?" He demanded, biting off the words.

Amy eyed him for a minute, then nodded. "Okay. Easily ten hours a week on the phone for a few months, plus going out to New Jersey to look at locations and meet with caterers and florists and other people. I'd have to add it up."

"So, you were Brittany's wedding planner."

"I'm her maid of honor."

"Trust me. Most maids of honor just show up for the dress fitting and the rehearsal party. They create work, in my experience, because they don't like anything that doesn't make them look fabulous even though they're not the star of the day."

"That's mean."

Ty took a sip of wine. "Maybe I'm not so nice after all."

Amy considered him for a long moment, long enough that he wondered what she saw, then picked at her salad. "Well, I was just trying to help." She looked a little bit lost, and Ty could imagine how anyone might respond to the chance to be involved in a family function once all the family she had known was gone.

He still didn't like it, but it wasn't Amy's fault. "Fair enough," he said more gently. "But wedding planners are expensive. They should pay you for taking on all of this responsibility."

Amy laughed. "That'll never happen."

"Maybe I'll ask for you," he threatened and her eyes went round.

"You wouldn't! Not at the wedding!"

"I might, if I like them as little as I think I'm going to."

Amy seized her glass of wine and took a big sip. "Maybe this fake date isn't such a good idea after all."

"On the contrary, it's a great idea. We're going to have a fabulous time, so fabulous that they'll all be insanely jealous of you. Do you know how to foxtrot? We'll tear up the floor and leave them all drooling in envy." He toasted her.

Amy giggled. "You're wicked."

"I'm trying." Their gazes locked and held for a potent moment and Ty felt more than admiration for the woman opposite him. "What color are the dresses?"

All the color left Amy's cheeks, then she winced. "Tangerine," she admitted in a tiny voice.

"Ouch. Raspberry is one thing. Seafoam is another. But tangerine?" Ty shook his head as if burdened by the truth of it. "In this situation, I think it's only fair to go for blood," he said so solemnly that Amy laughed out loud.

"You're terrible!"

"No. I have it on very good authority that I'm *nice*."

She laughed harder then and he couldn't look away from the mischief in her eyes. He leaned closer, intent on prolonging her laughter, but someone cleared her throat beside him.

Dinner couldn't have come at a worse time, in Ty's view. With any luck, he'd be able to pick up where he left off.

But it wasn't dinner. Ty smelled a waft of a perfume he'd almost forgotten right before he heard a voice he'd never expected to hear again. That was when he knew he had no luck at all.

"Ty-lair! How wonderful to see you once again! And with another leetle seester. How *charmant* to dine *en famille.*"

Giselle.

Shit.

Little sister.

That was exactly how Amy felt when she looked up at the woman who spoke to Tyler.

That woman was sleek. Beautiful. All lithe curves and effortless style.

And French, too.

Her little black dress looked simple, but Amy was enough of her mother's daughter that she wasn't fooled. It had the sophistication that only exquisitely made clothes from a big designer could have. It must have cost a bomb.

The woman's make-up was flawless; her lips ruddy and full; her dark eyes hinted at intimate sensual secrets to be revealed—by invitation only. She moved with grace and elegance, but there was a little bit of viper in her gaze when it swept over Amy.

Then her attention fixed on Tyler and she smiled.

Wait. *Another little sister.* Could this be Giselle? If so, Amy couldn't imagine why Tyler wasn't seeing her anymore. She looked...perfect.

Amy felt plainer than dirt.

Ty stood up and made introductions. It *was* Giselle. That woman seized the opportunity to kiss Ty on both cheeks, then run a proprietary hand down the lapel of his suit jacket. Her smile issued several hundred simultaneous invitations, and Amy wished she could just disappear.

She realized belatedly that Ty was trying to end the conversation, asking after Giselle's companions at the other table and urging her politely back in their direction. Finally, Giselle gave a little fingertip wave and blew him a kiss, tossing her hair over her shoulder as she returned to her friends.

Three women, all just as gorgeous, and two men.

An odd mix.

"Flight crew," Ty muttered as he sat down. "I thought she'd never leave." He took a large sip of wine that was so obviously meant to be restorative that Amy might have smiled under other circumstances.

If she hadn't felt quite so much like a *little sister.*

The waiter brought their dinners, which looked wonderful. Amy didn't have as much appetite as before.

Ty, of course, noticed her hesitation to eat. He was attentive, and she appreciated it.

"I didn't plan that," he said with concern, his gaze searching. "I didn't know she'd be here. I haven't seen her in months."

"Since your grandmother's eightieth birthday party."

"Our one and only date. Big mistake. I've learned my lesson." Ty indicated the dinner she hadn't touched. "Is your steak cooked the way you like it?"

Amy took a bite and nodded. "It's wonderful. Thank you."

He smiled, at ease again. "Where were we?"

Amy wasn't ready to tell him more about herself just yet. "So, your whole family met her?"

"Pretty much. Briefly." Ty's gaze sharpened. "Why?"

Amy had already pushed her notebook aside, but now she put it back in her purse. "I don't think this is going to work at all." She eyed her dinner then averted her gaze. She felt a bit sick.

Ty beckoned to the waiter. That man took the plates and offered to wrap up the leftovers. Amy nodded that she'd take hers.

"I hate to see such delicious food wasted," she said and the waiter smiled.

She was aware that Ty watched her the whole time. When the waiter left, he leaned across the table and caught her hand in his. "Why not?"

Amy took a deep breath and pulled her hand away. Her throat was tight. She didn't want to answer him but she knew she had to. She swallowed. "They'll never believe that you picked me over her. Or even me after her."

There. She'd said it.

"Why?" Ty asked. "Because you're smart and funny and cute, and she's none of the above?"

"Ty!"

He lifted a hand. "You're nice. I'm officially nice. They'll believe that we're together."

"No, they won't."

His voice hardened in a very sexy way and he fixed her with an intent look that made her shiver. "Then we have to make them believe it, don't we?"

There were moments when Ty didn't seem like such a nice big-brother kind of guy. When he gave her a simmering look or his voice dropped low or he became resolute, it was easy to imagine him as a hot book boyfried—even though Amy knew it was just an illusion.

"I don't think it can be done," she protested. "I don't think that anyone sane would imagine that you with all your advantages would choose me." She shrugged. "I just don't."

Ty averted his gaze for a moment, but not in the direction of Giselle and her friends. He drummed his fingers once, then looked back at her so abruptly that Amy jumped. His eyes were vividly green. "I'll bet you a hundred dollars that they will."

"What?"

"A hundred bucks to you if you can convince my family that you and I belong together."

"I'm not going to bet on this..."

"Why not?" A daring gleam lit his eyes. "Afraid you'll lose?"

"I will if you take the opposite side and try to undermine it."

"Not me. I'm a believer. We might not have met the right way, but we should have. This is about you believing it enough to convince them." Ty leaned back then, spinning the stem of the wine glass between his finger and thumb, and Amy again felt a rush of desire. He looked dangerous. Confident. In control. Used to getting his way.

That realization made her sit up straighter.

"I won't lose. You'll lose."

"Then take the bet."

"I don't have a hundred dollars to waste on a silly bet."

Ty smiled. "Then you'd better win, Amy," he purred.

And in that moment, with that challenge in his expression and that husky catch in his voice, Ty convinced Amy to not only try, but to give it all she had.

"All right," she said and offered her hand. "All right! You're on."

His smile was quick and genuine, and the warmth of his hand around hers was enough to keep her awake all night. Amy wasn't entirely sure what she'd gotten herself into—or how big of a part the wine had played in her impulsive agreement—but she was determined to do her best to convince his family that their fake date was real.

She was in the cab heading home when she realized Tyler McKay was proving to be a little more naughty than she'd imagined.

Was he really doing it for her?

Ty watched the cab disappear into the evening traffic with satisfaction.

Amy didn't even realize the change in her posture after she took the bet. She didn't know how much he'd already built her confidence, and he'd barely started. He liked making sure that the good guys got whatever they deserved, and Amy had been served short too many times. No matter how long their fake relationship lasted, he was going to leave a lasting impression in her life.

He'd change her view and her expectations. He'd teach her to expect more, and maybe manage to ensure that she got it sometimes. It was enough of a noble pursuit to encourage him to whistle as he walked home.

Ty didn't know where Amy lived.

He still didn't have her phone number.

He didn't have one good way of reaching her over the weekend— except by showing up for the class in bondage she'd registered for at F5.

There was absolutely no way Ty was going to miss that.

Fitzwilliam's sixth sense about Amy's arrivals and departures was stronger than usual. She heard him mewling from behind the door even as she was fitting her key into the lock.

The cab driver waited until she had the door open, then gave a little honk. Amy waved and he drove off. She felt a bit pampered, first with Ty insisting on hailing the cab and paying for it, then the driver making sure that she was okay before he left. Ty had probably told him to do that.

Amy smiled at his protectiveness. It would be easy to get used to having someone like Ty in her life, but Amy wasn't going to rely on him. That would only make their inevitable parting more difficult.

She already thought it might not be easy.

Fitzwilliam rubbed against her legs with such enthusiasm that he nearly tripped her. He was yowling and talking to her all the way down the hall to the kitchen, giving her a lecture in Maine Coon that Amy was sure had a lot to do with the little box she was carrying. She put it down on the kitchen counter then went to hang up her raincoat and kick off her loafers. She cast her jacket across the back of a kitchen chair and smiled to find Fitzwilliam on the counter, perched beside the box. He straightened regally, wrapped his tail around himself and stared at her in obvious expectation.

"I left you kibble. I knew I'd be late."

Fitzwilliam emitted a mew of complaint, which effectively communicated his opinion of kibble. Amy saw that the contents of his dish were untouched. "For an abandoned cat who was eating garbage a year and a half ago, you've gotten pretty picky."

He audibly agreed and sniffed the edge of the box. His eyes glowed when he met her gaze again and the end of his tail flicked.

"All right, you can have a piece. But not all of it. This is going to be my dinner tomorrow." Amy got out her kitchen scissors and opened the box. Fitzwilliam sat a little taller in his enthusiasm. She snipped off a piece of meat, holding it in her fingers as she put the box in the fridge with the rest. Then she returned to the cat's side and snipped the chunk of medium rare beef into smaller morsels. She fed them to him one at a time.

"He's really nice, Fitzwilliam," she admitted, talking to the cat as she always did. "Even if I do feel a bit like I'm another one of his sisters, an honorary fifth. Giselle nailed that." She sighed and frowned, then said the thing that was bothering her. "I really don't want to disappoint him. It's nice that he believes his family will think we're really dating, but *I* don't believe it."

She gave Fitzwilliam the last piece of meat and it rapidly disappeared. The cat licked her fingertips, then began to groom himself.

Amy washed the scissors and put them away. "I could back out, but I don't want to." She pursed her lips and admitted another unwelcome truth. "It might be mean of me, but I want to see Aunt Natalie's face when I show up to Brittany's wedding with Ty."

Fitzwilliam leaped from the counter and surveyed the kibble in his dish. He hunkered down and began to eat it, one piece at a time.

Amy looked down at her skirt, hearing Giselle's "leetle sister" comment again. Was she really that sexless? Maybe so. It had been a while since she'd bothered much with her appearance. There had been so many other, more important worries.

But Ty had noticed her, even so. The realization was encouraging.

"All these sensible clothes and sensible shoes, Fitzwilliam. Mama would be disgusted. She always dressed so beautifully, no matter how little money they had. I wish I could sew like she did..."

Amy fell silent and stared at the cat.

Fitzwilliam stared back.

"Why didn't I think of that before?" Amy whispered, then got the key and hurried up the stairs. Fitzwilliam abandoned the pleasures of kibble and padded after her with obvious curiosity.

The house was a small Victorian, the oddball on the block. The one room in the attic had been a closet and dressing room for Amy's mom and was still filled with her clothes, purses, and shoes. Amy hadn't been able to think about cleaning it out.

Her mom had been a talented dressmaker. She'd sewn clothes for a number of regular customers, and in the course of shopping for them, found bargains at fabric stores for herself. Her taste ran to couturier clothes and she had the skill to replicate them. Amy had known she wouldn't get any money for her mother's clothes, as beautiful as they were, plus she couldn't bear to part with them.

The closet effectively hadn't been touched, not since Amy had chosen a dress for her mother to be buried in. She'd tucked plastic over the clothes and ensured the roof didn't leak on them, but hadn't really had the heart to spend time in the room, much less examine its contents.

Amy turned on the light and, as always, took a deep breath. She hadn't closed the door behind herself, so Fitzwilliam had followed her up the stairs. He'd never been in this room, so he prowled the perimeter, investigating.

The scent of her mother's favorite perfume still lingered. Amy buried her nose in a blouse, tears springing to her eyes at her mother's familiar scent. It was fainter, but she could still discern it. She eased aside plastic then ran her fingertips over the suits, silk and tweed and wool, then the blouses, silk and cotton. The shoes were on a rack to one side, and there was a full-length mirror at the end of the room. She smiled, remembering pinning a hem for her mother as she turned in front of this very mirror. How many times had her mother fitted a dress for Amy right on this spot?

Amy considered herself in the mirror. She was maybe an inch taller than her mother had been, but the shape of her body was similar. She was a little thinner, and she knew her feet were a size bigger. Her mom's hair had been darkest brown, and her eyes had been nearly as dark. Amy shared her mom's creamy complexion though her coloring was lighter, thanks to her father. She eyed the racks of clothes. She couldn't wear the red that her mother had favored. Could she wear black to a wedding or shower? Amy thought not.

She remembered her mom telling her that she could wear green, if it was the right green, and reached for a suit jacket in a green and gold bouclé. It was her mother's mock-Chanel suit, perfectly lined and trimmed.

Amy tried it on. Her mother would have said that the sleeves were a whisper too short but no one else would have noticed. It fit beautifully through the shoulders. Her mom must have made it in the late 80's but Amy liked that it looked a bit retro. Like she shopped in vintage stores. Amy chucked off her skirt and tried on the skirt that matched the jacket. It was slim and just barely covered her knees.

The suit looked so glamorous that she found herself twirling in front of the mirror. Her mom had also made a second skirt in a solid green that was flared a little bit more. There were three blouses that coordinated, and Amy tried on all the combinations with rising excitement.

But a suit at a summer wedding?

No. Amy needed a floaty dress.

Maybe a hat.

She remembered a dress that her mom had made for a wedding and quickly found it on the other side of the closet. It was in one of the fabric garment bags that her mother had sewn for her most treasured dresses. A larger garment bag hung beside it but Amy knew which dress had pride of place, and she wasn't going to look at her mom's wedding dress yet.

Amy opened the bag with the summer dress and caught her breath in wonder. Her memory hadn't done it justice. She'd definitely forgotten how pretty the fabric was. Rose petals of a dozen hues of pink were scattered over the silk chiffon, seeming to cluster at the hem. She knew that the fabric had been a border print, and that her mom had spent a lot of time planning how to cut it to get the effect she wanted. She remembered how the dress seemed to float—or her mother seemed to float while wearing it—because the fabric was so light. It had little sleeves and tiny buttons that were shaped like rose buds. Her mom had even made a silk slip to match.

Could she wear this color? Amy hung the dress beside the mirror and wondered. Her mom had had a hat to go with this. She dug in the hat boxes and found the broad-brimmed hat with the cluster of pink roses on one side. She tried that on and decided it was perfect.

"Mama would know immediately if it was a good color for me."

She fingered the hem of the dress. "I'll have to look at it in the daylight, Fitzwilliam," she told the cat. He cleaned his paw. "But I'll need shoes, even if it works. And I think it's too much for the shower on Sunday."

Amy surveyed the contents of the closet. Her mom had loved to dress up, so there were simple blouses and skirts for working at home, and glamorous garb for going out, and not much in between. She went through the rack of dresses again, peeking inside the garment bags, only to confirm that all the other options were either black or red.

This one or another solution. Amy closed her eyes for a moment and hoped that daylight proved she could wear the pink, then put the hat back and ushered Fitzwilliam out of the closet. She returned to the kitchen and yawned mightily. Between her week of late nights and the wine, she was ready to drop. And she had a class the next day, back downtown.

There was no way she could write any more tonight.

But she thought of Ty, arguing that she was being taken for granted and smiled at how resolute he'd been in her defense. She was meeting him at the office on Sunday at noon, and just thinking about him convinced her that she would definitely have sweet dreams.

She wasn't going to let him down.

CHAPTER FIVE

TY WAS UP at dawn. He checked the news as he always did, then headed down to the gym. He liked to work out early before it got busy, and Saturday was always a challenge. On this particular Saturday, though, he intended to do a bigger workout than usual. He swam twice his usual number of laps and pushed himself at the end to beat his best time.

He was thinking about Amy.

He was thinking about Kyle's class.

Most of all, he was thinking about Amy in Kyle's class.

The possibilities made him sweat before he even reached the weight room. He was pumped when he left the showers, but that nervous energy was still bubbling inside him. Ty was never agitated, so he didn't know what to do about it.

Cassie was at the main desk when he passed, and he was glad to see her dressed in her usual yoga gear. The last thing he needed to see was fetish wear. "Wow, you're really ripped," she said, giving him a thorough survey. She even came out from behind the desk to check him out. "And shaved smooth, too." She made a little growl in her throat. "You can drag me back to your cave anytime, Ty."

As if he didn't know that.

If she hadn't been acting the way she had lately, Ty might have asked for her advice. As it was, that was out of the question. "I think it's time we talked about something," he said gently and Cassie's smile turned philosophical.

"You knew all along?"

"Ages ago," he admitted, holding her gaze. "I just like being friends."

Cassie's expression turned rueful. "I thought maybe you hadn't noticed."

Ty shook his head.

She sighed, then nodded as she looked away. "Okay. Thanks for telling me."

"I'm flattered..."

Cassie lifted a hand. "Don't go there. It's okay." She met his gaze, a hopeful expression in her eyes. "Still friends?"

"Still friends," Ty assured her with a smile.

There was an awkward silence between them, then Ty cleared his throat. "Kyle promised a lesson review."

"You got it," Kyle said, approaching Ty from behind. He indicated one of the smaller rooms. "Just some basic knots and strategies, then we'll get you suited up."

Damon joined them then. "Class time?" he asked.

"It'll be easy," Kyle said. "Fifteen minutes, tops, then you can work on your costumes."

"I want to be Ivan the Terrible," Damon said, pretending to have a Russian accent.

Cassie placed a fluttering hand over her heart. "Say it again," she whispered. "I'm overcome with desire."

"I will make you my little *lisichka*," Damon growled, and tossed her over his shoulder. She squealed, just as she always did when the guys teased her, and Ty hoped things would be okay between them. "And you will serve my will all winter long."

"Yes, yes, yes," Cassie panted as he carried her into the room Kyle had chosen. "Take me. I'm yours!" She looked over Damon's shoulder and pointed to Kyle. "Or maybe yours."

"We will share the *lisichka*," Damon threatened.

Cassie wriggled as if she wanted to escape and kicked her feet, then spoiled the effect by laughing.

"Is that even a word?" Kyle asked.

"I didn't know you spoke Russian," Cassie said.

"Little fox," Damon translated. "I know endearments in forty-seven languages."

"You're ready for anything," Kyle said, obviously impressed.

"Or anyone," Ty added.

Damon nodded. "Listen and learn, my friends. Listen and learn."

"This is what he does on Friday nights," Kyle said as if he'd solved a mystery. "There's a little *lisichka* calling his tune."

Damon didn't admit to anything, his expression turning bland, and Ty wondered what secrets Damon was keeping. One thing was for sure, that partner wouldn't share until he was ready to do so.

Which might never happen.

At quarter to one, Cassie put the final touches on Ty's temporary tattoo. He could feel it, though he hadn't looked at it yet. He was tapping his toe, restless. The tattoo had to be enormous. He'd felt her creating it on his shoulder and bicep, then trailing onto his pec and even his back.

She gestured him to the mirror. "What do you think of your new bad-ass self?"

The dragon tattoo looked dark and dangerous, but not nearly as dangerous as the leather hood that Kyle had brought.

"I look like an executioner," he said when he had tugged it on, sure it was too much.

"Who better to administer *Pleasure and Pain 101?*" Cassie replied. "It's the danger that makes it exciting."

"Danger in a safe environment," Kyle added. "It's a game. You can explore scary possibilities without any risk of getting hurt."

"If people are stupid, they can always get hurt," Ty felt compelled to note.

"Which is why we're giving the classes," Kyle and Cassie said in unison.

"I thought he was smart," Kyle said to Cassie in an undertone.

"Me, too. Go figure," she replied.

Damon clapped a hand on Ty's shoulder. "I'm with you. It's weird. But if women like it, we could have an interesting hour this afternoon." He shrugged and pulled on his own hood.

"Now, we're twin executioners," Ty noted. His bad feeling doubled and then doubled again.

Cassie must have sensed his unease, because she patted him on the shoulder. "You should get into the part." She smiled. "Give yourself a name. An alter-ego with a different backstory. It'll help."

"Like acting a role," Damon reminded him.

"Exactly," Cassie agreed. "Indulge your own naughty fantasies."

"Please tell us you have at least one," Kyle muttered.

"You can't be Ivan the Terrible," Damon noted in his fake Russian accent. "That's taken."

On Damon's suggestion the day before, Ty had done some digging and created a role for himself.

"Matteo," Ty said. "Ex-con from California."

Cassie held up her hands. "Oh, we can't know that at F5. You must have lied to us. We don't hire people with criminal records."

"You might have to fire me, then." Ty held out his hands. "I need jail tats. Four dots in a square."

"California gangs," Kyle said, giving a low whistle.

"Now look at everybody's big brother," Cassie teased as she made fake tattoos on his knuckles. "Saving all of us naughty girls from ourselves."

Ty glowered at her and she pretended to swoon.

"Green eyes glittering with sensual intent, and danger." She fanned herself. "It's hot, Ty. Really hot. Little Miss Double-Check won't have eyes for anyone else."

Ty could only hope.

Amy was so excited that she could hardly keep still.

She sat cross-legged on the mat at F5, waiting for the class to begin. She'd been early, of course. She was always early.

It was a simple room, with high ceilings and yoga mats scattered across the gleaming hardwood floor. It had no windows, just a pair of doors that opened to corridors leading to men's and women's change rooms. Like the others drifting into the room, Amy wore her yoga gear. Her feet were bare and her hair was swept up into a ponytail.

The attendees were a mixed bunch. She hadn't been sure what to expect, but it hadn't been this. There were a number of couples, of all ages and shapes, including a gay couple. They barely glanced around, each one's attention fixed on his or her partner. They were probably as nervous as she was. Amy tried to guess who had instigated the registration for each couple. There seemed to always be one member of the team who was more self-conscious about their attendance.

There was, maybe predictably, one guy who looked shifty to Amy. It might just have been that he'd come to the session alone, but Amy didn't like the look of him—even though she'd come alone. She kept her distance.

And there was a healthy contingent of single women. Most were around Amy's age, but there was one woman with silver hair and a glint of mischief in her eye. She had a great laugh. The women were of all shapes and sizes, too, and she admired that most seemed to be confident in their own skins. It looked as if most of them had come in groups, with friends. She hadn't been able to convince Jade to come, so Amy stayed near the single women, feeling that there was some safety in numbers.

At two minutes before the start of the class, an incredibly good-looking guy strode into the room. His hair was dark blond and a little bit too long, his smile was confident and he had the look of just having come from the beach.

Amy was sure she'd seen him in an ad for F5 before.

"Hey, welcome!" he said, waving to the entire group with such cheerfulness that many waved back. "I'm Kyle. I'm one of the partners here at F5, and I'll be your instructor today." He braced his hands on his hips and surveyed them with a smile. "Are you ready to get naughty?"

There was a cheer of assent.

"I can't hear you," Kyle charged, then cupped a hand to his ear. "Are you ready to get naughty?"

"Yes!" This time, the call was much louder.

He clapped his hands. "All right, then. On your feet. Let's get that blood circulating." He started to jog in place.

"This isn't a step class," someone complained near the front.

Kyle laughed. "No, it isn't, but you're going to find that your ability to participate in sexual games will be improved with good health and fitness. After the class, I invite you to stop and talk to one of our counselors or a nutritionist, get a massage, take care of your body inside and out, and make positive change in your life. It's all part of what we do at F5."

Wow, he was a walking advertisement for the club. On the other hand, he pitched it with such ease and charm that Amy couldn't fault him for it. She was breathing a little bit more quickly than she thought she should be and realized that hiking back and forth to the subway wasn't giving her nearly enough exercise.

"A few stretches," Kyle encouraged. "Left hand down to that right toe. That's the way. Hold it for a minute, but don't bounce. Flexibility is also going to improve your enjoyment of these games, which are meant to enhance your pleasure. Right hand to the left toe and hold. Intimacy isn't just about what goes where." There was a little laughter in response to that comment. "It's about understanding what gives your partner pleasure and how best to deliver it. And up, stretch those hands high overhead. Lots of us like a little play acting, maybe a little bondage, maybe a spanking once in a while. Left hand to the right toe again and hold. Exploration also builds intimacy. Try new things, like this class, and talk about it. Stretch for the sky and really reach for it! One more time, right hand to the left toe and hold it. No bouncing. Feel that stretch. This isn't about being mean or hurting each other. It's about experimentation and sensation. It's about discovering what you like and sharing it with someone you like. Once more for the sky. Stretch tall, up on your toes, grab a few clouds and make them your own. Reach for it! Now, relax and shake it off. Walk once around the room, please, just take it easy."

There was a little murmur of conversation as the class attendees followed his instructions and more than a bit of anticipation in the air. When Amy returned to her place, she saw that a cart piled with silky ropes had been wheeled into the room while the group was walking. The ropes were coiled and loosely knotted. They were shiny and of various colors: black, blue, green, red, yellow.

Just the sight of them thrilled her.

Two men had evidently brought them in and were now standing on either side of Kyle. They wore black tights and leather hoods that hid their faces. They wore no shirts and both of them had large tribal tattoos on their upper arms. Amy's mouth went dry. They were large and buff, a little bit tanned, and could have been made of muscle. The one on the right had a dragon tattoo that Amy liked a lot.

"Meet my assistants," Kyle said, indicating his companions. He pointed to the guy on the left. "This is Ivan." He pointed to the one with the dragon tattoo and Amy realized that guy was looking at her. A quiver slipped through her but he didn't avert his gaze. "And this is Matteo. They're going to help me out today, so you can all work out the kinks."

The group groaned collectively at the pun, but Kyle just grinned.

"You'll need to pair up for our first exercises. Those of you who came with your significant other can make the predictable choice or mix it up." The couples laughed and did not mix it up. "Ladies, maybe you could find a wicked sister. Each couple needs to come up here and claim a hank of rope and a length of cloth." There was laughter as people chose a partner and some milling as they headed for the front of the room. Ivan and Matteo were distributing rope and cloth.

Amy turned to the woman on her right, but she was already

speaking to the woman on her right. The woman on Amy's left was laughing with the woman on her left. The single guy who gave her the creeps was heading straight toward Amy, and the women had all paired up.

"Perhaps you will help me to demonstrate," a man said in a deep voice close beside Amy. His accent was Spanish and sounded wonderful. Gravelly, just the way she liked. Amy turned to find Matteo beside her, his eyes gleaming through the holes in his mask as he studied her.

Her heart skipped. What harm could come to her in front of all these people?

Less if she was with Matteo than with the predator, for sure.

"Oh, okay," she said and smiled, certain her voice was a little higher than usual. She could see his mouth below the bottom of the mask and he smiled quickly, then put a hand on the back of her neck and guided her toward the front of the class. His skin was warm and the weight of his hand made Amy realize how much smaller she was than him. She felt claimed and that made her warmer than the exercises.

It was a delicious sensation.

The creepy guy, Amy noticed, was snagged by Ivan to be his assistant. The women in the class couldn't fully hide their amusement of that.

"The first thing to remember is that you're allowed to enjoy this," Kyle said. "People who don't enjoy it are always quick to speak up, and that's a good thing. But people who really do enjoy bondage are often afraid to admit as much. With your partner, in the safety of this room, you can admit that." His smile flashed. "We won't think any less of you." There was a little ripple of appreciation in the group. "Not every part of these games and rituals will work for everyone, but I'm hoping you'll take away something new. The important thing is to communicate with your partner."

He held up a finger. "Anyone know what a safe word is?" There was some murmuring. "It's a signal that you want to stop. You can use it any time, and part of what's key to making these games mutually pleasing is that the safe word has to be absolute. When it's uttered, the game stops. Right then. No hesitation or delay. Bonds must be loosened, gags and blindfolds removed, any discipline stopped. Using the safe word means it's all over and either of you can say it anytime. Got it?" Everyone nodded. "We're going to use 'Red Light' as a safe word today."

"Even though it's two words," Ivan muttered and Amy bit back a smile.

"It's simple to remember, but you might want to choose your own safe word for games with your partner. All together now. Red Light."

Amy added her voice to the chorus, liking the sound of Matteo doing the same. Kyle really was good at putting people at ease.

"First game," Kyle said, waving one of the lengths of black cloth. "Do you like to be blindfolded? Maybe you know and maybe you don't. Let's find out." He demonstrated, flicking the cloth over Ivan's head, then knotting it behind. "Your knots should always be readily undone, in case you have to free your partner in a hurry. I'm using a slipknot for that reason. If you don't know how to tie one, come and watch one of us do it. If you or your partner like blindfolds, you might want to invest in hoods or blindfolds with Velcro fastening. We have some hoods you can try, if that's your inclination."

"Would you like to try?" Matteo murmured to Amy, and she thought she could have listened to him forever. She nodded, her throat tight, and removed her glasses. He set them on the table, then flicked the cloth around her head. Unlike Kyle, he wrapped it around three times, then gave the ends a tug before securing it. He could have read one of her books. She was sure a dom had done it that way in one of her recent reads, and like the heroine in that story, Amy melted.

"Too tight?" Matteo murmured against her ear and Amy wanted to purr.

Instead, she shook her head. The cloth was some kind of stretchy velvet and it really did block out all of the light. She liked how it felt wrapped around her head, and how it seemed that her hearing was keener. She felt tingly and excited.

"I like it," she whispered, then licked her lips.

"See if your partner feels safe," Kyle encouraged. "See if you want to trust your partner when you're blindfolded."

Matteo's hands landed on her shoulders and he spun her in place a little. Amy felt reliant upon him and thought it was incredibly sexy to be both at his mercy and feel safe. She could smell his skin and feel the heat of his body, and it seemed that his fingertips caressed her a little as he moved her around. Tender and tough. He caught her shoulders in his hands when her back was to him and bent to whisper, his breath making her shiver in delight. "Red light?" he murmured.

"Green light," Amy said. "I'd like to try one of the hoods, if I can."

"Velvet or leather. You must choose."

"I want to try them both." The end of the cloth was tugged and she spun out of the blindfold, laughing at how much she was enjoying herself. There was a glint of humor in Matteo's eyes. Once again, he put his hand on the back of her neck, urging her toward the table to make a selection. There was a black velvet hood with lacing that would run down the back of the head when it was on. It would encase someone's head, with just the nostrils and mouth remaining exposed. The sight of it made her quiver.

Amy pointed to it, not trusting herself to speak.

"The elastic can be tightened and loosened," Matteo confided, and she watched him display the hood to her. He had beautiful hands, even with the crude little tattoos on his knuckles. At her nod, he slid the hood over her head. There was even a space at the top of the lacing for her ponytail to be fed through. When he framed her face in those strong hands and smoothed the velvet over her head, Amy thought she might come on the spot. She felt fragile and possessed, and was throbbing with an acute desire. Sound was muffled and her awareness of Matteo sharpened even more.

"I can see your pleasure," he murmured, and it sounded as if his lips were almost against her ear. His thumb slid over her mouth, roughly but gentle, too. Amy wanted to moan. "The darkness softens you," he whispered for her ears alone. "Like an angel opening her wings to the moonlight."

A lump rose in Amy's throat.

Oh.

She might get addicted to this class.

Or maybe to Matteo.

Where did that come from?

Ty didn't say shit like that. The words just fell out of his mouth, making him remember the poetry from that long-ago English Lit class. For a moment, he thought he'd pushed it too far, but Amy glowed.

She loved the compliment. And that made him glad he'd said it.

Ty couldn't believe the change in her. When Amy was blindfolded, she relaxed, and when she was hooded, the effect was even greater. He couldn't think of a better way to describe it than to say she

softened. It was as if her defenses dissolved. She was pliant—and
compliant—her lips fuller and softer, her movements more fluid. She
seemed to be more at ease with her femininity, more sensual. He'd
thought she was sexy before, but like this, she drove him crazy. Even
the way she stood invited his attention.

And his touch.

He had a hard time pretending he was less interested in her than
he was. He couldn't keep himself from running his thumb over her
mouth and the softness of her lips sent heat stabbing through him.
She shivered beneath his touch, which was really exciting. He wanted
to kiss her, slowly, savor her and tempt her to respond. He was pretty
sure he wouldn't be able to stop there, and would need to seduce her,
just as slowly, maybe spend a whole day and night at it.

Those lips enticed him. If she'd been wearing lipstick and they'd
been redder than they were now, maybe glossy, he might have lost it
completely. As it was, he couldn't stay away from her. He wanted to
touch her all over.

She smiled when he brushed his fingers over her shoulder again.

"You think this is funny, Angel?" he murmured in his best Spanish
accent.

"I think maybe you like me as much as I like you," she replied.

Ty blinked in surprise. So the blindfold made Amy bolder, too,
maybe a little more mischievous. He wondered how he could
convince her to try one on when she knew she was with him.

Next time, he wanted to take her glasses off himself.

He caught Kyle watching him and growled a little. "Back to our
lessons," he said to her. "You are not the only angel on this day." He
removed the hood and she smiled up at him, her hair tousled and her
eyes luminous, a sight that made him want to make their deal into
something more than it was.

A lot more.

She insisted on trying the leather hood. It was padded to heighten
the sense of isolation. He'd thought it might frighten her, but she
didn't use the safe word.

No, she seemed to revel in the feel of the hood.

And that did hard and thick things to Ty.

Amy went back to the velvet hood, which she admitted she
preferred, and Ty laced it snugly around her head. He ran his hands
over her again to smooth it, wanting to feel her shiver and loving
when she did.

"Who needs a spanking?" Kyle said and there was a roar of agreement. The attendees were getting more confident, which was great. Amy raised her hand as well. "Well, let's make sure you get the one you deserve," Kyle continued. "First, let's secure those hands." He demonstrated a knot, one that he'd shown Ty earlier. Ty bound Amy's hands behind her back, then knotted the rope around her waist to hold them in place.

As he bent over her repeatedly, Ty became aware that Amy smelled delicious. Like sunshine and soap. It was one Ty recognized but he had to think about it. Neutrogena, with that little undertone of ash. It figured that she used that brand. He could smell her perspiration, ever so faintly, and that turned him on.

But the scent that really finished him was that of her arousal. He could only smell that she was wet because he was so close, binding her and securing her. He was sure no one else could smell it. He would have killed anyone else who responded to it.

It meant that she was really enjoying the class.

And it meant that he was aroused, too. Thank God he'd worn a jock. No one else should know his reaction, and the tights Kyle had suggested left little to the imagination. Ty thought he was finally coming to understand what was so hot about these games. Even though they were complicated, if they worked for his partner, they worked for him.

Amy was humming with her anticipation. Ty was so transfixed by her that he barely listened to Kyle's patter.

Ty braced his foot on a stool, just the way Kyle had shown him earlier. He tipped Amy over his thigh quickly and lifted her so that her toes were just above the ground. His left hand was planted on the back of her waist, holding her in place. She gasped, not able to see it coming, and Ty chuckled. "Now, you will pay the price, Angel," he threatened and she kicked her feet.

"Promises, promises," she said, her voice a little breathless.

Cheeky little minx. Ty felt an urge to give her what she deserved.

"For the best spanking, we have to find the sweet spot," Kyle said. "It's right under the butt. So, if you're getting a spanking, lean forward a bit and arch your back. If you're giving the spanking, use a sweeping motion. You want to spank *up*."

Ty demonstrated, giving Amy a gentle smack.

She caught her breath, then laughed. "That's more of a tickle," she accused.

84

Kyle met Ty's gaze, then brought him a leather paddle. He winked at the class, then Ty used it to give Amy another smack. It was harder this time, and the leather made a loud crack when it collided with her butt.

She jumped, then he heard her giggle. "Better," she said, wriggling her hips in a very distracting way. "It makes me feel warm."

"Three hard blows, right on the sweet spot," Kyle said, and Ty leaned into it, making sure the paddle smacked hard. Amy jumped each time and he heard her catch her breath.

"Now, the tease," Kyle instructed. He was walking around the class. "It's mixing the pleasure with the pain that feeds sensation. If you're giving the spanking, caress that butt. Tickle it. Trail your fingers over it so that your partner shivers. You want to confuse the nervous system and have your pet find the pleasure in pain."

Ty trailed his fingertips across the sweet curve of Amy's butt. She shivered, then she trembled. She was fully covered, sheathed in cotton and Lycra, but he wanted to touch her.

He let his fingers trail into the crevice between her cheeks, just lightly, just for a moment. To his amazement, Amy moaned softly and parted her knees.

Ty blinked. He swallowed. His desire roared.

Then he spanked her again with the paddle, hard.

Her nervous system wasn't the only thing getting confused.

Amy was in heaven.

She floated out of the room after the lesson, well aware that Matteo watched her every step. She felt sexy. She felt empowered. She felt hot. Her butt was a bit sore and her sex was humming. She'd been blindfolded and hooded, spanked, hog-tied, and bound in a g-string tie. It had all been amazing.

Amy knew that was because of her partner. Matteo was strong but gentle, rough at the right time, mixing tender and tough in the way that made her crazy. She could have jumped his bones without a second thought and ridden him hard to their mutual satisfaction.

She felt more aware of her body, too, after the class. She noticed the feel of her breath across her own skin, the heat of the water in the shower, the smell of the coffee from the refreshment bar, the scent of sweat and excitement.

"Weren't you the lucky one today?" one of the single women said to Amy in the shower. "What a score."

85

"Matteo!" came the chorus from that woman's friends and one faked a swoon. "Have you ever seen a more gorgeous man?"

"I'm glad he picked me," Amy admitted, feeling herself blush. "I *was* lucky."

The woman waved off the comment. "He was watching you from the moment he walked in the door," she said. "Maybe you should get his number."

"Or come back for another class," suggested her friend.

The idea of seeing Matteo again was definitely appealing, but Amy laughed it off. The women talked bluntly about the creepy single guy in the class and there were many jokes about him being chosen by Ivan for the demonstration. They then planned to ensure that none of them could be followed from F5.

Amy's euphoric mood sent her floating down to the street to the subway station. The sun was shining. The flower vendors had set up their wares. There was a street fair across the way and she smelled roasted meat and heard a band playing. It seemed in this moment that anything was possible.

She just had to wish for it.

What she wanted most of all—well, besides Matteo finishing what he's started—was for Ty's fake date plan to work the next day.

That bet.

She needed to dress for success and look like a woman he'd choose.

Amy stopped beside a shop and looked in the windows. It was one of those designer clothing sales that popped up in empty retail spaces for a day or maybe two. Amy had passed the line of eager shoppers on her way to F5 earlier, but now there was no line. There were only a couple of women in the store, flicking through the garments on the racks, and a bored clerk examining her nails by the cash.

All the good stuff was probably gone.

It couldn't hurt to look.

On impulse, she turned into the shop.

"Can I help you?" It turned out there was a second clerk, who was one of the women going through the racks of clothes.

"I need a dress," Amy confessed. "Elegant. Conservative. With a bit of flair. I'm going to a bridal shower in Connecticut. Huge. Garden society ladies."

"Ralph Lauren," the clerk replied immediately. "Navy with polka dots." She pulled two dresses off an adjacent rack, both cut of the same microfiber fabric. One was sleeveless with a crossover bodice and a little flutter at the hem. The other had short sleeves, a deep V-neck and a flared skirt.

"That one," Amy said, pointing to the second. "Do you still have an 8?"

The clerk looked her up and down. "Only the 6 and the 10, but give them both a try. I would have guessed the 6 for you. There's an 8 in the other style."

Amy took the dress and glanced at the tag. It was priced at a fraction of the retail price, which was awesome. Maybe this *was* her lucky day.

The 6 fit, which was even better.

She spun in front of the mirror outside the change room, only to find the clerk watching her. "Red shoes or pink?" that woman asked. "I think pink with your hair."

Amy pivoted to face her. "You think I can wear pink?"

"Absolutely. That stuff about redheads and pink is a lot of crap." The clerk smiled. "Of course, I'm biased because we have Kate Spade shoes in pale pink with little kitten heels and bows on the toes."

"No."

"Yes."

"Seven and a half?" Amy asked, hoping.

"I'll see. And the matching clutch," the clerk said, returning in a heartbeat with both.

The combination looked perfect. Amy pushed up her glasses and had another good look at herself. "Pink lipstick?" she asked the clerk, who nodded.

"I'd get a French manicure. Just pearl earrings, if you have them. Keep it simple."

"Right." Amy added up the damage and nodded. Winning that hundred bucks from Tyler would put a big dent in the bill, and as she considered her reflection, she had to think that she'd just radically improved the odds of success.

It definitely *was* her lucky day.

She'd think about Matteo the whole way home and write like mad when she got there.

CHAPTER SIX

*A*RGENTA *was agile and quick, though not as quick as me. Even with my damaged leg, I am swift of foot. Her trepidation was no match for my resolve.*

Or maybe she wished to be caught. At the time, it did not occur to me, but now I wonder.

I ensured the chase was longer than it needed to be, for that is part of the satisfaction. I let her put distance between us time and again, then sped up to be fast on her heels. She was panting and flushed, and her hair still flowed loose behind her. Still, there was a fire in her eyes that made me certain I was not alone in my enjoyment. I do not know how far we ran, but we were both out of breath when she stumbled over a tree root.

I lunged for her, caught her around the waist, and rolled her beneath my weight. She struggled against me, but she had no chance to evade my intent. I had her wrists bound together in a flash, then stood up and cast the rope over the bough of a tree. I drew her up so that her toes barely touched the ground and she spun furiously in her attempt to escape. I adjusted my hood, ensuring that she did not see my face.

"You..." she began with anger and aimed a kick at my crotch. I caught one foot and then the other, holding them both in one gloved hand. The heavy jute rope was knotted around her ankles in a heartbeat. I dropped the end to the ground and stood upon it, securing it with my weight. I liked that she was stretched taut and at my mercy.

"You cannot do this..." she began, her eyes flashing. She watched as I pulled out my handkerchief and flicked it, then tied a knot in the middle. "You wouldn't..."

"I can and will," I retorted. She had time to take a breath before I shoved the knot into her mouth. Whatever she had meant to say was lost in the knot. I bound the handkerchief behind her head so it could not be dislodged.

Her eyes flashed fire still, which both intrigued and pleased me.

I bent closer to murmur to her and the vixen tried to peer into the shadows of my hood. Was there no limit to her audacity? I hoped not.

"There is a reason my handkerchiefs are so generously sized, and wrought of linen both thick and smooth." I ran my gloved fingertip over her mouth. "You cannot see but my monogram is over your lips, marking you as my own, and I like the sight well."

She wriggled furiously, clearly outraged. Her eyes had darkened to the hue of clouds burdened with snow. I could see that her nipples were as tight as pebbles, even through the cloth, and I could smell her heat.

It seemed that she liked my game as well as I did.

The realization was intoxicating.

Amy was home, seated at the kitchen table and writing as quickly as she could. The words were flowing like magic and she didn't want to even stop to make a pot of coffee. It would probably get cold before she finished it, anyway. Fitzwilliam was dozing on the other kitchen chair, having abandoned his attempt to convince Amy to appreciate his catnip mouse.

It rested beside her foot.

Her cell phone rang and she just about jumped out of her skin. The sky was dark outside the windows and the only light on in the house was the kitchen pendant overhead. The phone rang again and Amy raced for her purse in the hall, grabbed the phone and answered without taking the time to check who it was.

"Amy?"

Big mistake. Amy wrinkled her nose and returned to the kitchen. "Hi, Brittany. How are things?" She already knew from the high pitch of her cousin's voice that something had gone wrong.

"It's The Dress," Brittany said in a rush.

Brittany's wedding dress had been The Dress in Amy's imagination even before it had been ordered.

"Why? It's beautiful."

"No, it's not! We went to pick it up this afternoon and the sleeves are all wrong. They tightened them too much at the cuff and I couldn't even get it on! And they did something to the top of the dress..."

"The bodice." How could that be? Amy had been there for the last fitting and the dress had looked gorgeous.

"It's too tight! They insisted they hadn't changed it, but I can't breathe in it." Brittany's voice rose. "You should have been there..."

It was odd how influential Ty's comments about Brittany's wedding were. Amy found herself thinking about how much she'd already done for her cousin, for how little thanks, and didn't feel like signing up for more.

If the dress that had fit three weeks ago didn't fit now, that could only be Brittany's own fault, and Amy couldn't fix what her cousin put in her mouth.

"I had a class today," she said lightly. "There was no way I could have gotten to New Jersey, too."

Fitzwilliam wound around her ankles and mewed. Amy realized that she hadn't fed him, and she hadn't eaten either.

"Well, you could have canceled it," Brittany snapped. Amy refrained from pointing out that she couldn't or wouldn't have canceled a class to attend a fitting she hadn't known about. "You should have been there," her cousin repeated.

"You didn't tell me about it."

"You understand all this dressmaking stuff and know how to tell them what to do..."

"It's not that hard. You just point out what's tight or what's loose."

"Everything is tight!"

"You didn't happen to gain a couple of pounds?" Amy asked, because she was sure the dressmaker wouldn't have dared to do so.

"What if I had?"

"Well, the dress would be tighter then. It's not stretchy."

"And that's just the kind of snarky comment that doesn't help," Brittany snapped. "This is a *crisis*, Amy, and one that wouldn't have happened if you'd just been there...."

Amy opened the fridge with Fitzwilliam beside her. The only thing in it was the box of leftover steak from her dinner with Ty the night before. She wasn't giving the cat any more of that. It would be her dinner. She braced the phone against her shoulder and Fitzwilliam leaped to the counter to supervise. She took a can out of the cupboard and the can opener, serving Fitzwilliam's dinner as she listened to the latest crisis.

She really wanted to get back to Lothair and Argenta.

Brittany wasn't going to get to the end of her soliloquy anytime soon. She cried, then stopped, then cried again, then started the tirade about the dress again.

Amy interrupted her cousin. "Well, the way I see it, you have a few choices. You can ask for the dress to be altered again. You can choose another one. You can go on a starvation diet. Or you can find a girdle."

Brittany didn't think much of option number four. Amy put the phone down on the counter to put the food in Fitzwilliam's dish, because she really didn't need to listen to her cousin's response. *Bridezilla*, she mouthed to the cat silently, knowing that her cousin had it bad.

When Fitzwilliam was happily dining, she picked up the phone again.

"Did you hear me?" Brittany demanded. "I need you to come to the shop with me tomorrow and fix this."

"I can't," Amy said and was really glad it was true.

"What do you mean you can't?"

"I have a date."

Brittany was struck to silence for a long moment. Amy arranged her leftover dinner on a plate for the microwave, content to wait. "You're kidding me."

"No. I'll find out tomorrow whether he can come to the wedding. I'll let you know."

"You can't just invite someone to a wedding a week before. The meals are finalized..."

"My invitation was for myself and a date," Amy said, then took a breath and lied. "I was hoping Tyler would be able to make it, but you know, it's a big deal to ask someone to go to a wedding with you, especially if you're in the bridal party. I wanted to leave it as long as possible before springing it on him. You understand."

"How long have you been seeing Tyler?" Brittany asked.

Amy chose to take that literally. She'd been seeing him in the food court for a long time. "A couple of months, but you know how it is when everything's new. You kind of take it one date at a time."

"Yes," Brittany said, as if all the air was leaving her lungs. "You could have told me."

"I could have, but I didn't want to make any distractions when you were planning for the big day."

"That's true. You have no idea how much I've had to do."

Amy laughed, although she hadn't meant to.

"Why is that funny?"

"Because I've actually done a lot of it, so I do know."

There was a poisonous silence. Amy couldn't believe she'd just said something so very true, out loud.

She had Ty to thank for that.

"I see," Brittany said, sounding a lot like Aunt Natalie when she was in a snit. "I suppose I won't be able to count on you at all."

"I can't come to another fitting tomorrow, but I'll see you at the rehearsal. And you can always call me."

"For all the good that'll do," Brittany sniffed, then ended the call.

Amy ate her leftovers and marveled at the change in her own attitude. "For a nice guy, Ty is remarkably dangerous," she told Fitzwilliam. "I feel a bit mean, but not as mean as I would have on Thursday."

Fitzwilliam was busy eating.

Dangerous.

Hmm. Matteo was dangerous.

And the perfect inspiration for Lothair. Amy finished her dinner and sat down to write some more. It was going to be a late night.

Ty parked outside the office building where he worked. On a Sunday, no one would much care if his car was at the curb for a few minutes. He got out and stood on the sidewalk, waiting for Amy.

He was still agitated and he didn't like it. The class at F5 had shaken his assumptions—both about Amy and about desire. Her reaction had heightened his awareness of her, and awakened some urges in himself that he saw as ungentlemanly. He felt unsettled.

He was never agitated about a date.

But Ty stood on the sidewalk and even paced a little, jingling his keys in his pocket. Amy had liked that class. He knew it. He told himself that he was more troubled about the perils of her reaction than his own. How could he warn her away from men like Matteo? She could go down a path that led to a very nasty place, and his protective urges were roaring that he intervene.

Even though he had no right to do so.

Except as a concerned human being.

Maybe a friend, but that was stretching it. They worked in the same building. She said he wasn't her type, a detail that he found more irksome with every passing day. She wasn't one of his sisters, and he might not see her again after they officially broke up.

But Amy needed a protector, and Ty was inclined to volunteer.

Would she be offended if he said anything?

How could he say anything? He didn't officially know that she'd been to the class at F5, and if he revealed that he did, it would sound like he'd been spying on her. Or following her.

And—not to forget—lying to her by pretending to be Matteo so he could be the one to teach her about bondage.

It was all true that one lie led to another. He'd lied about Giselle. He'd proposed this deception of a fake date, and now, he had an alter-ego who had been to prison. Ty paced, feeling as if he'd slipped down a rabbit hole to a place where all the things he knew about himself were being turned inside out. Kyle had started it, with bad advice, but Ty had chosen to follow it and wasn't going to abdicate his own responsibility.

This recent run of celibacy, his dry spell, wasn't helping. It shouldn't have mattered. He was in control of his desires, but yesterday's class had shaken everything free. He wanted—but the only woman he wanted was Amy.

Ty itched where he'd shaved off his chest hair and he hated that he had a dusting of stubble. His skin was rubbed raw where he'd removed the tattoo—it might have been temporary, but it hadn't come off very easily either.

Complicated had nothing on this. Ty shoved a hand through his hair and practically walked a trough in the sidewalk, his train of thought doing nothing to diminish the turmoil.

At least it was a beautiful day. A little cool but the sun was out, so if Aunt Teresa had planned to let the party flow into her garden— which she probably had—that would work out well. He guessed that his aunt might have been ambitious with the guest list and miscalculated the number of people who would easily fit in her living and dining rooms, so the weather was a bonus.

He hoped Amy wouldn't be late. He'd checked the traffic and there were no accidents. He checked his phone for messages, then remembered that Amy didn't have his number. His mom hadn't called since the night before, which had to be some kind of record.

Or a portent of doom.

Ty glanced up to find Amy flying down the street toward him. He held up a hand even as relief flooded through him. "You don't have to run!" he called. "There's lots of time."

"I don't want to be late."

"You're not!"

"But you're waiting."

"I'm always early."

"Me, too! I'm never late."

Something else they had in common. "You aren't late now."

It was irrational, but Ty felt better because Amy was hurrying toward him.

Because she was in sight.

Amy laughed and slowed to a brisk walk. She was wearing her raincoat and carrying that familiar black tote bag. He saw a flash of navy when the raincoat parted to reveal a bit of her dress.

The loafers, regrettably, were present and accounted for.

He admired her legs all the same and recalled how trim and tight she'd been in her yoga gear the day before. Amy was hiding all the good stuff away.

Ty smiled and opened the passenger door when she got closer. She was wearing pink lipstick, which drew his attention to her lips. He remembered how soft they had been beneath his thumb and wanted to touch them again.

No, he wanted to kiss her.

What would she think if he acted like one of the guys in those books, if he locked her into his car and drove her to a sanctuary and made love to her all day and night long? It was a seriously appealing notion, even if it challenged everything he believed about consent.

No doubt about it, Amy had Ty all tangled up.

"I'm sorry," she said, as calm as if he'd been a doorman or a remote acquaintance. "The train was held up for something on the tracks. I didn't have your number, so I couldn't let you know."

"We have plenty of time," Ty said. He pulled out one of his business cards and wrote his cell phone number on the back. He handed it to Amy and she smiled.

"Thanks. I'm usually more organized," she said, then paused to look at his car. She was obviously impressed. "New?"

"Not really." He shrugged. "Pampered a little."

"Just a little?"

"Okay," he admitted. "A lot."

Amy smiled. "It's beautiful."

"Thanks. I don't drive it much. A little run will be good for the engine."

"Don't you drive it to work?"

Ty shook his head. "I live downtown, just a couple of blocks away."

"Oh." Amy slid into the passenger seat. She was reaching for her seat belt when Ty closed the door. He went around to the other side, got in, and started the engine.

He indicated the controls on the dash. "Too hot, too cold, feel free to change it." There was classical music playing and he turned it down a little, then glanced at her. "Or I can turn it off."

"It's nice," she said. "I like Mozart."

Ty nodded, biting back a comment about the word he was starting to hate, and pulled away from the curb. He was aware that Amy was digging in her tote bag and assumed she was going to review her notes. She was twisting around too much for that, though. He spared a glance her way when he could and saw that she was stuffing the loafers into her tote bag.

Hallelujah. Someone upstairs was on his side.

On his second glance, he discovered that she was wearing cute and feminine pale pink shoes.

"Thank God," he said, without meaning to do so.

Amy froze. "You don't like loafers?"

Ty winced that he'd spoken his thoughts aloud. "You'd probably be insulted if I admitted that I consider them a crime against humanity."

Amy laughed. "How so? They're just innocent little loafers. They haven't slaughtered the masses or dropped any nuclear bombs."

"But you have great legs. It's just wrong."

He could almost feel her smiling.

"But they're practical. I can run in my loafers." She indicated her pink shoes, turning her feet so she could admire them in a way that was very distracting. "I'd sit down and cry if I stepped in a Manhattan puddle in these, or if I caught the heel in a grate."

"I'm going to sit down and cry when you put them away," Ty dared to say.

Amy laughed again. "Maybe I won't, then." He knew she was looking at him. "Or maybe I will, just to see you cry. Do you?"

Ty held up four fingers, knowing what her reaction would be.

Her burst of laughter gave him more pleasure than he'd expected. "Right, four sisters. I bet they taught you well. How many chick flicks have you been compelled to watch?"

"Dozens. *Pride and Prejudice* is the universal balm."

"Which one?" she demanded, but Ty knew the right answer.

"Colin Firth."

"Excellent choice."

"I know his lines better than he ever did."

Amy laughed a little. "I'll bet." She was switching out her bag, and he realized she meant to leave her big tote bag in the car, with the loafers. When she was done, she had a small pink purse in her lap, one that matched the shoes. "Do you cry at weddings?"

"No. But I always bring five handkerchiefs even so."

She thought about that for a second. "Your mom?"

"Weeps inconsolably at weddings. My dad's handkerchief resources are always exhausted. You'll see."

"I'm looking forward to it." She was watching him closely again, so closely that he could almost feel her gaze upon him. Her voice softened. "Are you? Or are you dreading the performance?"

Ty smiled to reassure her. "The only thing I'm dreading is you winning that hundred bucks today."

"Then you shouldn't have made the bet."

"Are you letting me back out?"

"No way. I have plans for that money."

Ty liked the sound of her confidence. "You haven't won it yet," he teased.

"Just watch," Amy said with resolve, and Ty knew that he would. "I studied," she admitted, and he wasn't surprised this time that they thought similarly "Go ahead and quiz me."

"Sisters, youngest to oldest."

"Easy," Amy replied. "Katelyn, Paige, Stephanie, Lauren." She took a breath. "Married to, respectively, Jared—well, not for another month—Derek in 2015, Trevor in 2016 and Mark in 2014. Only Paige and Derek have a child, Ethan born last November. I'll bet your mother gave thanks for that." Before Ty could ask, she continued. "Parents, Colleen and Jeffrey; helpful aunties Teresa and Maureen. Teresa has nine grandchildren but you didn't tell me about your cousins, except Maxine, Maureen's daughter. And uncles. Wait." She turned to him and touched his hand, the brush of her fingertips sending a thrill through him. "You never told me. Are the perilous aunties widowed?"

Amy had never been in such a gorgeous car.

96

Ty's car was sleek and silver, a two-door sports car with a throbbing engine. The upholstery was black leather and every bit of the car gleamed. He could have just driven it off the showroom floor of a dealership. It had a teeny tiny back seat, but it was really built for two.

It was comfortable, too. Amy felt insulated from the world as Ty drove. She could almost hear her dad saying "Well, this is how the other half lives," and smiled at the memory.

Ty was a good driver, too—but then, she wouldn't have expected otherwise. He drove with a confidence she knew was characteristic, born of knowing the vehicle and its capabilities as well as his own. He didn't take chances, and she felt safe riding with him. She relaxed by the time they were on FDR Drive, headed north. He chatted easily with her, filling in some of the gaps in her knowledge about his family, and Amy realized she was enjoying herself.

It didn't hurt that she was in the company of such a handsome man. He could have stepped out of a GQ ad—for Italian suits. Ty was wearing a dark suit that was as perfectly tailored as the ones he wore to work. His white shirt looked crisp and he was wearing a tie, too. Amy was glad she had her new dress. At least she looked as if she might visit his zip code sometimes.

The car, however, had nothing on his aunt's house, which was in the old part of Greenwich.

Aunt Teresa's home was an enormous Shingle-style house, set back from the road with massive gardens. It had to have ten times the square footage of Amy's house in Brooklyn, and her entire lot would have fit in that front perennial garden. Every inch of the yard was perfectly tended, and the driveway was filled with luxury cars. They were parked on the street, too, and Amy realized it was going to be a really big party.

Her confidence faltered, just a little.

Ty idled beside the driveway for a moment, considering the cars. "So, how comfortable are those shoes?"

"Not bad," Amy said because they *were* new. She'd worn them for exactly thirty minutes, in the car. "Why?"

"We have two choices. I can let you off here, then go park the car somewhere between here and Boston. That will toss you to the wolves for at least ten minutes, maybe more, and there's no telling how hungry they are." His eyes widened in mock horror of that prospect, and Amy fought a smile, knowing he was trying to make her feel better. "Or, you can stay with me while I park, but then we'll have to walk back."

Amy looked at the full driveway and the silhouettes of people in the doorway. She was really tempted to stay with Ty, but his family would be nice. She didn't need a bodyguard to enter a bridal shower.

"I'll go in," she said before she could change her mind.

"Are you sure that's wise?"

"How bad can it be?"

"You'll probably have to face the Mommy Test," he said, looking solemn.

"I'm not afraid of mummies," Amy said, deliberately misunderstanding him. "I've been to the Metropolitan Museum."

Ty laughed and she liked that she'd surprised him.

"Suit yourself."

"What's the Mommy Test?" she asked, but Ty had already gotten out of the car. He opened her door and offered his hand. She liked that he was always a gentleman. It made her more aware of the sensual possibilities.

Even though officially there weren't any.

When he looked at her the way he had when she'd met him today, though, she wondered. There'd been something in his eyes. Relief. Appreciation. Awareness. It had been very sexy, for as long as it had lasted. Had she just imagined it?

"What's the test?" she asked again, and knew her suspicion showed. She took his hand and got out of the car, pleased by the way his gaze swept over her legs. His appreciation was obvious and that made her flush a bit.

She hadn't imagined it and she was glad.

"I tried to defend you," Ty said. She knew it wasn't anything that dire, thanks to the twinkle in his eyes. He was just teasing her. "But you want to be a hero and go it alone. I salute you." He opened the trunk and removed a large parcel wrapped in silver and white. "Maybe I shouldn't be surprised that you're so fearless, since you do have excellent taste. Presenting her heart's desire to Katelyn would give anyone confidence."

"What did you get them?"

"We," Ty corrected as he gave her the box. It was heavier than she expected. "Don't you remember? It was your idea, just another sign of how perfect we are for each other and what an intuitive understanding you have of my sisters."

Amy laughed. "You can't do this. You can't change the rules and introduce new information without giving me time to prepare."

"Why not? It'll be more fun that way. More risky. I thought you liked risk." He leaned closer, his eyes gleaming in a way that made Amy's heart skip and her mouth go dry. "Haven't you introduced any new information?"

Amy bit her lip. "Guilty as charged. I told my cousin last night that we'd been seeing each other for months."

Ty grinned. "Technically true," he agreed. "But thanks for warning me."

Another car honked behind them and Ty waved. "Cousin Maxine," he said under his breath.

"But what's in the box?" Amy demanded.

Ty strode around the car and winked at her before he got back in. "I'll be as quick as I can." He winced. "Whatever you do, don't drop it. And please, don't fail the Mommy Test. It'll unleash a storm of meddling if you do, one that will ensure we never make it to the wedding."

And then he drove away, leaving Amy standing at the end of a stranger's driveway holding a large, elaborately wrapped gift. Maxine slowed down to take a good look at her, and Amy smiled before the other woman drove on, presumably also looking for a parking spot. She looked down at the gift. There were glittery silver butterflies on the top, and they looked like they were fluttering around the massive bow.

Either Ty had unexpected talents or the shop had wrapped it

She shook it a little and wondered whether it was an appliance of some kind. Why had Ty said she'd chosen it? It must be practical. A coffeemaker? A toaster?

Amy turned and looked at the door, noting the sound of many people laughing and talking.

It was no big deal. They were having a good time.

She could do this.

Amy walked up the driveway and wondered about the Mommy Test. She reviewed her mental summary of her notes about Ty's family. By the time she rang the bell, she was pretty sure she knew what the dreaded challenge would be.

Ty's mom had one grandchild and wanted at least nine more.

Amy had a good idea which member of the family she was going to meet first—and who Ty's mom would introduce her to next.

When a tall woman with silver hair answered the door, Amy could see the resemblance to Ty in her eyes. "Amy?" she asked. "Could you be Amy, dear?"

"I am," Amy replied. "Ty's parking the car. Are you his mom?"

"I am, dear, and I wanted to make sure that you felt welcome. You can call me Colleen. It can be a little bit daunting to step into a family gathering as large as this, so I'll just introduce you to a few people to get you started."

"Thank you."

"Teresa? Could you take the gift, please? Amy, this is my sister, Teresa, and now where is Paige?"

Paige. Amy bit back a smile, knowing she'd nailed it in one.

She surrendered the parcel and her raincoat, glad that she liked babies.

Ty wasn't kidding about the Mommy Test. He would have bet his last buck that his mother would be hovering by the door, waiting to pounce on Amy. She would interrogate his date in his absence and throw her toward Paige and Derek—no, she would put Ethan in Amy's arms, preferably with a dirty diaper, and see how Amy responded.

When he was driving away, he realized his mistake. He should have given Amy a better warning. He should have thought of it sooner. He'd been thinking they'd walk into the shower together and that he'd be able to defend her, but of course, there were dozens of cars. Ty blamed his uncharacteristic agitation, and the fact that Amy had surprised him again by abandoning those loafers.

He parked the car two blocks away and strode back toward the house as quickly as he could. On the way, he saw his cousin Maxine again, and he paused at her gesture to guide her into a spot that was a tight fit. They walked back to the house at a crisp pace, Maxine practically trotting to keep up with Ty.

She told him some story about something, but he barely listened.

He'd left Amy for almost fifteen minutes. Ty rang the bell and his Aunt Teresa opened it, then cooed over him in the foyer. He was surrounded by relations, and there was no prospect of immediate escape.

Ty scanned the assembled guests, only to discover that his suspicions had been right on the money. His mother was talking with great animation to a woman in a navy dress with white polka dots, a woman who had her back to him and her hair twisted up to show her sleek neck to advantage. The dress was very flattering to the woman's slender curves—which were familiar to him, thanks to the class the day before.

Amy turned then, as if she sensed his arrival, and looked over her shoulder at him. Their gazes locked from across the room. Her smile was full of mischief, as well as the conviction that she'd surprised him, and the sight sent heat through him. Ethan was in her arms, trying to grab her glasses, but her expression filled him with relief.

She'd guessed and played it well.

Ty smiled and raised a fist to his heart. Amy laughed. He eventually made his way across the room, shaking hands with relatives and being hugged by cousins. He scooped Ethan from Amy's arms when he reached her side and held him high, which made his nephew chortle.

Then release a huge gob of saliva.

"Spit string," Paige cried and grabbed it out of the air before it could collide with Ty's suit or tie, then laid claim to her son. She made a face. "Oh, that diaper!" Ethan giggled and blew some bubbles. "I'm sorry, Amy! Excuse me, I'll be right back." She gave Ty a kiss on the cheek before she left and whispered the word "keeper" in his ear before she carried her son away.

"Tyler!" his mom said from behind him, her voice warm with predictable approval.

"I thought you weren't going to be mean to Amy," Ty complained as his mom hugged and kissed him.

"Mean?" She laughed at him. "What's mean about introducing her to the newest member of the family?" Her gaze was knowing, though. When Ty sighed and shook his head, his mother laughed again. Her delight was clear. "Are there small children in your family, Amy?"

"I have friends with babies."

Ty shook hands with Derek, waved to his dad, then dropped his hand on the back of Amy's waist. He bent down to whisper into her ear. "I'm guessing you aced the test," he murmured.

Amy gave him a disparaging look. "Is there a shred of doubt in your mind?" She arched a brow. "The stakes are considerable, after all."

Ty smiled. "I thought you'd be surprised."

"I figured it out on my way up the driveway. We're at Aunt Teresa's house, after all." She scoffed, her eyes dancing. "Piece of cake."

"I've been dating dumb women, clearly."

"Time to lift your game."

Ty met Amy's sparkling gaze, then looked down at her lips. He wanted to steal a kiss, a celebratory one, but tried to satisfy himself by keeping one hand on her waist. A pair of young kids raced past them, one in hot pursuit of the other, and several wine glasses were nearly spilled.

"Two of nine," Ty murmured. "My mom is already crazy for you."

"I'm feeling richer," Amy teased in a whisper.

"It's all yours, but if I give it to you here, people will get ideas."

Amy laughed. "Very bad ideas."

"Completely inappropriate ones." Ty grinned and traced a circle on the back of her waist with his thumb before he realized what he was doing. Amy froze, then she took a breath and stepped a little closer to him. Her gaze flicked to his, her eyes glowing, and he couldn't have cared less whether his mom was watching them. He stared down into Amy's eyes and his heart thumped. He bent and touched his lips gently to her temple. "I'm officially in awe," he whispered and she giggled.

Then she blushed.

There was absolutely no missing his mom's satisfaction with that.

"Let me get you a glass of wine," he said and Amy nodded.

"Thank you."

"You'll need it. We've got three hours to go, easily." He made a face. "But I'll be leaving you at their mercy."

"I'll survive, even without a champion."

"But then you won't miss me."

"Oh, but I will." Amy's smile flashed as their gazes clung again. Ty left her side reluctantly, well aware that his mom brought Maxine to be introduced.

He had fourteen seconds at the bar to feel smug about the likely success of his plan, before his sister Lauren appeared at the bar by his side. She had a determined look about her, and Ty had a very bad feeling.

His feeling got worse when she topped her wine glass to the rim. He could see by her eyes that it wasn't the first, or maybe even the second glass.

What was going on? He gave Lauren a kiss of greeting and complimented her, well aware of how her gaze was following Amy on the other side of the room. Amy was talking to Derek about something, her house maybe, and she looked animated. Happy.

Gorgeous. Ty could have watched her all day.

But Lauren was watching him. "Kind of amazing, big brother, that you have this great girlfriend no one has heard anything about until now."

"You can't blame me for wanting to defend her from all of you."

"Or is it the other way around?" Lauren murmured. She turned a smile on him before he could answer. "So, how did you two meet?"

Ty remembered a little too late that he and Amy hadn't worked out all the details of what she called the meet-cute yet. Caught without a plan, he did the only thing a team player could do.

He tossed the question to Amy.

"You've got to ask Amy that," he said cheerfully. "She tells the story so much better than I do."

Lauren gave him a considering glance. "You'll have to introduce us, then." She crossed the room with the focus of a heat-seeking missile and Ty's heart sank like a rock. If Lauren was determined to dissect their so-called relationship, his fake date plan didn't have a chance.

He really hoped Amy could think on her feet.

CHAPTER SEVEN

AMY HADN'T counted on Ty acting like they were dating.
No. She hadn't counted on him acting like they were in
love.

In hindsight, it was a stupid oversight. Of course, he would stick close to her, put his arm around her, stare into her eyes and even kiss her temple. Of course, he would act as if he was crazy about her. It probably wasn't a bad thing that his touch had such a powerful effect on her, given how closely his mom was watching them.

But still. Amy was rattled. She felt as if she had a full-body blush from the moment he arrived, and it wasn't fading at all. Having his hand on the back of her waist, his thumb tracing those little circles that made her skin heat, was more distracting than anything she could imagine him doing. When he'd given her that survey across the room and his gaze had heated, her mouth had gone dry. When he murmured to her, her heart leaped for her throat, then raced like crazy. She could have lost herself in his eyes, and even thought about dragging him into her house when she got home and having her way with him.

Her nipples were tight, for goodness' sake.

And other bits of her were similarly...aroused.

How would Tyler McKay kiss? Amy really wanted to know. She realized that if he had ever been set on courting her—or even seducing her—she wouldn't have had a chance.

But this was a fake date.

And she was smart enough to not forget that bit.

Maybe.

Even if her body wasn't.

The thing was, she'd been sure Ty was a lousy liar, and that disconcerted her even more. Had she misread him? He couldn't be really attracted to her, could he? That would have been an introduction of new information—even though he had admitted the night before that he liked their lunch conversations.

Amy did, too. She needed time to sort through everything he'd said and done to decide what the truth was, but instead she was at a bridal shower with his family. She had to make it look good and remember what she'd studied.

She'd have to analyze Ty's words later.

Amy tried to have a coherent conversation with Derek, as Ty went to get her a glass of wine, and was sure she failed. It seemed that everyone in the room was checking her out, and Amy wasn't used to being the center of attention. On the other hand, it was reasonable to expect her, as a new arrival, to be a little overwhelmed by his family.

"Do you live downtown like Ty?" Derek asked, when Paige had left to change Ethan's diaper.

"No, I have a house," Amy admitted. "And it's close enough to the city that I can commute."

"Good for you."

"It was my parents' house," Amy admitted. "I inherited it."

"Even better," Derek said with an easy smile. "How old is it?"

She recognized that he was trying to put her at ease and appreciated it. "It's Victorian. It was built in 1899."

Derek's eyes brightened. "Go on! I love old houses. Paige is determined that we'll buy one and renovate it completely." He rolled his eyes. "I don't know where she thinks I'll find the time. I'd have to run my crew hard to even afford one of those places, then there's the cost of the renovations."

"Tell me about it."

Ty returned with her wine and Amy tried not to jump when he put his hand on her back again. She smiled up at him, knowing that her cheeks were warm. His eyes were twinkling and his dimple was in view, so she knew he was just waiting for another chance to tease her.

If only he knew that her reaction wasn't very sisterly.

"Where is your house?" Derek asked. Paige returned and they traded off, her taking his glass of wine and him lifting Ethan out of her arms. "Amy has a house built in 1899," he said to his wife, who gasped with delight.

"I'm officially jealous," Paige said. "Tell us all about it."

"Well, it needs a lot of work right now."

Derek waved this off. "All the keepers need work. But the bones of the old places are incredible."

"And the details," Paige added. "Where is it?"

"In Brooklyn," Amy said, well aware that Ty was listening. "Flatbush, actually."

Derek and Paige exchanged a glance. Paige asked if it was on a street, which was Amy's street, and named a cross-street.

Amy was startled. "Well, yes, it is."

Derek leaned closer. "Tell me it's not number 304."

Amy looked up at Ty, a little bit freaked out. He appeared to be interested but there was something else. What did that gleam in his eyes mean? He seemed more focused than he'd been before. She realized that there was another woman with similar eyes standing behind him, watching her avidly. "What if it is?" she asked.

"*That* house!" Derek and Paige cried together.

"I love that house," Paige said. "I *want* that house."

"Hey," Ty said as Amy stiffened and she felt him draw her a little closer. "Take it easy, Princess Paige."

"I just love it, that's all," Paige said, her voice rising with her enthusiasm. "It has that porch, which is wonderful and the bay window and the little turret roof." She sighed with rapture. "Oh, it's perfect in forty-six thousand ways."

"Hardly," Amy said, feeling uncomfortable to hear her house discussed in such terms by strangers. "As I said, it's due for a lot of work."

"Like what?" Derek asked. "The porch? Those wooden porches are always in need of maintenance."

"Yes, that. The most urgent thing is that it needs a new roof."

Derek reached into his jacket pocket and removed a business card. He beckoned to Ty, who gave him a pen, and he wrote another phone number on the back. "Ty must have told you that I have a construction company."

"He did."

"We do a lot of renos, including roofs and porches, but I really like working on the older houses. My goal is to build a reputation for sympathetic renovation of those places." He handed her the card. "So, I'd be honored to have a chance to bid on your roof."

Paige nudged him hard.

"And I'll give you a family discount, just to sweeten the deal. Name the day and I'll come and have a look."

"And Paige will come, too, so that she can poke around inside your house," Ty said wryly.

"Ty!" Paige protested.

"Tell me that's not the plan," he said, and Paige blushed a little.

"Well, it did occur to me that I could talk to Amy while Derek was up on the roof."

"She's shameless," Ty said to Amy. "You don't have to let her in. Make her sit on the porch."

"That porch!" Paige nearly swooned.

"Even better, make her stay in the truck."

"Ty!"

"I have tenants, so I can't show the whole house to anyone anyway."

Derek's brows rose. "Was it always duplexed?"

Amy shook her head, still hating that she'd had to do it. "It was the only way I could keep it."

"You know, if you ever want to sell it," Paige began, but Ty held up a hand.

"Give it a rest, Paige," he said sternly, his tone firm enough that Paige complied. "Amy's been here five minutes, survived the Mommy Test, and you're already trying to buy her house from underneath her." His fingers tightened briefly on Amy's waist. "And now Lauren wants her turn at the interrogation." He turned and introduced the woman who had accompanied him.

Amy remembered the list of details.

Lauren. Oldest sister. Ty's unofficial favorite. Married to Mark in 2014. Hairdresser with her own salon.

But Amy would have guessed that part. Lauren's hair had that effortless beauty of a fabulous cut and artful coloring. It swung around her shoulders, gleaming and bouncing slightly. It was hair to envy.

Amy swallowed when Ty kept her tightly against his side. She could smell his cologne and that combined with his attention, his heat and his thumb doing those little circles on her back made her knees weak. Her reaction was just about the most inappropriate one at a family event like this, and she wondered whether Ty had any idea what he was doing to her.

"Lauren wanted to know how we met, but I said you had to tell the story." His hand slid up her side as he smiled down at her in apparent adoration. "You do it so much better than me."

Amy's mind went blank. His hand dropped to rest on the back of her waist again and her heart slowed its palpitations. She was aware that everyone in the little group was watching her, waiting.

And she needed a meet-cute involving an elevator.

"In the elevator," she said, then laughed a little. "It was really silly, which is why Ty doesn't want to tell it." She spared him an adoring look, which prompted his dimple to reappear. "We work at firms in the same building, and one day, we ended up being the only two people in the elevator."

"So, you started a conversation," Paige concluded.

"Not until the elevator got stuck," Amy admitted.

Ty chuckled and the pressure of his hand increased ever so slightly. "What's a guy to do when he's trapped in an elevator for ninety-seven minutes with a beautiful woman?"

Amy blushed at his compliment, but his siblings loved it. There was a collective "awwwww."

"She had a book," Ty continued, his voice very low. "And I asked her if it was any good."

Amy's gaze flew to his only to find his eyes sparkling again. He *was* teasing her. He was talking about *that* book. She lifted her chin, more than ready to participate in this version of their first meet. "He couldn't understand why a woman would read an erotic romance, so I set him straight."

Paige laughed and saluted Amy with her wine. "Good for you. Taking on Ty the tiger on a first meet."

Ty the tiger. Interesting.

"Who won?" Lauren asked softly.

"Amy," Ty said quickly. "I couldn't summon a word in my own defense." She glanced up at him again and the twinkle was gone from his eyes. He looked deadly serious. "Book, line, and sinker," he murmured with such conviction that even Amy considered believing him.

She took a large sip of wine and wondered what the hell she'd gotten herself into.

"Come on, Amy," Ty said as the conversation continued around them. "Let's check out my aunt's garden. She won an award from the horticulture society last year."

"Really? How wonderful." Amy excused herself from the others and let him lead her away. She sighed when they were a few steps away.

"Sorry," he muttered when they were out of earshot.

"I just had complete deodorant failure."

"I didn't want to screw up the story, so that seemed a good way to be on the same proverbial page."

Amy nodded agreement. "Lauren looks skeptical."

"I'll call her later this week and push the story."

"No," Amy said. "If you do that, it'll only feed her suspicions. Wait for her to come to you."

"All right." Ty opened the door to an expansive patio, lush with potted floral arrangements. "And I'm sorry about the house thing. Paige is a bit of a pitbull when she latches onto something. There's a reason we used to call her Princess."

"Ty the tiger?" Amy asked.

His smile was quick. "Okay, so there's more than one stubborn soul in the family."

"It is kind of nice to hear that someone admires your house. I was just surprised. I didn't realize it had fans."

"I guess you know who to call if you ever do want to sell it."

"I'll never sell it," Amy said, and only realized how fiercely she had spoken when Ty looked down at her in surprise. "It was the house my parents bought when they got married. It's filled with memories for me, and with their love. I can't imagine ever surrendering it willingly." She lifted her chin. "They'll take me out of it in a box."

He nodded understanding as they crossed the patio. It was a lovely yard, and very serene, even with guests milling about and chatting. There was a little waterfall near the house and the water flowed around the patio into a pond. Amy spotted koi swimming in the pond and admired the variety of exotic plants around the lip of the pool. They crossed a little bridge to a gazebo that was empty for the moment and she took a deep breath.

"You're doing great," Ty said.

"It's intense."

"They don't mean to be."

She nodded understanding. She could feel the love in this family and the concern they had for each other. She wouldn't think about her own situation in contrast, not until she was home alone again. "They just want you to be happy."

109

He opened his mouth, then closed it again, so clearly at a loss for words that Amy smiled. His gaze met hers and he smiled. "You keep doing that," he mused.

"Doing what?"

"Throwing me off guard." He brushed a fingertip across her cheek, launching a thousand shivers. "It's disconcerting."

"I'll stop."

"No, don't." There was a heat in his eyes again, one that prompted tremors with her.

Amy had to look away from him for a moment, because she was so disconcerted.

The garden had been cleverly designed so that it was hard to tell exactly where the property lines were, though Amy had no doubt it was an extensive property. Large trees blocked the view of other houses. She wondered that there wasn't a pool, because the house seemed to have everything, then saw the glass conservatory that enclosed the indoor pool.

"So, you have tenants." Ty was leaning against the pillar of the gazebo and she realized that he'd been watching her compose herself.

As if he really was smitten.

"Good ones," she said, hearing the doubt in his voice. "I went to high school with Lisa, and she teaches now at the primary school. When her parents split up, her mom moved in with her, then they moved into my place. They have the second floor of the house, and it works out pretty well for all of us."

"That sounds official and cheerful. What aren't you saying?"

Amy grimaced and decided to admit the truth to him. "I hate the extra doors."

"What doors?"

"To give them privacy and security, I had a door installed at the bottom of the stairs, blocking off the main floor. There's another new door at the top of the stairs, securing their apartment." She wrinkled her nose. "The doors just look wrong. The house used to be so open and inviting. Now it doesn't feel the same."

"And you only have half your house to yourself."

"Which is better than not having it at all."

He smiled. "Always making the best of whatever comes your way, aren't you?"

"Am I?"

"I think so. It's admirable, Amy, but wow, it makes me want to help you out."

"We've made our deal," she told him sternly. "And you gave me your friend's number at the bank." He arched a brow. "I'm going to call him this week." She saw something dawn in his eyes and shook a finger at him. "No making arrangements behind the scenes. No pity funding. No mercy meddling."

"You're taking all the fun out of it."

Amy refused to be charmed. "No upping the ante. No changing the rules. I'm not a charity case."

Ty sighed theatrically and she found herself smiling. "I guess another friendly bet is out of the question, then?"

"Like what?"

"Like... Derek will quote the roof to you at cost and plan to do it himself on a long weekend."

"That sounds like you know him well enough to anticipate what he's going to do, which doesn't make it much of a wager."

"True. You could negotiate with my inside information, though."

"How so?"

"If Paige is going to torment you the whole time, they should pay you."

Amy bit back a giggle. "She's not so bad."

"She was only getting warmed up."

"She's just enthused."

"Is that what you'll say when she's trying to peel your wallpaper to see the plaster, or pull back your rugs to check the floors, or pushing aside your clothes to assess the size of your closets?"

"You make it sound as if I need to be defended from her."

Ty lifted a hand. "Consider me a volunteer. If you want me to play defense when they come, just let me know."

Amy's heart warmed despite herself. "Do you protect all the women in the world?"

"Just the ones I like." Their gazes met in that electric way once more and Amy almost forgot to breathe.

"Let me think about it," she said lightly. "Shouldn't we go back inside?"

"Definitely. I need more wine for round two. You?"

"Yes, thanks." She must have straightened visibly, because Ty claimed her hand and gave her fingers a squeeze.

"You're doing great. I can already hear the accusations of what an asshole I am to have let you go."

Amy knew she shouldn't have felt flattened by the reminder, but she was. She forced a smile. "Let me be the bitch instead."

"We'll argue about the details later. Come on. Maybe half an hour more, then the gifts will be opened and we can leave."

"No. Your aunt is putting out a buffet."

"I was going to take you out for dinner to compensate for pain and suffering." He arched a brow. "To have you to myself."

"I think we should stay and do it right." Amy squeezed his hand. "Besides, I'll get mine back soon enough."

"All right. Definitely more wine." Ty held tightly to Amy's hand and led her back to the house. "Then you should meet the bride and groom."

"And Stephanie and Trevor."

Ty nodded and led her back to the house.

"One down, two to go," Ty said when they were driving back to the city. He had tapped in Amy's address into the GPS once they were in the car, having committed it to memory when Derek and Paige worked it out of her. She'd watched but hadn't protested. He took that as a good sign that she was trusting him more.

"Four to go," Amy corrected. "Two rehearsal dinners and two weddings."

"I forgot the rehearsal dinners. You're right again." He spared her a glance. She didn't look as if she'd been too shaken by his family, which was a relief. "How do you think we did?"

"You want a score?"

"Absolutely. On a scale of one to ten."

"Eight," Amy said without hesitation. "We nearly blew it on the meet-cute."

"Even with your brilliant variation on the truth of the elevator meet." Ty shook his head. "At least a nine." Amy didn't say anything and he wished he wasn't merging into traffic and could turn to look at her.

"It was clever to mix it with part of our actual first conversation."

Ty nodded. "I knew that if they heard you'd told me off, they'd like you and believe that you caught my interest."

"You make it sound like they think you terrorize them."

"I have been told that I'm bossy."

He smiled at the sound of her giggle. "How was it my idea to get the Keurig?"

"Hot coffee. You said you only like it hot, and I remembered Katelyn complaining that every time she makes a pot, it gets cold before she remembers to drink it."

"She seemed pleased."

"You're one of her favorite people forever now," Ty said with satisfaction. Could he give Amy a similar coffee maker without insulting her?

"Was the necklace she was wearing one of her own pieces?"

"Yes. You can tell because it was all twisty wire and asymmetrical." Amy chuckled. "I liked it."

"I guess I'll have to look at it again, without my preconceptions." He felt Amy's satisfaction with that and liked it a lot.

They rode in silence for a few minutes, and Ty watched a pair of black SUVs in his rearview mirror. They were swerving in and out of lanes, and looked like they were racing.

They were closing fast.

He wondered whether their course was erratic because the drivers were drunk. Either way, he was going to get Amy out of harm's way.

"You know, we never finished our discussion about those books," he said, not wanting Amy to notice the SUVs.

"You're right. Did they change your mind about the genre?"

"Not a bit. Take that first one, the new release with the naked guy on the cover."

Amy named the title.

"Right. Castration would be too good for that guy."

"So you said. Why didn't you like him?"

Ty pursed his lips and quoted. "'You're at your most beautiful when you're struggling to survive.' Seriously. How is it sexy that he likes to take her to the brink of death, then save her? Again and again and again?"

"It's about control and trust."

"It's twisted. Lock him up and throw away the key."

"Like in one of your thrillers."

"Absolutely. 'The good ended happily and the bad unhappily. That is what Fiction means.'"

"Who said that?"

"Oscar Wilde, and it's true. This genre is screwing with my conviction that the good guys win." One of the SUVs cut off the other one and nearly missed a sedan in the lane behind Ty. He gripped the stick, assessing the traffic ahead and hoping for a gap to open.

"How so?"

"If this is what women want, then a normal guy, with normal appetites, hasn't got a chance."

"Maybe it's what women like to fantasize about."

To Ty's relief, the SUVs weren't catching up that quickly. They were both changing lanes rapidly, swerving right and left, but the volume of traffic was holding them back. Brakes squealed behind them and a horn was honked. Ty spoke quickly to keep Amy from looking back. "Maybe it's a bad sign for society at large if that's the case."

Amy straightened, as provoked as he'd hoped. "How is it up to you or any other men to decide what's right for women to fantasize about?" she demanded in a hot tone that made Ty wish he could look at her. "We're not property or chattel who need our thoughts managed. Men fantasize about all kinds of stuff that I'd call twisted..."

"Not most of us," Ty felt obliged to note. One SUV was zooming up the lane to their right, but the gap between the cars ahead wasn't quite wide enough yet.

"But some of you do, and that's apparently okay, given what's in the magazines at the corner store." Amy was indignant. "But if a woman fantasizes about being dominated or about being taken in a rough way or about bondage, then it's assumed there's something wrong with her." She took off her glasses and shook them at him. "There's *nothing* wrong with fantasy..."

Ty wanted to look at her so badly it hurt.

"What about that book? You know, the one that sold a bazillion copies," he asked, wanting to keep her from looking behind them. "The one that was a movie."

Amy exhaled in exasperation. "No one who has criticized that book has read it. It's not my favorite, but neither is it about what everyone assumes it's about."

"What's it about?" Ty asked through his teeth. He silently urged the sedan ahead of him to move just a little faster...

"Consent and trust. And love healing wounds."

"Seriously?"

"They have a contract and a safe word!" Amy cried. "If you actually troubled to read the book or paid attention to the movie, instead of making assumptions about its content, you'd realize that *she's* the one who's in control of the situation, and that's what's so powerful about it! Besides, it's *fiction!*"

The second black SUV was behind the first one, waiting to pass on the right and swerve ahead. The first one accelerated, then swerved toward Ty's back right bumper.

The sedan ahead changed lanes.

"Hold on," he muttered, shifted down, and floored the accelerator. Amy gasped and dropped her glasses into her lap. The car shot forward like a rocket, exactly as Ty had planned, passing the sedan. He changed to the lane on his right, then the one to the right of that, giving the SUVs lots of room. The first one raced past them, weaving between the two lanes.

Amy picked up her glasses and put them on, then twisted in her seat to look out the back window. She then peered into the side mirror.

Ty took an exit, choosing an alternate route to leave the other SUV behind forever, then slowed to a sedate pace in the middle lane.

"Okay?" he asked when Amy remained silent.

"Were they racing?" she asked.

"And too close for comfort."

She nodded. "Were you listening to me at all?"

"Yes. Not particularly well, but I was listening." He cast her a smile and saw that her lips were tight.

"I don't believe it," she said, folding her arms across her chest. "You were just trying to distract me."

"Well, maybe a little."

"Don't you think that's condescending?" she asked coldly, and Ty knew he was in trouble.

"How is it condescending to protect someone?"

"I'm an adult, not your *leetle seester,*" Amy said. "Why wouldn't you tell me what was going on?"

"I didn't want you to worry."

"So you deceived me."

"Deceive is a little strong..."

"You didn't tell me the truth because I'm just a woman, and I can't be relied upon to remain calm in a bad situation?"

"That's not what I meant."

"I know you're a good driver. I've seen that already. And you're not a risk-taker or a daredevil, either."

Ty felt his temper rise. "Funny how those don't sound like good traits."

"I know you'd do your best to keep us safe, but I'm not a child. I deserve to know what's going on around us."

"I don't think it's wrong to be protective!"

"And I don't think it's wrong to be told the truth. Do you seriously think I don't know anything about danger or death or taking risks to survive?"

Ty would have admitted he was wrong if she hadn't continued.

"And I don't think it's wrong to expect to be treated as a responsible adult and an equal!"

His temper flared. "How does that mesh with all those naughty fantasies?"

"Perfectly well."

"Really?"

"Really. They're games. They're explorations and role playing— and they're done in an environment of complete safety."

"In an ideal world," Ty muttered. "So, is the guy who likes to see his beloved struggle to take another breath only sexy because he doesn't fuck it up and leave her to fight for too long? Because she doesn't actually—*oops*—die?"

"Pretty much." Her tone was considering and he wondered why. "It's his perfect control that's hot."

"Control," Ty muttered. "And which universe do these people live in where anyone has perfect control?"

"A fantasy one," Amy acknowledged. "That's the point." Her voice hardened. "It's *fiction*."

"It's a slippery slope."

"Not for me."

Ty bit his tongue.

Hard.

A terse silence filled the car then, and Ty gave all his attention to his driving. There wasn't a lot of congestion, but he was furious with Amy for refusing to see how dangerous all of these ideas were. It *was* a slippery slope, in his opinion, from consenting to naughty games and women being shipped in boxes against their will to serve as sex slaves.

She waited until they left the freeway completely, then cleared her throat. "These discussions are a bit lop-sided, aren't they?"

"What do you mean?"

"What are *your* fantasies?"

"Oh no, we're not going there."

"Why not?" she challenged. "Afraid I'll think castration is too good for you?"

No, just that she'd think he was boring. Predictable. Safe. Vanilla. Fucking *nice*.

"I never thought you'd be a big chicken," she taunted.

"I'm not afraid. Just private."

"Uh huh." Amy made a clucking sound and Ty saw red. He pulled into a parking lot, squealed the tires, and put the car in park.

Then he gave Amy his undivided attention, along with a healthy dose of honesty. "Okay, you want the truth. Here it is. All this bondage stuff seems unnecessarily complicated to me. The role-playing, the knots, the games, the mind-fucking. And I think it *is* a slippery slope to tendencies that aren't nearly so much fun. What if your hot dominant lover decides to ignore the use of your safe word? There's too much latitude for abuse, and the person who's going to be on the losing end of that is, nine times out of ten, going to be the woman." Ty shook his head and held up one hand for a moment. "Don't say trust again. I hear where you're coming from, but I'm not sold. Not every guy *listens*, especially in the heat of the moment."

Ty realized that a lot of the vehemence of his reaction came from his concern that Amy would explore the games more, and he wouldn't be able to ensure her safety. That worried him enough to make him be so forthright.

"You're stalling." Amy had folded her arms across her chest. "You haven't 'fessed up to anything."

Ty gritted his teeth. He might as well lay it all out. He was damned if he did and damned if he didn't, at this point. "What works for me is really simple. I like what my partner likes. Whatever excites her works for me, because there's absolutely nothing hotter than a woman who can't get enough of you or can't have you fast enough." Ty held her gaze, and saw her eyes widen. He leaned closer, watching how she quickly licked her lips, hearing her breath catch, wanting to touch her more than anything in the world. He dropped his voice to a purr. "Not. One. Thing."

Amy swallowed. "What if your partner liked you tying her up? What if it made her wild to have her wrists bound or to be blindfolded?"

"I guess I'd have to get out my old Boy Scout manuals and practice my knots."

"Says he with a decided lack of enthusiasm," Amy said, her disgust clear. She shifted her legs, the way she did when she was reading, but Ty didn't think it appropriate to admit his enthusiasm was greater than she realized. "I think you're full of it. I think you'd tell her that her fantasies were wrong and refuse to play along."

Amy looked out the window then and Ty couldn't think of a thing to say in his own defense. Well, except to admit the truth and that wasn't going to save his butt.

He waited, but she didn't look at him.

He took a deep breath and left the parking lot, squealing the tires a little bit. If he drove too quickly down her street, that was just too bad.

The thing was that he hadn't told her the whole truth about his fantasies. He remembered his hour as Matteo, the softness of Amy's lips beneath his thumb, the sweet curve of her butt under his hand, and the intensity of the desire he'd felt for her in that session. It had been incredibly hot—and they'd practically been in public and had been mostly clothed. The possibility of doing the same things naked and in private—let alone doing more than that—was enough to make him dizzy.

All because he knew Amy liked it.

"There," she said, pointing to a house a hundred feet ahead. "You don't have to get out to open the door."

"It's what I do," he retorted.

"Don't bother. I can manage a big car door all by myself."

"Amy!"

She was opening the door before Ty could think of an argument in his own defense, and she got out of the car so fast that he barely managed to pull out his wallet to pay off their bet.

"Thanks." Amy plucked the bill from his fingers and slammed the door hard. She walked away, without giving Ty a chance to continue their conversation.

He sat and watched until she was in the house, his blood simmering with more than frustration. He wanted to follow her. He wanted to try to convince her to believe him with his touch. No, he wanted to back her into a wall and kiss her until she couldn't think about any other guy or any other fantasy lover than him.

The simple fact was that he felt protective of Amy because he liked her.

A lot.

Enough to want more than a few fake dates.

But now that he'd stepped square in it, even those fake dates were in jeopardy unless he found a way to apologize.

Ty's hundred dollar bill was so crisp and new that Amy didn't want to break it.

She showed it to Fitzwilliam, who was unimpressed. He sat beside his bowl of kibble, his expression expectant.

Amy still felt a little agitated that Ty knew where she lived. She was more agitated that they'd argued. She could see his point, but it infuriated her that he refused to see her point.

Despite herself, she liked that he'd waited until she was inside before driving away.

And when he was gone, Amy's world seemed a little less colorful.

She couldn't stop thinking of how Ty had looked when he'd accelerated to get them away from the drivers he didn't trust. His eyes had glittered and his lips had thinned. He'd looked like a different man than the charming one who met her for lunch. A decisive and commanding man.

A demanding one. The sight had worked for Amy in a big way.

Never mind his intensity when he parked the car and gave her a serving of truth. And when he told her what he liked... well. Amy wondered whether she might have ovulated in that moment. He was really really hot and she'd hoped that he might act upon his urges.

But he hadn't. He'd kept everything under control, except his voice.

He had dropped the f-bomb twice. She'd never hear him do that before.

There had been a moment when he'd come up behind her and put his hand on her back at the party, that she'd thought of Matteo. She'd been almost startled when Ty's murmur had been in her ear, instead of Matteo's gruff Spanish accent.

Not significantly less aroused, though.

Maybe she was mixing them up, which was a troubling possibility. Amy changed and washed out her new dress, then went into the kitchen. The fridge was depressingly empty and she regretted eating so little at the buffet. She'd been too nervous to indulge, although everything had looked delicious.

"I need to have a cooking day," she told the cat. "Like Mama and I used to." She frowned. "Maybe next weekend."

She opened a can of cat food for Fitzwilliam, and a can of soup for herself. While it was heating, she walked around her part of the house, imagining what Paige would notice about it. It was still beautiful, despite the extra doors needed for the duplexing, and the main rooms were generously proportioned. The living room at the front had a bay window that looked over the porch and a fireplace, which Amy used in the winter. The mantel was original and lavishly carved. She ran her hand along it as she passed. She'd always liked the tiles in the fireplace, too. Her parents' dining suite was still in the room, although Amy seldom sat in there.

There were two bedrooms on the main floor as well as the kitchen and a full bath. The kitchen was smaller than would have been ideal— Amy remembered her mom joking that there could never be enough counter space in any kitchen—and had been renovated the last time in the seventies. It was sufficiently vintage to be due for an update. One bedroom, the one immediately behind the dining room, had always been Amy's dad's library. It had built-in bookshelves, still full of his books, and a fireplace, as well. There were two chairs in front of the fireplace and Amy remembered many winter nights spent there, reading with him.

The back bedroom was chilly and had been used as a storeroom when Amy's parents had been well. They'd used it as a bedroom when someone was sick, and technically it was Amy's bedroom now. She often slept in the living room, though, on the couch, or in her father's library. She couldn't rearrange the other main rooms without disturbing her good memories, not any more than she could empty the attic, so she made do.

Was Ty right that she was always making do? There was a germ of truth in that, for sure.

The second floor had four bedrooms and a full bathroom. The bedroom immediately over the kitchen had been turned into another kitchen. Lisa and her mother used the largest room as a living room and ate in their kitchen. The other two rooms were their bedrooms.

The stairs continued past their door to the attic, to her mom's dressing room and closet and lots of buckets catching rainwater.

One of Amy's favorite daydreams was how she'd fix up the house if she won the lottery. Her mom had always wanted a larger kitchen and they'd talked about integrating that back bedroom into the kitchen, since it hadn't really been in use anyway. That changed when her mom became ill. It was still a good plan, though, because it would mean that the back end of the kitchen would open into the yard.

The back yard had never been given much attention as a living or entertaining space. Amy's mom had grown a lot of vegetables when Amy was small and much of the yard had been in production. If the kitchen opened to it, though, Amy could imagine a patio, maybe with grapes trained over a trellis and paths between the vegetable beds. Flower beds, too. She was inspired by the house she'd visited that day with its beautiful yard.

There was a garage at the back of the lot, one that defied gravity by remaining upright and provided accommodations for wild creatures. It could be rebuilt, if it was done before it fell down, but without a car, Amy's priority was the roof.

The fact was that even at cost, she doubted she could afford the roof. She wouldn't phone Derek until she had some idea of where to find the money. In the morning, she'd call Ty's friend, just in case there were more options than she realized. It really couldn't hurt to find out.

She put Derek's card into the drawer that held all her household bills and estimates, then went to eat her soup. She plucked one of her mother's favorite recipe books off the shelf to browse as she ate, because she was due to fill the freezer with pre-made meals.

Amy was yearning for a taste of home cooking.

Her mother's cooking.

As soon as she'd served the soup, her phone rang.

Of course, it was Brittany.

Amy only half-listened to all the drama of the day, because evidently the dress had been fixed. When the call ended, Amy realized that her cousin never asked about her own date, and knew that Ty had called the relationship right without even meeting her cousin.

His family was big and they liked to razz each other, but there had been an incredible sense of love between them. Amy had seen how they supported each other, and provided for each other, in the same way that her parents had supported her. Ty's safety net would never be gone, though, unless the Apocalypse came.

There were so many of them.

She could be a little bit jealous of that.

Or she could use it. *The Dark Prince* himself was alone in Amy's story, reviled by those around him because of his scars. Lothair was too embittered himself to reach out for help. He didn't even think he needed any assistance.

But his slave, Argenta, knew better.

She challenged his expectations.

Amy thought about the Oscar Wilde quote and knew that her story was going to deliver to that expectation. She seized her pen and the pad of paper and began to write.

The prince lifted my chin with one gloved fingertip, and I could feel the weight of his gaze upon me.

Then he let his hood slide back a bit so I could see his face. I knew he expected me to avert my gaze but I didn't. I looked. His one eye was patched and judging by the scars, I wagered that his eye was gone. I had glimpsed the deep wound that etched his cheek, pulling down one corner of his mouth. Another scar, or perhaps more of the same one, erupted from the top of the patch, and carved a line to his temple, pulling up the end of his dark brow so that he looked diabolical. On that side, I could see that his scalp was red and marred, as if he had been burned. On the other side, his hair was as dark as ebony, thick and wavy. His eye was as green as new grass.

He had been handsome before his injuries, and even now, I found his face arrestingly beautiful. If he had expected me to quail in terror, he was doomed to disappointment. The scars on his flesh showed his valor to me. They showed that he had faced an ordeal and survived it. They were a mark of his venturing beyond the borders of Euphoria. I wanted desperately to know where he had been, what he had seen, what it was like beyond our borders.

I wanted to go there myself.

Clearly, there was peril to be found in such distant lands. Someone had disfigured him deliberately, so savagely that I wondered why.

I looked my fill and sensed his surprise.

"No pity," he said softly.

I shook my head, holding his gaze.

Something changed in his expression. If anything, he became more intense. We stared at each other and the air seemed to heat between us...

CHAPTER EIGHT

A MY WORE the green suit to work on Monday.
Because she was going to call Red. She didn't know much
about money and banks, but she knew that her chances of
being loaned any money were much greater if she didn't look as if she
needed it so desperately.

The suit gave her confidence, too.

She dug in her own closet and found a pair of black pumps she'd
bought ages ago—for her mom's funeral—and hadn't worn since.
They were black and the heels weren't too high. They were Italian and
leather, a tribute to her mom's affection for quality. She'd thought
them elegant then, and they didn't look dated at all. She wore the
loafers to work, then changed.

Mrs. Murphy looked her up and down, but Amy was saved from
any interrogation by the ringing of the phone. She'd already made an
appointment with Red—who sounded very nice, and knew nothing
about her, which was proof that Ty wasn't organizing things for her
behind the scenes—when the flowers were delivered.

For her.

It was a beautiful spring bouquet, with lilies and roses and more, in
shades of pink and purple and white. Amy was astonished, because no
one ever sent her flowers.

She opened the card and her heart stopped for a moment.

I'm sorry was written inside. *I was wrong. Give me another chance at lunch
today?*

And it was signed by Ty.

Amy took a shaking breath and stuffed the card into the pocket of her suit jacket. He'd apologized and she was completely seduced.

He probably didn't need to know that she'd been planning to give him that chance at lunch today anyhow. She knew it was important that he'd lost his temper and that he'd sworn.

Amy put the flowers in pride of place on her desk and enjoyed how Mrs. Murphy regarded them with suspicion.

The morning flew by.

Ty was looking forward to lunch on Monday.

No, he was looking forward to seeing Amy again.

He wanted to provoke her to defend her favorite genre again, just so he could watch her without distraction. He wanted to make her laugh. He wanted to learn more about what she liked and why.

Mostly, he wanted to apologize in person.

He worried about the flowers, that he might have made a bad choice of color or that she might have allergies. He worried that she might dislike getting them at work, but he wanted her to receive them before lunch. He worried that she might not give him another chance and watched the minutes tick by with painful slowness.

He had to get her phone number because it killed him that this apology had had to wait.

Reviewing April reports for his best clients that morning didn't captivate his attention. His mom had called the night before and again that morning, gushing about Amy and what a marvel she was. Ty had no disagreement with anything his mom said.

Hook, line, and sinker sounded like the truth.

Ty was early to the food court and claimed a seat at Amy's usual table. He was starting to think of is as *their* usual table. From his place, he could watch the elevators. He opened his book but glanced up at intervals. Even though he was waiting for her, he was startled when she appeared.

Amy wasn't wearing navy.

She wore a suit he hadn't seen on her before, with a tweed jacket in green and gold and a skirt in solid green. The hem swung around her knees in a fabulous way. The loafers were gone, and instead, she wore a demure pair of black leather pumps.

He swallowed and stared.

Amy smiled and spun in front of him before taking off her jacket and sitting down opposite him. "What do you think?"

"Gorgeous," Ty said, and meant it.

Amy blushed, right on cue. "My mom was a dressmaker. I still have all of her clothes but I didn't really think about us being the same size. I'm a little taller than her, but that's it." She smiled and stroked the tweed. "I remember her making this."

The love she had for her mom shone in her eyes, and it was enough to break Ty's heart.

"It suits you," he said. "Great find."

She grinned impishly. "Don't you miss my loafers?"

Ty considered them. "I only regret that you didn't give me the chance to burn them."

"Never! I need them for the trip home."

She crossed her legs, giving him an ideal view. "You are killing me," he murmured. "Is this how you're going to get even with me?"

"Liar! You're too nice a guy to ogle women's legs."

"You might be surprised," Ty growled and she eyed him for a minute.

She started to blush and he watched. "Thank you for the flowers," she said quietly.

"I am sorry."

"Me, too. You really made me mad."

"We have that in common, then," he acknowledged and she smiled.

"My gentleman was quite annoyed that he didn't have my undivided attention when I got home," she said, surprising Ty with that confession. Her eyes sparkled when she looked up at him. "He doesn't take well to being left home alone on the weekend."

"Your gentleman?"

Maybe her role-playing at F5 wasn't the only surprising thing about Amy.

"Fitzwilliam gets disgruntled if dinner isn't in his dish on time."

If she was talking about a man, she had some kind of strange domestic life. "Fitzwilliam?"

Amy laughed and Ty knew his confusion showed. "He's a cat, a Maine Coon. When I first found him, I thought he was a brooding type, but he was just suffering."

"Found him?"

"They left him!" She confided, outrage putting an enticing spark in her eye. "When the neighbors moved, they left him behind. He was abandoned with no food and was eating garbage if he could find it. I heard him yowling before the new people moved in."

"And he wasn't theirs?"

"Their children have allergies. They couldn't keep him. I took him home."

Of course, she had.

"I knew where the first people had moved and I called them, thinking it was a mistake, but they said they didn't want him anymore." Amy's eyes flashed. "They couldn't even take him to a shelter or a vet, so he could have a new home. He was just left behind. They didn't even think about him dying there!"

Ty was intrigued. "So, you kept him?"

"Well, I took him to the vet and they said he was undernourished but otherwise healthy. They said that adult cats don't get adopted very often, so I couldn't take him to the shelter." She made a face. "They kill them, you know. They have to, because there are just too many cats without homes."

Ty knew she was trying to hide her tears. "You had to save him." She had a soft heart. He liked that she was so giving.

He had to figure that it was part of the reason she was allowing him another chance.

"I did, even though he had an attitude problem. He'd glower at me when I was home, but he ate when I left the room. I didn't even know his name, or how old he was or anything, but I couldn't exactly call the former owners again." Her lips tightened. "They weren't very nice the first time."

"Because you were reminding them that they'd been callous."

Amy thought about that for a minute. "Maybe. Anyway I had to give him a name, so Fitzwilliam seemed the obvious choice."

"Which one? Darcy or Colonel?"

Her entire face lit with a joy that made Ty feel like a star. "Does it matter?"

"It'll tell me everything I need to know," he said, because it was true.

Amy's smile turned mischievous and the sight made Ty's chest tight. "Then guess."

Ty thought for a moment. "'My disposition could be said to be resentful,'" he quoted. "'For my good opinion once lost is lost forever.'"

"You've seriously watched it so many times that you have it memorized?"

"Maybe, but I also took nineteenth-century English literature as a breadth course."

"But you're a money guy."

"The cute girls are in English lit classes."

She laughed at that. "But now, like Mr. Darcy, he's warmed up considerably. That's a nice change after Riordan."

"Vanity Fair?"

She nodded and sighed. "It was the perfect name for him. A reckless gambler, and a handsome rogue. He had charm and good looks, but a conviction that he could beat the odds of crossing the street."

"He showed up on your doorstep wounded," Ty guessed.

Amy nodded. "And I couldn't just leave him. The thing was that after the surgery, he wouldn't stay in the house. He made us crazy with his yowling and his escape acts."

"He had to be who he was."

"And he'd come crawling home, bashed up in one way or another. He cost us a fortune. I think Dad and I paid for the renovation at the vet's offices."

"But you couldn't turn him out."

She blushed a little. "He was very charming." She sighed and twisted the container from her sandwich. "But when they found the cancer, it was too advanced. We just kept him comfortable for as long as possible." She shed a tear, and Ty felt like he should console her in the same instant that he feared it would be inappropriate.

"I'm sorry," he said, feeling it was inadequate.

"Do you have pets?"

"No. Never have."

"You should think about it," Amy said. "I didn't plan to have another cat after Riordan, given how much trouble he'd been." She smiled a little. "But Fitzwilliam charmed me."

"'But I think Mr. Darcy improves on closer acquaintance. In essentials, I believe he is very much as he ever was. I don't mean to imply that either his mind or manners are changed for the better, rather, my knowing him better, improved my opinion of him.'"

"Wow."

Ty shook a finger at her. "But that's not what it says in the book, actually."

Amy propped her chin on her hand to study him. "I don't remember. What's in the book?"

127

Ty cleared his throat. "'When I said that he improved on acquaintance, I did not mean that either his mind or manners were in a state of improvement, but that from knowing him better, his disposition was better understood.'"

"You are good at this," Amy said, then met his gaze with a sparkle of challenge in her own. "I should have called him Algie."

"'Anyone who knows me really well knows that when I'm very upset, I refuse everything except food and drink,'" Ty guessed, quoting Oscar Wilde.

"You must have gotten great marks in that class."

"Kyle and I had an incentive." At her glance, he clarified. "Friend of mine. That's where we met. We'd both chosen the course for the same reason and were the only two straight guys in the class. We had to stick together, and we had to ace the course." Ty smiled and continued. "Four sisters means I had an advantage."

She laughed. "How many times *have* you seen *Pride and Prejudice?*"

"I've lost count. Fifty or sixty. They wore out one DVD set."

"So, is it true that a man in possession of a fortune, or at least a decent job, must be in need of a wife?" Amy asked.

"My mother thinks so," Ty confessed and she smiled at him in the way that set his blood on fire.

"I suppose it's not all bad for a man to be protective."

"I suppose it's not all bad for a woman to have naughty fantasies," he countered.

She raised her gaze to his. "Maybe it would be smart, though, to only act them out with a man she trusts completely."

"Definitely smarter," Ty agreed. They stared at each other for a sizzling moment, one that made him hope about possibilities, then Amy unwrapped her sandwich.

"Do men really look that much?"

"All the time."

"Not just legs?"

"Nope." Ty hesitated. "How honest should I be?"

"Completely. I can take it."

"That pink lipstick of yours yesterday was very distracting."

"Really?" Amy didn't look displeased by the revelation, which was good.

"Absolutely."

"What about you, with your hand on my back?" she replied, then rolled her eyes. "And your thumb."

128

"The first time was an accident," Ty admitted. "But I liked it. Did you?"

Amy averted her gaze, then looked him square in the eye. "Yes."

They stared at each other for another hot moment and Ty's throat was tight. He was about to make a suggestion when that Mrs. Murphy began to shout at Amy. "Not again," he muttered.

"All the time," Amy replied in an undertone.

"We've got to find you another job."

To his surprise, her eyes were dancing. "I think I have an idea."

"Tell me."

She shook her head. "Not yet."

"Don't you trust me?"

Her expression turned fierce. "I don't want you fixing it."

"You know me already."

Amy grinned.

"I promise to stand back unless my assistance is specifically requested."

"Deal." She offered her hand and they shook on it.

Ty wasn't in a hurry to let her hand go.

"Amy!" Mrs. Murphy interjected, appearing suddenly beside them. "Mr. Forsythe just called. His flight was canceled because of thunderstorms and he's stuck in Dallas. You know he has to get to Denver today..." She frowned down at their clasped hands and Ty hoped the gesture gave her something to worry about.

"I thought it would be better if he changed at O'Hare," Amy said, already gathering her things.

"Well, it isn't up to you, is it?" Mrs. Murphy snapped.

"Then maybe it can be fixed after Amy has lunch," Ty suggested more mildly than he felt. "I doubt the storms will stop soon."

Mrs. Murphy looked him up and down, then spoke to Amy again. "You need to come and do this now. Mr. Forsythe has gone to lunch and expects this to be solved by the time he's done."

He went to lunch and left his travel arrangements to be solved by Amy? Irritation rolled through Ty. It would be much easier for this Forsythe to step up to the desk in Dallas and sort out his own flights.

Ty opened his mouth to comment but Amy got to her feet. "I have a secret weapon you don't know about," she said with a smile and hastily put her lunch back in her tote bag. "I'll see you later."

She was gone before Ty realized he *still* didn't have her number.

Amy's dad would have loved how much Ty knew about nineteenth-century literature, too. Ty might have taken the course for the women, but Amy liked that he retained so much of it.

And that he watched chick flicks with his sisters. He was such a nice guy.

It wasn't quite as sexy as being a dangerous man, but it was still good.

If he'd let that inner tiger of his out more often, she might have been in serious trouble. Amy supposed she should be grateful for small blessings. This fake date plan would be easier to end if there weren't any emotional complications.

She told herself that it was good that Ty wasn't really her type.

She wasn't sure she believed it.

Once Mr. Forsythe's travel plans were rearranged, Amy was called into the older woman's small office. "We might as well get this out in the open," Mrs. Murphy said. "Are you considering leaving us? Is that why you're dressed up, and you were lunching with that man?"

She'd witnessed the handshake and thought it meant a different kind of deal.

"I really don't think it's something I should discuss," Amy prevaricated.

"Well, I would have thought that you'd have spoken to us first if you were unhappy."

"I'm not unhappy." It wasn't exactly a lie.

"But you think you can do better." Mrs. Murphy exhaled. "I will see if anything can be done to give you a small raise, since Mr. Forsythe depends upon you so much. I trust you will show the courtesy of not accepting another offer before I get back to you on that."

"Of course not."

The two women eyed each other, and Amy realized her request would only fan the flames. "I do have to leave a little early today, if you remember. I mentioned this morning that I had an appointment..."

"And I assumed it was a doctor's appointment, not another interview," Mrs. Murphy huffed. "I won't make it easy for you to complain about us here. Go to your appointment, but be sure everything is done before you leave."

"Of course." Amy bit back a smile as she returned to her desk. It would be wonderful to get even a small raise.

Maybe she would be able to afford that new roof after all.

There was an obvious step Amy had to take, although it made her nervous.

So, she avoided it.

She went to her appointment with Red and had to think it went reasonably well. He was dressed as well as Ty, but wasn't as handsome or as trim. His hair was as red as could be expected, and he wore a gold wedding ring. There were pictures of three red-headed kids on his credenza and a pretty woman with them.

Red was quick to put her at her ease, and after reviewing the information she'd brought, he had a few suggestions. He wanted to have the house assessed, because he thought its value was probably low. It made sense that if her only asset was worth more, Amy might be able to borrow a little more. Red was positive about her prospects and promised to call her in a few days.

Bolstered by that, Amy made the plunge. She went to the copy shop and made copies of her book pages. She'd miss the train she usually took, but this had to be done. Amy needed to know whether she was on the right track with her book, and that meant showing it to someone else.

Someone who understood the genre.

Jade.

Even if the prospect terrified her.

One good thing about running late was that there was little chance of running into Ty at the bookstore.

To her relief, he wasn't there.

On the other hand, she was a little disappointed to have missed out on another glimpse of him.

Jade waved to her from the horror section and Amy hurried toward her friend. She'd put the copies in an envelope and handed it to Jade before she could reconsider. "I'm doing it," she said in a rush. "I'm writing a book. Could you read it and tell me if it's good?"

Jade's eyes lit. "No way. Really?" She accepted the envelope with a kind of reverence. "It is evil of you to bring this now when I have to work until nine-thirty tonight."

"I hope you don't mind."

"Are you kidding? I can't wait to read it!"

"You have to be honest," Amy insisted. "Totally and utterly honest."

"Absolutely," Jade said. "I'll tell you the truth." Then she bounced a little. "This is so exciting, Amy!" They hugged quickly, then Amy crossed her fingers and left for her train. When she glanced back, Jade was peeking inside the envelope.

Amy couldn't read on the train on the way home. She kept thinking of bits she should have changed, or additions she could have made, or how the book could have been better. It seemed that as soon as it left her hands, she had a million more ideas.

She reminded herself that it wasn't published, or even sent to an editor.

Her book was safe with Jade.

Even so, Amy made a lot of notes when she got home. So many notes that Fitzwilliam had to remind her about dinner, more than once.

Then she read the last bit of the book again, reviewing what she'd written. It was the scene where Lothair claimed his prize. It should have been really intense.

It seemed thin to Amy.

Lacking in sensory detail.

It was evidence of her lack of experience. How long had it been since she'd had sex? And she'd never had hot sex like this, let alone sex in a bondage scene.

She had to come closer than her own experience to improve this part of her book.

Amy took a deep breath. She retrieved the flyer from F5 and read the bit on the back again. *Private sessions available.* How much would one be? She had to invest in her research. She had to find the money for it.

She had to give the book its best shot.

She pulled out her phone and called F5, hoping that Matteo was available for private instruction.

Ty was heading upstairs from swimming laps, daring to hope that he was making some progress with Amy. She hadn't gone to the bookstore after work, and he felt cheated of her company. He told himself that he'd see her the next day, but he was restless.

"No, I think he's probably gone for the day. Can I take a message?" Damon was on the phone at the desk and Ty waved to him on his way to the elevator. "Wait!" Damon said, then beckoned to Ty. "I see him now, just coming out of the pool."

Ty frowned. Who would call him at F5?

"Matteo!" Damon shouted and Ty understood. "Call for you!"

But who would call Matteo?

Only one person.

Ty crossed the lobby fast and took the phone. "Hello?" he said in his deepest voice, trying to imbue the single word with his Spanish accent.

"Hello, Matteo," Amy said, her words falling quickly. "You probably don't remember me..."

"Of course, I remember you, Angel," he said.

She exhaled and he realized she was nervous. Why was she calling?

"Oh good, because I see on the flyer that F5 offers private instruction, and I wondered if we could, if you could, I mean, if it was possible..."

"There are private instruction rooms on the sixth floor," Ty said smoothly, uncertain whether to be annoyed with her for taking such a chance or thrilled by the prospect of such intimacy with her. She was screwing with his assumptions one more time.

Damon grinned and turned to answer a question from a staff member.

Ty folded his arms across his chest, the image of Amy, probably barefoot in her kitchen, making his gut clench. "If you would like a session, Angel, I can indulge you for an hour for fifty dollars."

Damon gasped in outrage from behind him and tapped the price list on the counter with an emphatic fingertip. Ty waved him off. Amy wasn't going anywhere else to get this kind of private instruction from anyone else. He would subsidize it and she'd never know.

"That's all?" she demanded. "Oh, well, that's wonderful, then. Could we book a session?"

"The week after next..."

"This week," she insisted. "Wednesday night?"

Ty was startled but he tried to hide it. He checked the schedule. "Of course, Angel. Room 612 is available at seven on Wednesday night."

"Oh, good. Do you need a credit card to make the reservation?"

"You are on file here," Ty said evenly. "It can be paid at the time."

Damon spread his hands, shaking his head.

Ty waved him off again.

"Oh, good."

"Do you have *preferences*, Angel?"

"Um. Everything we did before, but in private," she said hurriedly. "I want to see what it feels like without so many people around."

"It will be more intimate," Ty said, his own body reacting to the prospect. "It will feel riskier."

"Good," she said with a little rush of breath that put fire in his blood. "Good. That's exactly what I want."

Damon shoved a sheet at him and Ty eyed it, then nodded.

"You should stop in at the club, Angel. They have consent forms and check sheets for private clients, the better to ensure that everyone is satisfied."

"Good idea," she said, her anticipation clear. "I'll do that at lunch tomorrow."

Ty winced that he'd be missing another chance to talk to her.

On the other hand...

"Thanks, Matteo. I'll see you then."

"Of course, Angel." Ty ended the call and stared at the phone for a moment.

"You know we have fixed rates," Damon began.

"And you know you can charge the difference to me," Ty replied crisply.

"Maybe there's going to be rain in the desert after all," Damon teased.

"Maybe it's not your business." Ty heaved a sigh and turned to the store. It was time for some more research.

There was no way he was going to take a chance on disappointing Amy.

Ty studied.

Research was how he confronted every challenge in his life. He researched, he studied, and he aced the exam. He researched, he studied, and the stock portfolios under his management were the most profitable ones. He researched, he studied, and he won. Over and over again. The strategy worked for everything else: it had to work for sexual games.

He didn't have performance anxiety, especially about sex. Ty knew he was a good lover, at least when he knew the lady's expectations. What concerned him about Wednesday night was his lack of certainty over Amy's expectations.

And his determination to give her exactly what she wanted, whatever it was.

What options was she going to choose? He had to be ready for all of them.

On Monday night, Ty had watched a ton of the instructional videos that were for sale in the club's shop, and read the instruction books, too. He was looking for diversity, and for games he'd never played before. There was a surprisingly high number of them. Some variations made him feel that he'd lived a very sheltered life—human pony training was oddly fascinating—and he was surprised to find some images titillating.

He crashed late, rose early, and told himself that it was a good thing that Amy wasn't meeting him for lunch. He wouldn't be at his best.

He took his e-reader with him and picked up a couple of digital books in the store, then read them at lunch. Anaïs Nin was a gimme. He was studying, but it felt covert.

Illicit.

Cassie was waiting for him in the lobby of F5 when he came home Tuesday night.

That gave him a bad feeling.

It wasn't just that Cassie looked like the proverbial cat who had swallowed the canary. The way she waved her tablet at him seemed portentous.

Had Amy canceled?

"Your girl came to fill in her forms," she said, much to his relief.

"Really?" he replied, trying to sound casual and indifferent when he was relieved—and not.

"Really," Cassie said with conviction. "Check out the lady's preferences. Pretty conservative, if you ask me."

Ty hoped so. He said a silent prayer that it wasn't too heavy of a scene Amy wanted, shoved a hand through his hair, and looked.

Spanking

Bondage.

Blindfold, hood, and/or gag.

He dared to be relieved. It *was* just like what they'd done in the class, but in private.

Still fully clothed, too.

Okay. He could do this.

"She's not much of a risk-taker," Cassie said, drawing her fingernail along the row of options. "But some women like the tease."

"It's not bad to be cautious," Tyler found himself saying.

"Maybe that's what you two have in common. Nice people making cautious moves."

"Maybe I'm not as nice as you think," Ty replied, knowing he wasn't nearly as nice as Amy thought he was.

Cassie flicked her finger to make the display scroll. "Don't miss the best bit. It surprised me."

Shibari.

"Should I know what that is?" Ty asked warily.

Cassie smiled. "The Japanese art of binding captives, often suspending them."

Ty caught his breath.

"It's a tricky one," Cassie confided. "No pressure, but the captive can get badly hurt if the person tying the knots doesn't know what they're doing." She practically strutted to the gift shop as Ty's heart stopped cold. She picked up a coffee table book. "The only reference we have, but she had a good long look at the open copy."

It was titled simply *Shibari* and had an image on the cover that was artfully lit. The nude woman had been photographed from behind, her hands bound behind her back with heavy jute rope. The knotting was elaborate, from shoulder to wrist, ensuring that her arms remained outstretched behind her in a precise position. Her legs were crossed in a way that looked uncomfortable to Ty and, judging by the shadow beneath her, she was suspended from the three ropes that stretched upward.

"Complicated," Cassie mused without sympathy.

"Fuck," Ty said under his breath.

Cassie laughed and shook a finger at him. "No, no, none of that. This isn't a brothel, you know. It's about the sizzle, not the steak."

He gave her a glare that could have melted glass and seized the book.

Cassie pretended to swoon. "Put that in the jar and it'll rain for forty days and nights in the desert," she said, but Ty was already striding across the lobby.

Shibari.

What was in Amy's mind?

How was he going to master this ancient art in one night?

Mild panic set in. Ty blew off his work-out and headed upstairs to cram. He hadn't gotten through half of the materials he'd taken the night before, and there wasn't much time left to get it right. He had to multi-task.

SIMPLY IRRESISTIBLE

Upstairs, Ty loaded another DVD. This one was about pain and pleasure. The narrator had a British accent. He couldn't decide whether that made it more ridiculous or less so.

"Trace the letters of the alphabet on her clitoris, with your finger or tongue..."

The video showed just that, a drawing of a clitoris with the letters of the alphabet being languidly traced over it. They were in lower case.

This would be the pleasure bit.

Ty had this covered. He opened the *Shibari* book and flipped through it. He'd choose one pose and master it. They were both beginners, after all. Just one, an easy one. The narrator droned on as Ty sought a comparatively simple option.

He was irritated when his door buzzer sounded and snapped "What?" over the intercom.

But it was Lauren and even over the intercom, she sounded odd. Upset, maybe. She never came by his place unless there was something really wrong. Ty buzzed her in.

He opened the door to the corridor to wait for her to step off the elevator, wanting to make a guess at what was bothering her before she put a good face on it. Her head was bowed, her long hair obscuring her features, but he was sure that when she glanced his way, she blinked back tears.

Her smile was certainly forced.

"What's up?" he asked, keeping his tone light.

"I need a reason to visit you now?" she asked, a break in her voice.

"Of course not, but it's been a while."

"You just don't like having anyone in your cave."

"There is that," he admitted, then made a guess. "How's Mark?"

"Fine." Lauren seemed to bite off the word. Mark might be fine, but Lauren's view of him wasn't. She slipped past Ty into his apartment and stopped dead. "Who are you and what have you done with my brother?"

Shit. Ty realized that his study materials were strewn all over the coffee table, couch, and dining room table. There was a drawing of a clitoris filling his television screen. Ty felt the back of his neck heat even as he cleared the coffee table.

At light speed.

"J. K. L." continued the voiceover with the British accent, at least until Ty shut off the video with a savage gesture.

137

"Seriously," Lauren said. She propped her hands on her hips and gave the apartment another look. "You, of all people, are into this? And so into it that your pristine retreat is—be still, my heart—a mess?"

"It's not a pristine retreat," Ty said with some irritation. "And it's not a mess."

"Sorry to correct you, bro, but you're wrong on both counts." Lauren picked up a black leather flogger and tried it against her palm. "I find it really hard to believe that Amy is into this." She spared Ty a glance. "Or are you seeing someone else on the side?"

"It's really not your business." His look should have warned her to let it go, but Lauren wasn't daunted.

"Oh, but it is." She lounged in one of the leather chairs that was still clear, crossing her legs and bouncing one foot. "Seeing that Amy is going to be my sister-in-law any minute now."

Ty nearly dropped the stack of books he was moving to the floor. They did land harder than he'd planned. "I beg your pardon?" he said with care.

If he had proposed, he would know it.

Lauren leaned forward, eyes sparkling. "I should warn you. Mom is seriously planning to put the moves on her at the wedding. She says it's high time you settled down, and if you won't put things in motion, she will." She leaned forward. "Amy didn't even flinch when they tossed Ethan at her with a loaded diaper. What did you expect?" She started to hum *Here Comes the Bride* and he chucked a book at her.

She caught it, turned it over and her eyes widened. "Who are you really seeing?"

"Amy. Why?"

Lauren tossed the book on the coffee table. It was the one featuring the guy Ty didn't like, the candidate for castration. "Because she's totally not your type."

"I like women. She's a woman." He raised a hand.

"No, you like *gorgeous* women. Sleek, polished women who could be models. But they're not. They're all super-ambitious career machines with hearts of ice." Lauren made a face. "Barracudas, every one of them."

Ty was startled. "That's a bit harsh, don't you think?"

Lauren shook her head. "Take Giselle. She had you in her sights like nobody's business. I think you were the airline retirement plan."

"Maybe."

"What made you finally realize that I have shoes with greater empathy?"

Ty sighed. "I knew that right away. I only ever went out with her the once."

"Really? To Grandma Trixie's eightieth birthday? Strange choice for a first date."

"It was an act of pure desperation."

Lauren pointed at him. "That I understand."

Once Ty started to confess, the truth came easily. "I was on the flight home from Beijing. Giselle was the stewardess in the first class cabin. Very pretty."

"She is that."

"Charming. Interested."

Lauren rolled her eyes. "Proof only that she was heterosexual and had a pulse."

Ty ignore the implied compliment. "Mom called before we pushed back. Mom called again when we landed." He met Lauren's gaze steadily. "Mom had an agenda item to resolve."

His sister grinned. "Grandma Trixie's eightieth birthday party. And more importantly, the great showdown between the Preston sisters." Lauren sat back and nodded, then mimicked their mother expertly. "You know, dear, that Aunt Teresa's children are all married and she has nine grandchildren already..."

Ty made a dismissive gesture. "I knew before we even got to the party that I'd made a mistake."

"Kudos to you for that." His sister toasted him. "I was afraid you might have been thinking with your dick."

"Thank you very much." Ty sighed and shoved a hand through his hair. "I've been listening to Kyle for too long. It seemed like a good idea at the time."

"Even pretending you were still seeing her?"

"Even that. Kyle thought it was brilliant. Me, not so much."

"Good. The longer I heard about Giselle, the more I worried about you." Lauren folded her arms across her chest. "Are you still taking advice from Kyle?"

"Why?"

"How could you bring home a woman who looks like a kindergarten teacher and expect us to believe it's love?" She shook her head. "Seriously?"

Amy had been right about Lauren's skepticism. Ty had some

damage control to do. He sat down opposite his sister, intent on making a case that his sister found persuasive. "Seriously. Amy's different and that's the point."

"How so?"

"The others were predictable," Ty explained, having analyzed the heck out of his own dating dry spell. "I knew exactly what they'd do when and how the relationship would evolve. I knew when the demands would start, and the arguments, and the shrill bits."

Lauren seemed to be fighting a smile. "The shrill bits?"

"I hate the shrill bits," he admitted and she chuckled. "So, I'd break it off a week or two before we got to that part. I'd meet someone else, sparks would fly, and the whole thing would progress *exactly the same way*. I could see Giselle starting down that path before we even got to the party."

"Your future unfolded before your eyes."

"Sure. The hot sex after the party. The forgotten something or other in my apartment. The phone calls, the dropping by, the contrivance of coincidence."

"And then the shrill bits."

"Inevitably." He shook his head. "Only truly stupid people keep doing the same thing and expecting different results. Something had to change. I didn't know what, so I stepped back."

"To analyze and assess."

"Call it a weakness."

"Until you got stuck in an elevator with a woman who looked like a plain little mouse but ended up setting your straight."

Ty smiled, recognizing a truth when he heard it. "It *was* different."

"I'll bet."

"And Amy's not plain."

"I know that, but most men wouldn't notice. Those cheekbones are awesome, and her complexion..." Lauren rolled her eyes. "I'd love to get my hands in that hair. How long is it?"

"Just past her shoulders," Ty guessed, remembering the length of her ponytail in the class.

"Lots to work with. Feel free to give her my number." Lauren winced. "But be smooth so she isn't insulted."

Ty nodded, although he had no intention of stepping into that minefield. He knew well enough that suggesting a different stylist to one of his sisters carried the possibility of launching the nukes. "The thing is that the more I look, the more I see. Her eyes are like Sophia

Loren's. She has opinions I don't expect. She's not innocent, but is vulnerable. Yet she's worldly in ways that I'm not. She surprises me..."

"And so she's a riddle you feel compelled to solve."

"Exactly." Just uttering the word sent a rush through Ty, and that was when he knew.

Amy was the one.

He'd found Ms. Right, in the most unlikely of places, when he wasn't even looking for her.

CHAPTER NINE

A S TY CAME to terms with his revelation, Lauren kept talking.
"Have you considered that you might be married with a couple of kids by the time you figure out the enigma that is Amy?" she teased.

Ty laughed, not having a problem with that at all. "I might have already sent them to college. I might *never* be able to anticipate her." He shook a finger at his sister. "And that makes me determined to see her again."

"And again and again and again."

"Yes. Even when she sets me straight."

"She did it again?"

"Sunday. I distracted her when it looked like an accident would go down on the freeway. I didn't want her to worry about it. When we got out of there and she figured it out, she said I'd been condescending."

Lauren gave a low whistle. "Well, it is, when you think about it."

"But I hadn't. I was just trying to protect her from the truth, but she doesn't want to be protected like that."

Lauren smiled at him. "What if she doesn't actually need you, big bro?"

"Then maybe I need to convince her otherwise," Ty said with resolve.

That was the nut of it. He looked around his apartment, amazed by the truth that had just fallen from his own lips. It gave him a new sense of purpose.

He looked at Lauren. "Your turn. Why are you really here? Something up with Mark?"

She winced. "Right to the chase."

"You want a drink?"

"Definitely. If you still have some of that single malt Scotch that Katelyn bought you for Christmas, make mine a double."

Ty did. When he came back with the two drinks, Lauren was playing with the flogger again. He took it out of her hand and gave her the drink instead. "Cheers," he said, lifted his glass and savored a substantial sip.

"To Giselle and her usefulness," Lauren said and took a sip. At Ty's glance, she nodded sagely. "Giselle *was* useful, and not just in changing your priorities. The idea of her was useful, so long as she didn't need to show up anywhere. You had almost five entire months without the matchmakers coming after you."

"That was the plan," Ty started, then bit his tongue. He'd been about to say that if not for the wedding, he wouldn't have talked to Amy.

Lauren eyed him. "What aren't you saying?"

"If not for the wedding, I wouldn't have introduced Amy to all of you," Ty said, which was true but not all of the truth.

Lauren nodded agreement. "I hear you. I sometimes wonder if I only married Mark to stop Mom's pestering." She sipped her drink and stared out the window.

"She means well."

"Yes," Lauren said in a long exhalation. "That's always the rationale."

"Anything you want to talk about?"

"Bumps in the road," she said lightly and he knew she wasn't ready to tell anyone more. "We'll work it out." Her words didn't ring with her usual cheerful confidence, though. She claimed the flogger again and spun it around, flicking it in the air. She snapped it against her palm. "It does sting a bit." If it was an attempt to distract Ty, it didn't work.

"You know where I am if and when you want to talk."

Lauren widened her eyes and brandished the flogger. "But you might be all tied up when I need you."

"Ha ha."

"Seriously, what *is* this about? Is Amy the damsel you want to distress?"

Ty ducked that question, his urge to protect Amy and her reputation amongst his family not something he could dismiss. "I'm curious," he said. "The club is offering classes and they're really popular."

"Let me guess. Kyle's idea?"

"Yes, and it's amazing how well it's working."

"Changing the tone of things a bit?"

"In surprising ways. We have a lot of older couples signing up. A new demographic for us, and a profitable one."

"Kyle was probably just thinking about the sex."

"Don't be so hard on him. He's the most honest person I know."

"Maybe you should get out more."

"Maybe you should give credit where it's due. Kyle is absolutely up-front about his disinterest in commitment. When it comes to romance, he's in for a good time but not a long time, and every woman he dates knows it in five minutes."

"He's going to get a disease one of these days."

"And when he does, he'll be direct about that, as well." Ty frowned and shook his head. Lauren had always been hard on Kyle, and he didn't understand it. "I'm sorry you two never saw eye to eye."

"Since he's one of your oldest friends." Lauren smiled. "Who says opposites don't attract?"

"He's brilliant at identifying new trends," Ty said, then grimaced when his gaze fell on the *shibari* book again. "But I don't get this one."

"And in true Ty fashion, you're going to analyze it to the smallest molecule and figure it out." Lauren's manner turned thoughtful as she studied the flogger. She sipped her Scotch. "Want to know what I think?"

"Sure."

"It's probably about different things for different people, but I wonder whether the abdication of responsibility is the appeal for some women."

"Excuse me?" There were times when his sister sounded more like a psychologist than a hairdresser, but then, maybe that came with the territory.

"Think about it. A lot of women solve everything for everybody in their lives. Their own needs come last, if at all." Lauren waved her glass. "I see it all the time at the shop. They think they're being self-indulgent by taking half an hour to get a haircut instead of running

144

errands or getting things done for their family." She lifted her glass, watching the amber liquid swirl in the light. "I wonder sometimes what their sex lives are like."

"You don't." Ty wasn't really shocked.

"I do." Lauren met his gaze. "I mean, what if it's all about the mister getting it off? What's left for her? Is it just wham, bam, and hey, the game's back on? If a haircut is an indulgence then I can believe an orgasm would be a bigger one." She leaned forward again, as serious as he'd ever seen her. "What if the fantasy is less about the nuts and bolts of it all, and more about being completely irresponsible and self-absorbed? Of thinking of nothing but their own pleasure? Of having a man determined to ensure their sensual satisfaction at any cost, maybe instead of the one they do have?"

Ty had to wonder whether she was talking about herself and Mark.

He had to wonder whether that was the appeal to Amy. She'd taken care of two dying parents and now was trying to keep her house, alone, with a crappy job. How often did she indulge herself?

He thought of that one hot coffee every Friday at lunch and knew she deserved a lot more.

Lauren sipped before she continued. "It would be a powerful idea, especially if that kind of indulgence never happened in real life. It explains the need to submit and surrender, too, as part of the compact. The situation is out of the woman's hands but still under her control, because she's named the terms. All she has to do is feel." She sipped again. "And luxuriate. What's not to love about that?"

There was a moment of silence between them, the lights of the city twinkling far below. A siren echoed from the street and Lauren cleared her throat. "Every day, I see so many women melt at the smallest sensual pleasure. I watch them close their eyes when I massage the shampoo into their hair. Some of them shiver. Some of them sigh. Most of them capitulate and their bodies show it in ways they don't realize." She met Ty's gaze, her own filled with concern.

Did she see her own future in her clients?

Ty made a joke because he needed to see his sister smile. "And the guy has to be a billionaire so he can pay someone else to do all those errands."

Lauren laughed. "Staff to pick up his shirts, take his kids to swimming class and soccer games, do the grocery shopping and the cooking. Maybe." She took another sip. "Or maybe wealth is a fantasy all in itself." She looked around his apartment with admiration, but her next words surprised him. "Always the neat freak."

"What?"

"Your room was always organized and tidy. Military precision when you made your bed. Mom was always so proud that your room wasn't a pit, like Katelyn's." Lauren pursed her lips. "I always figured you had a secret. I imagined some pretty good ones over the years. You might have been secretly gay."

Ty gave her a mock scowl. "Seriously?"

"If so, you did a really good job of hiding it. I've never met anyone so obviously heterosexual."

"Is that a crime?"

"No. It's reassuring." She brandished the flogger. "But this goes well beyond anything I suspected in the secret department. And unless I miss my bet, you're curious for a different reason than you say, big bro. There's a woman feeding your curiosity, and I'm already dying to meet her." She finished her Scotch with a flourish, looking much happier than when she'd arrived.

She stood up and put down the glass on the coffee table. "In fact, I wonder if I already have," she said and tossed the flogger at him.

Ty caught it and shoved it under the couch. "You want me to come down and get you a cab?" he asked, his tone businesslike.

Lauren laughed again. "Which is another way of saying don't let the door hit you in the ass. I'm going, Ty, and I'll get my own cab, thanks." She walked back to the door, humming *Love is All Around*, then paused to wave from the threshold. "Thanks for the drink and the conversation. It was exactly what I needed." Her smile turned mischievous. "Maybe you're a natural for the all-knowing dom who sees the secret desires of his beloved and makes them come true."

"I didn't give you that much Scotch," Ty grumbled and his sister laughed.

He did go down to the lobby with Lauren and he did flag her a cab. He paid for it as well, waving off her thanks. Then he stood on the curb, the city swirling around him, and watched the cab's tail lights as it headed uptown. Lauren waved from the back window, then the cab merged into the traffic and he lost track of it in the throng.

He'd never told her as much, but he really didn't like Mark. Never had. Never would. If their marriage was falling apart, Ty wouldn't cry. In fact, if their marriage was falling apart because Mark didn't treasure Lauren, then the bastard didn't deserve her. Ty's mom would see things differently, but divorce might be good for Lauren.

It might give her a chance at real happiness, and he wanted that for her, and all of his sisters, as much as he wanted it for himself.

Ty strode back to his apartment, reviewing their conversation, seeking clues as to what was really bothering Lauren. What resonated in his thoughts instead was her speculation about the appeal of bondage.

The abdication of responsibility.

Was that part of the allure for Amy? Ty thought of her references to her cousin's wedding plans, and her role in making that particular dream come true. It had already seemed to him like she was the one running that show, not the cousin or the aunt. He thought of her leaving college to take care of her parents, and never having the chance to go back. He thought of the woman from her office interrupting Amy's lunch so she could fix the copier, a job that surely could have waited or one that somebody else would have solved. He thought of Mr. Forsythe, going for lunch when his flight was canceled in Dallas and letting Amy sort it out for him, instead of walking up to the service desk and solving it himself.

Was Amy the one who fixed everything for everyone else?

Did Amy's dreams and desires come last?

Did they have to?

If this private lesson at the club was her attempt to put her own desires first for a change, Ty was going to make sure she got exactly what she wanted. He would give her a taste of pleasure that would haunt her, maybe even compel her to put herself first.

He cracked open the *shibari* book and chose a pose that required a harness. He was sure they had these in the shop.

Ty could do this.

He *had* to do this, for Amy.

And he would do it, because the one thing Tyler McKay did best of all was to succeed.

It was crazy.

It was thrilling.

It was probably the most daring thing Amy had ever done in her life. It was certainly the most daring thing she'd done in years, and her adrenaline was pumping. Amy reminded herself that it was also *safe*. She was at F5, one of the biggest and most successful deluxe fitness clubs in Manhattan. Nothing bad would happen to her.

She might just learn something.

And she would see Matteo again. That alone made her body hum.

She was early, which wasn't surprising given how fired up she was. She looked at all the merchandise in the shop and her heart skipped in anticipation. She flipped through the *shibari* book again and felt faint at the prospect of trying it herself. Finally, she went to the desk and got directions, then found the change room on the sixth floor. She located the assigned room and knocked.

There was no answer so she opened the door.

The room was a good size, probably as big as the living room in her house. The light was indirect and the walls were padded. They were also black, covered with something that felt a lot like leather. Maybe it even was leather. When she shut the door behind herself, she couldn't hear any of the sounds from the gym or the elevators anymore.

There was a box in the middle of the room, upholstered in the same black material, and about waist-high. There were steel loops embedded in it, below each corner and more just above the floor. Amy hooked her finger through one and gave it a tug. It didn't budge.

She shivered. On the far side of the room was a shelf, with an array of gear displayed. There were several hanks of the same shiny rope that they'd used the previous Saturday, and it was blue. There was a velvet hood like the one she'd tried on, and a blindfold. She fingered a leather harness with a ball gag, and a length of thick hemp rope like that used in the *shibari* book. There was tape, about three inches wide and the kind that doesn't stick to skin. There were a pair of ankle shackles and a spreader bar. She swallowed and continued along the shelf.

She stopped cold in front of the nipple clamps. They shone silver, looking small and wicked and so thrilling that her hand shook when she reached out to touch one of them.

There was a rap on the door and she jumped, then spun to face the door.

Matteo opened it, appearing to be larger and more dangerous than he had in the classroom. He was wearing a sweatshirt that was zipped so she couldn't see his tattoo, just a bit of his bare chest. He wore the black hood, just like before, and a pair of black jeans and black boots. "Good evening, Angel," he said in that scrumptious voice, then stepped into the room.

"Good evening, Matteo," she whispered.

He shut the door behind himself and turned the lock with a decisive click. "No one will hear us in this room." He ran a hand along the wall as he walked toward her. "It is designed for complete privacy."

"Like a dungeon," Amy said softly.

"Exactly like one," he agreed. "And once you are bound, you will be trapped here with me, until I choose to let you leave."

Amy's heart fluttered. "Yes," she managed to say.

"Tell me that this is your desire, Angel."

"It is," she said, finding her voice. "I want to be a captive sex slave. Your captive sex slave."

The air sizzled between them, then Matteo took another step toward her. He was bigger than she remembered. Taller and broader and infinitely more intense in private quarters.

Perfect.

"Turn around," he commanded and Amy did as instructed. "Take off your glasses."

Amy did. She folded them and put them on the shelf, then removed her earrings as well and put them beside her glasses. They were a favorite pair that she'd worn for luck. There was a trembling in her belly. Had she ever been so excited? Things were a bit blurry but she saw Matteo pick up the velvet hood.

"You came back for more," he murmured. "Are you a naughty Angel, then?"

"I think so," Amy admitted.

He chuckled and the sound made the hair rise on the back of her neck. "So, shall I teach you to be more naughty? Or should I punish you for your wickedness?"

"Maybe both," Amy said, then the velvet hood slid over her head. She melted when Matteo wrapped his hands around her head and smoothed the cloth down to her neck. He tugged the laces at the back, securing the hood, and gave her a little jerk before he fastened the lace. Amy stumbled a bit, but his hands landed on her shoulders.

They were strong and warm, and he lifted her to her toes, drawing her back against him. His chest was as hard as a rock. "Such a naughty angel," he murmured in her ear. "My favorite kind." He wrapped one arm around her there and it was like a steel band trapping her upper arms against her sides. His other hand rose to touch her chin, then his thumb moved across her lips. It was a caress but an emphatic one, one that pulled her mouth and left her feeling a little disheveled.

"Such a mouth is made for kissing, Angel," he whispered, then tipped her head back so that her cheek was against his chest. He brushed his lips over hers.

A jolt of lightning shot through Amy at his touch, electrifying her and heating her blood. She heard herself gasp and Matteo chuckled again.

"So naughty," he whispered. "I look forward to teaching you to behave."

Amy's heart was thundering.

His hands slid down her arms, then he bracketed her waist in his strong grip and held her against him. "And so you looked at the toys," he mused. "That is good. We will choose favorites."

Favorites. More than one.

Amy swallowed.

"Which rope, Angel? Or do you prefer the tape?"

"The blue rope first," she said, hearing how breathless her voice was. "Although I'm curious about the tape, as well. And, well, the jute, too."

"So very wicked," he whispered. "Any special requests? Or do you abandon yourself to me?"

Amy shivered at that. Then she thought of her book. "I'd like to be stretched taut and captive," she said, hardly daring to believe she'd said the words aloud.

"Your wish, Angel, is my command." He left her standing there and moved away. She thought she heard something fall and wonder if he'd taken off his sweatshirt. She wished she could see him.

He reached around her from behind to knot her wrists together in front of her and Amy felt like she was standing in his embrace. It felt like he was using the heavy jute rope, which made her think about that book. She felt his bare skin against her back and dared to lean against him.

"No hair," she whispered, without meaning to do as much.

"I shaved for you, Angel," he said quietly.

"You shouldn't have. I like when men have hair, if it's not too much."

"This is good to know." He moved slowly and steadily as they talked, wrapping the rope around her wrists over and over again. When they were securely bound together with at least a dozen wraps of the rope, he lifted them over her head and stepped back. Her wrists were behind her head. He must have knotted the rope again, because he wrapped it around her ribs, just below her bust, knotting it again at the front so it wrapped around her.

"Like this?"

Amy wriggled and the realization that she couldn't free herself made her breath hitch. "Yes," she managed to say. "Is this *shibari*?"

"Not yet." Matteo wrapped the rope around her, knotting each loop at the back and encasing her down to her waist. It surrounded her like a corset, but one made of rope. He worked steadily and slowly, his deliberation making her aware that she was being bound, and that she was letting it happen.

No, she'd asked for it to happen.

She'd paid for it to happen.

Her heart was galloping, but she didn't move away.

"And this is a good time to talk of our safe word," Matteo said quietly. "What is your choice."

"Red light is good," Amy said, her voice a little higher than it had been.

"And right now?"

"Green light," she said, trying to fill her voice with authority.

"Good," Matteo purred, then tied the last knot more tightly. "I think you like this, Angel." He ran his hands over her, his touch proprietary and firm. "You are not quite helpless."

"I could run."

"But you will not."

"I could scream."

Once again he rubbed his fingers over her mouth in that proprietary gesture. "But you will not, Angel."

No, she wouldn't.

She wouldn't do anything that might make him stop.

His lips must have been against her ear when he whispered again. "What else?"

"The nipple clamps," Amy said before she lost her nerve.

Matteo paused for a heartbeat, then moved behind her. "Well, well," he whispered in her ear, then cupped her breasts, one in each hand. He pinched the nipples and drew her to her toes. Amy squirmed in delight. She could feel the hardness and the heat of his body behind her and something against her butt that could only be his erection. If he was enjoying this half as much as she was, then maybe they were made for each other.

Then Matteo rolled each nipple between one finger and one

thumb, pinching them with the perfect exquisite amount of pressure, and she thought she might melt with the pleasure.

And that was before he made the torment complete by fastening on the clamps.

Ty would never forget his first glimpse of Amy in that room, or the way she jumped a little when he opened the door. There was a moment when he was afraid she would recognize him, but she didn't.

He made sure she didn't have much chance to do so, by lacing on the hood that she liked so well. Her mouth softened as it had before, and he wished she was wearing that pink lipstick. He couldn't resist the urge to touch her and to taste her, and barely kept himself from doing more.

It was titillating to bind her wrists and secure them, to truss her to her own specifications and with her compliance. The game was effective, as far as Ty was concerned. He wanted Amy already, but this tease was making him much more desperate to have her.

Repeatedly.

The space felt charged with sexual energy. He felt keenly aware of every breath she took, every glance she cast his way, and thought he could hear the nervous flutter of her heart. He could smell her perfume, a subtle floral scent, mingling with the leather that upholstered the room. He'd been certain she'd use the safe word, but when she was completely bound, he heard her quick intake of breath.

He smelled her arousal.

Then she asked for the nipple clamps.

Ty thought he would explode.

He savored the chance to fondle her breasts. Her nipples were already hard, but he remembered the lessons from the video and didn't just caress them to be tighter. He pinched them hard a couple of times, as well, mixing the pain and the pleasure. Amy's lips were parted and she was breathing quickly by the time he fastened on the first clamp. She shivered, from head to toe, licked her lips, then straightened for the second one.

There was heat coming off her in waves. She had to be slick and wet and ready. Ty could have tossed her over that box and stripped off her yoga pants, then given them both what they wanted, but there were rules.

His rules, ironically enough.

Tonight, it had to be about the sensation and the tease.

The sizzle and not the steak.

The fact was that he wanted Amy more than he'd wanted any woman in his life, and Ty already knew that wasn't going to change anytime soon.

"I want you suspended," he said, keeping his voice gruff. "So, that you swing from your bonds and are helpless to my will."

She swallowed. "Yes, please," she said, her voice breathless and uncertain. He was sure he didn't imagine that she trembled just a little.

"And then I will spank you, my naughty Angel."

"Yes," she said, her voice more faint. Ty recognized that she needed some reassurance. Tender and tough. That was the combination. He let his fingers trail along her jaw, his thumb sliding over her mouth in that slow caress. She trembled, the fight going out of her body, and her mouth softened.

Invitingly.

He brushed his lips across hers and tasted her gasp of delight.

"But you must beg me first and convince me," he murmured against her mouth.

"Please," she said, then licked her lips.

He licked her lips and she shivered with pleasure. "Matteo," he said, framing her face in his hands.

"Matteo," she echoed, her throat working. "Please make me helpless and use me for your pleasure, Matteo."

Her mouth was too enticing to resist. He kissed her again, lingering over the embrace, feeling her lean against him. It was a long, slow, sweet kiss that only got more intense, the way the best kisses could. "And then what, Angel?"

"Discipline me," she demanded, her voice husky. "Teach me the price of being naughty, Matteo."

"And then?" He claimed another kiss.

"Keep me captive and do it again."

"You will not escape me, Angel," he growled and she quivered in anticipation. "Do not move."

"No, Matteo."

He reached for one of the short chains secured to hooks in the ceiling and let it rattle as he unfurled it. Amy practically stood at attention. He fastened a leather harness to it, then belted it around her waist securely. Amy caught her breath and Ty lifted her to fasten the belt to the chains on her sides. He stepped back and checked that her toes just barely brushed the floor.

He gave her a push and she swung, powerless to stop herself.

The books said that being aware of the futility of the situation heightened the thrill.

"Fight it," he commanded. "Break free."

Amy tried, without success, and he saw a flush rise over her skin. Her mouth was open then, her breath coming quickly, and he could see the pulse at her throat.

He got the leather paddle and abruptly caught her ankles in his hands, then held them in one hand. He spun her around, pulled up her feet and smacked her bare soles hard. Amy jolted and shook, then Ty bent and kissed the bottom of her foot. He slid his fingertips across the bare flesh, following the smack with a caress, and she quivered.

She was practically humming and they'd barely started. They were complicit in exploring her fantasy, a delicious and forbidden one, and he felt an intimacy that he hadn't anticipated.

He wasn't going to disappoint her.

Ty stood behind her and closed his hands over her breasts again, teasing those nipple clamps. He could feel the anxious skip of Amy's heart, but he knew it was a good kind of anxiety, an anticipation that he wasn't going to disappoint.

"We have only begun, my Angel."

"Yes!" she said, the word falling from her lips in a single rush.

"And what do you want?"

"More!" she declared. "Don't stop, please, Matteo!"

When his own heart pounded faster, Tyler couldn't believe that he'd been missing out all this time.

There was more to these games than he'd ever guessed.

It was a sensual adventure.

It was dangerous.

It was incredibly, utterly hot.

Amy couldn't believe that her heart could race so quickly. She hadn't known she could ache so hard for a caress. She didn't know she could feel as if she was on fire from head to toe—and be kept in that state of delicious torment for what seemed like an eternity. Matteo knew her body better than she did. He urged her to greater heights of pleasure, then pulled her back. He mixed pain with pleasure so adeptly that she couldn't keep them straight anymore. She was floating. She was in heaven. She was waiting for whatever he would do next.

Desperate for his touch.

She couldn't stand the fact that there wouldn't be any release for either of them, but Matteo had planned otherwise. She felt him step away from her and struggled in her bonds, disliking his absence for even a moment. The sound of his chuckle reassured her, but the feel of his hands on her body was even better. He stood behind her again, his breath in her ear and his warmth wrapped around her. There was no better place to be, in Amy's view.

He was doing something, his hands moving in front of her, but she couldn't see what. She had to trust him, and she was surprised to realize that she did. Then a rope went around her waist and was knotted securely. She was used to that, although she wondered what he had planned. She felt the rope brush her thighs, then his arm was around her waist. "Legs apart," he commanded and she complied. She felt the rope pass between her thighs, then he spun her around and drew it up taut.

Amy gasped as what had to be a knot collided with her clitoris. Even through the cloth of her yoga pants, she could feel that it was the heavy jute. Matteo hooked the end of the rope through the loop already knotted around her waist, then tugged it. The knot drove against her, making Amy twitch with desire.

"Naughty Angel," he said. "Now the punishment begins." When he had pulled the knot against her, he bound the rest of the rope around the top of her thighs. She thought of a picture in the *shibari* book and was thrilled that he'd read her consent form.

"Struggle," he commanded and Amy twisted. She couldn't move the knot away, and in fact, every move she made only increased the torment. She caught her breath as it rubbed her just right and felt her color rise. It was infuriating that her feet were free but all she could do was kick them in the air. In a way, that made her feel more captive.

He pushed her and she swung, completely helpless to do anything about it.

"Red light?" Matteo asked, and the direction of his voice revealed that he was walking around her.

And looking at her.

Amy smiled and arched her back. "Green light," she gasped.

"You bad, bad angel," he murmured, then the leather paddle cracked across her butt. Amy might have cried out because the pain was sharp, but Matteo caught her face in one strong hand and kissed her. She kissed him back, hungrily, desperate for more.

"You should know better than to surrender yourself to me," he said, his voice rough. "Where do you think I got these tattoos, Angel?"

"I don't know, Matteo."

"Prison," he growled. "Where violence is not a game."

"You must have been innocent," she said, but he only laughed.

"There are no innocents there." The leather cracked against her butt once more and Amy gasped. This time, it was his fingers rubbing roughly across her lips and she opened her mouth to run her tongue across his knuckles. "There will be no innocents here when I am done," he continued and her heart leaped. She nipped at his hand with her teeth and he chuckled darkly. "Wicked angel, I will give you what you have come for."

His kiss sent fire through her blood, his need feeding her own. She wanted him, though she knew it couldn't happen here, but her desire was so primal that she couldn't think beyond it. Their kiss was open-mouthed, devouring, so furious that she moaned and he swallowed the sound. She felt his hand close around her nape, holding her captive to his kiss, and she reveled in it.

All too soon, he stepped back and she felt bereft.

She whispered his name.

"We count to twenty," he said harshly then stepped back and spanked her again, the blow stinging and making her swing. Amy moaned from the depths of her soul.

Then another soul-melting kiss and his hands, his wonderful strong hands, roving over her.

Like she was a prized possession.

A captive treasure.

A hunger he could never satisfy.

Matteo stepped back and Amy braced herself, but it wasn't enough for the smack across her thighs. She jumped and the knot pressed against her sex and she trembled with need even before he kissed her again.

Amy made it to seven, which she thought was some kind of miracle. When Matteo locked his hands around her head and kissed her that time, she came in a tidal wave of pleasure, bucking against him in her release.

That she heard him moan only made her orgasm last longer.

Then there was only Matteo, his solid strength, his warmth and power as he held her close and kissed her deeply. He swallowed her ecstatic cries and she was dizzy with the potency of his touch.

It was perfect.

Even before she caught her breath, Amy knew she wanted more.

"Bad Angel," he whispered against her ear, his voice hoarse. "We must begin again."

And she moaned, because he had guessed her desire so well.

Ty was raging.

He swam fifty laps, lifted weights for an hour, and still couldn't put his desire for Amy out of his mind. He stood in his apartment, looking over the city, doing serious damage to that bottle of Scotch.

Amy had demanded Matteo's phone number at the end of the session. Ty had stalled, astonished by her request, and she'd jammed a piece of paper with her number into his hand. She'd been so nervous that she'd left in a hurry and forgotten her earrings. Ty had taken them and now considered them, sitting on his counter beside the crumpled note.

Call me.

Fuck.

How was he going to give her back the earrings? He should turn them in at F5's lost and found, but he wanted to make sure she got them back. They were elegant and simple. They were also 18K gold. Plain hoops with a little pearl dangling from each one. He had a feeling they might have been her mother's or a gift from her parents. They were as eloquent an expression of Amy's nature as the way she'd come trembling in his arms.

What had been in his head? Why had he pretended to be Matteo?

It was true what they said, that every lie led to another, but now he was caught in a tangle of his own making and unsure what to do.

How could Ty *not* have pretended to be Matteo? How could he have let any other guy play those games with Amy?

Telling her the truth now couldn't possibly be a good thing.

Continuing the charade could only be a mistake.

Call me.

Ty replayed every minute of their private session and wanted her more and more.

Her orgasm had nearly finished him.

On the one hand, Ty didn't know how he'd survived that hour without stripping Amy naked and giving her what they both wanted.

He hadn't lied to her: there was nothing more sexy than a woman wanting him. It had just about killed him to make her writhe—and come—but be unable to do more than that.

On the other hand, he hadn't wanted their private session to end. It had seemed like an hour stolen out of time, when it didn't matter that she didn't know the truth about who he was and there was only pleasure to be shared.

But it did matter.

It mattered a lot.

If she ever found out he'd really been Matteo, she'd despise him.

If he apologized, would she be relieved or furious?

Ty hated having any deception between them. It wasn't in his nature to deceive, and he knew he wasn't good at it.

If Amy didn't find out that he'd really been Matteo, she might pursue a relationship with his alter-ego instead of with him. The very idea was strange and troubling.

Surely Amy was more practical than that.

Surely Ty could make sure she was more practical than that.

He drained the Scotch. He'd buy a burner phone for Matteo and make sure.

CHAPTER TEN

HOME AGAIN after the best hour of her life, Amy was exultant. She knew she should write, but she was too excited to sit still. Matteo had been everything she dreamed of, and more. Her sensual adventure and experiment had practically blown her mind.

She'd brought Ty's flowers home the day before and they perched on her kitchen table like a silent accusation. He would be completely shocked by what she'd done.

It was almost worth telling him, just to see his reaction.

Almost, but not quite.

Amy eyed the flowers and felt guilty, as if she'd lied to Ty.

Although she hadn't.

They were only having a fake date, after all.

Well, a few fake dates.

She squirmed a bit, feeling that wasn't all of the truth, but there was no way she'd confess her secret desires to him.

Even though she'd called him a chicken.

Amy determinedly pulled out her pad of paper and got her pen. She had writing to do.

Inspiration had, after all, been fed by her research. Lothair was in agony, and only Argenta had the audacity to reach out and help him. Now, Amy knew how to make that scene better.

The castle was silent, save for the crown prince's agonized cries. I darted through the corridors that led from the kitchen to the hall, following the sounds of

159

his pain. As I ran, my outrage grew that not one soul lifted a hand to help him. They feigned ignorance of his suffering, and I knew that even if I had been commanded to do so, I would have defied that instruction.

No one should suffer so alone. I did not care what his sins had been

There were two flights of stairs rising from the hall, one on either side of the massive hearth. Dogs lay before the glowing coals on that hearth, though they were not asleep. I could see the gleam of their eyes and their readiness.

The crown prince's cries troubled them, at least.

The stairs to the right were narrower and appeared to twist more, but his cries came from their summit. I shielded the candle with my hand and darted up the stairs. They were crooked and narrow, and the stone steps were cold beneath my feet. Near their base, there was dust upon them, and I glimpsed spider webs in the corners, and my indignation at the crown prince's expense grew.

Who served him?

What was the merit of being the heir to the king, if he was shown no greater care than an abandoned dog?

The stairs seemed to be endless, winding high into the sky. I thought of the single spire that graced the keep, the tower that rose high above its squat companion, and guessed my destination. The air chilled with every step and the darkness seemed to grow. The crown prince's shouts were louder and made the hair stand up on the back of my neck.

And that was before a chance gust extinguished my candle.

I stumbled and almost lost my balance, well aware of the long fall behind me. I gripped the steps, the shadows pressing against me on all sides. I felt my palms go damp and smelled my own perspiration.

My own rare nightmares have been of falling endlessly, the deepest of terror fed by the certainty that there was no one to pluck me out of the abyss. These stairs could have been my nightmares come to life. I was alone. No one would aid me. This was abandonment of another kind.

My spirit quailed and I might have huddled there trembling until the dawn, but the crown prince cried out again. He, too, was lost in an abyss that terrified him. My mother had always tugged me back to the light with her touch, arousing me from sleep and banishing my terror.

I could do that for the crown prince.

Someone should.

Ty went to the bookstore on his lunch. He wasn't entirely certain he could face Amy and not give away the truth, at least not yet.

And he needed a new book anyway, one without any BDSM. Even one without any sex. A nice tidy thriller, with a diabolical serial killer and a sleuth who figured out the truth in time. That would be perfect.

He heard Jade's voice when he walked into the store, but headed for the mystery section.

"It's fabulous," Jade enthused. "And it was six kinds of wicked for you to give me this much and not the ending. This is the best erotic romance I've read all year. I nearly died Monday night when I realized I didn't have it all. If I'd had your number, I'd have called and woken you up."

Ty glanced up at the excitement in Jade's voice.

"Where *were* you this week?"

"I had appointments," a woman said and Ty's eyes widened in recognition of her voice.

Amy?

"Well, hand over the rest. I need to know how it ends."

Ty ducked down to consider a book on a lower shelf and shamelessly eavesdropped. Amy was writing an erotic romance?

He wasn't sure whether to be shocked or thrilled.

Titillated. He was definitely titillated.

And relieved.

"It's not done yet," Amy said. "I still have to write the dark moment and the big finish..."

"And here you are talking to me when you could be writing!" Jade complained. "Go finish the book."

"You're sure it's good?"

"Yes! Lothair is so hot and damaged and violent, but Argenta brings out the tenderness in him." Jade sighed. "You can see right away that no matter what he does to her, he isn't going to break her, and that she's the only one who really understands him."

"Do you believe she can heal him?"

"I know she can! Now write it already. I want to know what happens when he has her tied down in his tower room."

Ty leaned back against the end cap as relief surged through him. Matteo was *research*. Amy was writing an erotic romance, so she was doing research at F5. He was more reassured than he could have believed possible.

But why *should* he be relieved? His reaction lasted only seconds. She had a perfect right to have fantasies and explore them, just as she'd insisted to him on Sunday. Whether she wrote about them or not was immaterial. In fact, now that he'd explored some of them with her, he was more than ready to investigate more. There was a lot to be said for the safe investigation of fantasies.

But he was still relieved. Ty smiled that his relief was because Amy was doing exactly what he would have done.

Research.

Which was just more evidence that they were right for each other.

Ty looked around the end of the shelf but Amy was leaving, carrying a large envelope that had to contain her book manuscript.

Would she confide in him? She'd said she had a plan for a new job. Was this it?

Would she let him help with her research?

Maybe he didn't need a new book so badly, after all. Ty grabbed one blindly off the shelf and paid for it, then headed to the food court in the hopes of lunch with Amy.

It had to be her guilty conscience, but Amy could have sworn that Ty knew what she'd done with Matteo. There was a knowing gleam in his eye when he sauntered into the food court, so unpredictably late that she halfway thought he'd been at the bookstore, too.

But she would have seen him, surely.

He dropped a paperback on the table, its spine uncracked.

Had he been in the bookstore? The possibility of him knowing about her book was almost as worrisome as him learning about Matteo.

"New book?" she asked, hearing a strain in her own voice.

"Yeah, I picked it up last night but haven't started yet." He eyed the large envelope containing her book manuscript. "You?"

Amy rummaged in her bag and pulled out the first book she grabbed. It didn't have a cover on it.

"I thought you finished that one."

"Reading it again," she said. "It was that good."

"But not covering it up. Interesting."

Amy had nothing to say to that. She felt herself blush, though, because she'd been caught and she had a feeling he knew it.

Ty sat down opposite her instead of in the spot diagonally across from her. He unwrapped his sandwich, then picked up his own book. He stretched out his legs and crossed them at the ankles. Amy looked down. He'd never done that before and it kind of barricaded her into her spot.

It looked possessive to her in a way that Ty usually wasn't.

She looked up to find him watching her, but he glanced

immediately down at his book.

What did he know?

"I have a theory for you," he said lightly. "A quote from Oscar Wilde."

"Another one." Amy smiled at his nod.

"'Everything in the world is about sex except sex. Sex is about power.'" Ty arched a brow. "Maybe that's what those books are about."

Amy propped her chin on her hand to consider this. "Maybe. But maybe not the kind of power you think."

"What kind of power am I thinking about?"

"Physical power. Control."

"Not emotional power? Control over the relationship and its direction."

"I'm thinking of the power of a woman's desires and fantasies. Taking control of those and exploring them, regardless of what other people might think."

"It could be the same thing."

"Not to some people. For some people, sex happens a certain way, by the man's choice, because that keeps women in their place." Amy made curly quotes with her fingers around the last three words.

Ty shook a finger at her. "Freud said that the largest sexual organ was the mind."

Amy smiled. "I like that. I think it's true. Fantasy and desire are more potent than sensation and what goes where."

"And both together make for better sex, as well as greater intimacy." He nodded. "I like it."

"Me, too," Amy said and they shared one of those smiles that could launch an inferno. "I've hardly seen you this week," she said then, and he looked down at his lunch.

"Well, you'll have a big break from me next week. I'm going to Tokyo on Monday."

Amy's heart sank. "Japan?"

Ty nodded easily. "We meet with other bankers in other markets periodically. The senior partner, Mr. Fleming, is cutting back on his traveling this year, so has been handing trips off to me."

"Beijing in February," Amy said, remembering how he'd met Giselle.

Ty nodded. "Right. Prague in April, Tokyo this month, then Paris and London in October."

"Glamorous life," Amy said, not wanting to ask about their fake date for Brittany's wedding. The last thing she wanted was to sound like a nag.

"It has its perks," Ty said, then leaned across the table. "I'll be back for Brittany's rehearsal dinner on Friday night."

"Are you sure?"

"I promised and I'll be here," Ty said, interrupting her with resolve. He met her gaze steadily. "I might be jet-lagged and a little wrinkled, but I'll be here."

Amy smiled at the notion of Ty being disheveled. "Okay. Thanks."

"Look," he said, leaning across the table. "You have my number but give me yours so I can call you when I land on Friday. I can pick you up here and we'll drive out to New Jersey together."

"Okay, but I should give you the address for the church, too," Amy said. "Just in case, you're running late."

"Sounds good. And you still have to walk me through your family tree."

"Right," Amy said. "Well, there's my cousin, obviously..."

"No, no, no," Ty said. "My family tree deserved a dinner and so does yours. Tomorrow night? We can go to the same place or somewhere different. Your choice."

"You should let me treat."

"No way."

"That's not part of the deal."

"Sure it is." He smiled, looking unrepentant and a little bit wicked. Resolute. Amy's heart skipped a beat, even though she knew that Ty could never be wicked, much less dangerous. He might be a fake rake, at worst, an apparent rogue with a heart of gold. Yes, that was it. "Six?"

"I'm going to cook for you one of these days."

"Is that a threat or a promise?"

"A promise. I'm a very good cook. Mama taught me."

Ty smiled. "Then I'll definitely be taking you up on that." He glanced at his watch and his eyes widened. "I've got an appointment. See you tomorrow?"

Later that afternoon, Amy realized she'd left her favorite earrings at F5, in the private room. It said something for how distracted she'd been about Matteo and the inspiration he'd provided that she hadn't thought of them immediately.

She stopped at F5 on the way home, but they weren't in the lost and found. The girl on the desk took her name and number and said she'd have the room checked. She promised to call if they turned up.

Amy tried not to think about losing them forever.

They'd been her mom's.

Instead, she went home and wrote. She wrote and wrote and wrote. The story was really coming together and she was motivated by Jade's praise. She just wanted to get it all down, while it was perfect in her thoughts.

It was after nine when Amy's phone rang. She retrieved it from her purse, but didn't recognize the number. She answered anyway.

"Hello, Angel," Matteo growled and she smiled with pleasure. "I have a phone now, just for you."

Amy frowned, wondering whether she'd misunderstood him. She couldn't be the only one who felt the power of the attraction between them.

Could she?

Did he have other women who requested private sessions?

The idea bothered Amy.

A lot.

He gave her the number. "Call anytime, Angel. I will always talk to you."

She copied down the number. "I forgot my earrings last night, Matteo. Did you see them?"

"I have them, Angel," he said and she breathed a sigh of relief. "Should I leave them at the desk for you?"

"Why don't you keep them until we see each other next?" she dared to suggest.

Matteo didn't answer for a moment, as if he'd been surprised. "I did not think there would be a next time, Angel."

"Of course, there will be," Amy had time to say before she heard a phone ring in the background.

"Calling late is better, Angel. I will dream of you," Matteo vowed, then was gone.

Amy programmed his number into her phone, thinking about what he'd said—and hadn't said. She had a bad feeling.

Just how many angels did Matteo have?

Amy was up late enough that it seemed she'd just put her head on the pillow when the alarm rang. She could hear the rain and wanted to just burrow beneath the covers and stay in bed.

Preferably with someone else.

She forced herself out of bed and headed off to work. To her surprise, the morning was awesome. Mrs. Murphy offered her a small raise and Red called with good news.

The end of the buckets in the attic was in sight.

Amy's heart gave that little skip when she came down for lunch and saw Ty waiting for her. Would she ever get used to seeing him there?

He glanced up and smiled. She got her Friday coffee, liking how he put his book aside and rose to his feet when she approached the table.

A perfect gentleman, every time.

"Good news and bad news," Amy said by way of greeting. She sat down and Ty did the same.

"Good news first, if I have a choice," he said. "I'll have time to brace myself for the bad."

"It's not that bad."

"Phew." He wiped a hand over his brow and she laughed at him.

"I heard from Red this morning," she confided.

He glanced up, his eyes bright. "And?"

"He's arranged a line of credit. It's not huge but I think it's enough for the roof, which is really all I wanted."

"That is good news. Congratulations." He toasted her with his bottle of water, and Amy lifted her steaming cup of coffee. "Dinner will be celebratory, then. We have to go to my favorite place again."

"That's the bad news," Amy said. "I can't go for dinner."

"Why not?"

"Because I want to have a party, and I'm going to have to start cooking tonight."

Ty sat back to study her. "Am I invited?" he asked with a smile.

"Yes! That's why it's not such bad news."

"Here I thought I was being punished for something."

"You told me you thought that stuff was too complicated," Amy teased and he gave her a simmering look. She had a sudden thought. "I hope you didn't make sure this worked out with Red's bank."

"No." Ty shook his head and held up one hand. "Scout's honor. I just gave you his card and that's it. Whatever was accomplished, you did it yourself. You and I made a deal."

When he looked at her so intently, Amy believed him.

"What about this party?"

"Well, I was thinking of having Derek look at the roof this weekend."

"Good idea. He won't be working with the holiday. The weather is supposed to be good, too."

"And since Paige is going to want to come, maybe you would, too."

Ty smiled. "To defend you against the curiosity of the princess."

"My mom used to have a yard party every year on Memorial Day. It was wonderful, kind of the launch to summer each year. She asked friends and neighbors, and we always had such a good time."

"And it's a tradition that has lapsed," Ty guessed.

"Until now," Amy said. "I want to do it again this weekend, but with you going to Japan, it'll have to be Sunday. Do you think that's too short notice?"

Ty chuckled. "You could call Paige right now and she'd be tapping her toe on your porch when you got home, no matter what else she was doing when the phone rang."

Amy laughed. "Will you come?"

"Absolutely. Will you have enough time?"

"I'll shop tonight and have a full day in the kitchen tomorrow. I have lists already, and it'll be a lot of work, but I'm excited. The house hasn't seen a party for a long time." She looked up to find Ty watching her warmly.

"You don't have to cook."

"Actually, I do."

"Need some help?"

"No, thank you. I might get weepy, going through my mom's cookbooks. She always wrote little notes in them. Probably better if it's just Fitzwilliam and me."

Ty gave her a considering look, then nodded. "All right. What can I bring?"

"Oh, nothing..."

"What about the wine?" Ty lifted a finger when she would have argued. "They'll see it as a couple thing, as us inviting them, so you have to let me help, either with the cooking or with the set-up or with the supplies." He arched a brow. "Or with everything."

"Can you cook?"

"I follow directions well..."

"You do not!"

He chuckled. "I do some basic cooking."

Amy smiled and leaned over the table. "I'll be making pasta."

"From scratch?"

"It's the only way."

"Now I'm impressed. Making pasta is way out of my league, though."

"Once you've had it this way, you'll never be happy with the dried stuff," Amy said.

"No, I have a feeling there's no going back," Ty murmured and she glanced up at him. His eyes were twinkling and she had the definite sense he wasn't talking about food. "You have a preference for the wine?"

"There's a red table wine that my parents liked..."

Ty enjoyed watching Amy as she talked. She was more animated than when he'd first met her and he liked to think he'd played a part in that. She trusted him, and she was becoming more confident in herself.

And today, triumphant in getting the financing she needed and planning a party, she was glowing. Ty was captivated.

"You never quite get around to telling me about your family. Is your cousin that scary?" he teased, wondering if there was something more serious at root.

"She has got a Bridezilla thing going on."

"Ouch."

Amy wrinkled her nose and put down her sandwich. "The thing is that my parents were estranged from my dad's family all my life."

"Because your dad married your mom."

"Not just that. I guess my dad didn't follow his parents' plan for him. My grandfather was an electrician and he started a business that he wanted to pass down. It's still pretty successful. They do work for the trade, but also have a consumer side."

"That's where your aunt works?"

"Yes, she runs the lighting stores. My cousin took some interior design classes, then started to work for Aunt Natalie a few years ago."

"And your dad?"

"He was the only son, and the oldest, but he didn't want to be an electrician or take over the business. He went to college and became a high school English teacher. He wrote poetry."

"Ah, a free spirit."

"In a way, he was." She smiled with obvious affection. "He always said that people should follow their dreams and make themselves happy first."

"Good advice," Ty said, glad that Amy was writing her book. "Are you doing that?" he asked gently.

"I wasn't," she admitted. "But I am now." She hesitated, adorably uncertain. "I didn't tell you before," she admitted in a rush. "But I'm writing a book."

"Really?" Ty was ridiculously pleased that she'd confided in him. "Should I ask what genre?"

Amy laughed. "You can guess."

"You suggested a different ending for that one book."

"And Jade practically dared me to write it. I decided to write another story, though, one that's all my own idea. She's reading it as I go."

"Going well?"

"She likes it so far." She bit her lip. "Would you read it when it's done?"

Ty was jubilant that she'd trust him with her book. "I'm not as familiar with the genre as Jade."

"But you understand stories and books. You can tell me if the structure is good, and the pacing." She sighed. "I would ask my dad to do that if he was here."

"Even in this genre?"

Amy smiled. "When my dad caught me reading Anaïs Nin, he told me to be sure I read Henry Miller, too. He showed me where to find *Tropic of Cancer* in his library."

"And you were how old?"

"Fourteen." Ty knew his surprise showed because Amy laughed at him. "My dad believed that a good book was a good book, regardless of genre."

"He was right."

"Would you?"

"I'd be honored," Ty said and meant it.

"Well, you can't see it until it's done."

"Fair enough."

"So, back to my family," she said and he sensed her relief. "My dad's parents weren't pleased with his choice, I gather, and they were less pleased when he met my mom. She'd just arrived from Italy and he taught a class at the school for people learning English as a second language." Amy smiled. "He always said it only took one look for him to fall hard."

Ty understood that well enough.

"And your mom?"

"She called it *colpo di fulmine*." Ty knew he looked blank. Amy smiled. "Love at first sight."

"It sounds better in Italian."

"Most things about love and romance do."

"So, she taught you Italian?"

Amy nodded. "But I haven't spoken it since she died. Those actually were the first Italian words I've said in years." She looked a little sad but took a steadying breath and smiled at Ty. "I always thought I'd speak it again when I fell in love."

"And teach your kids."

She nodded and he pretended not to have noticed that she swept away a tear.

"What about your mom's family?"

"She didn't have any left. Her brother had been killed in an accident and her dad died of grief. Her mom didn't survive long afterward. My mom decided to start fresh in a new place and moved here by herself."

"That's a bold move."

"I know." He watched pride fill Amy's expression and his chest tightened. "She was fearless. I can't even imagine getting on a plane with five hundred dollars, the clothes on my back and my wits, but she did it."

"And you said she was a dressmaker?"

"She did beautiful work and she understood how to make people look their best. My dad was so proud of how quickly she built up a business."

"And she married him."

Amy shook a finger at him. "Not so quickly as that! Her mom had been completely reliant upon her husband for everything, and as much as she loved them, my mom said a woman had to have her own resources, her own skills, and her own money. She wanted to be independent, even though she loved my dad from the first, too."

"She wanted to establish her own financial footing."

Amy nodded, then she sighed. "They'd known each other seven years by the time they got married. I wonder if they'd have married sooner if they'd known what was ahead of them."

"Maybe, maybe not. It sounds as if they were a couple even before they were married." Ty shrugged. "Sometimes a marriage certificate is just a piece of paper."

Amy gave him a considering look. "I thought you'd be all for tradition."

"I'm all for true love conquering all obstacles. The legal details are less important than the love and trust of two people being together who are right for each other."

"I think you might be right." Her smile turned mischievous. "My mother was pregnant at the wedding."

"With you?"

"With me. At any rate, I understand there was a big fight when they got married and no one from my dad's family attended. They were complete strangers to me until about a year ago."

Ty thought it was pretty harsh that her father's family hadn't even reconciled with him before his death, never mind that they'd never helped Amy with the burden of care, but she had become quiet and he wanted to coax her smile.

There was no point in dwelling on the past. "So, walk me through the family tree. Your dad was oldest and the only boy."

"Right. He has three younger sisters: Pauline, who is divorced from Craig, Natalie, who is married to Tom who runs the family business now, and Sara, married to Daniel."

"The bride-to-be, Brittany, is Natalie and Tom's oldest?"

"She's their only child, and just between you and me, she's a bit spoiled."

"I would never have guessed," Ty murmured and Amy smiled.

"Pauline has a daughter and two sons, all of whom are married with children. Rachel married Duane, who works for Tom, Jake married Kirsten, and Mike married Marie most recently. I can't keep the kids straight, although I have it all written down. Sara had two boys: Andrew and Thomas are just a little younger than me. Andrew just got his certification as an electrician and Thomas is still serving his apprenticeship."

"Everyone into the family business."

"Seems like it."

"And the groom?"

"Nick. His dad's a real estate developer."

"Sounds like a corporate merger."

"My aunt and uncle are pleased with the marriage." Amy shrugged.

"I get the impression that Nick's parents aren't so thrilled."

"Why?"

Amy lifted her hands. "The seating plans were a nightmare. Aunt Natalie and Nick's mom had all these lists of who should sit with whom."

"And a lot of the choices were mutually exclusive?"

Amy nodded wearily. "I was trying to negotiate compromises, then they both started to call the venue independently to force their changes."

"You had to go and sort it out, I'll guess." Ty felt that simmer begin, the one he felt whenever Amy talked about her family.

"I had to go and keep the venue from chucking their deposit money back at them. One wedding isn't supposed to be a full-time job for their catering manager." She took a deep breath. "To be honest, I'm kind of expecting someone to explode at the wedding."

Ty was glad he'd be there. Amy might need a defender. He'd guess that if anything went wrong, they'd blame her. "It'll be fine. I'm sure you did a great job organizing it all."

"And they'll undo it," she said, proving that their expectations were shared. "Just watch."

"But, we will have a fabulous garden party on Sunday, in your mom's tradition," Ty said, raising a finger.

Amy's smile was brilliant and immediate. "We will!"

"Let me call Derek and Paige. You have more than enough to do."

"Thank you." She reached out quickly and touched his hand. "I'll see you Sunday."

"Heartless," he murmured with a shake of his head. "Here I was planning on a great dinner tonight with the best company, and I'll be eating alone."

"I'll make it up to you on Sunday," Amy promised.

"I'm going to hold you to that," Ty vowed, and she laughed before she hurried back to work.

She thought he was just teasing, but Ty was serious. He was disappointed about dinner, and he was even more disappointed that he wouldn't see Amy again until Sunday. Who would have thought that she would have such a hold on him in such a short time?

It must be love.

He could have been glad about that, if it hadn't been for Matteo.

What was he going to do about that loser?

Kyle leaned against the wall in his office as his mom scolded him yet again. It was Friday night at F5 and he had a party in the club to heat up.

Instead, he'd been caught by his mother, whose calls he'd been ducking on his cell phone. She knew him well enough to know where to find him on Friday night.

And Cassie was merciless. She hadn't covered for him at all.

This was what friends were for.

"Your brother is five years younger than you, but he's married with a son and another baby on the way," his mom said for the hundredth time that month. "My younger sisters have three grandchildren each. Kyle, I want to have grandchildren while I can enjoy them."

"Enjoy Dave's kids."

"I do! But it's not just about me. It's about you, honey. You need to have someone in your life..."

"Mom, I'll let you know when I meet the right woman."

"I know, honey, but I'm not at all sure that you're doing anything about meeting women. Every time I talk to you, you're at work..."

"It's a gym, Mom. It's *full* of women." Kyle admired a woman walking past him on her way to yoga class. She cast him a flirtatious smile and he smiled back at her, enjoying the view until she was out of sight.

"But maybe the right kind of women aren't interested in a fitness instructor. Maybe you need a better job, honey. I mean, this was all fine when you were younger, but women might not find it enticing. I don't want to insult you, Kyle, but women have to be practical. If they're going to have children and stay home with them, they need a man who can provide for them..."

"Mom, there are so many assumptions tied up in that sentence, that I don't even know where to start."

"Assumptions?"

Kyle winced at his mom's tone.

Now he'd done it.

"How is it an *assumption* that the woman you love and marry will want to have children, or that you'll have lots of children, or that she would naturally want to spend their formative years with them?"

"Well, there's three assumptions right there, Mom."

"If you mean that fertility might become an issue when a woman is over thirty, then you're right, honey, and that's all the more reason to get serious about finding a wife and partner..."

"Mom, I've got to go and teach a class."

"*Liar*," Cassie mouthed as she passed his office door.

Kyle made a face at her and she grinned.

"Well, think about it, Kyle. I picked up some brochures at the local college about skills improvement that I think might be interesting to you..."

"I make enough money, Mom."

"Enough money for you is not the same as enough money to support a family, Kyle. Trust me. I know!"

His mother had no idea how much money Kyle made and he wasn't going to tell her. California wasn't nearly so far away that she couldn't inflict herself on him with short notice and try to fix his social life.

"Class, Mom. Gotta go."

"And that's another thing. You really need to start thinking about your own health, honey. All this exercise seems excessive at your age..."

"Bye, Mom!"

Kyle ended the call, feeling just as annoyed as he had after every single phone call he'd had with his mother in the past ten years. He exhaled steadily and slowly, using some of the Tantric breathing exercises he taught to calm himself down.

"When *are* you getting married, honey?" Cassie taunted, interrupting his thoughts with her perfect imitation of his mother. She put a new flyer design on his desk for consideration. "You're not getting any younger."

"That's what I hear," Kyle said. "She thinks I need to make more money to improve my appeal to women."

Cassie laughed so hard that a tear worked its way free. "Poor Kyle. Slumming in the big city for minimum wage when you could retrain to be a"—she cast around for a suitable occupation for him—"a licensed plumber!"

"Did you see the bills from the trades? Don't under-estimate their earning power."

"I just can't imagine you getting mucky. It might mess up your hair."

Kyle laughed despite himself. "She never gives it up."

"She probably wants grandchildren. Mine does."

"She has grandchildren. Dave is working that angle."

"Mine doesn't," Cassie said with a sigh.

Kyle remembered that Cassie was an only child and felt bad for complaining. "What do you tell her anyway?"

"About what?"

"Your job."

"I work in a private gym, teaching exercise classes for executives."

"Well, that's kind of true. It's pretty much what I say, but she acts like I'm still teaching summer lifeguard classes at the Y."

"I'm guessing you didn't do that for the money."

"I would have paid them." Kyle put a fist over his heart. "Teaching mouth-to-mouth resuscitation to a dozen cute girls at a time. Those were the days."

Cassie laughed again. "Funny how things don't change, isn't it?"

Damon paused in the hall and glanced into Kyle's office. He was bare-chested with a towel slung around his neck. "Is the joke good enough to share?"

"We're whining about our mothers," Cassie said and Damon's mouth tightened. "What do you tell yours?"

"About what?" Damon was always hard to read, but he seemed a particularly wary to Kyle.

"About love and romance, marriage, and grandbabies," he said, turning it into a joke.

"I told her years ago that I was gay."

Kyle was astonished.

"No!" Cassie protested in shock. "Who would believe that?"

"My mom, evidently," Damon said.

"Seriously?" Kyle asked. "You let even your mom think that?"

"Well, she was halfway there. She had some magazine with an article 'is your son gay?' and she'd left it out on the coffee table. The quiet type with few friends in school was one of the possibilities." Damon shrugged. "I just went with it. It seemed easiest."

Kyle shoved a hand through his hair. "I don't think it's worth it. I don't think I could tell anyone that I was gay."

Cassie rolled her eyes at that.

"She doesn't ask about grandbabies anymore," Damon said. "And nobody in my family fixes me up."

"Not without advantages," Cassie said. "The people they pick when they fix me up." She shook her head. "It's scary sometimes."

"Deeply scary," Damon agreed. "I was motivated to find another solution."

DEBORAH COOKE

If Kyle went home at Christmas without bringing a date, they'd all move into action. "What was the name of that magazine again?" he asked, already thinking of working through the holidays.

Cassie and Damon cracked up.

"You'd better get to the club," Cassie said to Kyle. "The music isn't nearly loud enough yet."

"Are you coming?" Kyle asked Damon, who shook his head. "You never come to the club on Fridays. What's the deal?"

"I've got a date," Damon said, his manner secretive.

"Who would date you?" Kyle said, razzing him the way he always did. "You *always* say you have a date on Friday night and I think it's crap. You're just leaving all the work to me."

"All the work you want," Cassie noted.

"Jealous?" Damon teased.

"No, skeptical. You probably just say that because it gets you out of working a weekend shift, leaving more for me to do."

"You *are* jealous," Damon replied, then taunted Kyle. "Her name's Natasha and she's a dancer. She has legs..."

"That's why you know endearments in Russian!" Cassie said.

"You're going to have to tell your mom about Natasha, though, right?" Kyle asked. "Isn't that going to blow your perfect cover story?"

His partner turned away. "Maybe, maybe not. We'll see."

"I'm surprised Damon has to explain to you that it's not always about marriage," Cassie said.

"Well, it isn't for me. I thought Damon played by different rules, though."

"Just proves you can't know all of anyone's secrets," Cassie said lightly and left Kyle wondering what his buddy wasn't telling him. He'd bet good money that there was something unusual about this Natasha story.

Kyle was headed to the club when he passed Ty, who was coming home. Ty was slinging a briefcase and looked a bit defeated. His tie was even loosened. Kyle stopped to look, interested in the change, and Ty pointed a finger at him.

"You. Owe. Me." He bit off the words one at a time.

Kyle grinned. "Did you finally get caught about Giselle?"

"Not in the way you think. But now there's the fake date with Amy that I want to be real, and there's Matteo." Ty winced and Kyle laughed out loud at his expression. "It's what my parents always said.

176

One lie leads to another. It's a great big slippery slope leading to nowhere good..."

Kyle tapped his buddy on the chest, interrupting him. "Tell her the truth."

"She'll hate me."

"Maybe for a while." Kyle winked. "Maybe not if you beg for mercy."

Ty seemed to be considering that possibility. "I should never have listened to you in the first place."

"It was the tequila."

"Also a bad idea, and also, as I remember, your idea." Ty made a sound of frustration that sounded like a growl. "The only mercy is that you stayed away from my sisters."

Kyle left that one alone. "But you did listen, and now the truth is the only thing that can save you."

"Which again, would be advice from you." Ty shoved a hand through his hair and Kyle knew his friend had it badly.

Of course, he'd known that in the Saturday class.

No, he'd known it when Ty had gotten all hot under the collar about this Amy taking the Saturday class, so bothered that he'd actually agreed to participate. Kyle had always thought that when Ty wanted something, he was fierce in its pursuit, and he'd seen that Ty wanted Amy in spades.

The pair of them had nearly melted the yoga mats.

"Beg for mercy," Kyle said, patting Ty on the shoulder. "Trust me. She won't be able to resist you."

Ty gave him a searing look, just as he anticipated. "I should be so lucky."

"You might." Kyle left Ty standing there, and whistled *I Miss the Rain in Africa* on his way to the club. He heard Ty growl in frustration and laughed, his good mood restored again.

Marriage. As if. His mother had been the one to teach him that "forever" didn't last and Kyle had taken the lesson to heart.

CHAPTER ELEVEN

F OR ONE precious evening, Amy almost forgot about
Brittany's wedding.
        It was glorious.
    She shopped on the way home from work Friday night, checking
her lists twice. She went to the shops her mom had favored, and it
was good to chat with the owners again. It felt good to be preparing
to cook, and that she'd be hosting a party. Optimistic. Celebratory.
Happy. She planned to have some things delivered Saturday morning
and would invite some of her neighbors to the party when she saw
them.
    She was at the butcher shop, deciding if she'd forgotten anything,
when the guy behind the counter fixed her with a look. "Aren't you
Mr. Thornton's daughter?"
    Amy blinked. He was maybe ten years younger than her and
vaguely familiar. "I am. Were you one of his students?"
    "One of his projects, more like," the guy admitted with an easy
smile. "He was a good teacher. I was sorry to hear he got sick."
    "Me, too."
    "I should have come to the hospital." He gestured to her
purchases and Amy shook her head, because she had everything she
needed. He carried her choices to the cash and she sensed that he had
more to say. "I came to the funeral, but you probably don't
remember."
    "Sorry, I don't." Amy had been too upset to be aware of everyone
that day. She smiled. "A lot of people came. It was a nice tribute."

"Well, he made a difference, you know. He was the first person who believed in me, the first one who challenged me to try." The younger man shrugged. "I was hanging out with these guys. I thought they were cool, but your dad didn't. He told me I was too smart to just go with the flow, that I should figure out what *I* wanted and chase that."

"That's what he did," Amy said.

"Yeah. That's what he said. That you have to have the conviction to go after your dreams, because that's the only way they come true." He smiled, then wiped his hand before offering it to her. "Name's Jesse. I'm very sorry for your loss. I should have gone and told him that he'd helped me change."

"I bet he knew," Amy said, her tears rising.

"Maybe," Jesse acknowledged. "You need anything, I'm here to help."

"Thank you, Jesse." Amy was touched by the reminder of her dad's influence. Jesse's words just made her more determined to return to the land of the living, to stop marking time and keep chasing her dreams.

She arrived home, laden with groceries and filled with plans. She put the eggs in the fridge then climbed the stairs to invite Lisa and Mrs. P. to the party before she started to cook. She fed Fitzwilliam, then changed her clothes and began on her prioritized list.

Lothair and Argenta would have to wait a few days.

Amy felt as if her mom was standing behind her, one hand on her shoulder, giving advice about when the dough was just right, when the filling had enough seasoning, when the sauce was thick enough.

She thought about Ty and couldn't suppress a little shiver of anticipation. He'd be here at her house, in her kitchen, acting like they were a couple again. If he wasn't so nice, she would have jumped his bones.

Doing so would undoubtedly shock him.

On the other hand, she did enjoy shaking up his assumptions a bit. Maybe she would jump his bones.

Amy thought about Matteo and what they'd done this week and felt a different kind of tingle. The danger certainly gave her an adrenaline rush.

Was he as bad as he tried to appear? Amy couldn't believe it. He'd touched her so gently. So reverently. He'd just had bad luck, she was sure of it.

Maybe he just needed someone to believe in him, the way that her dad had believed in Jesse.

Maybe he needed the love of the right woman.

Maybe that was thinking too far ahead, but by the time the lasagna noodles were hanging to dry and the ravioli had been filled, Amy knew what she had to do. She washed her hands and got her phone. She hesitated for a moment because it was late. She glanced at the night sky beyond the window, then took a deep breath and called Matteo.

Ty was sorting out his files for the trip to Japan, ensuring that he had the phone numbers and emails for all of his contacts programmed into his phone, and double-checking his reservations when the burner phone rang.

At first, he wasn't sure what the sound was. It chirped, a completely different ring tone from his own phone. By the third ring, he realized what it was and dove into the kitchen to snatch it up before Amy abandoned the call.

She'd called Matteo.

At midnight.

"Hello, Angel," he purred into the phone, even as he wondered what was going on.

"You knew it was me," she said and didn't sound entirely surprised.

"I told you. I got this phone for you."

"How many phones do you have?" she asked with a welcome suspicion.

"I cannot share all of my secrets, Angel. Is there a reason you are calling?"

"There is."

He heard her take a deep breath, as if to steady herself.

"Talk dirty to me, Matteo."

Ty blinked even as a jolt slid through him.

"Tell me what you'd like to do to me, in complete detail," she continued, her voice strengthening with conviction. "Every naughty little bit. I want to hear it all."

Every naughty little bit.

Shit.

Ty hurried across his apartment to dig out the books he'd put aside. He reminded himself that Amy was doing research, but this didn't feel like any research he'd ever done.

"Matteo? Are you there?"

"I am deciding, Angel, how naughty you wish me to be."

"Very naughty," she said, her tone husky with need. "I want wicked and I want outrageous, and I want it now."

Ty flipped open a book, scanning the text in desperation. "Tell me what you are wearing first, Angel," he said, to stall for time.

"A T-shirt and jeans."

Ty considered this. "Naked, Angel," he said, letting his voice turn harsh. "I want you naked, now."

"Yes, Matteo."

"I want you in your bed, blindfolded, naked, and waiting for me."

"Oh, yes, Matteo."

Ty took advantage of the few moments required for her to follow his instruction to locate a sexy scene in one of the books he'd picked up. He'd thought at the time that taking the woman captive and using her as a sex slave had been a bit over the top, but if they were exploring forbidden fantasies, this looked like a good candidate for the dirty talk Amy wanted.

"Imagine that you are waiting for me," he said, making his voice low and silky. "Imagine that you have left the door unlocked and prepared for me, following my instructions perfectly."

"Ohhhh, yes," Amy said, exhaling the words in a way that got Ty right where he lived.

Maybe Matteo didn't have to die just yet.

Maybe he'd survive this phone call, just to see how far Amy wanted to go with this.

Wherever she wanted to go with it, Ty had a feeling he'd be right there with her.

Amy was done.

She surveyed her kitchen with satisfaction. She'd worked all day, but it had been joyous work. Her back ached a bit, but her counter was covered and her fridge was full. Everything was ready, and it had come out brilliantly.

Because she'd had her mom's notes.

It was only eight on Saturday night, but she was going to crash so that she'd be fresh and ready the next morning. She was heading for the shower when her phone rang. She snatched it up, hoping it was Ty, then saw that it was Brittany.

"Hi, Brittany." Amy winced when her cousin's triumphant laughter echoed in her ear.

"I changed everything!" Brittany declared. "You said it couldn't be done, but I fixed it all."

Amy sat down hard, a cold knot in her stomach. "What exactly did you fix?"

"The menu, of course. I *never* wanted chicken..."

"But your mom did."

"Who cares what she wants? I wanted roast beef and so does Nick, and so I went there today and changed everything to what I want. It's my wedding, isn't it?"

Amy rubbed her forehead. "And what are the vegetarians going to eat?"

"I don't care." Brittany paused. "They can have the salad, or the shrimp appetizer."

"Vegetarians don't eat shrimp," Amy said wearily. "Neither will the guests requesting kosher meals or the ones with shellfish allergies."

"Then they can eat the pecan pie."

"That'll work for the diabetics, too." Amy knew her sarcasm was unkind but Brittany missed it.

"There are diabetics?"

"Twenty-eight diabetics, eight vegetarians, six vegans, two rawists, twenty-three lactose-intolerant guests, and forty-seven requesting gluten-free." Brittany seemed to be startled to silence by this, so Amy continued. "Twenty-one shellfish allergies and thirty-seven nut allergies, the majority of which are listed as anaphylactic."

"What does that mean?" Brittany demanded with suspicion.

"They can die. People with allergies that severe don't even need to eat the substance in question." Amy took a deep breath, not feeling particularly inclined to be nice to her cousin. "The catering manager and I planned a menu with no trace of any of those substances because I assumed you wouldn't want anyone to get sick or die at your wedding." She paused for a minute. "My mistake."

"Oh. My. God." Brittany whispered. "Well, you have to fix it!"

"No," Amy said, bracing herself for the tears.

They came in a torrent.

Amy held the phone away from her ear when Brittany wailed.

"My wedding is going to be a disaster and it's all your fault. You were supposed to be helping me, but now my dress doesn't fit and someone's going to die and the flowers are all wrong..."

"What happened to the flowers?"

"*His* mother changed her corsage, because it won't match her dress and now it won't match anything else..."

"The mother of the groom's corsage doesn't have to match the other flowers," Amy said with more patience than she felt.

"Yes, it does! Of course, it does!" The tears began again. "I thought my wedding was going to be perfect but every bit of it is going to shit. I should never have trusted you!"

Amy finally snapped.

"And I should never have expected you to delegate the arrangements and leave them alone," she replied.

"What's that supposed to mean?"

"That even a big wedding like this shouldn't have been this much work. That I shouldn't have spent so much time on the phone or on my way to New Jersey or negotiating between you all over trivial details."

"Trivial!"

"Trivial," Amy repeated. "They do say that no good deed goes unpunished, and I guess that's true. I did this because you're my cousin and I wanted to be helpful, but I'm done. Fix it yourself."

"I can't fix it myself! Amy, you have to help me."

"See, that's just it. I don't have to help you and if you don't ask me nicely, I won't."

"Bitch!" Brittany screamed and ended the call.

Amy knew her cousin well enough to anticipate that she'd call back within five minutes and try to change Amy's mind. She turned off her voice mail, knowing she had to call someone.

If she called Ty and told him what had happened, he'd be proud of her. The problem was that she was pretty sure she would ultimately cave in and fix the arrangements. Even though she was frustrated with Brittany, she liked to finish what she 'd started. Ty probably wouldn't like that.

Better if he didn't know at all.

No, what she needed was a treat.

An indulgence.

Something sinful and naughty.

A forbidden pleasure.

The choice was obvious.

Amy dialed and spoke as soon as he answered.

"Talk dirty to me again, Matteo," she whispered. "Tell me the sexiest thing you've ever done with a woman."

"Such a naughty angel," he purred and she shivered with delight. "I will tell you the harshest punishment I ever gave a woman, and how she loved it."

"Yes, please," Amy said.

It was research, plain and simple.

But when Matteo murmured to her in his deep gravelly voice, Amy's reaction didn't feel plain or simple at all.

Talk dirty to me.

Amy was driving Ty crazy.

He'd thought the first call was bad. This one had gone right off the rails to uncharted territory. He was wound up, and aroused, ready to get in his car and go to Amy's house to do all things they'd just talked about.

Because she loved it.

Or at least the idea of it.

Ty paced his apartment, replaying her words in his thoughts.

Because Amy had talked dirty to him this time. Really dirty. And it thrilled him, even though she thought he was another guy. Who was actually him. The whole game was fucking with his mind and his assumptions, yet it was addictive all the same.

He wanted to call her back and go another round.

Worse, what he wanted to do to Amy was even naughtier.

He wanted to make her fantasies come true.

He wanted her to know it was him doing as much.

But if he told her the truth, she might break off the fake date or even stop speaking to him. It was a mess.

A beautiful, exciting mess.

He doubted that begging for mercy would make one bit of difference if he confessed the truth. She'd never forgive him if she knew what he'd done, and he couldn't imagine being without her in his life.

Ty was never going to sleep.

He decided to go down and swim laps, but he took the burner phone with him, just in case.

Sunday dawned sunny and warm, as if Amy had ordered the perfect weather.

Or Ty had ensured it was right for her party.

She accused him of that when he arrived and liked how he laughed. "I don't have that much influence," he said. "Now, what can I do?"

He'd arrived first, of course, dressed more casually than Amy had ever seen him before. He wore jeans that fit in all the right places and had brought the wine. He got her dad's collection of wicker furniture out of the garage for her and hung the lanterns on the clothesline before Paige and Derek arrived.

By then, he was doing it again.

He touched Amy casually, keeping up the show for Derek and Paige. It seemed he was always behind her, always dropping his hand to her waist, always brushing his fingertips across her cheek or tucking her against his side. Worse, he kissed her on the temple and the cheek, stirring her emotions and making her flustered, then watched her intently.

With that delicious little smile tugging his lips and revealing his dimple.

He was driving Amy crazy. Two long, hot calls with Matteo had left her itching for satisfaction, and Ty wasn't helping with his light caresses. She wanted sex more than she'd wanted it before in her life, and thought she'd scream if she had to hang on any longer. The tease was monumental—and the day had barely begun.

Amy was sure that if he kept this up, she wouldn't manage to take a complete breath all day. Ty made such a good show of adoring her that even she was halfway convinced. She blushed more than she thought humanly possible. Derek and Paige clearly loved the display, and Amy supposed that her reaction only added to their conviction that she and Ty were deeply in love.

Paige stepped up to help Amy as the guys got Derek's ladder from his truck, fastening down the tablecloth and admiring all the food.

"No paper plates?" she asked.

"My mom always said guests should get real dishes," Amy replied with a smile, and began to carry her mom's party collection out to the one long table.

Ty spotted Derek on the ladder when he went up to check the roof, and Amy showed Paige the main floor of the house before the other guests arrived.

Paige was smitten with the fireplace in the living room. They shared ideas of how the house could be renovated, and Paige did have some great ideas. The two women exchanged numbers and email addresses, Paige clearly assuming that Amy and Ty would be together for the duration. She also gave her the number for Lauren's shop, pointing out that if Amy ever wanted a cut or color, Lauren was the best.

By then, Derek was sitting with his laptop in the corner of the kitchen. He compiled his estimate, then showed it to Amy on the laptop screen.

"I'll email it to you, too," he said. "A little higher than I thought, but you need some point work done on the chimneys. We'll put caps on them while we're there, and new flashing, of course." He indicated a separate line item. "That's for new gutters. I think you're due, and it's a lot easier to do them the same time as the roof. I know a coppersmith who can probably fix the cap of your turret, too, rather than needing to replace it. I made a guess on that cost here."

Amy stared as her heart soared. Even with the extras, it was lower than the old estimate in her kitchen drawer. She wanted to hug somebody.

It could also be put on the new line of credit that Red had set up for her and wouldn't even take it all.

"That must include a big discount," she said and Derek grinned.

"Like I said, family price." He pushed his hand through his hair. "A little better, actually, in exchange for having my sign on your front lawn for a couple of weeks." He watched her closely, so obviously wanting the work that Amy smiled.

"Deal," she said, offering her hand. "When can you do it?"

"Fourth of July weekend? We're taking Monday and Tuesday off, but a couple of the guys are always ready for some overtime. Even with a smaller crew, we can get it done in four days if the weather is good."

"Sounds good to me."

"I'll check the long distance forecast and confirm with you closer to the date."

"Wonderful. Thank you." Amy realized that Ty had been watching her the whole time so she smiled at him across the kitchen. *And thank you*, she mouthed, though Paige noticed. Amy saw the smile she exchanged with Derek.

"Hello!" someone called from the backyard and Amy hurried to greet her guests. A new roof just six weeks away.

That was something to celebrate!

It was a great day.

Ty couldn't remember a party he'd enjoyed more. The food was awesome and plentiful. Amy hadn't been kidding about her cooking abilities. There were two kinds of lasagna, plus handmade ravioli, a soup made from scratch, several salads—one leafy and one with legumes—and delicious garlic bread. There was tiramisu for dessert and zabaglione and fresh fruit and cookies that the kids couldn't resist.

Amy had really knocked it out of the park. She was glowing in the praise from her guests and Ty enjoyed watching her.

The weather was perfect, with no chance of rain. The wine flowed as well as the conversation, and it was a successful party by any accounting. He met the guy next door and his mother, Amy's tenants, and a number of her old high school friends. The affection between them all was clear, and Ty understood why this house was such a home for Amy. He realized that she did have an excellent support network, even without her dad's family, and was glad.

In fact, her family was notably absent and he was glad about that, too.

Amy looked wonderful, her hair in a swinging ponytail and her eyes sparkling with laughter. She wore jeans that hugged the sweet curve of her hips and Ty wanted to touch her more than he'd wanted to do anything in a long time. He was haunted by her phone calls to Matteo, and that night at F5. He couldn't stay away from her and was sure Paige noticed.

With glee.

No doubt his mom would be getting a report, but Ty didn't care. He was already sold.

They eventually put the food away then sat in the yard under the lanterns swinging on the clothesline, drinking wine, and ignoring the growing chill in the air. The neighbors drifted home as the sky darkened. Ethan fell asleep in his carrier but Derek and Paige lingered, chatting, when Ty just wanted Amy to himself.

When Lisa and Mrs. P. retired, Amy kissed them and thanked them for coming.

Ty sat back, sipped his wine, and let his admiration show. Amy noticed, of course. She'd been as aware of him all day as he'd been of her. Her gaze flicked to him frequently and her cheeks often burned pink, as if she knew his thoughts were more naughty than nice.

But she kept smiling and kept looking.

And he kept touching and looking, wanting to do more than that.

He was starting to think that his sister would never leave.

"It was awesome, Amy," Paige said. "Ty never mentioned that you're such a great cook."

"He didn't know," Amy admitted, mischief in her eyes. "He keeps taking me out."

"That might change," Ty threatened and she laughed.

Their gazes met over the table, still littered with plates and napkins and crumbs, and that electric awareness crackled between them.

Ty smiled slowly.

Amy blushed slowly.

"Good thing you have F5 to keep you trim," Derek teased and Amy's gaze snapped to him.

"F5?" she echoed with alarm. "Isn't that the fitness club downtown?"

She was concerned, and Ty knew why. He straightened, preparing for damage control.

Too bad Derek and Paige hadn't left already.

"Ty's one of the fabled five," Derek said, saluting Ty with his glass.

Amy looked alarmed.

"Silent partner," he said to her. "Only three of us actually work at the club." He kept his tone casual. "I just go there to work out."

"Oh." Amy sat back.

He shrugged. "I'm the numbers guy."

"Oh," she said again, her relief more obvious.

But not complete.

"Keeping secrets from Amy, Ty?" Paige teased.

"We're working through each other's secrets," he said evenly, then claimed Amy's hand. "It's the thrill of discovery."

She blushed right on cue, and he could have guessed the direction of her thoughts.

"Soon enough, there won't be any secrets left," Paige teased. "Get ready for my brother to get you under his microscope, Amy, if he hasn't already. He'll have you analyzed and all figured out before you know it."

"Maybe I'll beat him to it," Amy said and Ty chuckled. Their gazes locked again and the evening didn't seem so chilly after all.

Paige reached for the wine and Ty cleared his throat.

"That's a hint, sweetheart," Derek said cheerfully.

"About the ninth one," Ty muttered and Derek laughed.

"Only nine?" he said. "I counted at least twenty."

"We can help clean up," Paige said, reaching for plates.

"I've got it," Ty said firmly. "Take Ethan home to bed."

"Me, too," Derek said and Paige laughed.

"I hope you like it when he gets bossy," she said to Amy. "He does it all the time with us."

Amy smiled at Ty. "I love it," she said and heat surged through him. Their gazes clung again and this time, his sister seemed to notice.

"Oh, yeah, we really do need to go," she said to Derek.

Ty refrained from noting that it was about time. He followed them to the truck, holding fast to Amy's hand. They stood together in the driveway and waved as the pair left. "I thought they'd never leave," Ty muttered.

Amy giggled. "Funny how I picked that up."

"Funny," he echoed, then turned to face her. He could have drowned in those sparkling eyes. He put one finger beneath her chin and bent to brush his lips across hers. He'd meant it to be a quick little kiss, just a taste to sustain him, but Amy sighed and leaned against him. She seemed to be inviting his touch, and Ty couldn't resist the temptation. He slanted his mouth across hers in a sweet potent kiss that was all too short.

Because Amy stepped back.

"The dishes," she whispered.

"The dishes," Ty agreed easily, more than content to let the tension build between them.

In fact, he'd give it some help.

It might have been Amy's imagination, but she and Ty seemed to clean off the outside table with record speed. He gathered all the trash and sorted the recycling after she'd taken the plates and glasses back into the kitchen. She stacked dishes by the sink as she stole glances of Ty working in the yard.

That kiss had been wonderful.

Was it possible that it hadn't *all* been for show?

Paige and Derek proved to be good company and good fun, and Amy did enjoy the way Ty and his sister teased each other. Ethan was adorable and enough of a mischievous child to steal anyone's heart away. She felt the beginning of a family's embrace closing around her, and she liked it very much.

She liked Ty even more.

Even though he was part-owner of F5. It seemed strange that she didn't know that already, but on the other hand, when would they have talked about it? They really were just getting to know each other. Could he know about her taking that class? Or meeting with Matteo? Did he know Matteo? He was completely at ease, which would seem to be unlikely if he did know.

His kiss had left her yearning for more.

For him.

Ty locked the door behind himself when he came into the kitchen, as if he meant to stay. Amy's heart fluttered that he was so open about his hopes. Then he picked up a dishtowel and came to her side.

"No dishwasher," she said, her hands in the suds.

"No problem," he said easily and began to dry glasses. He lined them up on the cleaned counter as they were finished, and the neat rows made her smile. Her kitchen felt smaller and warmer with Ty in it, and even more intimate when he opened cupboard doors and began to put things away. He brushed past her so often that it couldn't be an accident. He touched her shoulder and her back, and when she felt him draw one of those circles, she knew their thoughts were as one.

She had a feeling he'd wait for her encouragement, for as long as it took.

She was in control.

Why was she hesitating? A fake date with benefits wasn't any more serious—or binding. Ha.—than a fake date without them. They could enjoy each other without pledging to be together forever.

Ty wanted her.

She wanted him.

Why was she making it complicated?

Amy couldn't think of a single reason.

"Penny for your thoughts," Ty said when she was drying her hands.

"I thought you were just making it look good today but now I wonder."

He granted her a glance that spoke volumes. His eyes were intensely green and his gaze was hot. "I don't like to do anything just for appearances," he murmured and Amy's knees weakened. "Sooner or later, I'll convince you that the whole Giselle thing was out of character."

"And the fake date plan?"

"An excuse, in hindsight." Ty mused, in a low voice that started earthquakes inside Amy. He smiled that slow smile and her mouth went dry. "What exactly is making you wonder?"

The wine made Amy bolder than she would have been otherwise, and she dared to say it out loud. "You didn't have to kiss me in the driveway."

Ty nodded. "Oh yes, I did." He chucked the dish towel on the counter and closed the space between them with a single step. Amy thrilled at his resolve and liked even better when he trapped her between his hips and the counter. "Just like I have to do it again right now." He considered her, then lifted off her glasses and set them aside. "I've been wanting to do that forever," he murmured.

Things were a bit blurry, but Amy could see that dimple.

And she could feel his interest.

Ty cupped her face in his hand, tipped up her chin and kissed her sweetly.

Sweet was good, but she wanted more.

"I think we should make a deal," she said when he'd lifted his head.

"Anything you want."

"Don't you think you should know before you agree?"

He kissed the side of her neck, then her ear. "Nope. I trust you completely."

"It might be naughty."

"A guy can hope."

Amy smiled, then she pulled back to look into his eyes. "I want to be honest with you."

"Okay."

"Completely honest."

"Okay."

"I want a hot kiss, a long wicked possessive one, after the nice ones."

Ty smiled slowly. "You're on," he murmured, then slid his hands into her hair. He framed her face and lifted her a little, crushing her against the counter. He bent his head and caught her mouth under hers.

Amy's heart thundered. She slid her hands up Ty's chest, over his shoulders and around his neck. This time, she pushed her fingers into his hair and opened her mouth to him, arching against him and demanding more. Ty made a little growl—a very satisfying sound—then locked his arms around her and deepened his kiss. It was the hottest and most passionate kiss they'd ever shared and Amy wanted only more.

Ty broke their kiss and ran a hand over her cheek, pushing back her hair before claiming her lips again. Amy felt treasured and precious, also confident that she could call a halt with a single word or touch. Ty would stand back and walk away, leaving the choice up to her, and she loved that.

When he lifted his head, his eyes were blazing. When he whispered her name, his voice was husky and uneven.

This was her chance.

"I like this honesty," he whispered.

"I have more."

"Go for it," he invited, his eyes shining.

"I want you, Tyler McKay," Amy said with heat and liked how he caught his breath. "I want all of you and I want you now."

His eyes blazed. "Does your fireplace work?" he asked.

Amy blinked. "Absolutely. There's wood in the living room..."

"Don't move," he instructed and left her there. She could hear him setting the fire and smiled at the thought that he was using his scout skills.

"We could just use the bedroom," she called.

She heard him strike a match and the wood begin to crackle. She saw his silhouette as he strode into the kitchen, then blinked when he flicked off the light.

"Live dangerously with me tonight and try something different," he said. Amy laughed but Ty didn't give her a chance to argue. He kissed her again and swept her into his arms. He headed for the living room with a purpose that made Amy's heart race in anticipation.

For the first time in a long, long time, Ty felt some concern about sex.

He wanted Amy. She wanted him. He had condoms and everything should have been perfect. But he couldn't help thinking that he had to ensure he gave her as much pleasure as Matteo had. No, he had to give her more. He had to be better than his alter-ego, and that was just weird.

Not only was it bizarre to be competing with his own past performance, but Ty already knew many things that Amy liked. He hoped like hell he didn't reveal his own disguise and ruin everything.

He hoped he could pull it off as lucky guesses or intuitive understanding or something like that.

He would tell her the truth.

Just not right now.

The prospect of making love to her was too sweet to sacrifice.

Later, he'd confess and beg her forgiveness. He had to believe that this was an opportunity to gain some goodwill.

Beyond that, Ty couldn't think much at all.

The firelight made Amy skin look more golden than usual, an exotic beauty waiting for him. He lowered her before the fire and kissed her again, then removed the fastener from her hair. Her hair fell around her face and to her shoulders, soft and gleaming. "I had this idea," he said, coaxing her to her back. She kissed him, so soft and inviting that he nearly lost the train of his thoughts.

"An idea?" she echoed, kissing his ear. She grazed his ear lobe with her teeth and he caught his breath, then did it again when she laughed and her breath fanned his skin.

"An idea." He slid a hand down her length, then under her shirt. He spread his fingers wide and inched his hand higher.

"Only one?"

"It's a good one, I think. Simple."

Amy smiled at him, then crossed her arms in front of herself and peeled her shirt over her head, casting it aside. Ty stared at the way the dark lace of her bra contrasted with her creamy skin.

"Navy," he murmured, wishing he'd imagined that she wore navy lace lingerie as well as sensible separates in that color.

"You don't like blue?"

"I like it better all the time."

Amy smiled and rolled toward the fire, displaying the clasp on the bra to him. Ty wasn't one to decline such an invitation. He unfastened it, then smoothed the elastic over her shoulders, taking the chance to run his hand up her back to her nape. Her hair tangled around his fingers like silk, and Amy rolled to her back again, flicking the bra aside. He bent and kissed one nipple with reverence, and then the other. Her breast filled his hand perfectly, and he liked the idea that they might have been made for each other. She sighed beneath his caress and stretched out beside him, and he remembered his idea.

He caught her wrists in one hand and guided them to the leg of the sofa. "Don't let go," he instructed her. Amy's eyes danced with anticipation. He unfastened her jeans and stripped them off, then slid

193

his hands beneath her panties to discard them as well.

"You could tie me here," she said playfully, but Ty shook his head.

"Too complicated. I'm going to show you the appeal of simple."

"Simple," she repeated. "Well, I can't see much without my glasses."

"Close your eyes. That way, you won't be able to see anything."

She looked as if she might argue, but changed her mind and did as he'd instructed. Ty ran his hand over her, admiring her beauty. He eased his fingers between her thighs, discovered that she was as excited as he was, and moved to be between her knees.

"What are you doing?" she asked, tension in her voice.

"Something simple to make sure you're pleased," he said, then eased her thighs wide apart. When Ty closed his mouth over her, Amy gasped.

And then she surrendered to him, uttering only one small delicious moan in capitulation.

Amy came, after it seemed like Ty tormented her for a thousand years. He didn't stop, though, but kept teasing her with his tongue and teeth, ensuring that her orgasm lasted so long that she was breathless. Her heart was hammering when he moved to tear off his jeans, and she saw the tension in his movements.

"Good idea," she whispered.

"Don't move," he said, his voice a little rough, and Amy obeyed. She realized he was getting something from his jeans and smiled as she guessed why. He returned to her side with a couple of foil packages and opened one, eyeing her as he smoothed on the condom. No wonder he looked so good in his suits. Even without her glasses and even with him still wearing his T-shirt, she could see that he was toned and fit. He'd need to be part owner of a gym to spend that much time there.

Or rich.

She felt a combination of excitement and a little trepidation when he stretched out beside her again and she felt the size of him against her thigh. The fire crackled on her other side and she felt warm.

"It's been a while," she whispered.

"Me, too," Ty admitted, trailing his fingers over her. Amy felt tingles run over her flesh and stretched beneath his caress. "A bit of a dry spell."

"I like that we have that in common."

"Me, too. But I don't want to disappoint you."

"I don't think you could," she confessed and earned a thorough kiss for that. "But you had condoms. Does that mean expectations?"

"Preparations in a spirit of optimism," Ty admitted, kissing her again before she could laugh aloud. The weight of his hand was on her hip and her waist, then rising to her breast, brushing over the nipple, and sliding up her throat. He kissed her ear, stroking her all the while.

"Sit on me," he invited in a throaty whisper. "I want to see you." He pulled back to look into her eyes. "And you'll be in charge, which I know you like."

Amy didn't need to be invited twice. She straddled Ty and he caught her waist in his hands. She watched him inhale sharply as she took him inside, and teased him a bit by withdrawing before she drew him deeper. He whispered her name and his grip tightened upon her, but he waited for her move. She saw his jaw clench. She saw his nostrils pinch. She felt his muscles go taut. But he let her set the pace, even though his eyes glittered when he looked up at her.

"Planning to kill me?" he whispered.

"Slowly," Amy said, catching her own breath as she lowered herself to take him completely inside her for the first time. She leaned her forehead on his chest and he pushed his hand through her hair, drawing her close for a sweet hot kiss.

"I want nine lives," he murmured against her cheek. "And I want to be finished off this way every single time."

Amy laughed, then moved again, rocking her hips a bit. She liked how Ty caught his breath and how he gripped her tightly. She knew he wanted her, but she was in command.

They found a rhythm together easily, so easily that they might have made love a dozen times before. There was something right about their connection, and Amy welcomed that sense of coming home. The heat rose between them and Ty's fingers dug more deeply into her waist with every stroke. He pulled her forward, so that she was rubbing against the strength of him and Amy shivered with delight. She caught his face in her hands and kissed him deeply as she rode him, his hands locked on her hips and increasing their pace. She closed her eyes and simply felt the power of his body and the pleasure of being with him, hearing her heart thunder and her breath race.

"Amy!" He locked one arm around her waist and rolled her partway beneath him, kissing her deeply. She could feel his heartbeat against her own and his heat filling her and knew there was nowhere else she wanted to be. He drove deep, then moved his hand between them. One strategic flick of his finger and Amy came again, crying out in her pleasure and digging her nails into his shoulders as Ty came and came and came.

Cuore mio. The words flitted into Amy's thoughts with the resonance of truth. *My heart.* An endearment of the most powerful kind.

Could it be true?

Of course not. This was just a fake date with benefits. Amy knew that, but wondered all the same.

CHAPTER TWELVE

Y OU NEVER took off your shirt," Amy complained in the aftermath, when they'd cleaned up and Ty carried her to her own bed. She gave the hem of his T-shirt a tug when he laid down beside her. "Don't tell me you're shy."

"No, of course not," he said, but his hand closed over hers. To stop her.

Amy leaned over him and grabbed her spare glasses, put them on and smiled at him. "You have a secret, then," she teased. "It must be a great big tattoo."

"No!"

"I want to see it." Amy pulled her hand free again and reached for the hem. Ty stopped her again.

"No, you don't need to see," he protested and she would have bet that he was embarrassed. That made her only more determined.

She clucked like a chicken, poked him hard with one finger and when he exhaled, she slid her hand beneath his shirt. He froze, watching her.

"You have *stubble!*"

Ty's gaze slid away from hers and he gave it up. "Yes."

Amy pushed up his T-shirt and ran her fingers over the line of short dark hair. Ty shivered.

"It itches," he said through his teeth.

"You shaved it. Why?"

He gave her a simmering look. "My buddy Kyle says that women prefer smooth skin. I believed him."

"Again, you believed him? This is the guy who suggested the Giselle ploy, right?"

Ty winced. "Right." He slanted a glance at her. "I need someone to give me better advice."

Amy braced her elbow on his chest and dropped her chin to her fist. She was fighting a smile because he had maybe a quarter inch of growth. This had happened recently. "Any particular woman whose preferences you were worried about?"

"You know it was you," he growled.

She tapped a finger on him. "When did you do this?"

She was thinking he might say before the bridal shower, but he frowned and looked away again. "Before our dinner."

"You thought on a first date, on a first *fake* date," Amy started, but Ty interrupted her.

"No! I had no expectations." He surveyed her warmly and lifted one hand to her hair.

"What then?"

"Preparation in a spirit of optimism."

Amy laughed.

"Seriously, you surprise me, especially in matters sexual. I never know what to expect."

"In matters sexual," Amy echoed.

Ty looked a bit exasperated. "I wanted to be ready for anything."

Amy slid her hand under his shirt again, pushing her fingers through the stubble. "But not today?"

"You surprised me," Ty admitted. "Again." He leaned back, not looking very troubled about that situation. "I should get used to it."

"Even though you were trying to drive me crazy?"

"I had no idea whether it would work."

"So, it's not a bad thing for me to command a performance?"

He lifted a brow. "What did I tell you?"

"About matters sexual? Hmm, only that there was nothing sexier than a woman wanting you?"

"Exactly." Ty rolled her to her back, then removed her glasses and put them back on the nightstand. "And now I'm thinking that it's time I surprised you."

"I don't know that I can be that easily surprised."

"No?" He laced his fingers through hers and drew her hands over her head, holding her wrists captive there. Was he holding her down? Amy thrilled at the possibility. His other hand was on her waist, his fingers splayed wide, and he held her firmly against him. Ty touched his lips to hers, before whispering in her ear. "What if I show you that I'm not quite as nice as you seem to think?"

Amy shivered a little in his grip, liking that she couldn't pull her wrists free. She swallowed as Ty trailed kisses to her nipple, then gasped when he dragged his teeth across it. He kissed it then, teasing it to a point, holding her exactly where he wanted her.

Stretched taut.

Captive to his caress.

"I think that would be fine," Amy managed to say before Ty hooked one foot around her ankle and eased her legs apart. Her heart leaped but she loved it.

"I have to go to Japan," he whispered against her skin. "I don't want to."

"I don't want you to," Amy managed to whisper.

"So, let me give you something to think about this week." Ty leaned over her so that her leg was trapped beneath him, and eased his fingers between her thighs. He caressed her, still kissing her nipple, and though it wasn't as naughty as what Amy wanted, she appreciated his determination to please her. He touched her boldly, kissing her sweetly all the while, and Amy surrendered to the pleasure Ty was determined to give.

Ty was restless. He knew he should have told Amy the truth.

He should have laid it all out for her and come clean.

But he hadn't.

It had been so good that he hadn't wanted to compromise anything.

He stood in his apartment, looking south to Brooklyn, nursing another double shot of that Scotch, and thinking of Amy.

Admitting the truth would have been the right thing to do.

Begging for mercy might not have been all bad.

But he hadn't wanted to take any chance of destroying what had been so wonderful.

Something so fragile and magical had to be protected.

The truth, Ty was sure, would trash everything. He'd deceived Amy. There was no getting around that. She wouldn't be glad to learn the truth. No one would. He had to hope that she'd forgive him, but he knew it would take time.

Time he didn't have when his flight for Japan left in seven hours.

He drained the Scotch, called himself a chicken-shit, and resolved to find the right moment as soon as he got back.

The burner phone rang as he was putting down the glass and he spun to face it, incredulous.

What the hell? She'd just made love to *him*. He'd just made love to her. He'd just tried his best. He knew he'd pleased her. He'd left her sleepy and satisfied.

And she was calling Matteo?

Ty threw back the rest of the Scotch and strode across the room to answer the phone.

Amy sat in her darkened bedroom and wondered.

Making love with Ty had been awesome.

It had been safe.

She had felt cherished and treasured and completely connected with him. Vanilla hadn't been boring at all.

But she felt conflicted. As good as making love had been, and as much as she admired Ty, Amy wasn't entirely sure she could surrender the adrenaline rush of being with Matteo.

The thrill of risk.

At the same time, she knew she couldn't ask Ty to play erotic games with her. He wouldn't approve. He would probably think less of her. Was it possible that she could love him but that her truth would destroy any love he felt?

Was their relationship doomed before it really got started?

Should she tell Ty about Matteo?

Amy disliked the idea. She knew Ty would take it badly.

What was she going to do?

She should get Matteo out of her system, have him and be done with it. Explore naughty and move on, hopefully with Ty. She might not like the reality as much as the fantasy. It might just be a forbidden temptation, one that didn't deliver in real life. She knew she had to know, so the sooner she found out, the better.

Amy's hands shook when she picked up her phone and called Matteo's number. She felt like she was betraying Ty, but she wasn't really.

Was she?

Matteo answered after two rings and sounded so pissed off that her heart skipped.

"I want another private session," she admitted in a rush. "But here, at my house, for real."

There was a long silence that seemed cold to Amy.

"Impossible," he snarled.

"It's not impossible. I'll give you the address..."

"It is impossible because I am leaving. I have a job to do."

His voice sounded so hard that Amy feared the worst. "What kind of job?"

"The kind of job I do to earn a living. You don't think that playing with little girls at F5 gives me the kind of money I need, do you?" His tone was so mocking that Amy was shocked. He'd never talked to her like this before.

"What else do you do?"

He took a deep breath, as if deciding whether to humor her or not. "I am not of your world, Angel. A man must make choices in my world. I have friends, who demand loyalty from me. I do not betray them."

"What kind of friends?"

"The kind of friends it is foolish to offend."

Amy thought about his tattoos and his earlier comments. "Why were you in prison?"

"I am what is called a mule, Angel. I make deliveries."

"Of drugs," Amy breathed, then she realized he'd used the present tense. "You're not doing it again?"

"I am what I am, Angel. I do what I do. I will not be caught."

His confidence was undeserved, in Amy's opinion, and she wanted to save him from his own impulses.

"You were caught before."

There was another cold silence and she feared she'd said too much.

She really didn't know much about him.

Still, Amy tried again. "If you need a place to stay, I can help..."

"I will not be caught, Angel," Matteo said harshly, interrupting her. "Because I ensured the man who betrayed me last time could not betray me again. He speaks no more."

"He's dead?"

"We shared a woman once, so I trusted him. But he betrayed me. When I was freed, I wrung the life out of him with my bare hands," he said. "And I was not caught."

He'd killed someone?

"You have to stop, Matteo," Amy spoke sternly. "You have to

refuse to make another delivery...

"No," he snarled, sounding completely different from the man who had pleasured her and touched her so gently. Had the connection she'd felt with him been a complete lie? "I leave tomorrow. I will be gone many days."

"Matteo, you have to give yourself a chance..."

"Goodbye, Angel," he growled, then ended the call.

Amy stared at the phone. She redialed his number, but was informed that the customer was unavailable.

He'd turned it off.

I want another private session. But here, at my house, for real.

Ty paced his apartment, more agitated than he'd been in years. Amy wanted to have sex with Matteo. He would never have believed it, but she'd said it aloud, to him.

If you need a place to stay, I can help...

What was in Amy's mind? She would invite a guy with a criminal record to stay at her house? He'd been sure she was more sensible than that. And what happened next? What they talked about in the phone calls would happen in real life?

He couldn't talk to her again, not as Matteo.

He couldn't fix this before he left for Japan.

He couldn't tell her the truth, not without being sure that she wouldn't put herself in a dangerous situation with some other guy like Matteo.

Ty folded his arms across his chest and glared out the windows of his apartment, wanting to see all the way to Brooklyn. Amy's research had him all tangled up inside, never mind the effect of Amy herself. Making love to her hadn't been nearly enough. He hadn't even left on his trip and he couldn't wait to get home again, to see her again.

As much as he wanted to crush that burner phone, Matteo had to survive until Ty got home and told Amy the truth.

She was going to despise him and he didn't blame her, but this couldn't go on.

He had to hope that begging for mercy would work.

It was a bad moment to realize that this strategy had been Kyle's advice.

Amy Googled Matteo's tattoos and found the four dots on Wiki. They were a gang mark from California, for the Norteños, who trafficked drugs. Amy chewed her fingernail as she thought.

It appeared that there was a lot she didn't know about Matteo.

She couldn't dismiss the memory of his touch, though, or the power of those two hot scenes.

It was almost like he was two different people.

Fitzwilliam sauntered into the room and leaped onto her bed, fussing with the covers before he laid down. Clearly, hosting a party—enough though he'd hidden in her dad's library for all of it—had worn him out.

Amy thought of her dad, reaching out to the kids in his class who were heading into trouble. She thought of him believing in them and sometimes making a difference, as he had with Jesse. She didn't believe that Matteo was truly bad. He might have been in bad circumstances, but he'd been gentle with her.

More gentle than Lothair had been with Argenta.

Surely his actions revealed the truth of his nature?

But then there was the harsh way he'd talked to her tonight.

"Would it help if I believed in Matteo?" she asked the cat. Fitzwilliam cleaned his paw, not in the least bit interested in the emotional torment of anyone other than himself.

"In a book, it would make all the difference," she mused. "Lothair needs someone to trust him, in order to be healed, and in my book, Argenta's trust will heal Lothair."

Fitzwilliam yawned mightily.

Would Amy have any chance to show her trust of Matteo?

Could she stop him from making a bad choice?

She didn't know. She tried again, but he still had his phone turned off. There was nothing she could do for Matteo immediately.

But Amy could write about trust healing a hero's wounds.

On impulse, I tipped her head forward and unlaced the hood, tugging it from her head. Her hair was left disheveled, glimmering like moonlight, and her cheeks were flushed.

Against my every expectation, she smiled at me, untroubled by the sight of my ravaged face—much less to discover it in such close proximity. "Thank you, my lord."

I lifted the hood. "You don't like it?"

She averted her gaze, her lips curved in a mischievous smile, then she eyed me anew. "It makes me feel wanton, my lord." Her eyes were dancing.

Wanton. There was a word to make me hard again. Temptress.

DEBORAH COOKE

"How so?" I had to ask, though the words did not fall easily from my lips.

She frowned a little, considering the question. "I feel more in the absence of my sight. It seems my skin is more sensitive when I cannot see what touches it." Her gaze collided with mine once more, unflinching. "Is it so with you, my lord?"

I avoided the question, by reaching down to tug that rope again. Her eyes widened as the knot eased past her clitoris, which I had to guess was hard and throbbing. "Does this make less impression now than before?"

She gasped, her lips parting in the way I found more inviting. "I cannot be sure, my lord."

I raised a hand to one pert nipple, caressed it, then pinched it. "And this?"

She moaned a little, her hips moving against the pillar of the bed. "I think not, my lord."

I kissed that nipple then, savoring her agitation. "And this?"

"No less than before, my lord."

I lavished attention upon that nipple then, suckling it and drawing it to a point, then grazed it with my teeth. She gave a delicious shiver, one that claimed her from head to toe. "Then maybe you are a wanton," I whispered against her flesh.

Her gaze locked with mine. "Only for you, my lord."

I straightened and spun away from her.

Did she flatter me with a lie?

Or did she truly have some affection for me?

I knew what I wanted to believe, but forced myself to accept what had to be truth. She was a beauty. Her heart would be snared by beauty. She was, however, my captive, and it was only clever of her to court my favor.

"You're a fool to give anything to a monster," I said tightly.

"You are not a monster," she retorted. "You choose your torments from your own experience, but the way you grant them reveals your true nature. You beat me, but you don't injure me. You burn me, but with candle wax that cools quickly. You use a knife to shave me, not cut me, and you do so with great care. You teach me of pleasure. You're the only one of royal blood who thinks of anyone beyond himself! How does that make you a monster?"

I was shocked, thrilled and determined to put an end to any romantic notions she might hold. She was my Mark. She was mine to take and mine to abandon at Beltane. I would be compelled to choose a husband for her from the village, and already guessed it would be her rustic companion. I would be obliged to watch her in my kingdom, wed to him, bearing his children, unavailable to me after she was dispatched from the palace.

Already, I disliked this and dreaded the spring day when she would leave.

It would be better if she had no tender feelings for me. There was an irony in

204

the fact that she of all people should have any affection for me, but it must be destroyed. She must be happy with her peasant husband, not yearning for what neither of us could have.

My yearning would suffice for both of us.

"You think better of me than I deserve." I spoke with an indifference that cost me dearly.

She caught her breath and glared at me. "You think worse of yourself than you deserve," she snapped, her eyes afire and her chin high. I couldn't turn away from the sight of her.

We stared at each other for a long moment, one that made my heart sing.

Amy spent Memorial Day writing.

She tried to call Matteo repeatedly, but there was no answer and no voice mail available. She paced, reading through her story, knowing she needed a climactic scene, one that proved Argenta's trust of Lothair.

Matteo said he had been betrayed by a man he trusted, and that he had trusted because they'd shared a woman. A ménage scene could be hot. Amy heated up some leftover lasagna as she planned the scene. But who would Lothair trust in the first place? He was bitter and scarred.

It would have to be someone he knew from before he'd been wounded.

His brother!

Amy fell upon the pad of paper just as her phone rang. She snatched up the phone, scribbling madly, and didn't check the number.

"Amy!" Brittany whined. "You have to fix it!"

"Fix what?" Amy assumed her cousin meant the menu, but they hadn't talked in two days and it was always possible that her cousin had created more work for her.

"The menu for the wedding. You can't just let someone die."

"I wasn't letting anyone die. You messed it up. You fix it."

Brittany began to cry. "I trusted you! I wanted to have the most beautiful wedding and now it's all ruined and you won't fix it and someone's going to die..."

This could go on all night, and Amy was losing the thread of her story. "Fine," she said curtly. "I'll go tomorrow night, on the condition that you don't talk to anyone involved in hosting the wedding before the end of the reception."

"That's harsh, Amy."

Amy straightened. "That's the only deal I'm offering."

Brittany sniffled a little. "Okaaaaaaaay," she began, but Amy refused to listen to any more.

"Great. I'll let you know when the damage is repaired. Warn your mom that there might be some extra charges, and please point out to her that they're because of you."

"What?" Brittany began to protest, but Amy ended the call.

She called Matteo, partly because she wanted to talk to him and partly because she wanted her phone to be busy.

He still didn't answer.

Where was he and what was he doing?

It was bleak to have lunch alone again. Even the first day, Amy missed Ty's company with a vengeance. She found herself looking for him even though she knew he wasn't going to appear.

And calling Matteo.

Fruitlessly.

She even called F5 about him, but the person who answered the phone had no idea who he was.

That didn't bode well.

The only bonus on Tuesday was that Amy finished the book on her lunch. At least, she finished the first draft. She couldn't think of another thing to add, though she thought that might change, so she copied it after work and dropped the copy into Jade's outstretched hands.

After work, she decided to go to F5 and ferret out the truth.

To her relief, the main instructor from the class she'd taken was chatting to a woman with a blond ponytail at the front desk. He'd introduced himself as Kyle. Was this the same Kyle who'd suggested to Ty that he keep Giselle and get rid of his chest hair? Amy wondered but knew she couldn't ask.

She marched right to Kyle, and he spared her a glance. "Can I help you?"

"I took a class that you taught," Amy said and his eyes lit in recollection. "And there was another guy helping you."

"Ivan?"

"No, Matteo."

Kyle's expression immediately became guarded. The woman stepped away.

"I just need to see him."

"That's not going to be possible," Kyle said.

"I know it's against the agreement to meet socially between paid sessions, but I'll pay for a session. I *really* need to see him."

Kyle's eyes narrowed. "But he doesn't work here anymore."

"What do you mean?"

"I mean he quit." Kyle shrugged. "Actually, he quit because we were going to fire him."

"Can you give me his address or phone number?"

Kyle folded his arms across his chest. "You know that's a breach of confidentiality. I can't release any private information."

"But how will I find him?"

"Maybe you don't want to find him," Kyle said gently. "Maybe he's not who you think he is."

"I know he's been to prison."

Kyle's eyes widened. "Well, that was a surprise to us. He lied on his application, and we can't have that here at F5."

"I found the meaning of his tattoos on Wikipedia," Amy said. "Don't you check these things out?"

Kyle looked a little uneasy. "In this case, it slipped through the cracks."

"So you offered him the choice of being fired or of quitting?"

"We're not completely heartless." Kyle considered her. "Are you sure that no one else here can help you out?"

Amy thought for a minute about Ty being a silent partner. He could probably find out more about Matteo, but she wasn't going to ask him that. "No, thanks. I'll find him somehow."

"Good luck," Kyle said, as if she didn't have a chance.

Then she went to New Jersey, trying not to guess Jade's reaction or think too much about Matteo.

Amy had phoned first thing to make an appointment and the catering manager practically fell upon her in relief. She'd tried to undo Brittany's changes after talking to Amy in the morning, but they'd missed ordering deadlines for several food items. They made a few substitutions and reviewed the arrangements for the room and the schedule, and Amy knew she wasn't the only one who was reassured by the time she left.

She was riding the train home alone at nine, thinking that Ty wouldn't approve, when her phone rang.

It was Ty.

As if he could read her thoughts.

Amy's heart did that little skip and she smiled as she answered the phone. "How's Japan?"

"Crowded," he said and she closed her eyes, savoring the sound of his voice. "Fascinating. How's your week?"

"Busy. No rest for the wicked and all that."

He chuckled and that made her feel warm all over.

"We're going to lose the connection in a minute," she warned him. "The train's going into the tunnel."

"Train?" Ty echoed, his outrage clear. "Tunnel? Are you in New Jersey?"

"Not for much longer," Amy had time to say before the train went into the tunnel and Ty was gone.

She stared at the phone, pretty sure he'd call back. He was probably calculating her route and the time it would take her to change from the train to the subway at Penn Station. If he didn't have the schedule memorized, he'd look it up. And while she did find his indignation unnecessary, it was also kind of nice to have someone concerned about her.

Her phone rang again when she was fifty feet from her front door.

"Not dead yet," Amy said when she answered and heard him exhale. The connection was better than before, with no satellite delay and she wondered whether Ty had used the time to find a land line. "What took you so long?" she teased and smiled when he growled a little.

"Never mind that. Why were you in New Jersey?" he demanded.

"Because my cousin saw fit to change all the arrangements on Saturday and told me that night when everyone at the facility who could have fixed it was gone for the weekend."

"You could have left it alone," Ty said grimly.

Amy had anticipated that argument. "I could have, but I like to finish what I start. She messed up the menus, Ty, and there are a lot of guests with allergies and dietary restrictions. It would have been unpleasant."

"I thought I was the one who was nice."

Amy laughed. "Maybe it's a bigger club than you realized."

He made a disapproving sound, but she guessed that he was in a better mood. "You're home now?"

"Door locked behind me, no stalkers hiding in the closet, and Fitzwilliam complaining that dinner is late. Listen." The cat yowled right on cue. "See?" Amy chucked her coat and shoes without moving the phone from her ear.

"They're taking advantage of you."

"Of course, they are. I knew that from the start. I expected it."

"You did?"

"Nice doesn't necessarily equal dumb, Ty," Amy said as she opened the fridge. Leftover lasagna it would be.

"Not necessarily," he echoed, then laughed a little. "That's good to know."

"I knew when Aunt Natalie called that first time," Amy admitted. "It was like an undeclared price of admission. I was lonely enough to take the deal, just to have some family again."

"And if you'd known then what you know now..."

"I probably would have negotiated harder."

"Good," he said and the single word filled her with a warm glow. "How's the book?"

"I gave it to Jade tonight."

"Are you happy with it?"

"It probably needs some changes. Of course, now I've thought of a hundred things to tweak."

"She'll love it. I'm sure you did a great job."

"You have no idea whether I can write or not!"

"Doesn't matter. I believe in you, and that means I think you can do anything."

Amy didn't know what to say to that. She felt shy and tongue-tied once again, uncertain how to go forward. If this had morphed into more, how did her phone calls with Matteo fit into it all?

"Don't tell me that you're eating some of that fabulous pasta for dinner."

"Why not?"

"I'll curl up and die of envy."

Amy laughed. "Guilty as charged. You?"

"Fish," Ty replied and she guessed his opinion of that. "Noodles and rice."

Amy smiled. "I'll save you some lasagna. I'll put it in the freezer tonight."

"Temptress."

"Hardly."

"Don't sell yourself short, Amy," Ty purred and Amy's mouth went dry.

She sat down at the table and decided to be direct. "Are we still having a fake date? Or one with benefits?"

"I thought you'd never ask," he said smoothly, as if he had been waiting for the question. "How about we talk about it in person, this weekend?"

"Sounds good," Amy said, trying to keep her tone light. If Ty wanted to be intimate again, she knew what she'd say. She had a feeling, though, that Ty had more in mind than that.

If he wanted to get serious about their relationship, that would change everything. Amy knew what she should say, and she knew what she wanted to say, but those forbidden fantasies weren't going to be so easily dismissed.

And she knew what Ty would say about them.

Complicated.

After he ended the call, she stared at the phone. Would she be happy with simple and vanilla for the duration? Amy wasn't sure.

She called Matteo's number again, with no more luck than the other times.

Amy's phone rang Thursday evening, just as she was sitting down to write. She'd bought herself a new laptop on the line of credit because there was enough money left over after setting aside the money for the roof. She'd already typed in all of Lothair and Argenta's story and was considering whether to start her revisions.

Or should she wait to talk to Jade the next day?

There had been a note slipped under her door from Lisa when Amy got home from work, telling her that she and Mrs. P. were moving out. Amy went upstairs and heard the news about Lisa's brother and his wife in Orlando expecting a baby, and the plan to move closer. She was pleased for her tenants, but a little worried about finding another tenant. Red's financing plan wouldn't work out if she didn't have that rent money coming in. Lisa thought a co-worker might be interested in the apartment, so Amy was hoping for the best.

She was trying to not worry about it.

The phone rang before she decided whether to revise or not, and she smiled to see that it was Ty.

"Hi," she said, more than ready to hear his voice. "Aren't you on the other side of the world?"

"And stuck here," he admitted, sounding rueful. "Unless you'd care to use your super-powers for good."

"What happened?"

"The airline has one flight a day from Tokyo to New York. Yesterday's had a mechanical issue and is waiting for parts. So does the plane that just arrived. They don't know when they're going to get passengers on their way." Ty's tone revealed more than a twinge of irritation. "I've tried every counter and every phone number, but every seat is booked out until Sunday. You said you had super-powers when Mr. Forsythe had his flights canceled so I'm throwing myself at your mercy."

"I like the sound of that," Amy said before she thought about it.

There was a pause, during which she started to blush.

"Do you?" Ty murmured, his voice almost gravelly.

Amy caught her breath. "Don't go away."

"I'm not going anywhere," he replied, sounding tired and frustrated again. "Help me get home, Amy, please. I'll make it worth your while."

Amy smiled. "I'll need your itinerary and your credit card number.

"Yours," Ty said.

Amy took notes even as she called her friend Sandra on the land line. They'd gone to high school together and Sandra had trained to be a travel agent. She'd coordinated business trips for the executives at a Fortune 500 company, then built a travel agent business at home when she had her twin sons. Her specialty was getting business travelers where they needed to be, especially when things went wrong.

"Where is he?" Sandra asked immediately. Amy heard the chime of her laptop booting up.

Amy played intermediary, filling Sandra in on the details. She could hear the hum of the busy airport on Ty's end of the line, and typing from Sandra.

"Oh yeah," Sandra said. "That's one ugly mess."

Amy's heart sank. "They told him Sunday."

"Optimistically. There's a storm forecast for tomorrow." Sandra typed. "Everything is booked. It's crazy."

"Sandra said there's going to be a storm there," Amy told Ty. "And that the flights are full."

"The airport is full," he agreed. "I've never seen so many people in my life. Tourists and luggage everywhere!"

Tourists. Amy opened her browser and began to search on tourism from Japan.

"Every US-destined flight is booked," Sandra said. "The airline must have grabbed as many seats as they could from the other airlines to get as many their passengers on their way as possible."

"That's what they said," Ty agreed when Amy shared that. "I just don't have enough miles to have been one of the lucky ones."

"You might have to get comfortable," Sandra said and Ty groaned when he heard that bit of news.

"There has to be a way," he said, just as the results of Amy's search filled her screen.

"Tourists," she said, scrolling then clicking on one. "Did you check charters, Sandra? Because I'm looking at a ton of last minute deals on charter flights from Tokyo to Honolulu. This one goes later today."

There was a moment of silence on both phones.

"Brilliant," Ty breathed.

"Honolulu," Sandra said, even as she started to type at manic speed again. "Once there, it's easy-peasy to Los Angeles, then on to Newark. Lots of choices, without even going to Las Vegas."

"There is a god and she loves me," Ty said.

"We can do this. It won't be pretty, and it won't be business class..."

"Just find me a seat," Ty muttered. "I'll sit in the john if I have to."

"That's against FDA regulations," Sandra said when Amy repeated his comment. "But tell him to move it. He's going to have to pay to check his bag on this one, and he needs to get to this counter in forty minutes. Give me his credit card number, but he'll have to verify it at the counter with the actual card."

"Forty minutes should be do-able," Amy said and told Ty where he had to go.

"I'm on my way," Ty said.

"Do you know how big that airport is?" Sandra said. "Tell him I've got an alternative routing departing two hours later if he misses this one."

"Give me your email," Amy said to Ty. "We'll send you a new itinerary. You should have it by the time you get to Hawaii."

"I think I love you," Ty said and Amy's mouth dropped open.

Then he ended the call, leaving her staring at it in wonder.

She almost forgot to check Matteo's number at midnight. It rang and rang, and she laid awake for long hours, afraid of what kind of trouble he'd found.

And whether she could have made a difference.

Late.

Ty hated being late.

Even if it wasn't his fault.

Maybe especially if it wasn't his fault, because he couldn't fix it. The flight was late leaving LA and missed its landing slot at Newark, which meant they circled for what seemed like an eternity before finally landing. Ty shot through the terminal and grabbed a cab, only to be caught in the jam of Friday night traffic heading into the city. F5 was lit up and the cab inched along the street toward the building. He finally paid the driver and walked the last two blocks, pushing through the crowds with his briefcase and suit bag.

He had to go back to New Jersey, but he wasn't going to meet Amy's family looking the way he did now. He was charging to her defense, and he was going to look like a champion who had at least a chance of kicking butt and taking names.

He'd had a sense ever since leaving Tokyo that he was coming home, not just to New York, but to Amy. He'd called her at each connection point and savored the sound of her voice. She'd been writing and he could hear the thrill in her voice at her accomplishment. He was proud to have been even a tiny part of that, to even be able to observe her taking charge of her life again, and he was looking forward to another night in Brooklyn.

At Amy's house.

Ty was going to make sure she knew how much he appreciated her help.

The burner phone was still on the kitchen counter. Ty checked and it had thirty-seven missed calls. That did just about nothing to improve his mood. He called Joe and told him he'd need the car in fifteen minutes.

Ty had a shower and shaved again, dressed in a crisp white shirt and navy suit. In thirteen minutes, he was standing at the exit of the private lot and garage where his car was pampered.

"Ooo, hot date tonight," said Joe with a low whistle of appreciation.

Ty smiled and tipped him, then roared toward New Jersey.

And Amy.

What was she doing calling Matteo thirty-seven times? That was worse than her going to New Jersey alone on Tuesday night.

It was past time for the truth.

There was no sign of Ty.

And Matteo was still AWOL.

Amy feared the worst. She'd talked to Ty when he was in Hawaii and he'd called again from LA to say that flight was late. Ever since, there'd been silence. She'd called him and gotten no answer. She'd called Matteo—repeatedly—and no one picked up.

Jade loved the book but thought there was something missing. She and Amy had talked about some possibilities on Amy's lunch break Friday, but none of them felt right to Amy. She needed to think, but she wasn't feeling creative with so much before her.

She hadn't heard from Lisa's co-worker about the apartment and though it hadn't been long, the prospect of not having a tenant worried her.

Amy left the office at the last possible minute on Friday night and took the train to New Jersey. She'd gotten a ride to the church from her uncle, who was disgruntled that she hadn't made better arrangements.

That would be arrangements that didn't inconvenience him.

Amy couldn't decide whether she wanted most to see Ty or to inhale a glass of wine. Brittany was in full Bridezilla mode, Aunt Natalie was snapping at everyone, and the minister was trying to get Josh to repeat his vows.

"I thought you had a date, Amy," Brittany said with a smile that wasn't very kind.

"Ty's flight is late," Amy replied smoothly. She saw the two bridesmaids, Tamara and Brigid, exchange a knowing glance.

She was so tired of all of them.

Amy sat down, wondering whether she'd ever see any of them after the wedding was over.

"You're probably wondering if it was worth it," Aunt Pauline said quietly, taking a seat beside Amy.

Amy glanced up in surprise and her aunt smiled. The oldest of the three sisters, Pauline had to be close to sixty. She was slim and tall, and something in her features reminded Amy of her dad. The touch of silver at Pauline's temples was a painful reminder that her dad hadn't had time to get gray hair and she looked down again, her heart in her throat.

"I would have told you to run and not look back, if you'd asked me." Pauline sighed. "You were free of it all." Her gaze roved over her mother and siblings, then returned to Amy. "You didn't have to follow anyone's advice and that must have been wonderful."

Amy wasn't prepared to look at her sole care of her parents in such good light. "How could I have asked you?" she said, her tone carrying a challenge. "I had no idea how to find any of you."

"True," her aunt admitted. "Not a one of us was there for you, and that was just wrong."

"What was wrong was that you weren't there for Dad," Amy said.

Her aunt flicked a look at her. "So, they didn't tell you after all," she mused. "I wondered whether they would."

"Who didn't tell me what?"

Aunt Pauline sighed. She indicated her mother with a fingertip. Amy still couldn't think of Helena as her grandmother, although she was. "My father—your grandfather—had very firm ideas about the world, and his wife was the one most expected to adhere to them. We all were. We all were trapped. I even stayed in a terrible marriage, just to keep from challenging his notions." She gave Amy a look. "Good women don't get divorced, you know."

"I see."

"About a year after my father died, I finally filed for divorce from Craig. It was the most liberating thing I'd ever done and I regretted not doing it sooner. I spent more than thirty years of my life miserably unhappy. Sure, I have three wonderful kids, but our marriage was terrible. But I stayed, rather than defy my father's expectations." She nodded. "I defied him once, though, and he never found out."

"Really," Amy said, wondering what this had to do with her.

"I adored Peter," Pauline admitted, tearing shining in her eyes. "We were only two years apart, but he was my big brother and I thought he could do anything. In the end, he did the impossible. He refused to become the heir to the throne. He wrote poetry. He went away to college and didn't come back. He made his own future, independent of the one my father insisted he should have." She took a deep breath. "And he married your mother because he adored her. They were happy. I could see it and hear it. And no one, not even my father, was going to make Peter give up Gabriella. It was like a fairy tale."

"It didn't end like one," Amy felt obliged to note.

"No, it sure didn't." Pauline swallowed. "Peter called to tell me about Gabriella, and I could hear how devastated he was. I cried with him, because I'd always believed that love conquered all and he was living the proof of it. It wasn't right that she died so young. Then he told me about his own diagnosis and I cried even more. I've never felt so discouraged as I did that day." Her throat worked. "But he tried to console me. He told me that if you follow your heart and pursue your dreams, there can be no regrets."

Amy looked down at her hands, because she was afraid she would cry.

"I thought about that for a long time. Too long, really. Then my sixth grandchild was born and my seventh was on the way, and I wondered what kind of example I was giving to all of them. I went to the house, but the neighbor said Peter was in the hospital. I went to the hospital and checked with the nurses' station. They said you were running errands that afternoon and wouldn't be in to visit until later. I made them promise not to tell you I'd been there. I wasn't sure whether they'd do it or not."

Amy was astonished. "I'm glad you went to see him," she said. She'd really had no idea.

Pauline nodded. "It was so precious to spend time with him. I went four times in all, and then he died." Amy watched her aunt's tears well. "I was such a coward, Amy. I thought you would hate me for not coming sooner. I passed you in the corridor that last time, and I didn't have the nerve to speak to you. I didn't want to start something that I might not be able to finish. My father forbade us all to go to the funeral. I couldn't defy him that time either." Her tears fell and Amy took her hand. "And Peter was right. I didn't follow my heart so I have plenty of regrets. Once Father died, I was able to change, but I regret all those lost years and lost opportunities. I regret not having known Gabriella at all."

"She was wonderful."

"I know, because she raised a wonderful daughter, and she made my wonderful brother happy." The two women smiled at each other, and Pauline took a shaking breath. "I'm still not very good at following my heart. But I wanted to tell you that I'm so sorry. And I would like to know you better. We can't make up for all the lost time, but I would like to have you in my life."

"Dad would like that, too," Amy said, her voice thick.

"He would."

They smiled at each other, then Pauline kissed Amy's cheeks. The minister cleared his throat with impatience and Amy stood up again, ready to continue with the rehearsal.

Follow your heart.

It was advice to live by, and Amy was going to do it. She'd made a good start, thanks to Ty's encouragement, and no matter what the future held for the two of them, she was going to pursue her dreams, wherever they led.

"Oh!" Aunt Natalie said suddenly and Amy saw that she was looking toward the back of the church.

Amy turned to find Ty striding down the aisle looking as confident and polished as ever. If he was wrinkled, she couldn't see where. He walked straight toward her, ignoring everyone else, halted before her and tipped her chin up with a fingertip.

"I'm sorry, sweetheart," he said, then brushed his lips across hers. His gaze brightened and she knew he'd noticed that she'd been crying a little. "You look gorgeous," he murmured, smiled just a little, then bent to kiss her.

Thoroughly.

And Amy didn't care if it was for the benefit of her relatives or not.

CHAPTER THIRTEEN

AMY HAD been crying.

And that meant Ty was ready to slaughter whoever was responsible.

He was well aware of her relatives watching them and he felt their astonishment, but he'd planned for that. After he'd given her a kiss that should have made his intentions clear, she smiled up at him. He'd kissed off a lot of her lipstick and a strand of her hair had slipped free. Her eyes were shining so brightly that his heart thundered.

He had missed her so much. In this moment, he just wanted to scoop her up and carry her off to a private corner, at least until they had all the truth on the table between them and he'd convinced her to let him be part of her life.

But that would have to wait.

Again.

"Ty, this is my Aunt Pauline," Amy said, turning to make introductions. "I just found out that she visited my dad near the end."

That explained the tears.

And that made Ty an instant fan of Aunt Pauline.

Maybe he wouldn't have to kill *all* of them.

He shook the aunt's hand and let himself be introduced all around. The bride was as pouty as he'd anticipated, clearly disliking that he and Amy had stolen even an increment of the attention she felt she deserved. The groom looked as if he were attending on sufferance, which was strange. If he was reluctant to marry Brittany, why was there going to be a wedding?

218

Ty noticed that Josh's parents stood back a bit from Brittany's family and sensed their disapproval. The tensions were really odd, and he'd been to enough weddings to be aware of the ones that should have been present.

He looked again at Brittany and noticed that her breasts were straining her dress, as if they'd suddenly become larger. She looked more tired than was typical for a bride, and seemed more inclined to become emotional than all the women he'd known in his life.

If she was pregnant, that would explain a lot.

By the time the rehearsal and the dinner were over, Amy was worn out. Ty put his arm around her when they left the restaurant and she found herself leaning against him. She'd never expected to come to rely on him so much, but he'd been great. He'd charmed them all, answered their questions, and diverted their rude comments. He made it look like he and Amy were madly in love and she felt the change in how her family regarded her.

She was feeling pretty smitten herself.

Amy slanted a look at Ty and felt a little hum of pleasure to be in his company again. He looked tired, though he was trying to hide it. Her heart squeezed that he'd made such an effort to keep his promise to her.

She could love this man.

She was pretty sure she already did.

The question was whether he could love her, if he knew the whole truth about her desires and fantasies? Amy had a pretty good idea of the answer to that, but they should talk about it.

When they weren't both so worn out.

"Did you give up on me?" Ty asked when they were on the road.

"I was afraid you'd arrive after we'd gone to the restaurant." Amy stole another glance at him. "And I hadn't given you that address. I tried to call you."

"My phone died, and there was no time to charge it in any of the terminals."

"Lots of running?"

"Lots. I got my workout for the week without getting to the gym."

"Thank you for doing it. I was really glad you came."

"I would have done more than that," Ty admitted and cast her a look that made her simmer. "The way you smiled when I walked into that church made it more than worthwhile."

219

Amy felt herself flush. "I'll bet you say that to all the women who use their super-powers for your benefit."

"If so, it would be a very select group of women."

"Is that right?" Amy knew he was teasing her and she liked it.

"It is. In fact, I can only think of one person in that group."

"That *is* very select."

"Picky, that's me."

"Discerning, maybe?"

"Definitely." He drove, and she watched him, admiring how he made everything look easy. "So, we have a deal," he began and Amy smiled.

"Several, actually. Which one do you mean?"

"The 'no intervening on my part without asking permission' one."

Amy's smile broadened. "Oh, that one."

"Yes, that one."

"The one that's killing you."

"Pretty much." His sidelong smile was conspiratorial and that dimple had reappeared. "So, I need to ask permission."

"For what?"

Ty grimaced. "I hate to say this, but I like your family about as much as I expected to."

"Except for Aunt Pauline."

"Right."

"You can't make a scene at the wedding."

He shook his head slowly. "I really, really want to defend you here."

"I'm not sure I need a champion."

She got a quick bright look for that. "I don't like how they talk to you. I don't like that they're taking advantage of your kindness and think it's okay."

"It'll be over soon."

"Just let me do one thing." Ty spoke quietly but with resolve. "Just one."

"Not to Brittany. She wasn't this awful before, and it will be her wedding day."

"No, not Brittany," Ty agreed easily. "Aunt Natalie." He bit off the name with satisfaction and Amy had to tease him.

"That wouldn't be nice."

"No, not at all. But what goes around comes around. I'd really like to make the delivery." His tone dropped to an entreaty. "Please?"

"You're not going to tell me what you're going to do, are you?"

"Nope. It'll be a surprise."

Amy only had to think about it for a moment. "Okay."

Ty grinned. "If I weren't driving, I'd kiss you."

"Promises, promises," Amy teased and liked that she made him laugh out loud. They rode in companionable silence for a few moments, a little hum of awareness crackling between them. She was thinking about dragging him into her house and having her way with him, just to check whether vanilla was as hot as she remembered...

Then Ty cleared his throat. "Can I ask a tacky question?"

Amy laughed. "You?"

"Me," he agreed.

"Go on then."

"Is the bride pregnant?"

Amy's lips parted in shock. She thought of the dress being too tight, repeatedly, after so many fittings. She thought about Brittany's emotional state, which she'd attributed to wedding nerves. She thought about Josh's sullen participation and his parents' resentment of every little decision. "She might be. I never thought of it. They've been engaged for ages, though."

"So, maybe the groom had second thoughts. His family doesn't look too happy about the match."

"You think she tricked him?"

"I don't know. It doesn't seem as if it would be out of character."

Amy chewed her lip, thinking. "No, it wouldn't be. Not if her perfect wedding might be canceled."

Ty shook his head. "Bad idea to try to make it right with a pregnancy."

Amy was intrigued by his pessimism. "Because they don't really love each other?"

"Doesn't look like it, does it?"

She had to agree with that and it made her sad. Ty's comment about Brittany and Josh made Amy think about her own choices and taking responsibility for them. If she made love with Ty again, she wanted to be absolutely sure of her choice. It would be so easy to invite him in and spend another night together.

But was the easy choice the right one? It seldom was.

She wanted what her parents had had. Complete confidence in each other. Love and happiness and the conviction that they were pursuing their dreams together.

No regrets.

They drove in silence for a while, then Ty turned down her street. "Tired?" he asked.

"Exhausted," Amy agreed.

He cast her a very hot look as he parked in front of her house. "Did you forget that I promised to make it worth your while?"

"No," Amy admitted. They needed to talk and Amy wanted to do that when they'd both had enough sleep. When this wedding from hell was over. "But I can't tonight. You must be even more tired than me."

Something flicked in his gaze, then Ty smiled. "Of course. What time should I pick you up in the morning?"

"I'll take the train."

His eyes flashed but Amy lifted a finger and spoke before he could. "You just traveled halfway around the world, in a hurry, to keep your promise to me. I appreciate it so much that I don't want you to have to get up early, then find something to do in New Jersey for four hours. Sleep in, please. I'll see you at the wedding."

The corner of Ty's mouth quirked. "Sounds like you're being nice."

"I hear it's contagious."

He chuckled, then got out of the car, coming around to open her door for her. When she was standing right beside him, Amy couldn't resist. She stretched up and kissed him, showing her gratitude with her touch.

And maybe a little more than that.

Ty inhaled sharply when she ended their kiss and his eyes were dark. His arm was locked around her waist, keeping her on her toes and crushed against his chest.

It was a very good place to be.

Amy's resolve wavered. She doubted that she'd regret another night with Ty.

"I want to talk to you about something," he said and she smiled.

"It doesn't feel like you want conversation."

Ty brushed her hair away from her cheeks with his fingertips, and the tenderness of the gesture made Amy's heart clench. "You do look tired."

"So do you."

"Until tomorrow then," he said, his voice tight. "And we'll talk."

Amy's chest was tight. "Yes, sleep well."

Ty snorted, as if that was out of the question, and kissed her again, slowly enough to warm her all the way to her toes. Amy wondered whether she was insane to not drag him into the house, but knew she'd think more clearly in the morning. She left his embrace with reluctance.

Ty stood watching until she was in the house. She heard the sound of his car driving away and looked down at Fitzwilliam, whose tail was flicking.

"I know. Another late dinner. You're going to have to fire the staff."

He complained, then led the way to the kitchen, his tail waving like a rallying banner.

"What if I got pregnant?" she asked the cat. "Condoms are hardly reliable. Would Ty want to do the right thing? Would I even want to get married to keep up appearances?" She followed the cat to the kitchen, thinking out loud. "No, but neither would I want to raise a kid alone."

Amy pondered that as she put kibble in the cat's dish. "Mama was pregnant, but she knew she loved Dad with all her heart before that happened. Is it wrong to want to be as in love as Mama and Dad were?"

It wasn't. Amy knew it. She didn't want to compromise anything. She wanted it all.

Amy shook her head at her own whimsy.

Fitzwilliam hunkered down beside his dish, the image of disapproval.

"The thing is, Fitzwilliam, that Ty is just fine. He doesn't need me, not like Matteo does. Maybe he doesn't need anyone." Amy found a can of the cat's favorite food and showed it to him. "I think he likes me. I know I like him. That's all good. But I'm worried that other things I like will eventually drive us apart. You know?"

Fitzwilliam fixed her with a look of disdain that she should be so slow.

"I think it's important for love to heal people's wounds, but I don't think Ty has any. That's a good thing, I know. He's normal. He's reliable." She sighed. "He's wonderful, actually. I don't want to ever see him disappointed in me."

Fitzwilliam wound around her legs, purring vigorously.

"And what about Dad's legacy? Shouldn't I try to make a difference, even if it's not the easy path? There's something about

Matteo that gets to me and I can't ignore that. My heart tells me that I should reach out to him."

After she fed Fitzwilliam, Amy tried Matteo's number again.

Twice.

And worried what kind of trouble he'd found.

Ty awakened to find the sun shining into his apartment. He felt roughly a thousand times better than he had the night before. As much as he hated to admit it, Amy had been right.

Tonight was another story.

Tonight would be the night they straightened out everything, for once and for all. Ty had to hope that tomorrow morning, she'd be right beside him when he woke up.

He rolled over and stretched, then eyed the clock and winced. He'd slept much later than he'd expected. He still had time to go down and work out a bit and shake off a bit of his jet lag.

He thought about calling Amy, but knew she'd be busy this morning.

The burner phone was still on the kitchen counter.

Five more missed messages.

Two had to have been right after he left. Another in the middle of the night. Another at dawn. Another just five minutes before.

Fury shot through Ty's body. Amy had been exhausted. She'd sent *him* home. But she'd been calling Matteo all night long? If he could have incinerated the phone with a look, he would have done it. Instead, he marched down to F5 and worked out hard.

He would solve the Matteo problem today.

Forever.

The wedding, to Amy's relief, went off without a hitch.

Even if Ty's eyes did twinkle when she floated down the aisle in a horrific mound of tangerine chiffon and tulle. She despised the dress and she was pretty sure he knew it. He winked at her as she passed him and she felt her cheeks heat, but she didn't miss a step.

He looked wonderful, of course. How many suits did he own?

She'd been peeking at her cousin all day, when they visited the hairdresser and the make-up artist, and as they dressed at the house, wondering. Was Brittany pregnant? Her dress was so tight across her breasts that Amy thought she'd pop a seam, and it had been altered less than a week before.

Her tummy was round and soft, too, rounder than Amy remembered.

And there was the zit on her chin. The make-up artist teased her about it, saying that all brides got either a zit or their period, and that the zit was the easier choice. Brittany's expression had turned sly, as if she knew she wouldn't get her period.

Hmm.

At least Josh had warmed up to the proceedings a bit. He didn't stammer over his vows and he looked at Brittany as if he felt something for her. Amy chose to take encouragement where she could find it. The weather was perfect, so the plan to go to a local park with pretty gardens for the pictures was a go. The catering manager met Amy at the facility when the wedding party arrived, and they confirmed a few last details.

The meal was delicious.

The speeches were awful.

And finally, the dancing began.

Amy wasn't really surprised to see Ty striding straight toward her, intent on claiming her first dance. Her aunt Pauline looked on with pleasure.

There was a tension in him, though, one that she hadn't been aware of until he touched her. "What's wrong?" she asked when he'd swept her onto the dance floor.

"Not a thing." He looked down at her and with proximity she could see his intensity. "Yet."

"You're up to something," Amy accused.

"You have a suspicious mind," he countered.

"You look far too innocent. Are you going to do more than we agreed?"

"No way." He gave her a hard look that was thrilling. "We have a deal."

"That sounds more ominous than reassuring."

He surveyed her and smiled, that teasing twinkle back in his eyes. "Aren't you lovely," he said.

Amy knew he was quoting a movie and she knew which one.

"You're blind, Tyler," she said, doing her best imitation of Kristin Scott Thomas. "I look like a giant meringue."

"But a citrus one. That's different."

"Different isn't always good."

"No." He looked at the dress again. "I doubt you'll even get use of it at parties."

Amy giggled and Ty swirled her past her grandmother in that moment. Helena looked up. "Not any parties I want to be invited to attend."

"The ecclesiastical purple and the pagan orange," Ty began, then shook his head. "I forget the rest of that bit.

"It's okay. I forgot a purple sash." She smiled up at him, feeling much better than she had all day, just because he was determined to make her smile "So, *Four Weddings and a Funeral* was another popular choice with the sisters?"

"Of course. Hugh Grant, you know. But that song." Ty rolled his eyes. "I already have the earworm."

"I bet they play it tonight."

"I bet they do, my Tangerine Queen."

Amy laughed. "You're just trying to make me feel better."

"Yes." He bent down and whispered in her ear, the feel of his breath doing shivery things to her. "Because it's a hideous dress. Probably the most hideous bridesmaid's dress I've ever seen, and I've seen quite a few."

Amy sighed with mock relief. "Thank you for that. Help me take it to Goodwill?"

"No. I'll help you burn it."

"Too much synthetic. I'm not sure it'll burn. It might just melt and make a lot of smoke."

"Great, it's an environmental hazard, too."

She looked down. "I could maybe save the shoes. They could be dyed black..."

"Shoes and dress are destined to be together forever." Ty raised his brows. "*Everything* burns."

"But..."

"You'll agree with me when you realize the shoes have turned your feet tangerine today."

"How do you know these things?"

Ty put her hand on his shoulder and held up four fingers. *Four*, he mouthed and Amy laughed again.

The music changed but Ty kept dancing.

"But here's the thing," he continued. Amy realized all of her female relations were watching, obviously wanting desperately to know what Ty was saying to her. "It's not a coincidence that your cousin chose this color."

Amy pulled back a bit to look at him. "What do you mean?"

"I don't think she could have picked a worse color for you."

"But it wasn't about me..."

"Wasn't it?"

"You can't just say something like that and look all wise and not tell me what you're talking about," Amy complained.

"I wondered, but I knew for sure last night, at the rehearsal dinner."

"How so?"

"Didn't you see the look on the bride-to-be's face when we said hello after a long week apart?"

Amy felt her cheeks heat. "I was busy, being kissed."

Ty smiled. "Complaints?"

She smiled back at him. "Not one."

"You should know that the groom was checking you out and your cousin looked murderous."

"Tyler!"

He held up a hand, scouts' honor. "All true. You're much prettier than Brittany, and nicer, too." He shook his head. "If you ever figure that out, it might be the end of you being unpaid staff."

"I can't believe she'd do that," Amy charged, but there wasn't as much heat in her words as there might have been a week before. "It would be petty and mean."

"Which doesn't make it untrue," he murmured. He kissed her cheek as the song came to an end. "And now, I'm going to dance with your aunt Natalie."

"What have I agreed to let you do?"

"I'm just spreading joy and goodwill everywhere I go."

That would be a feat, but Amy had no chance to tell Ty so before he winked and headed for her aunt. She bit back a smile that the DJ was playing *Love is All Around*. She couldn't look at Ty, because she knew she'd laugh too hard.

It *was* an earworm. She'd be feeling it in her fingers for a week. She'd even feel it in her toes.

Aunt Natalie was like putty in Ty's hands. He'd planned this moment and it worked out even better than he'd anticipated.

There was a certain irony in the song that played as they danced. As far as Ty could see, love was AWOL at this particular wedding.

"I'm so glad to finally meet you all," he said with false cheer.

DEBORAH COOKE

Natalie regarded him with suspicion. "Amy has talked about us?"

"No, not so much. She's very discreet, but we have talked about the loss of her parents." Ty shook his head, and spoke from the heart. "I wish I'd known her then and could have helped her out. It must have been very tough for her."

Natalie averted her gaze. "It must have been," she agreed without much enthusiasm.

"Thank goodness she had all of you to support her," Ty said, knowing it was just the opposite. "It's so great when families stick together and help each other out."

"Isn't it?"

"Like this wedding. Amy hasn't mentioned it, but I have to think that she's done so much for Brittany to return the favor to all of you." Ty smiled and shook his head, aware that Natalie was staring at him. "That's what family is all about, isn't it?"

"I suppose."

"My sister used a wedding planner last year and it cost her eight thousand dollars." He felt Natalie flinch. "The wedding didn't go as smoothly as this one. It's so great that Amy offered her organizational skills to help Brittany avoid that kind of expense." He sighed. "She's just amazing, isn't she?"

Natalie's eyes narrowed. "I'm glad you think so highly of her," she said, her tone a little sharper than it had been. "I'm sure she has plans for you."

"Plans for me? What do you mean?"

Natalie smiled coldly. "You look like you have a good income, Tyler. I don't doubt that Amy learned her tricks from her mother."

Ty's heart clenched and he felt cold. He wouldn't have believed that Amy's aunt would say anything so nasty, but realized he was wrong.

"Tricks?" he echoed, pretending he didn't understand.

He wanted her to say it out loud.

Bitch.

And then he wanted to make sure that what went around came around.

Natalie, oblivious to his thoughts, smiled. "My brother was compelled to marry Amy's mother after she got pregnant. She knew that no one in our family approved of the match, but she tricked Peter, and she got what she wanted. At his expense."

"I don't think she had to trick the man she loved to convince him

228

to marry her."

"You weren't there!"

"No, but I know that Amy was raised by two people who loved each other, two people who followed their hearts and their dreams."

"It wasn't Peter's dream to marry an immigrant," she snarled.

"Was it Josh's dream to marry your daughter?" Ty asked quietly. "Because unless I'm very mistaken, the bride looks pregnant."

Natalie stared at him in astonishment. The music ended. Ty turned to the newly wedded couple, just in time to see Brittany barf on Josh's shoes.

It looked like wedding cake.

"Brittany!" her mother screeched. "Are you pregnant?"

Brittany turned red, as clear an answer as she could have made aloud. Josh looked as if he wanted to disappear and his parents turned away in disgust.

And that was enough.

Ty strode across the room to where Amy stood, one hand raised to her lips. He claimed her hand with a flourish and spun her into his arms. "My work here is done. Come on, my Tangerine Queen. We've got a dress to burn."

"That was wicked," Amy said when she finally stopped laughing.

"Impossible," Ty said, changing gears with a vengeance. "I'm *nice*."

That set Amy on another bout of laughter, one that made her cry so much that she had to take off her glasses. Her mascara ran and she used up all the tissues in her little clutch before the mess was cleaned up. She saw white and realized Ty was offering her a handkerchief. "I must look like a raccoon."

"No. There are no orange raccoons. They're black and a tasteful taupe."

Amy giggled again. "You shouldn't have done it."

"No, I shouldn't have. But I enjoyed it." He shook a finger at her. "And you laughed."

"It was too perfect."

"They had it coming."

They sat in companionable silence as Ty drove and Amy smiled at the realization of how much she enjoyed his company. It was easy to be with him but a little bit electric, too. She thought of Matteo, then, and how incredibly hot the scene with him had been, and yearned for a little bit more than even this.

She was greedy.

"Penny for your thoughts," Ty said.

"Nothing important," Amy lied and pretended to yawn. "Just worn out."

"You're shifting your legs," he noted. "I thought maybe we were thinking about the same thing."

Amy looked to find Ty smiling. He wasn't looking at her, but that slow smile still did things to her equilibrium.

"There's something I wanted to talk to you about," he continued easily, sparing her only the barest glance. His gaze was warm, though, and his voice had dropped low.

Amy's pulse increased.

"What would you think about making this fake date real?"

"What do you mean?" she asked, her voice a little higher than would have been ideal.

"I mean that we'd actually be seeing each other. Dating. Not pretending to date."

"I'd think that would be complicated."

Ty chuckled. "No, I think it would be simple. Simpler than a fake date with benefits." He stopped in front of her house and fixed a look on her that was so intense that she simmered. He reached for her hand, and his fingers closed over hers. "What do you think, Amy?"

"I'm surprised," she admitted, because she was caught off guard by the turmoil his question launched inside her. On the one hand, she wanted to accept. On the other, her forbidden fantasies weren't going to go away anytime soon. She had to believe that they'd ultimately drive Ty away.

"I'm not," he said. "I knew from the moment you started to tell me off that I was in deep trouble." His gaze was locked on hers and she was keenly aware of how close they were together.

Amy caught her breath. She tugged her hand from his. "I don't think I can, Ty."

"Excuse me?"

"There's someone else. It's complicated. I don't want to break my promise to you about the weddings, but I can't just abandon him. I need to see it through, even though I don't know where it's going. It might not go anywhere, but I have to finish what I started."

There she'd said it, and not well.

Ty straightened and his eyes narrowed and for a moment, Amy had an intriguing glimpse of the domineering billionaire book boyfriend in him. "Someone else," he echoed, clearly incredulous.

"Someone else." Amy forced a smile but she felt awful. "I'm sorry. I didn't think it mattered since ours was just an arrangement. If we'd really been dating, I would have broken this off ages ago."

Ty appeared to be stunned.

Amy guessed that he didn't get turned down very often.

"So, um, thanks for today. I really appreciated you coming, and I'll return the favor next weekend."

He didn't say a word.

She thought he was just shocked but when he turned to face her, she saw that his jaw was clenched. "Who is he?"

"I don't think that really matters," Amy said. "You wouldn't know him. Not in your social circle at all."

Ty's eyes narrowed. "Amy..."

If he tried to change her mind, if he touched her or kissed her or did that thing with his thumb, Amy was pretty sure he would convince her to choose him. But it would be only for the short-term and it would hurt more when it came to its inevitable end.

When she disappointed him.

She was trying to do the right thing. Why was it so hard?

Amy flung open the car door, not waiting for him to come around to open it. If he touched her, she'd be lost. "I'm sorry, Ty. Good night."

She was running away and she knew it, but Amy couldn't see another option. Her hand shook as she got out her keys, but she didn't look back. She could feel Ty watching her, his gaze practically boring a hole in her back, but he'd get over it. He didn't like being declined. No one did. But he'd find someone else easily.

Amy didn't think that Matteo had the same advantage.

He needed someone to believe in him. It might not be enough to matter, but she was going to try, just like her dad always tried. She had to trust the power of their connection, or at least give it a chance.

Amy shut the door behind herself and leaned back against it, fighting a sense that she'd just done a cowardly thing. She felt all mixed up, and reminded herself that it was only natural that she find Ty attractive. He had everything.

Even the fact that he wanted her didn't mean that she was the woman for him.

And that was when she knew exactly what scene her book was missing.

She kicked off her shoes and fed Fitzwilliam. She got her laptop and typed like a madwoman at the kitchen table.

Argenta had to heal Lothair with her trust.

"You have yet to learn the lesson taught by pain," I said softly, feeling her still. I knew she watched me. "You have yet to learn that there is more to fear from the presence of others than their absence."

I stirred up the fire in the brazier, feeding it until the flames leaped high. I tugged the signet ring from my finger, the gold one that indicated my rank as heir. I placed it upon a hook, one used to hold a vessel of wine or milk while it heated, and dipped it into the flames. It was not long until the metal began to glow. I knew Argenta watched me intently.

"I pledged to teach you of pain," I said, through my teeth. "Pain has shaped me and I have shown you how. You are right that I was cut, I was shackled, and I was burned. Perhaps I was too gentle with the wax for you to heed my lesson. Let us return to burn." I lifted the hook from the flame and the ring glowed hot. I donned my glove as I carried the ring toward her.

Her gaze flicked between it and my face, but her defiant expression didn't change. She glared at me, defying me to do it, to prove myself to be that I was less than she believed me to be.

I would take her dare.

I donned the glove. She didn't flinch.

I took the ring between finger and thumb, and the heat passed even through the leather. She lifted her chin.

I placed the ring over her breast, planning to Mark her where the brand of my insignia would always be seen.

She stared at me, proud and defiant.

Trusting.

I moved the ring over her flesh, choosing my spot. The skin turned rosy even when the hot metal was close, but Argenta kept her chin high and her gaze locked upon my face. Her confidence was absolute.

And confronted with the steely challenge in her eyes, I realized she was right.

I couldn't do it.

I spun and flung the ring across the chamber, not caring where it fell. I cast the glove aside, and removed her gag with rough gestures. I kissed her hungrily as I unfastened her bonds, my hands shaking with my need to possess this warrior maiden who had stolen my heart, against all odds.

By mirroring my truth in her relentless gaze.

I wasn't surprised in the least that she welcomed me, meeting me touch for touch, driving me onward until we were consumed together in the storm we had built.

No?

No?

Ty drove back downtown, more furious than he'd been in a long time. Maybe ever. Amy had turned him down? Ty could live with that, but he knew she'd chosen Matteo, a loser with a jail record, over him. He knew Amy was smarter than that.

He could have changed her mind. He could have overwhelmed her with his touch, followed her into the house, persuaded her to surrender to him. But she said no and no meant no.

No matter how much it pissed him off.

This wasn't over, not by a long shot.

Ty knew that Amy liked to help people. In hindsight, he saw that he'd created Matteo to be a little too much in need of a good woman. He'd tried to solve things for Amy, in the mode of Mr. Darcy making all come right for Elizabeth, never anticipating that she'd choose the rogue Wickham in the end.

That wasn't how the story ended.

Ty had seen it enough times to be sure.

It wasn't how this one should end either.

He parked in the entrance to the private garage, still simmering, and tossed the keys to Joe, who owned it. The older man watched him, undoubtedly discerning his mood. "I shouldn't park it tonight, Joe," Ty said and Joe smiled.

"No problem, Mr. T. You know, my boy Noah is home from college this weekend. He's coming in at midnight to give me a break."

"He's a good kid, Joe." Ty took a steadying breath.

"And he loves this car." Joe ran an appreciative hand over the hood. "If you don't mind, I'll leave it for him to park."

"I don't mind. Tell him to take it around the block first."

"You were always good to Noah, Mr. T. If it weren't for that summer job you gave him at F5, I don't think he'd be going to college."

"Noah's smart, Joe. I always said we'd all be working for him one of these days."

Joe chuckled, his pride in his son more than clear.

Ty was still riled as he rode the elevator to his apartment. He knew it would take a hundred laps to calm him down. Maybe that wouldn't even work. How could he convince Amy? She had to know how good

233

they were together. She couldn't really believe that Matteo could offer her a future.

He refused for the moment to consider that he was also Matteo, and how deeply screwy that was.

He'd played it all wrong, and that was a good part of what made him so mad. He couldn't blame Kyle for giving him bad advice. This situation was entirely his own making and he had to make it right.

The burner phone was still on the counter. Of course. Ty flicked the door shut and marched toward it, hesitated only a moment, then turned it on.

Two more missed calls.

His lips tightened.

Then the phone rang right in his hand.

Ty glared at it.

Here was his chance to kill Matteo, for once and for all.

Ty unlocked the door of his balcony and stepped outside, cleared his throat, and answered Amy's call.

Amy sat back.

She read the scene again. She knew truth when it fell out of her fingertips.

It was perfect. It was romantic and ideal and just so perfect.

Jade would love it.

Amy seized her phone and called Matteo again. She got up to pace in the kitchen. She'd called so many times that she wasn't really expecting him to answer.

She jumped when he did.

"Angel," he said in his deep dangerous tone and she sat down hard. "You should not call me."

"I needed to know that you were all right." She could hear the faint sound of traffic and wondered where he was.

"I have been better."

"I need to see you..." she began but he interrupted her.

"No."

"But I can help."

"You cannot help. I am running, Angel, because I have been betrayed again."

"I told you before that I can help. You should come here."

"No!"

"You're protecting me, and that's sweet, but we have to work together..."

"Sweet?" he snarled. "I am not *sweet*, Angel. I play games at F5 and give women what they want, but it is a game. I might have played it longer with you, but it was always a game and it was always going to end."

"Not necessarily," she argued.

"Absolutely," he said. "You are tempting. You are a little tease. You could never satisfy me." His voice dropped lower. "No one woman can."

"Maybe you should try being with one woman before you decide that."

He laughed harshly, then caught his breath. "No," he whispered and she knew he wasn't talking to her. He swore in Spanish, then his breath worked as if he was running.

"Matteo? What's going on?" Amy stood up, clutching the phone. "Matteo?"

He roared as if in pain, then his voice grew more distant. The sound of traffic grew louder and there was a sound like rushing air as Matteo's cry faded away.

Amy jumped at the crash of the phone impacting something.

Then the connection was lost.

She called again immediately, but the line rang busy.

Amy sat down at her kitchen table, horrified. What had happened to Matteo?

Ty knew as soon as he heard the phone hit.

No. Not his car.

It had been irresponsible to throw the phone, and he knew as much, but he was so livid with Amy that he hadn't considered his choice more than to chuck the phone in the direction of the roof of Joe's garage. There was never anyone there.

He'd been hoping it would hit the pavement and shatter.

But as soon as it left his hand, he knew his aim was off.

When the phone crashed on something metal. Ty knew what it had to be. He winced and leaned over the railing to look.

Sure enough, the silver roof of his car had a dark star on it now.

Shit.

Joe was standing beside the car, frozen in horror. He looked up and Ty knew he had to go down and reassure the older man.

Admit it was his own fault.

One thing was for sure. He'd smash that fucking burner phone to cinders first.

Then he'd make this right.

The truth would be told, in all its horrible glory, and the game would be done.

Someone knocked on Amy's door hard about half an hour after she talked to Matteo. It was past midnight and the sound echoed through the house with force.

But Matteo didn't know where she lived.

She ran to the living room and looked out the window. Ty's car was parked in front of the house, the engine running. Why was he back?

She opened the front door, only to find him waiting with obvious impatience on her doorstep. He'd loosened his tie and looked positively wrinkled, his gaze snapping as it swept over her. His hands were balled in his trouser pockets and he looked more furious than she'd ever seen him.

She felt bad for having turned him down.

"I'm sorry," he said tightly. "I'm sorry to be back in the middle of the night, but I owe you an apology and it can't wait even if you don't want to hear it. It's not one I'm going to deliver over the phone."

Amy watched him, thinking how hot he was when he was intent like this. "Okay."

"I deceived you. That wasn't my plan, but that's how it worked out, and then I couldn't tell you the truth because I was sure you'd be angry with me and I didn't want to risk you walking away. You would have been right to be angry. You'd be right to be angry now. I fucked up." He shoved a hand through his hair and glared at her. "I never meant to lie to you. I never meant for it to go so far."

Another f-bomb. This was serious. Amy leaned in the door frame and crossed her arms across her chest. Her heart was racing. It would be so easy to drag him inside and have her way with him, or let him have his way with her, but if there was a next time, it had to be right. "Should I understand what you're talking about?"

Ty pulled his hand from his pocket, then took her hand and pressed something into her palm. Something small and metal. He kept his hand locked over hers so she couldn't look. "I couldn't let any other guy do that to you," he murmured. "I'm sorry I lied about it."

Then Ty stepped back, watching her. Amy opened her hand to

find the earrings she'd lost at F5 cradled in her palm. She frowned. "But how could you have had them? I left them at F5..."

She blinked. Matteo had said he had them.

She looked up at Ty, her lips parting. Matteo was about the same height as Ty. His shoulders were the same breadth. His eyes were green.

And now that Ty's mouth was a taut line, the similarity was striking.

"I kept them for you," Ty said tightly. "I thought they were important to you and didn't want anyone else to take them from the lost and found."

Amy still couldn't believe what he was telling her. "But that..."

"It means I was Matteo," he said, then his voice dropped lower and he spoke with a Spanish accent. "Angel."

Amy gasped in astonishment and heat surged through her.

Ty was Matteo.

Matteo was Ty.

She didn't have to choose.

Amy could have it all.

Relief nearly took her to her knees, a thousand details and impressions suddenly making perfect sense. Ty was Matteo. He'd been the one to touch her at F5. She'd called *him* to talk dirty.

And he'd done it so very well.

Oh.

Ty looked away again, his annoyance clear. "You're probably really pissed off at me, and I don't blame you for that, but if you could ever give me a chance again, you know where to find me." He gave her a hard look and she wondered how she'd missed the truth.

"I would do anything to make this right, Amy. Anything." He turned away then and strode back toward his car, as if he had no expectations of a reprieve.

"It's cute how protective you are," Amy said.

Ty granted her a smoldering look over the top of his car, which had a dent it hadn't had before. "Cute," he repeated with precision, his opinion of that adjective clear.

"Adorable, then."

"I am not adorable," he growled.

"You must be." Amy smiled. "Because I adore you." She took a deep breath. "*Cuore mio.*"

Ty froze.

"What does that mean?" he asked softly.

Amy raised a fist to her chest. "My heart."

Ty stared at her.

"It's what you call your beloved in the language of love and romance." Amy smiled despite the lump in her throat. "It was always you, my own *colpo di fulmine*. I just didn't want to disappoint you, with my wicked fantasies."

"They're very naughty."

"They are."

Ty began to smile slowly as he strolled back toward Amy, his gaze locked upon hers. "But they have a certain appeal."

"Do they?"

"Absolutely." He paused in front of her, then took her hand in his. "There's a kind of nexus where what you like meets what I like, and it's very hot."

"Very," Amy agreed and swallowed.

"Say I'm cute again and I take no responsibility for the consequences," Ty warned her.

Amy smiled. "Are you suggesting that would be naughty?"

"Very naughty," he agreed, surveying her with a hungry smile. His expression made her want. "Very, very naughty."

"Maybe you'll have to do something about that."

"Maybe?" Ty framed her face in his hands then lifted her to her toes. His grip was possessive, tender and tough all at once, and Amy loved it. "I'd say definitely, *cuore mio*."

Amy loved how the words sounded on his lips. "Your place or mine?" she asked, hearing how breathless she was.

"Lady's choice. Always."

"But the lady has chosen. The rest is just detail."

"Mine," Ty said with a satisfactory vehemence. He bent to whisper in her ear, and his words sent shivers down her spine. "I want you in my bed this time." Then he claimed her with a kiss that made her heart soar and her blood boil.

"Lock the door, sweetheart," he said roughly a few moments later. "We've got places to go and things to do."

Amy had no argument with that.

CHAPTER FOURTEEN

C ALL IT A weakness," Ty admitted when they were driving back to the city. "But I can't manage complicated tonight." He cast a glance at her, hoping she wasn't too disappointed.

The air between them was charged with sexual energy, and he couldn't drive back to F5 fast enough. The last thing he wanted was a ticket, though, so he used the cruise control. Amy had packed a small bag while he'd put out kibble for Fitzwilliam.

He couldn't wait to peel her out of that hideous dress.

Maybe he'd rip it off her. She'd packed a change of clothes, after all.

She might like that.

"Why not?" she asked now, and the way her eyes sparkled told him that she knew the answer already.

"I'm too relieved," he confessed. "I won't last."

"I see." Amy crossed her legs very deliberately, and Ty growled a little that she kept messing with him. She sighed with mock forbearance and trailed a fingertip up her own thigh, pulling up her skirt. "Then maybe you're not the man for me, after all."

Ty looked and the car swerved. He looked back at the road, then at Amy's delicious thighs again. "Are you wearing stockings?" he asked, hearing the tightness of his own voice.

It wasn't as tight as his trousers.

Amy pulled up the hem of her skirt to reveal the lace tops of her stockings—and the expanse of soft, bare thigh above them. Ty's gut clenched.

He wasn't going to last two minutes.

"I thought I'd give you something to look at."

"We're going to end up in the ditch."

"I hope not. That's a different kind of complicated."

"You were wearing those all day?"

"Preparation in the spirit of optimism," Amy said. "If you hadn't gotten all serious..."

Ty accelerated, needing to get her home as soon as possible. "Timing appears to be an issue for me tonight."

Amy laughed. She trailed her fingertips over his hand where he held the gear shift. "I'm still wrapping my mind around the fact that you were Matteo. I had no idea you could be so dangerous." She leaned over and kissed his ear, her breath sending a jolt through him. "So hot."

"I'll show you hot."

"Did you at least keep his hood?"

Ty stopped at a red light and gave her a look. "Yes."

Her smile was playful and her eyes danced. "Good."

Joe gave a low whistle when Ty parked in the drive to the garage again. "Had to guess it'd be a woman."

Ty tossed him the keys and ignored the older man's comment, waved, then guided Amy to F5.

Amy looked up at him in confusion. "What are we doing here?"

"Going home."

"You *live* here?"

"Yes. Penthouse."

"Of course," she murmured beneath her breath.

They walked through the empty lobby of the club, past the closed gift shop and the vacant reception counter. Their footsteps echoed on the tile and he could smell the salt from the lap pool. The bar was closed and the building was silent. He tried not to think about the fact that he had the keys to the naughty shop in his pocket.

Simple first.

"It's my favorite time to be here," he told her. "I love having the place to myself."

"Is that when you work out?"

"Not always. But I often swim laps late at night."

"There's no one else here?" she asked.

"Maybe a janitor or two."

"Who else lives in the building?"

"No one, yet. We're going to sell apartments but are still waiting on permits. Then there will be contractors to schedule and the nightmare will begin." Ty led her to the private elevator to the far right, and pushed another card into the slot. "This one services the higher floors," he said. The buttons for the floors above the ninth floor only illuminated after he inserted the card in the panel inside the elevator. He pushed the button for the penthouse and the elevator began to smoothly ascend.

Amy slid her hand into his and leaned against him, her breast crushed against his arm. "How many people have keys to this elevator?" she asked in a whisper so wicked that he felt he was being warned.

"Just me, right now," he said, wondering. "Eventually, there will be other tenants..."

Ty didn't have a chance to finish because Amy ambushed him. She pushed him against the elevator wall, caught his face in her hands and kissed him thoroughly. Ty might have been surprised, but he didn't hesitate to respond. She wanted naughty and sexy, and he was going to ensure that she knew he'd deliver. He lifted her against him so that only her toes were on the floor and their kiss turned incendiary. She wrapped one leg around his thigh and he thought about those stockings, or more precisely where they ended and the bare skin began, and groaned.

"We could do it here," Amy whispered when he broke their kiss.

Ty inhaled sharply. He thought about pulling out the key, making the elevator stop, having her against the wall of the elevator, and nearly lost it completely.

"Not the first time," he replied tightly as the elevator doors opened. "I'll make sure the cameras are disconnected before you add another episode to our elevator stories."

Amy might have argued, but he tossed her over his shoulder and headed for his apartment. She kicked her feet playfully, clearly pleased with her situation. Ty had the door open and locked behind them in record time, then Amy was sliding down his chest in a pile of tangerine. She looped her arms around his neck and held his gaze, smiling as he tugged down the zipper at the back of her dress. She slipped her arms out of it and let it drop, then stood before him in creamy lingerie and thigh high stockings.

It was a much better view than the orange monstrosity.

Ty swallowed and hooked a finger under one garter.

"Complicated," he said and she laughed at him.

"You think everything is complicated."

"I think skin is simple." Ty shed his jacket and tie while Amy watched him. "I think having you naked and wet and ready is simple." His shoes, socks, and trousers were cast aside, as he held her gaze. "I think making you scream with pleasure is simple." He took off his watch slowly, then tugged his T-shirt over his head. "I think ensuring that you can't think about anything other than this, or me, is simple."

He stopped in front of her and lifted off her glasses, setting them on the coffee table. Then he freed her hair, pushing his fingers through it with a proprietary ease that thrilled Amy. He caught her close and kissed her deeply, holding her on the tips of her toes, and kissing her until she shivered with pleasure. Then he ran his thumb across her swollen lips and felt her tremble.

"That's my kind of simple," Amy whispered.

"Then come here, Angel," he invited in his Matteo voice. "And let me give you the pleasure you deserve."

Amy felt as if she'd stepped into the heart of the sun.

And she wanted to stay there.

Making love with Ty might have been slow and sweet that first time, but this time was hot and fast. He was tender and tough, gentle and strong. He felt so good, filling her up and stretching her, moving with exquisite control.

And rubbing her in all the right places. She was on the verge of orgasm for longer than she would have believed possible.

She did scream when she came.

And he roared just a moment later.

They collapsed onto the couch, limbs entangled, and their breath coming quickly. He laced his fingers between hers and kissed her palm, then put her hand over the thunder of his heart.

Amy sighed contentment, then really looked at his apartment. The furniture was substantial and simple, but she could see with a glance that it was high quality. One wall was almost all windows, with a fabulous view of the city to the south. She wondered how far she'd be able to see into Brooklyn on a clear day. There was a pair of black leather couches in the living room, a large television mounted on the wall, a glass coffee table in between. The layout was open, so she could see the stainless steel appliances and granite counters in the kitchen to the right, and the massive four-poster bed in the bedroom to the left. The floors were dark hardwood with creamy Persian rugs in the living room and bedroom. It was neutral and elegant—and fastidiously clean.

Except for the clothes tossed all over the living room, and her own bag dropped just inside the door. Amy smiled as Ty stirred. He pushed the hair back from her temple and gave her a kiss. "Okay?" She could feel his voice rumbling in his chest below her breasts. "Or too fast?"

"Perfect. I like that you were almost but not quite out of control." She nestled against him. "It made me feel sexy."

"You are sexy." He rolled over so that she was beneath him, then kissed her slowly. "Maybe we can try simple one more time before we get complicated."

Amy teased him, just because she could. "I want to call Matteo. He *likes* complicated."

"I can't believe you invited him to your home."

"I had an intuitive trust of him," she admitted. "I wonder why."

Ty stole a kiss. "About those phone calls..."

"That's what it was," Amy said, snapping her fingers. "The phone calls. Mmmm. I'd have to invite any man to my house who talked dirty to me like that."

"Consider it done," Ty growled with mock ferocity, then stood up and lifted her in his arms.

"Another round so soon?"

"Won't take me long." He squeezed her in his embrace a bit. "I love doing it in the shower, don't you?"

"I don't know. My shower's too small for two people."

Ty raised a brow. "I see renovations in your future."

Amy's surprise must have shown, because he gave her another one of those bone-melting kisses. "I'd never ask you to give up the house," he whispered. "I know what it means to you."

"Which reminds me," she said. "I need to find another tenant. Lisa left me a note that she and her mom are moving out."

"Found. I'll move in."

She smiled that he was so resolute about it. "And renovate my shower." She kicked her feet playfully. "Your sisters are right. You are bossy."

"And you like it."

"I do."

"You must have plans for what you'd do to the house if you didn't have tenants."

"Of course."

"So, carte blanche. Do whatever you want. My only request is a shower like this one." He stepped into the bathroom and set her down, then flicked on the lights with a fingertip. It was a large bathroom, tiled in marble, with a huge walk-in shower in one corner. There were two big showerheads and a lot of smaller ones mounted in the walls. Amy could imagine many interesting possibilities, but she couldn't resist the chance to tease him.

"I don't know," she said with a frown. "It looks so complicated."

Ty caught her close. "Let me convince you," he murmured in her ear. A second later, Amy was crushed into the wall and kissed until she moaned. She closed her eyes and surrendered, forgetting all about the shower as Ty eased one finger between her thighs and caressed her. She sagged against the wall when he stepped away, shook his head and watched him turn on the water.

"It takes up an awful lot of space," she said, not wanting to give him an easy victory. She could already imagine turning the smallest upstairs bedroom into a shower similar to this one. "I'm not sure it's really necessary..."

Ty glanced over his shoulder and gave her a very green look. "It's critical." He beckoned to her with one finger, his smile turning wicked. "You're going to really like some of these side sprays. Let me show you."

Amy wasn't surprised that she found herself readily convinced.

Amy awakened on Sunday morning with the delicious awareness that she'd been savored. She stretched, realized she was alone, then saw the note beside the alarm clock. Her glasses were there, too, although she knew she hadn't left them there and she smiled at Ty's thoughtfulness when she put them on.

Back in Five was what he'd written.

It was just seven, which proved that she'd wake up early no matter what happened during the night.

There was a brand new toothbrush on the lip of the sink that Amy broke out of its package. She got the hair brush from her bag and laid claim to a soft bathrobe that was hanging on the back of the door. It was much too large for her, and smelled of Ty's cologne. She was knotting the belt when the lock on the door clicked.

Ty smiled at her when he stepped into the apartment. He was

wearing jeans and a T-shirt and a pair of loafers. He was carrying a shopping bag, but Amy couldn't see what was in it.

It wasn't take-out coffee.

"Good morning," he said and backed her into the wall, spearing his fingers into her hair before he kissed her with the thoroughness that made her heart race. Would she ever get enough of him?

"It is a good morning," she agreed when she had a chance. "You taste minty fresh."

"Mmm, so do you." He kissed her again, taking his time about it.

"And all dressed," she complained, plucking at his T-shirt.

"That can be fixed easily enough. I couldn't scare the locals when I went shopping, though, could I?"

"Where did you go shopping at this hour?"

He kept his arm around her waist. "I was feeling ready for complicated."

Amy met the twinkle in his eyes. "Really?"

"Really. You?"

"I'm always ready for complicated," she admitted and blushed when he grinned.

"So naughty. What am I going to do with you?"

"Teach me a lesson?"

"Great minds think alike." He guided her to the coffee table and put down the bag, then carefully reached into it so she couldn't see the contents. He was holding a pair of black leather wrist shackles when he removed his hand. They were lined with soft fur, and about four inches wide, with heavy buckles and embedded d-rings. They weren't clipped to each other.

Yet.

Just the sight of them made Amy weak in the knees. She swallowed and took one from Ty, feeling how smooth and strong it was. She had to sit down on the couch, and couldn't stop stroking it.

"I figured I should go for the top of the line, since they'll likely get a lot of use."

"Yes," Amy whispered.

"I hope I got the right size."

"Me, too."

"They did have a pair of handcuffs lined with pink fur, like the ones on that book cover. I liked the idea of them, since that was how we met, but they felt flimsy to me." Ty locked the second cuff, then tugged on it. Hard. "The way I see it—the whole point is that you can't break free."

Amy nodded, her mouth dry. "For someone who doesn't like complicated, you really get it."

Ty chuckled. "I also think that it'll be hotter if you help."

"Help?" Amy repeated.

"Help me to tie you up. That way, you're choosing it." He lifted a brow. "Participating."

"Surrendering."

Ty kissed her temple then spoke a little more roughly. "Put them on."

Amy flicked a glance at him, liked how hot his gaze was, and did as she was told. They were snug but not tight, the fur making them feel luxurious against her skin. She felt captive even without them being secured to each other or anything else. "Tender and tough," she said, barely recognizing her own voice. "The perfect combination."

"They make you look delicate," Ty said, his voice husky, too. He ran a fingertip over them. "Captive."

Amy's gaze clung to his. "Yes."

"Chances are good that you'll like these, too." Ty presented a matching pair of ankle shackles. They were larger and looked meaner somehow. Amy felt a little bit dizzy at the sight of them.

"Where did you go?"

"The gift shop for the club."

"It can't be open yet."

"No, but I have keys. And a standing account." He handed her the ankle bonds. "Put them on," he commanded.

Amy decided to surprise him. She untied the belt of the robe, then removed it, flinging it across the leather couch. She perched on it, nude, giving Ty something to look at as she fastened the ankle shackles. She preened before him, liking that he didn't even seem to blink. "What else did you buy?"

He removed a black velvet hood from the bag, like the one she'd tried in the class. "I thought you liked this."

"I did."

"And this." He had a black leather paddle.

Amy caressed it, remembering how smooth and cool it felt against her skin. How it smacked and burned. "Yes," she whispered.

"And these." He removed two hanks of the silky bondage rope, both blue, from the bag. "I'm starting to realize why nightstands have so many drawers."

Amy laughed. She hurried to her purse, though, and got out her pink lipstick, then went back into the bathroom. The sight of herself in the mirror, wearing only the cuffs with her eyes sparkling, was exciting. She applied the lipstick and put her hair in a ponytail in anticipation of their games. Her hands were shaking but she was thrilled already.

And Ty hadn't even touched her yet.

He was leaning in the doorway, watching her. He'd taken the last item out of the bag. It was a small box, like one for cufflinks, but he didn't open it. "And a surprise." He arched a brow. "Red light?"

"Green, green, *green* light," Amy said, not troubling to hide her enthusiasm.

He pointed to the bedroom. "You're going to be tied up this morning."

Amy could hardly wait. "How?"

"On your back, legs wide, hands over your head."

"Yes, sir."

They shared a hot kiss then, one that Amy thought would melt more than her knees, then Ty lifted his head and growled. "Now. Take everything with you."

"Yes, sir."

In moments, Amy was perched on the smooth sheets of Ty's bed. She eyed the windows.

"Tinted glass," he said. "No one but me will see how wicked you are."

"Good thing you have the perfect bed," she said, admiring the steel-framed four-poster again.

"Must have had a premonition," Ty said, then his voice hardened again. "Kneel and put your wrists together."

Amy watched him tie the cuffs together with the blue rope, then she was urged to her back. The other hank of blue rope was cast over her waist, and she loved how it spilled loose around her. The rope binding her wrists went to the top of the mattress and was secured so that her hands were stretched over her head.

"You wanted to be stretched taut before," Ty murmured and she saw him look over her in admiration. She knew by his expression that he'd noticed how her nipples were beaded.

"Yes."

He tugged back the top sheet and duvet, casting them to the floor, then claimed one ankle. Once he'd tied the end of the blue rope to the shackle, he tugged it slowly to the lower corner of the bed on that side. Amy enjoyed the feel of sliding over the smooth sheet and the sense that she could struggle but not escape. Ty stretched her out before knotting that ankle down. She struggled, but she couldn't break free.

She was already desperate for him.

"Time for your present," he said softly. He placed that small box on the mattress. It did look a bit like a jewelry box, but Amy couldn't figure out what might be inside it.

"I thought you needed your own set," he murmured, then leaned over to open the box and show her.

Amy swallowed at the shiny pair of nipple clamps nestled inside. They glittered coldly, looking both mean and wonderful.

"Oh," she whispered, her voice trembling a little.

"New arrivals," Ty said. "They have fur inside."

"Oh," Amy whispered again, and felt her cheeks heat.

"I was thinking of how you wanted the other ones on when you were stretched taut." He went around the bed and picked up the other end of the blue rope. It slid across Amy's belly in a slow caress. "How about I make sure you can't get away first?" He tied it to the other shackle, then tugged her foot toward that corner of the footboard.

She'd be spread wide when he was done.

Tied down.

Exposed.

Amy's face heated. She'd be open and available to him, unable to move away. "Yes, please," she whispered, so he had no doubt that she was loving this game. She had only an inch of leeway or so, enough to feel the limits of her bonds.

"I read that it's more of a tease if you can move a little."

"It's perfect," Amy admitted, thinking it was very good to have a partner who did his research.

Ty tugged off his T-shirt as he walked around the bed, just looking at her. She had a great view of him, and the chance to admire him again. He kicked off his shoes, then his jeans and briefs. Amy smiled at the evidence that he was enjoying their game as much as she was. "I thought you found this complicated."

"You've converted me," he said as he stretched out beside her. "But then, I told you before that there was nothing hotter than a partner who wanted you badly."

"I do," Amy whispered.

"I know. But let's make you want me even more." Ty's thumb landed on her mouth, caressing her bottom lip in that possessive way that drove her wild. "You relax when you know you're helpless," he murmured, his gaze locked upon her. "It's like you surrender to sensation."

"To you," Amy corrected.

"It's very hot," he said and slid his thumb across her mouth again. "So's that."

Ty's dimple made an appearance. "And I can do this in public."

She groaned a little. "It's bad enough that you put your hand on my back and move your thumb there."

"You like that."

"It makes me melt."

"So, you've said. I'll have to do it more often," he mused and she knew he would. He ran his hand down the length of her, then circled her navel with his thumb. Amy squirmed and he speared his fingers into her pubic hair. He didn't touch her, though, and she bucked her hips a little, impatient for the pleasure he could give. "Naughty, naughty."

"You knew that ages ago."

"True. It wasn't the first surprise you gave me, though." He smiled. "Hood or not? It's your choice."

Amy's heart skipped. "Will you smooth it down with your hands?"

"You like that?"

Amy nodded again. "It makes me feel like a possession." Ty slid the hood over her head and fitted her ponytail through the opening in the back. She was engulfed in darkness and felt as if every other sensation was heightened. She could smell his skin and feel the sheets, the fur in her shackles, the tightness of her bonds, the wetness of her sex. Amy inhaled deeply in pleasure when Ty's hands bracketed her head, smoothing down the velvet. He gave the elastic at the back a little tug, ensuring that it was snug and she shivered with delight.

He rolled over her, crushing her a little bit, trapping her beneath the heat of his body from shoulder to knee. He kissed her then, one of his slow and potent kisses, the ones that made Amy's heart race and she kissed him back hungrily, wanting only more. His hand landed on her breast and he rolled her nipple between his finger and thumb, teasing it so that it tightened even more. He pinched it a bit and Amy moaned, then he broke their kiss and took her nipple in his mouth. He tormented her even more, drawing his teeth over that tight peak and flicking his tongue across it, driving her crazy with need. Tender and tough.

She thought about those nipple clamps and wasn't sure how she'd stand it.

She moaned Ty's name and he lifted his head. She felt his weight move and knew he was getting the box. Her heart leaped as he rolled the nipple again, and she gasped when he gently fastened the clamp onto her nipple.

Amy froze. She choked. She felt heat surge through her veins and knew she was impossibly wet.

"Nothing like the satisfaction of a perfect gift," Ty murmured. "Comes with a chain and some weights, too, but maybe we should work up to that."

The idea made Amy dizzy. Weights?

"Maybe," Amy managed to agree.

"Maybe you can wear them to the wedding," he suggested and panic slipped through Amy. "It would be our little secret."

Her lips parted but no sound came out.

He wouldn't.

He couldn't.

He might.

And she would adore it.

Meanwhile, Ty's hand moved to her other breast and he braced his weight on his elbow to watch her. "You like this."

"You're getting really good at complicated."

"I'm motivated. I've done my research."

"Don't we have to go somewhere today?" Amy whispered.

"Nowhere at all." She inhaled as he teased the second nipple a little more roughly than the first. "Does that possibility of being trapped here worry you?"

"A little."

"Should I stop?"

"No!" Amy gasped.

Ty continued to torment her as he talked. "You know, I was thinking about that Oscar Wilde quote and you might be right."

It took Amy a minute to recall the quote he meant. That Ty took her nipple in his mouth didn't help.

That he grazed it with the edge of his teeth, then flicked it with his tongue, really didn't help.

"'Everything in the world is about sex except sex,'" she managed to say. "'Sex is about power.'"

"That's the one." He applied the second nipple clamp with care and Amy had palpitations.

She squirmed a little, then struggled outright against her bonds, discovering that she couldn't do anything about her situation. She was trapped in the most exquisite way, and would be for as long as Ty wanted her that way.

She hoped it was forever. She felt him move back and hoped he was looking at her.

Savoring her as his prize.

"But maybe sex isn't always about power," Ty mused. "Maybe when sex most appears to be about power, it's actually about trust."

The mattress dipped, as if he got up.

"You aren't going to leave?"

"Of course not. I'm just going to look." She heard his steps as he walked around the bed, as if considering her from every angle. Amy found herself arching her back a little and displayed herself to him. "What do you think?"

"About this? I like it."

"About the quote."

"I think you're right."

"What do you think I'm going to do next?"

Amy smiled. "I don't know, but I trust you. I'm pretty sure I'll like it."

"I'm thinking we'll both like it," Ty murmured, then she felt his hands on her knees. "I'm going to practice my alphabet."

Amy couldn't make any sense of that.

"You'd better hang on until we get to z, Angel," he growled in his Matteo voice. "Because we're going to do the alphabet over and over until you get it right. And if you're really naughty, we might miss work tomorrow."

"Practice," she whispered.

"Discipline," he corrected.

Amy sighed when Ty's mouth closed over her and pleasure flooded through her body. His hands were on her thighs, his shoulders against the inside of her knees. Then the tip of his tongue moved against her clitoris. The pattern wasn't accidental although she was too excited to make sense of it right away.

The first leisurely stroke started at the top then eased down one side. It took a million years, give or take, and sent a thousand shivers through Amy by the time it was done.

The second stroke was even slower and much more agonizing. Ty traced a little circle, from that side across her clitoris and below it, to join the end of the first stroke.

Amy gasped aloud when she understood.

He'd drawn an 'a'.

The alphabet.

She was already on fire and there were still twenty-five letters to go.

Maybe she'd call in sick all week.

It was a glorious week.

Amy couldn't remember ever being so happy.

She had lunch with Ty each day and spent each night with him, either at her place or his. They read each other's books and cooked for each other, and Ty began to explore her dad's book collection. Fitzwilliam tolerated his presence. She teased Ty as he fielded calls from his mother, and accepted an invitation from her aunt Pauline to bring him to dinner. She taught him some Italian phrases and wasn't surprised that he learned quickly.

He said he was motivated.

On Thursday, she knew from his expression when he came to lunch that something was up. "Dinner tonight?" he asked, and Amy knew her answer was more important than he was letting on. She agreed, and was surprised that evening when he guided her to F5.

She thought again about jumping his bones in the elevator, but Ty gave her a warning glance.

She could smell something delicious when they got off at his floor and immediately saw that the door to his apartment was open. He had his hand on the back of her waist when they entered and she caught her breath at the sight. Hundreds of candles had been lit, more of them clustered around the table and chairs by the windows beside the kitchen. The city sparkled, seemingly at their feet. The table had been set for two, with a long white tablecloth and gleaming china. A chef lit the candles on the table at their arrival and removed a casserole from the oven. Ty hung up Amy's coat and checked the arrangements before the chef left.

"Smells like osso buco," she said when they were alone.

Ty was removing the cork from a bottle of red wine. "I'm sure yours is better."

"From your favorite restaurant," she guessed.

"A perk of being a regular."

"We could have just gone there again."

"Not tonight," Ty said. "I wanted this to be a dinner to remember."

She had no chance to ask why because he turned to her and caught her hand in his. "Marry me, Amy," he said and her heart stopped.

"Is that a question or a command?" she teased and Ty smiled. His gaze was serious, though. "A request, because I love you."

"Since when?"

"The first day, when you told me off," he admitted. "We might have met because of a plan for a fake date, but I would have asked you out even if no one was getting married."

Amy smiled. "Book, line, and sinker."

"*Colpo di fulmine.*" His fingers trailed over her cheek. "I'm a sucker for a clever woman who defies expectation."

"Will I defy it if I accept?"

"No, but I can live with that."

"Good. Because I'd love to marry you, Tyler McKay."

Ty kissed her sweetly then, with that mix of tenderness and force that she was finding addictive. When he lifted his head, Amy smiled at him. "When you came to the bookstore, I knew I was in trouble," she whispered.

"Oh, you are in trouble, now, and will be for a long time."

"That's just the way I like it."

"Good." They shared a simmering glance, then Ty removed a small box from his pocket. "I hope you like it."

Amy opened the box to find a ring with a large sparkling square-cut diamond. It was surrounded by little sapphires and was the most beautiful thing she'd ever seen. She offered her hand and swallowed as Ty slipped the ring onto her finger. "I think we should put that casserole back in the oven," she whispered.

"Not hungry?"

"I want to celebrate in another way first," she said, then pulled his head down for another hotter kiss. She backed him toward the bedroom and Ty didn't fight her at all.

"Now, who's bossy?" he teased, but then he couldn't say anything for a very long time.

Ty was the luckiest man in the world.

There was no disputing it.

He sat with Amy with candles flickering all around them and served the dinner that would have been better an hour before. Neither of them cared much. She was wearing his bathrobe and her hair was loose. He thought she looked fabulous. Her eyes were sparkling and he knew that under the bathrobe, she wasn't wearing anything except his ring.

That suited him just fine.

"I was thinking..." he began.

"I doubt that," Amy replied. "You've been too busy to think."

Ty grinned. He leaned over the table to run a fingertip down her cheek, liking how she glowed with satisfaction. "I'm thinking a good philosophy might be to do unto others before they do unto us."

"I don't understand."

"You'll be going to my sister's wedding with that ring on your finger."

"Your mother!" Amy whispered in understanding.

Ty grimaced. "As soon as Katelyn drives off into the sunset with Jared on Saturday, less than forty-eight hours from now..."

"Your mom will have a new project." Amy nodded. "We need to make plans first, if we're going to make the plans at all."

"Exactly." Ty flicked a finger across the end of her nose. "Brilliant *and* beautiful. I didn't have a chance."

"Any particular ideas?"

Ty sighed. "As much as I'd love to elope, I doubt we can really evade the big family wedding."

"You can't steal all the fun from your mom."

"So a big wedding it is. Can we manage sooner rather than later?"

Amy nodded. "September is nice for a wedding."

"And in October I've got a trip to Europe." He filled her wine glass. "You could come along."

"But my job..."

"Seriously? You don't have time for that job anymore." He gave her a stern look. "Don't tell me it's going to break your heart to quit it?"

"No, it'll just be odd, not to have a pay check."

"So, how about this? You take time off to plan the wedding, start the renovations on the house, and finish your book, then when we come home from Europe, you can decide what you want to do."

"Do you always plan everything?" she asked, not looking very troubled about that at all.

"Preparation in a spirit of optimism," he admitted and she smiled. He lifted his glass to her. "To September weddings, successful books..."

"And fake dates that lead to happily-ever-afters," Amy concluded, raising her own glass. "Whether the participants are naughty or nice."

"Maybe that's what makes them simply irresistible," Ty said, loving when Amy laughed.

EPILOGUE

COLLEEN'S worries about the weather proved to be unfounded and Lauren was glad about that. It was a glorious day and the ceremony had been held in the garden as planned. Katelyn was radiant and Jared was clearly smitten.

Lauren, though, found herself watching Ty and Amy instead.

She didn't know how she'd ever thought that Amy and Ty didn't belong together. The heat between the pair of them was enough to boil asphalt in their vicinity. When their gazes met across a crowded room, Lauren felt like a bolt of lightning flashed between them.

Watching them made her own toes curl.

But she couldn't stop. It was intoxicating to see two people so wildly in love, especially her big brother. She'd always known that if and when Ty fell in love, he'd fall hard.

And she'd been right.

It should have made her happier than it did. The truth was it made Lauren realize how empty her own marriage was.

By the time dinner was served at the reception, Lauren was watching the pair outright. It wasn't as if Mark was interested in anything she might say or do. She was at the family table, and Amy was seated across from her. Ty, as one of the groomsmen, was at the head table with the rest of the wedding party. Amy looked amazing, so much more confident and lovely than when they'd first met. She was wearing a beautiful dress and had a hat at the wedding service, a combination that made her look like a model. Ty had been right about her resemblance to Sophie Loren. She'd come to Lauren for a haircut

256

the day before and it had been transformative. Lauren didn't need to be told the power of a good cut, but she knew there was more responsible than that.

It was love that made Amy glow.

Too bad Lauren could barely remember the sensation.

Mark was making short work of the roast beef dinner and not troubling with conversation at all. Uncle Lionel was seated on Lauren's other side, but he was talking to Aunt Maureen.

Lauren had noticed that Amy spent a lot of time with her phone while the pictures were being taken, and had thought she was just one of those people who treat a cell phone like another appendage.

But now she guessed that something was being orchestrated.

If Ty and Amy were as perfect for each other as she suspected they were, something was in the works.

She wanted to know what it was.

Not for the first time, Amy paused in her tapping and cast a sidelong glance at Ty. Ty started, then reached for the interior pocket of his tux, the one where his phone was. He pulled it out of the pocket just enough to read the screen, then glanced at Amy, his look hot enough to singe her panties.

He smiled a secretive smile, then quickly tapped a reply and dropped the phone back into his pocket.

Lauren heard Amy's phone chirp. Amy had it under the table and then she smiled a similarly mysterious smile. She bit her lip, flicked a glance at Ty, and nodded minutely.

Ty looked satisfied.

What *were* they up to?

Lauren wouldn't know until ten that night, when the dancing was well underway and the happy couple had departed for their honeymoon. The band was playing *Love is All Around* and Amy and Ty were dancing together, laughing at some private joke. That just made Lauren feel more lonely. She was still watching them and having yet another glass of wine. Mark had disappeared somewhere, possibly down the hall to the bar where the game was playing.

Amy and Ty both pulled out their phones, as if on cue. They both tapped once, then put their phones away.

And the music was interrupted by the chirping, ringing, beeping and music emitted by at least a hundred cell phones receiving a message simultaneously. Ty and Amy grinned at each other in triumph and kept dancing, maybe a little closer than before.

Lauren pulled out her phone, and knew she shouldn't have been surprised that it was a wedding invitation, from Tyler. He and Amy were tying the knot on September 16, apparently, and the arrangements had been made. The hotel and the church were listed, as well as a date to RSVP.

This was what Amy had been doing.

Evidently, the two of them had planned it out in advance. Lauren saw her mother's joy, then her disappointment that she wouldn't be organizing the festivities. She watched Ty and Amy dance, so delighted with each other that it made her heart ache.

Her brother had taken his time, but he'd found his perfect partner.

As glad as she was to see Ty so happy, Lauren wished she could have said the same thing for herself.

.

HER DARK PRINCE
By Ella Ardent

In the lost realm of Euphoria, royalty command all to serve their pleasure, but passion is the greatest power of all.

Can Beauty tame this Beast?

A defiant beauty is claimed for the annual village tithe to the ruling family of Euphoria, whose crown prince desires only the satisfaction of his own dark desires. He gets far more from his captive lover, whose talent for unveiling his secrets leaves them both wondering who is master and who is slave.

Her Dark Prince is the first book in the Euphoria series of fairy tale romances by Ella Ardent. (The excerpts in **Simply Irresistible** are used with Ella's permission.) You can find out more about Ella's books on her website: http://EllaArdent.com

DEBORAH COOKE

Read on for an excerpt from Kyle and Lauren's book

Addicted to Love

#2 in the Flatiron Five Series

Kyle wants it all...
Kyle Stuyvesant doesn't believe in love and romance. His parents taught him that there's no such thing as forever, and he took the lesson to heart. After all, there's only one woman who ever tempted him to more than a single hot night together. Fortunately for his convictions, she's married to another guy. Problem solved—until Lauren's marriage collapses and Kyle isn't just the bearer of bad news, but the man she turns to for comfort.

Lauren demands it all...
When Lauren's marriage implodes, she wants to lose herself in pleasure and sensation. Who knows that territory better than Kyle, the eternal playboy, who seduced her so deliciously years before? It was a night Lauren never forgot, and now that she wants to forget everything, Kyle is the only man she wants. Will she be able to accept his terms of no love or romance? Or will Lauren convince Kyle to take a chance on wanting more?

L AUREN came out of the back of her shop, drying her hands. Her feet were killing her. Fridays were just brutal. She was looking forward to having Saturday off for once and to trying to talk to Mark.

Maybe they'd finally get all their crossed signals sorted out.

It seemed like a long shot, but Lauren was nothing if not optimistic.

And stubborn. Marriage was supposed to be for keeps. No one worth anything just walked away when there was a patch of rough ground to be covered.

Even if it was more than a patch.

She stopped cold at the sight of a familiar man flipping through the magazines in the waiting area. As so often happened, Kyle seemed to sense her presence and looked up right away. As had always happened, one look from her brother's college friend and Lauren felt unsteady on her feet.

Kyle was way too good looking.

He was way too sure of himself.

But damn, he was easy on the eyes.

Just how long had it been since she and Mark had had sex? A hundred years?

"Look what the cat dragged in," Lauren said in the casual tone she always used with Kyle. The way she saw it, he didn't need anyone building up his ego. It was already sky high.

He grinned. "You have such a way with words. I knew you missed me."

Lauren rolled her eyes. "Seriously. What are you doing here?"

He lifted a hand to his tousled blond hair. "So hard to believe I need my highlights touched up?"

"You've never come here before."

"Maybe I wanted to spread the joy around."

She laughed despite herself. "You really should package that confidence and sell it. I'm sure you have more than enough to spare."

"Maybe," he said and sobered unexpectedly.

"We don't actually have any openings left today," she said, flipping through the massive appointment book. "No lies. It's been one nutty Friday, but thank God we close in half an hour."

Kyle looked up, impaling her on the spot with those baby blues. "I didn't come for an appointment, Lor," he said, calling her by the nickname only he ever used. His serious attitude gave her palpitations, but not as much as what he said next. "I need to talk to you."

"Sounds dire."

"You might think it is." He leaned back, watching her with an intensity more typical of her big brother, Tyler, than the happy-go-lucky Kyle she thought she knew.

"What is it?" she asked with new concern. "Is something wrong with Ty?"

"No, not that." Kyle shook his head, his gaze flicking to Marie at the back of the shop, who was finishing up with a client and probably was eavesdropping. "Not here." He stood up, then peered through the window at the little wine bar across the street. "That place any good?"

"Quiet until eight or so."

"Perfect. You said you close soon. When are you done?"

"In ten. I just have to clean up a couple of things."

"Then I'll meet you there in ten." Kyle cocked a finger at her, making her heart leap. "Don't stand me up. Remember that I know where you live." He winked, his reckless self again, blew a kiss to Marie, then left the shop.

Lauren watched his tight butt all the way across the street. He was fine. And she wasn't going to remember that one night...

No. Some things should be left perfect and that memory was one of them.

"Who's the delicious one?" Marie asked as her client came to the desk to pay.

"Friend of my brother's," Lauren said with an indifferent shrug that was just about the opposite of how she was feeling.

"The one who's getting married?"

Lauren nodded, coming up with a plausible explanation on the spot. "He's probably planning Ty's stag. I'll guess he wants help surprising him."

Marie rolled her eyes. "Men and their stag parties. You'd think they're afraid that once they got married, they'll never have sex again."

Lauren refrained from commenting on that. She cleaned up quickly and when she saw that Marie was done, too, locked up early. She made it across the street to the wine bar in eight and a half minutes. She'd always had a little bit of precognition and she had a bad feeling about Kyle's impromptu visit.

"Want a drink?" Kyle asked, feeling as if his usual charm had deserted him.

Lauren sat down, as gorgeous and as skeptical as ever. She was almost as tall as Ty, with the same chestnut hair and green eyes. Hers were thickly lashed, though, and her lips were full. Her hair was long and it bounced, like she should star in a shampoo commercial. She was slim in all the right places and curvy where it counted. There had always been something about Lauren that made Kyle's mouth go dry.

Even before their one night in paradise.

She fixed him with a look. "You're not going to just tell me, are you?"

He winced. "I think I have to work up to it."

263

"I'll have a coffee, please," she said to the hovering waitress. "Black."

"Double Scotch," Kyle said. "No ice."

"Bad news, then," Lauren said after the waitress left.

"I guess it depends on your perspective. Not happy news, that's for sure, but probably better to know sooner than later."

"You're not doing much to reassure me."

"I'm not sure I should." Kyle decided that a picture was worth a thousand words. He reached into his messenger bag and pulled out a brown envelope. The waitress brought their drinks then and he held on to it, the silence charging by the second.

"Thank you," Lauren said with a thin smile for the waitress. Then they were alone and there was no avoiding the inevitable.

Kyle put the envelope on the table between them, keeping his fingers on it. "I really recommend the drink first," he said.

Lauren scoffed and pulled the envelope from beneath his fingers. She opened it, clearly having some idea of its contents, but whatever her expectation had been, she was shocked. She flipped through the pictures in rapid succession, then again more slowly, her face becoming whiter and her lips getting tighter every second.

"Who took these?"

"Security cameras."

"How did you get them?"

"Seriously? That's F5."

Her eyes widened, and she put one of the images on the table. It was the bar shot, the one of Mark practically feeling up a hot young blonde. "Bad choice on his part to go there," she said quietly.

To Kyle's dismay, she wasn't surprised. He wasn't sure whether that made things better or worse.

Lauren's hands shook a little as she jammed the pictures back in the envelope. She took a gulp of her coffee and winced. "I know he collects porn. I know he goes out with his buddies. I know they visit strip clubs, too. None of that's a crime."

"No, it's not." Kyle took a sip of his own drink, then leaned across the table. "But there's more."

She exhaled and looked taut. "Why are you telling me this?"

Kyle went with the abbreviated version, leaving Ty out of it. "Because I offered to be the bearer of bad news when we saw the images of him at F5."

"Why?"

"I thought it might be better to hear from a friend."

"Is that what we are?"

"We can be."

"You seriously didn't bring me this in order to hit on me, did you?"

Her voice was sharp but Kyle knew her well enough to realize her anger wasn't really directed at him. "No. I thought you might want to talk about it, maybe in a way you can't talk to Ty. I knew you wouldn't want to talk to Cassie. I figured I was your best shot."

She bit her lip, considering this. "You can't prove anything..."

"I can, Lor," Kyle said interrupting her. "So, you can either trust me that I wouldn't shit you on something this important, or you can sign a confidentiality agreement and see it for yourself."

Her eyes narrowed. "Why do I have to sign anything?"

"Because there are other people in the film from the security cameras." He removed a second envelope from his messenger bag, a smaller one, and let his tone soften. "It's a loaded flash drive. You don't have to watch it."

Lauren's gaze lingered on the envelope. "Innocent until proven guilty," she said quietly.

"I thought you'd say that."

"Does Ty know?"

Kyle nodded. "I wanted to check that it was Mark."

"And?"

"I don't think he was any more surprised than you are."

Lauren took a shaking breath, then another gulp of coffee. "Do you have a laptop with you?"

"A tablet. You can watch it here if you want." At her nod of agreement, Kyle treated himself to another hit of Scotch.

She leaned across the table. "Does this happen on Friday nights? Like, every Friday night?"

"The F5 Club is only open Friday and Saturday nights."

Lauren faltered for only a moment, then she moved decisively. She pulled out the confidentiality agreement, read it twice, signed it in triplicate, and offered them to him.

"I already signed."

She took one copy, folded it, and put it into her purse. She took a large sip of his Scotch. "Bring it," she said, beckoning impatiently with her fingers. "I need to know."

Kyle booted up his tablet, slid the drive into the port and opened the file. He turned the tablet so she could watch her husband bang a blonde in the washroom at F5, then sat back to watch her.

"She needs her roots done," Lauren said softly.

"Ty said you'd say that."

She didn't reply, but then, Kyle knew that the video got rapidly worse. His Scotch tasted sour, only because of the way Lauren paled and her lips almost disappeared. She watched it all, though. No flinching from a McKay. But she looked drained when she was done, as if all the life in her was gone.

No. All the hope in her was gone.

The sight nearly killed Kyle.

"He took off his wedding ring," she said with no emotion at all.

"Yeah." Kyle wished he hadn't been the one to bring her the news, but on the other hand, he hadn't wanted anyone else to do it. "I'm sorry."

"You shouldn't be," she said, her eyes flashing briefly. She sat straighter and met his gaze as she handed back the tablet. "Not many people would have had the balls to tell me, let alone to take such a risk. My issue is with Mark and no one else."

Kyle had known she'd say that, but it relieved him to hear it. "And what are you going to do?"

"I'm long past getting mad," she said. "I think I'll try getting even."

"You need any help, just let me know."

She eyed him warily. "Filled with the milk of human kindness tonight?" she said, the first hint of her usual spark returning to her tone.

"He's an idiot," Kyle said and meant it.

A ghost of a smile touched her lips. "You're just saying that."

It would have been nice to reply that he never just said anything, but he did and Lor knew it. "Nope. Not this time." He shook a finger at her. "You weren't surprised."

"Not really. It's been shit for a while."

"You've only been married for a while."

"There is that." She met his gaze squarely, and he admired how direct she was. "You probably don't think I'm going to thank you, but I will. Thanks for telling me, Kyle."

"Like I said, anything I can do..."

"No, you've done plenty."

"That sounds like an accusation," he teased and to his delight, she smiled briefly.

She almost stood up, but then she sat down again. "You probably don't know this, but that night we had?"

That night. Kyle nodded, his throat tight.

"It's been a touchstone for me of how good things could be for two people. It's given me strength and hope in some dark times. So, thanks for that, too."

"'A thing of beauty is a joy for ever,'" Kyle said, nodding in understanding.

"That sounds like a poem."

"John Keats," Kyle agreed. "'A thing of beauty is a joy for ever: its loveliness increases; it will never pass into nothingness; but still will keep a bower quiet for us, and a sleep full of sweet dreams, and health, and quiet breathing.' Etc. Etc." He grinned at her obvious astonishment. "You think I'm uncultured?"

She considered him. "No, but I never associated you with poetry. Wait a minute. When did Keats live?"

"1795 to 1821."

She wagged a finger at him. "Nineteenth-Century English Lit. Ty took that course in his freshman year, supposedly as a breadth course but really to meet women."

"Where did you think I met him? He was a finance major. I was in athletics." He leaned across the table, determined to make her laugh. "We were the only two straight guys in that whole lecture hall. We owned that class, and we killed in our final presentation."

"Really?" Her lips were quirking, as if they wanted to smile but she had her doubts.

"Oh yeah. They were throwing panties at us for a month." Kyle heaved a sigh. "It was serious endurance training to make sure everyone got a turn in just eleven weeks. Big lecture hall." He saluted her with his Scotch. "But I tried. I really tried."

Lauren leaned across the table. "And how did I fit into that schedule?" she asked, a challenge in her eyes. "I seem to remember that was around the time of that one night."

Kyle sobered and for once in his life, he decided to tell the truth. "You ended it," he said with conviction. Her skepticism wasn't the best response, but Kyle knew he deserved that. He'd cultivated a reputation and let others make their conclusions, but there was one thing he knew without doubt.

It was why he'd taken on this job.

Maybe it was time to say it out loud.

He drained his Scotch and set down the glass on the table, his gaze unswerving from hers. "Because after you, Lor, there could be no other contenders. That's why this pisses me off so much. You're the most admirable and beautiful woman I've ever known."

She opened her mouth to protest but he held up a finger to silence her. "I'm not shitting you. This is the truth. That night was the very best night of my life, and you were the very best thing to ever happen to me."

To his surprise, he saw her tears rise but he carried on. Once the truth worked its way free, there was no stopping it. "I'm not just saying that. There have been women, lots of them, but it's never ever been like that night. Not even close. I'm not good enough for you, and I know it, but this bastard had the best and just threw it away. For cheap thrills."

He stood up as she looked at him in astonishment. "You need any help making Mark's life miserable, you just let me know." Before he could reconsider his choice, Kyle pulled out one of his cards, wrote his cell phone number on the back, and snapped it on the table in front of her. Lauren stared at it, as if it might bite.

As if everything he said was a lie.

That was the price of honesty. He wasn't even going to have a chance to throw himself at her mercy. She was too stunned. That was why there was no point in screwing around with telling people the truth. Kyle marched to the bartender and paid the bill. When he turned to leave, Lauren was already gone.

So was his card, but Kyle didn't know whether that was a good thing or not.

Three weeks after Kyle had given her the news, Lauren stood in Times Square, just letting the city flow around her. For the past few weeks, she'd felt raw inside, but now she felt empty.

Desolate.

Lonely.

It had been better when she'd had a list of jobs to be done. She'd cleaned out and sorted possessions. She'd removed Mark from her life with surgical precision. She'd parted their finances and hired lawyers and severed every connection. The work was done and she was alone again.

With the truth, that the past few years had all been an exercise in futility. She'd been stupid to hope for the best even when she knew her marriage was falling apart.

That was the worst part: she felt stupid for believing in happily-ever-after.

She was standing where she could see the enormous poster of Kyle. The perennial surfer boy, his hair tousled and his skin wet, a laugh just beginning to curve his lips. Honestly, she could see the twinkle in his eyes even from here.

Of course, the billboard was twenty stories high.

Get wet at F5.

Didn't she wish.

Lauren thought of one perfect night, of the weight of those hands on her skin, of the thrum of anger in his words when he'd told her about Mark. She hadn't thought that Kyle could be impassioned about much of anything. She hadn't thought he even remembered her much.

But she'd replayed his words in her thoughts a thousand times since.

That night was the very best night of my life, and you were the very best thing to ever happen to me.

She wanted to believe him, but she knew better.

It wouldn't be forever.

It would only be for now.

But that just might be enough.

Lauren pulled out the business card that she'd worn to softness and turned it over. She didn't really need to look at the number. She'd memorized it weeks ago. She liked the way Kyle wrote. Every character was filled with his confidence.

She wanted some of that.

She punched his number into her cell phone, and her heart leaped when he answered.

"Kyle here. What can I do for you?"

"You didn't look at the number," Lauren accused and felt his shock when he recognized her voice.

He recovered well, of course. Kyle always did. "No. I would have answered faster if I had, Lor. Where are you? It sounds noisy."

"Times Square."

"Oh." It had to be the first time ever that she'd heard Kyle at a loss for words.

"I've just been thinking that sometimes one thing of beauty isn't quite enough to provide joy forever," she said. "I've just been thinking that another one would be good."

For once in his life, Kyle was silent. She could feel him there, hear the faint sound of his breathing, and was aware of his attention.

"I know you can't give you what I really want, Kyle," she whispered. "But I also know you can give me what I need. I feel dead. I hate it. I want to feel alive again."

He cleared his throat lightly and she knew she'd surprised him. "Your place?"

"No. Mark is circling like a dog, double-checking where he crapped."

Kyle chuckled. "Not my place. No one goes there."

"Maybe it's time to change that," Lauren replied, wanting to convince him, not knowing what she'd do if he declined. "I'm taking a chance. How about you?"

Kyle didn't think about it long, much to her relief. He gave her an address on the west side. Hell's Kitchen, probably. She'd bet it was that shiny new building. "I'll be there in twenty minutes," he said, some of her own urgency in his tone. "If you change your mind, Lor, it's okay."

"I'm not going to change my mind," she said. "I'll be there." She ended the call and looked up at the billboard, welcoming the flicker of excitement in her veins. She hadn't even seen Kyle yet, but she already felt herself returning to life.

She knew that was just a hint of what was to come during the night ahead. That made her smile as she stepped to the curb to flag down a cab.

Addicted to Love
By Deborah Cooke
#2 of the Flatiron Five series of contemporary romances

Coming Soon!

ABOUT THE AUTHOR

Deborah Cooke sold her first book in 1992, a medieval romance called **Romance of the Rose** published under her pseudonym Claire Delacroix. Since then, she has published over fifty novels in a wide variety of sub-genres, including historical romance, contemporary romance, paranormal romance, fantasy romance, time-travel romance, women's fiction, paranormal young adult and fantasy with romantic elements. She has published under the names Claire Delacroix, Claire Cross, and Deborah Cooke. **The Beauty**, part of her successful Bride Quest series of historical romances, was her first title to land on the *New York Times* List of Bestselling Books. Her books routinely appear on other bestseller lists and have won numerous awards. In 2009, she was the writer-in-residence at the Toronto Public Library, the first time the library has hosted a residency focused on the romance genre. In 2012, she was honored to receive the Romance Writers of America's Mentor of the Year Award.

Currently, she writes paranormal romances featuring dragon shape shifter heroes under the name Deborah Cooke. She also writes medieval romances as Claire Delacroix. Deborah lives in Canada with her husband and family, as well as far too many unfinished knitting projects.

Learn more about Deborah's books at her website:
http://DeborahCooke.com

CPSIA information can be obtained
at www.ICGtesting.com
Printed in the USA
LVOW11s0800140617

538072LV00001B/30/P